About th

Mark co-wrote the movie *Robot* <u>   </u>
and it was selected for the 58th BFI London Film Festival; he also
wrote the film's novelisation, which was published by Gollancz to
critical acclaim. Mark is also co-presenter of 'The Bestseller Experiment' podcast, where he and Mark Desvaux challenged themselves to
write a Kindle bestseller in 12 months. Their novel, *Back to Reality*,
was an international bestseller in 10 categories.

Born in London, he now lives in Kent (it's the law, apparently)
with writer and YouTube gardener Claire Burgess, their kids, several
chickens and a murderous fish.

@markstay
markstaywrites.com

THE END OF MAGIC

THE END OF MAGIC

MARK STAY

Unbound Digital

This edition first published in 2019

Unbound

6th Floor Mutual House, 70 Conduit Street, London W1S 2GF

www.unbound.com

© Mark Stay, 2019

This book is a work of fiction and, except in the case of historical fact, any
resemblance to actual persons, living or dead, is purely coincidental.

ISBN (eBook): 978-1-78965-005-1
ISBN (Paperback): 978-1-78965-004-4

Maps by Kit Cox, based on sketches by Mark Stay
Cover design by Mecob

Printed and bound in Great Britain by Clays Ltd, Elcograf S.p.A.

For Mum and Dad and all those trips to the library

Dear Reader,

The book you are holding came about in a rather different way to most others. It was funded directly by readers through a new website: Unbound.

Unbound is the creation of three writers. We started the company because we believed there had to be a better deal for both writers and readers. On the Unbound website, authors share the ideas for the books they want to write directly with readers. If enough of you support the book by pledging for it in advance, we produce a beautifully bound special subscribers' edition and distribute a regular edition and e-book wherever books are sold, in shops and online.

This new way of publishing is actually a very old idea (Samuel Johnson funded his dictionary this way). We're just using the internet to build each writer a network of patrons. Here, at the back of this book, you'll find the names of all the people who made it happen.

Publishing in this way means readers are no longer just passive consumers of the books they buy, and authors are free to write the books they really want. They get a much fairer return too – half the profits their books generate, rather than a tiny percentage of the cover price.

If you're not yet a subscriber, we hope that you'll want to join our publishing revolution and have your name listed in one of our books in the future. To get you started, here is a £5 discount on your first pledge. Just visit unbound.com, make your pledge and type MARKSTAY19 in the promo code box when you check out.

Thank you for your support,

Dan, Justin and John
Founders, Unbound

Super Patrons

Julie Anne Bowden
Jon Appleton
Josh Atkinson
Graham Ball
Ian Ball
James Barclay
Richard Bat Brewster
Mitch Benn
Kit Berry
James Bleakney
Ray Bogdanovich
Paul Bulos
Alison Burke
Sally Busby
Joanna Carpenter
Stuart Cattermole
Iwan Clarke
Dylan Cross
Miranda Dickinson
Samantha Eades
Howard Ebison
Liz Fenwick
Rob Field
Naomi Floyd
Anne Fox-Smythe
Marcus Gipps
Ben Goddard
Sage Gordon-Davis
William Grupe
Philip Guest
Jac Harmon
Amanda Harris

MG Harris
Richard Hawton
Mark Hood
Paul Hussey
Jo Jacobs
Emma Jepson
Deborah Jessey
Tim Jessey
Gemma Johnson
Edward Kane
Jessica Killingley
Krys Kujawinska
Declan Kyle
Steven Lallt
Adam Le Dieu
Jack Logan
Darren Love
Fabia Ma
Jeffrey Marshall
Nic May
Marie McGinley
Mark McGinlay
Caroline Mileham
Morris Minor
Sara Mulryan
Ray Mutter
Andy Napthine
Kwaku Osei-Afrifa
Lucy Oulton
Lisa Pryde
Gavin Ralph
Gillian Redfearn
Adam Roberts
Bernadette Robinson
Steve Robinson
Lisa Rogers

Oliver Rowe
Tania Scott
Alison Sizer
Dominic Smith
Dylan Southern
Quentin Spender
Claire Stay
Derek Stay
Emily Stay
George Stay
Jenny Stay
Louise Stay
Patricia Stay
Catherine Stevens
Cameron Stewart
Louie Thomas
Bronwyn Thorburn
Cara Usher
Jonathan Wallden
Nick Walpole
Gareth Watkins
Jackie Wetherell
Lena Whitaker
Suzie Wilde
Graeme Williams
Paul Williamson
Jen Wilson
Simon Winsall

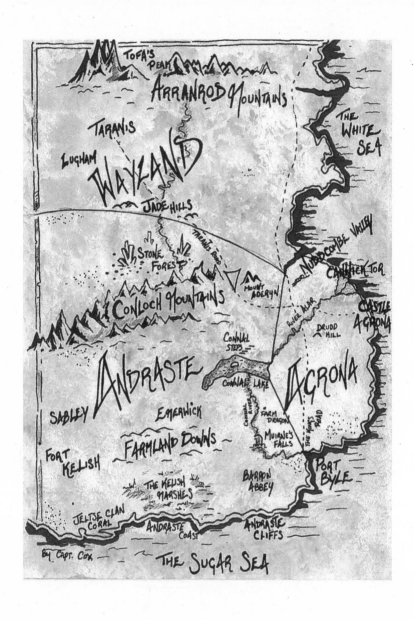

Contents

The Witch Who Thinks She's a Warlock

Rosheen was exhausted, sweaty and ready for a beer when a messenger from King Torren came begging for urgent assistance with the promise of abundant silver. She and her griffin Anzu had spent a whole day tracking a lost wild simurgh that had been picking off sheep in a hamlet near Emerwick. The dog-headed, winged beast had given Rosheen and Anzu the run-around all night, but between them, they managed to subdue it, cage it and release it back into its valley home by noon.

Rosheen needed a bath, but Torren's message was emphatic. Battle and bloodshed were inevitable and she had to come immediately. Even with Anzu's powerful wings, the flight to Canwick Tor had taken most of the afternoon. Now the sun was well on its descent to the horizon and Torren's men were flagging and close to defeat.

The battle had been raging all day. From their high vantage point on a winding path that led to the tor, Rosheen and Anzu found themselves watching the fighting below with creeping discomfort. King Torren's men, at least five hundred of them, clunked around the mud in heavy, glinting armour, performing well-rehearsed and somewhat predictable manoeuvres. Their opponents were fewer in number but wore only leather jerkins and attacked like packs of wolves, unbound by any rules of war. They were fast, bewildering and merciless. Rosheen was reminded of childhood games back in Eru, when huge herds of village children would charge each other, or chase a ball across hills and fields with no sense of purpose other than pure joy. But this was no game. Torren's men surged forwards, crashed into the immovable ranks of mercenaries, then were driven back again. Some floundered in the mud and were rewarded with an axe in the back or a broadsword biting into a limb. Cries of agony echoed around them, the voices of big men, professional soldiers, reduced to begging for death, weeping for their mothers. Children once more.

Apart from a few localised skirmishes, no blood had been spilled on Agrona's green and lush meadows in centuries. A battle between two armies of this size was unreal. 'There hasn't been anything like this since the Mage Wars.' Rosheen ran her hand through Anzu's feathers, something she caught herself doing when anxious. Anzu purred at her touch. 'It's like something from the Chronicles,' Rosheen said.

It's a slaughter. Anzu's thoughts came directly to Rosheen's mind with a voice that only the mage could hear. Anzu was six years younger than Rosheen, but like all griffins, her voice had an aristocratic air. *Who are these people? They look like mercenaries, but I've never seen paid men fight with such passion.*

Rosheen winced as she watched one soldier, wounded in the back and bleeding badly, trying to crawl from the thick of the battlefield. He was spotted by one of the mercenaries who strolled over calmly and stuck her sword into his ribs. The wounded man jerked and a moment later, his final cry of agony drifted up to the tor.

Oh gods. Do we have to watch this, Rosh?

Anzu wasn't squeamish, but this was unlike anything they had ever seen. Rosheen knew she shouldn't be dwelling on the carnage, but for a moment she felt like she was glimpsing the future. Prophecy wasn't one of her skills, but you didn't need to be a seer to know that things wouldn't be the same after this.

Rosheen!

'Uh, yes, sorry.' She shook herself back to reality. 'Let's find Torren,' she said.

A welcoming party of Torren's Royal Guard met them further up the tor road. They greeted her with courteous bows, though a couple of the younger ones glanced in open curiosity at her brown skin. Country boys. She doubted if many of them had ever left Agrona, let alone seen anyone from Eru before.

The older officers eyed her with suspicion. Mid-ranking officials generally didn't like mages, their authority threatened by a power they barely understood, and they had a singular disrespect for the younger, female kind. And so Rosheen – a woman in her thirty-third year, and a foreigner at that – embodied all their prejudices in one bundle.

A groom, more used to dealing with equine guests, reached for Anzu's reins. *Big mistake*, Rosheen thought. The griffin cawed and reared up, towering over them as her front feet with their razor-sharp talons stamped the ground.

The welcoming party quickly backed away. Griffins were rare enough around here, but all children grew up knowing that a griffin's talons could slash your belly open, and that their beaks could tear through flesh, snap bones and leave you with one limb less than when you first encountered it.

Do please remind them that I'm not some bloody horse. Anzu shook her wings and flexed her cat-like tail, filling the air around her with tiny hairs. One of the guards sneezed.

'I think they got the message.' Rosheen patted the mane around Anzu's neck.

After some quick apologies, the guards swept Rosheen and Anzu through King Torren's encampment to the edge of the tor, from where he was watching the battle unravel before him. Rosheen worked regularly with the old man, though she hadn't seen him for a month or so. He had always looked ancient, but he was haggard and beaten now, too, bent over on his grey horse as the wind whipped his long white hair around his face. One of the guards announced their arrival and he shifted in his saddle to greet them.

'We won't be killing anyone, Torren,' Rosheen said. 'I want that clear from the start. You know that's not—'

'My dear girl, you know me better than that.' Old King Torren usually welcomed them with niceties, good wishes and enquiries about the health of Rosheen's family, but there was none of that today. 'I simply need this to end quickly. These people are savages. Good day to you, Anzu,' he added, and the griffin respectfully bowed her head in return.

'Mercenaries?' Rosheen asked.

'Indeed, led by some chancer from the north. He's been making his way south through some minor skirmishes and made camp on our border. We asked him to leave, he refused, and so we... Well, we appear to have started a small war.'

'You're more of a wine-and-feasts king than a warmonger, Torren.' Rosheen liked the old king for his straightforward manner. He had little time for nonsense. He never bothered employing his own permanent mage, preferring to simply hire one, usually Rosheen, when necessary. 'This isn't like you at all.'

'Quite, but one must resort to rattling the sabre every now and then. Trouble is, these buggers are fighting like there's no tomorrow. I don't know what he's paying them, but they clearly think it's worth it.'

'Who is "he"?'

'A warlord named Frang.'

'Frang.' Rosheen swished the name around in her mind for a moment. 'Haldor Frang?'

'You know him?'

'He sent me word some weeks back that he wanted to hire me, but he wouldn't say what for,' Rosheen said. 'It was all a bit vague and he had no one to vouch for him, so I passed.'

'Hmm. He's been buying allegiances along the way south.'

'Glad I didn't follow it up, then. He's clearly off his chump to be taking on an army of the Newlands on their own turf.'

He's not doing a bad job of kicking their arses, though, is he? Anzu added, and Rosheen was relieved that only she could hear the griffin's voice in her mind.

'What do you want us to do?' Rosheen asked the king.

'Make it bloody stop.' Torren flourished a hand at the ongoing chaos. 'Preferably in our favour.'

'Our usual terms don't cover this – we—'

'Of course.' Torren beckoned to his guards and two of them brought forward a small wooden chest. They swung it open to reveal that it was brimming with silver coins. 'I trust this will be satisfactory?'

That's more than we've earned in the last two years combined. Anzu sounded awestruck to Rosheen. *He must be desperate. Think we can haggle for more?*

'I need to bring this Frang fellow to the table for parley,' the old king said. 'Can you do that?'

Rosheen looked out over the tor and across the field. With a roar, a few dozen of Torren's men charged around the mercenaries' flanks, trying to herd them like sheep. They were met immediately with fierce resistance, and soon the main bulk of them were split in two as the mercenaries cut a swathe through them.

If you think I'm going anywhere near that, you've got another thing coming, Anzu told her in no uncertain terms. *All it takes is one opportunistic loon with a bow and I'm done for. I don't care how much silver he's got.*

'It's okay, I know what to do,' she replied. She turned to Torren. 'We have a deal, good King Torren. Have your men fall back.'

The old man nodded. At his command, a horn sounded the retreat. Almost immediately, Torren's men peeled away, rushing back to the high ground. The mercenaries gave chase.

Rosheen moved to the edge of the tor, the wind whipping her cloak around, and closed her eyes.

She found the mercenaries' minds in the darkness. Bright little bubbles of energy. Rosheen knew that she wouldn't be able to send them to sleep – they were far too frenzied for that to work effectively. She would have to use their aggression somehow.

Later, when accounts of the Battle of Canwick Tor were gathered, a clearer picture began to emerge of exactly what happened. Torren's men said they saw all the mercenaries' eyes briefly roll back white, and then they turned on one another without explanation.

Those mercenaries who survived and were willing to talk about it told of a momentary loss of their senses. What followed was utter confusion and dread as their comrades transformed into undead creatures, living corpses of the last person they had slain in combat. They could hear their commanders crying, 'It's a trick! Magic! Do not be deceived, stand down!' But that's easier said than done when you find the reanimated rotting carcass of an old enemy rushing towards you with an axe.

Torren's men regrouped and attacked. They decimated the mercenary forces, sending them fleeing back across the field and over the River Can.

Rosheen opened her eyes, returning to the real world to find Torren clapping his hands delightedly. 'Excellent, splendid. What did you do?'

She didn't answer, but lowered herself to her knees and then rolled onto her back. Routine magic could make Rosheen feel a little light-headed sometimes, but she hadn't stopped for almost two days now, what with hunting down a simurgh, flying halfway across the country and sending an entire army packing. As she recovered, other people's voices sounded like they were in a bubble, and her mind was opening like the petals of a flower. She wanted to lie here and giggle like a child. She loved and hated this feeling. She was rudderless and vulnerable. It was known as the mage's delirium. Thankfully, it never lasted long.

'My dear Rosheen.' Torren looked worried. 'Are you hurt?'

Rosheen waved him away. 'Just… just give me a moment.'

Anzu gently brushed her beak against Rosheen's arm in sympathy. Rosheen ran her hands through the griffin's mane as they both looked up into the twilight sky, where they found the two moons Greystone and Lapis. One large, dull, rocky and lifeless. The other tiny in comparison and a dazzling blue. The Mages' Moon and the source of her power. Rosheen closed her eyes again, thankful as she basked in the strength it gave her.

The Moon Child

Oskar's mind wandered as he led Donella the donkey up the stony path from Sabley Village to home. Neither was in any hurry. Donella languidly pulled a cart laden with buckets brimming with urine and dung along well-worn wheel ruts, thereby avoiding the bigger rocks that might snap an axle or buckle a spoke, and the young man was so wrapped up in his daydreams that he didn't see the shepherd boy, or his two-dozen sheep, until they were on top of him. And so Oskar and Donella had to remain still as the sheep moved around them like a river around a boulder. Despite his poor eyesight and the twilight gloom, Oskar recognised the shepherd, a lad from the village a few years younger than him, and gave him a friendly smile.

The boy responded by sticking his tongue under the inside of his lower lip, crossing his eyes, waving his arms like a madman and making a horrible moaning noise.

A cruel mockery of Oskar.

It made Oskar's heart burn with shame, but he wouldn't let it make him angry.

Oskar was a moon child. Alby Clim had told him so, and how he was very special and unusual.

Alby was the village mage. A kindly soul who, many summers ago, had explained to Oskar's parents that while the boy could live a long and happy life, he would always need their care.

'There are few children like Oskar,' Alby had told them as Father sat by the fire and Mother poured sweet tea. 'Indeed, I've only ever met the one, and that's our boy here.' Alby scruffed Oskar's hair, which he hated, but his complaint merely came out as a groan. 'The Lapis Moon severely affects his speech, sight, hearing and understanding. Some days will be better than others, mind you. The moon moves around our world in a kind of egg shape, do you see?' Alby moved his hand around his teacup in an elliptical orbit. 'Oskar's best days will be when it's furthest away, but when it moves closer...'

Alby didn't have to say any more. They all knew that when the

Lapis Moon was close and twice as big, like today, Oskar could barely string together the thoughts in his head.

Father stoked the fire, stabbing it angrily with a poker. 'So it's not enough that I already have a daughter who brings shame to this family with her magic? Now you tell me my son is a cursed moon child?'

'Oh, it's not a curse, it's more of a... uh...' Alby wavered as Oskar's father angrily tossed the poker across the room and turned on Mother.

'This is your side of the family, woman!' he yelled at her, then spun to face to Alby. 'They come from old magic. Mylarian troublemakers. Tricksters and enchanters. Mother was right. I should never have married her.'

'The feeling is mutual,' Mother said with a sneer, leaning by the stove, unmoved by Father's hysterics.

'I know all about moon children, Alby Clim, you don't need to tell me,' Father said, jabbing a finger at the mage. 'Monsters, they were! Damned creatures that once threatened to destroy this world, and so the Goddess was forced to put the Lapis Moon there to ward off their evil!'

Alby lowered his teacup and frowned. 'I'm all for respecting others' beliefs, Mr Katell, but that is a somewhat unenlightened view of young Oskar's condition. It's true, there may be some part of him that isn't entirely human, but that should be a reason to celebrate his—'

'Celebrate?' Father's eyes threatened to pop from their sockets. 'He's lucky I don't sell him to slavers.'

'Mr Katell, I must object.' Alby stood slowly and the room seemed to shrink around him, and Oskar had wondered if he was using magic. Whatever the mage did, it worked, as Father shuffled back fearfully, his head dipped, his chin buried in his chest. 'Your daughter Rosheen is a fine mage and your son Oskar is a kind-hearted boy. You should be proud of both of them.'

'We are,' Mother said, raising her chin and chewing on her clay pipe.

'Very good, Mrs Katell, thank you.' Alby smiled and the room's dimensions returned to normal. 'I am always at your service should you need me, and do please send my best regards to Rosheen when you next see her.'

With that, the mage left. No one spoke for the rest of the evening.

Since that day, Father only ever looked at Oskar through narrowed eyes, as if the boy was going to turn him into a frog. Mother told Oskar that her love for him was bigger than the moons, the world and all the stars in the sky combined. Alby was always on hand to help, and Rosheen… She didn't come home often, and when she did, she always fought with Father, but she was always quick to embrace her brother.

'Hey, lackwit!'

The voice snapped Oskar out of his remembrance and he squinted to see the shepherd boy had something in his hand.

'You want some dung, numbnuts? I got some for ya!' The shepherd boy threw a clod of sheep manure that missed Oskar but hit poor Donella on the neck. The donkey brayed in hurt surprise and reared up. Oskar patted and stroked her to calm her down. That was too much. Oskar was used to being ridiculed, but there was no need to hurt his donkey. He cried out in rage, but instead of the angry words in his head, all that came out was a slurred moan.

The shepherd boy cackled and strolled away with his sheep into the next field.

Oskar held Donella close, humming gently in her ear as her breathing slowed down and she became less jittery. It wasn't long before they were back on the move, and once again, Oskar's mind was teeming with hopes, dreams and fantasies of travelling the world and seeing its wonders. And that's where they would always stay, trapped inside the mind of a boy who could barely speak.

Oskar worked for his father at his tannery in Sabley. Well, actually, due to the stench of piss and dung, it was way beyond the outskirts of the village on the other side of Gibbs' farm.

This meant a long walk for Oskar as he led the donkey and cart to the village each day to collect the pisspots left out for him. The tannery relied on a regular supply of urine and dung from the villagers, and Oskar was proud to help his father with such an important job. It also gave Oskar plenty of time to daydream. Today he was a mage fighting beyond Aeron's Wall, in the land where dragons slept. A gnarled stick he found under a tree was his magic staff and he swung it at imaginary foes as he danced around the plodding Donella. His sister had read him stories when he was little and they lit a fire in his mind, helping him conjure quests to embark on and fair maidens to rescue.

He and the donkey came to his favourite part of their walk as they rounded the valley path to see Sabley laid out below them. Nestled between two granite peaks, the village clung to the banks of the River Sable, glistening silver and blue under the moons. Oskar patted the donkey's rump and they continued their ascent up the winding path to home.

Oskar's life was not one of a mage's glory or fame. The most he could hope for every day was that Mrs Croup would have warm bread and butter waiting for him when he finished his collection and arrived at the tavern. In the summer, she would add plum jam.

He knew he was different from the other youngsters in the village. He couldn't think as fast as them, nor hear or see as well, and some, like the shepherd boy, would openly mock him whenever he came into the village. Alby Clim had tried to teach him his letters, but they wouldn't stay still on the page or leave any kind of impression on his mind, and when he tried to write, his hand trembled and the quill and ink would simply scrawl jagged lines on the parchment. When he heard others in conversation, he would have the words and ideas formed in his mind to join in, but when he tried to speak, all that came out were slow, slurred words in a jumbled stammer.

And so he chose to remain silent with a smile. He worked hard, and Mother and Father loved him, and he had his own room with his own wooden toy soldiers that Mr Doon had carved for him on his sixteenth birthday a few years ago. He may have been slow, but when he saw children with crippled arms and legs begging on the roadside, he thanked the gods that he was not as unfortunate as they.

He dearly wished that his sister Rosheen would come home more often, but the mention of her name would make Father angry and Mother would pull a sour face. Father, especially, would talk of a past that Oskar had never known, a home of deserts and mountains and griffins that flew as free as the birds in the sky, and how they had lost it all because of Rosheen and Anzu.

Oskar carried a likeness of her, carefully folded away in his top pocket. He recalled watching Mr Doon sketch it one summer afternoon, and seeing it come to life had been as wonderful as any magic by Alby Clim or Rosheen. With a few scratches of charcoal on parchment, Mr Doon's stained fingers had created a drawing of Rosheen so like her that Oskar half-expected it to turn and smile at him. Oskar had no doubt that when she returned, she would have changed some, so he would ask Mr Doon to sketch her again.

Oskar was so lost in his thoughts that he didn't see Alby Clim until one of the man's hands was on his shoulder, the other pointing back the way Oskar had come.

'Oskar, back to the village, lad,' Alby said, his breath wheezing. He turned the boy on his heels, but Oskar didn't understand. He gestured at the buckets in the cart that he had spent all day collecting, and to indicate that failure to bring them home would earn him a beating from Father. All that came out were those slurred words again.

'Please, Oskar, go! It's not safe,' Alby pleaded. 'Do you understand, boy? Hurry!' Alby was always happy and relaxed, and Oskar became anxious to see him so upset. He was shouting at Oskar now, shoving him back. Tears came to Oskar's eyes. What had he done wrong?

And then, with his blurred vision, he saw a pillar of smoke rising up the valley path. Flames licked at the roof of the tavern by the mill. Tiles were popping and cracking, black smoke pouring out of the windows, cheered on by men with swords and burning torches. Without hesitation, Alby Clim rushed towards them, summoning a whirling tornado. It towered over the mage, touching the ground on the path leading to the mill, drilling into the packed earth as it curved towards the men, who backed away, hands protecting their faces. The noise was deafening, even to Oskar's feeble ears, and the men's screams sent a chill through his body.

Oskar ran for home and the donkey followed. He ran past Alby and the screaming men, on and on, away from the village, up the hill, and even though his lungs burned and he had a stitch in his side, he didn't slow at all. All Oskar wanted now was Mother's embrace.

He knew he was close when the smell of the tannery started to make his eyes water. Heaving for breath, he staggered up to the squat stone building where they lived and worked. The raw animal hides pinned to the walls fluttered in the wind, but the rows of soaking barrels were unattended. Where was Father? Where were Jess, Gem, Pol and Dom, the ladies who laughed and gossiped and sang as they worked on the hides? He called for Mother, but there was no reply. He ran into the kitchen where pots lay cracked on the floor. Where were they all?

He dashed from room to room, calling for them with a frightened moan.

'Oskar!' It was Mother's voice, but thin and trembling.

He found them in the yard outside, where a fire burned in a brazier.

Father's blood was mixed in with the dust and the dung on the ground. It was thick and slow and steamed in the morning air. His body lay face down, a knife clasped in his hand. He must have tried to fight back. Oskar had seen that stillness in a body before when he watched Farmer Gerrit slaughter his spring lambs. With a gut-wrenching certainty, Oskar knew that Father wasn't going to be getting up again.

Jess, Gem, Pol and Dom lay dead in a pile nearby, dark, bloody stains on their shawls.

Mother was on her knees with a blade at her throat. Three men, dressed and armed like those who had set fire to the tavern, surrounded her. A noise wailed from Oskar, a mixture of confusion and despair. This didn't feel real. It was like a bad dream. How could everything change so suddenly?

The biggest one, a man with long white hair and jagged teeth, reached out and grabbed Oskar by the neck. His fingers dug into the flesh around Oskar's collarbone and the boy yelped in pain.

'Please!' Mother begged. 'Leave him alone, he's a simple boy, a moon child, he hasn't done anything wrong, please!'

'Who is he?' the man asked.

'My son, please, let him be.'

'Rosheen Katell,' the man said. His voice was strange, each word hacked out like a cough. Oskar had heard travellers in the tavern talk like this sometimes. He wasn't from around here. 'Is she your sister, lad?'

'He can't answer you,' Mother sobbed. 'He can't speak like others.'

'You're his mother, Rosheen's his sister, right?' The man was tired of the conversation already, and Oskar worried that meant he might kill them.

'Yes, yes,' Mother wept. 'Please don't hurt him.'

Oskar reached into his pocket.

'Careful, sonny!' Quick as a flash, the man had a blade pointing into the soft flesh above Oskar's throat. 'Don't make the same mistake your father did.' It stung and Oskar whimpered, but then the man followed Oskar's terrified glance and saw what the boy had in his hand.

He snatched and unfolded the charcoal likeness of Rosheen. 'Yeah, these are the ones,' he told his companions, shoving Oskar to his knees. The boy was facing Mother, both were sobbing, their bodies shuddering. 'Got a question for you two.'

'Please don't hurt us,' Mother pleaded. With a smack that made Oskar jump, the man backhanded her across the face. She froze in shock, wide-eyed, and coughed drops of blood from her mouth.

'Which of you two does Rosheen care for the most?'

'W-what?'

'Lemme put it like this…' The thick-lipped man crouched down on his haunches, grinning as he looked from Oskar to Mother. 'If she only had time to pull one of you from a burning building, which one would she rescue?'

Oskar was puzzled by the question, but a look of calm acceptance crossed Mother's face, like everything made sense and she understood the question perfectly. 'Oskar,' she said quietly. 'She'd rescue Oskar.'

'Good enough for me.' The man stood and turned to his companions. 'You sort her out and I'll take him back to the ship.' He kicked over the brazier, its flames catching on the hay scattered on the ground then licking up around the wooden kitchen door. Oskar sobbed as he watched his home burn. Then he screamed helplessly as he watched the man's companions drag Mother inside.

The man's hand gripped Oskar's arm, pulling him away from Mother. Oskar could hear her screaming, 'Don't hurt him! Please don't hurt him!' from inside, followed by, 'He's allergic to eggs, he can't keep them down, please, he—' And then she fell silent.

Only now, as Oskar was taken around the side of the tannery and thrown into a cage on wheels, did the words come. One word. The only one he had ever mastered. 'Mama!' he cried. The man got up on the biggest horse Oskar had ever seen, kicked its flanks and they were off. The cage was pulled along the bumpy road, dust getting in Oskar's eyes and throat as he called for Mother again and again and again until his throat was hoarse and he could speak no more.

Casual Racism in a Small Village Tavern

'I'm going to slice off your head and shit in your skull!'

And the evening had started with so much promise. Sander tried to recall how he and old Ragnall had come to this. The Jolly Cooper tavern was their first port of call tonight. Sander liked the place. It was always full but never too rowdy, and there was something about the smell of wet dog by the fire, combined with farmer's armpit and mouldy sawdust, that he found reassuring. And they served an incredible local black ale called Night Mary, which not only had the perfect balance of fruit and malt with a lingering after-taste but was also strong enough to get you perfectly merry in under a pint and a half. He and Ragnall had decided to kick off the Springtide weekend with a few drinks here, a little warm-up before the main event later, but Ragnall never could hold his ale and it wasn't long before he started spouting off.

'Kelish are a desperate lot. The marshes flood every year, so they build their homes on stilts. Why don't they just move? Idiots, every one of them. And have you ever tried trading with them? Shifty buggers. Can't trust 'em as far you can kick 'em,' the old man said as he downed his tankard, shaking out the final drops. He tossed it away and immediately started drinking from Sander's. 'And that lot up in Eriworth are no better. Place is a refuge for pig fornicators.'

Lugham Village was a crossroads for traders, and the Jolly Cooper tavern offered travellers a warm bed, cheap beer and the best sausage and mash in onion gravy in the Newlands. Looking around, Sander could see quite a few folk from Andraste and Eriworth and elsewhere, and they were glaring with tight lips and clenched jaws as Ragnall carried on with his rant. And most – if not all – of them were armed as they waited for some kind of signal for the fight to kick off.

It was the pig fornicator comment that made the big red-faced man step up and make the skull-shitting threat. Problematically, Ragnall was a hedge wizard, and most hedge wizards looked, and smelled, like tramps. And this being the Springtide weekend, Sander wasn't in his official robes, either, so this big fellow didn't know whose skull he was threatening to defecate into.

Sander stood slowly. Anxiety attacks had kept him up for most of the previous night; he was in no mood for any kind of fight, verbal or physical, so he raised a placating hand. 'Friend, I apologise for my companion's behaviour. Now, you've both had a lot to drink. Words were said, that's all, mere words, so let's put this—'

'Shut it, son, before I take your arms off and shove 'em up your arse!'

'That's a unique threat, and one I take seriously, of course, but you should know—'

'Any fights and I call the Guardhouse!' Astrid, the Jolly Cooper's owner, yelled as she pointed a many-ringed finger at the red-faced man. 'You. This one might look like a vagrant, but he's the King's Mage, and his mate is a mage, too, so you'd best kiss and make up like real men.'

Sander watched as the red-faced man tried to parse all this new information. 'This long-haired pissant is the King's Mage?'

'Sander Bree.' He extended his hand, but the red-faced man didn't take it. 'Certainly no vagrant, so thanks for that, Astrid, and yes… the hair is real.' Sander took great pride in his long blond hair; it hadn't been cut since he turned forty and reached to the small of his back. He gave it a shake in the hope of getting a laugh.

None was forthcoming.

'Uh… and I am indeed Mage to His Majesty King Steffen Henning Mathias Bhaltair of the House of Ultan. Or Bhalty, as I call him,' Sander continued, desperately hoping that levity would win the hour. The laughs still didn't come, so he waved the joke away. 'I don't. He'd kill me on the spot. Well, he'd *try* to.'

The red-faced man's eyes flitted from side to side. He'd made a fool of himself and was looking for a way out that would leave him with some shred of decency. 'And him, too?' His voice was dry and cracked now as he pointed at Ragnall. 'The one who smells of dung?'

'It's compost.' Ragnall exhaled heavily as he got to his feet. 'My own special blend. It's good for the mushrooms,' he added. 'And if you don't believe I'm a mage, then watch this…'

'Raggy,' Sander warned, 'don't do anything silly.'

Ragnall closed his eyes, slowly raising his arms to the sides like a bird's wings. Candles on every table shimmied and the hound resting by the fire perked up at some noise beyond human hearing. The crowd began to back away.

Ragnall's sandalled feet left the dusty tavern floorboards and he levitated into the air.

It was a simple piece of magic but one that never failed to impress ordinary folk. There were 'oohs' and 'aahs' from those gathered, and one person even tried to start a round of applause, but it soon faltered to nothing. Sander tutted and puffed like a parent with a boastful child. 'All right, that's enough, down you come, you big show-off.'

Ragnall rose above the wax-caked iron chandelier and soon found his head scraping against the timbers. He brought his hands together like he was cupping water to drink, then raised them slowly.

And everyone in the room rose with them. Including the dog.

People yelped in shock, dropping their tankards as their legs kicked in the air and flapping their arms as they reached for something to grab on to. A few began praying; others begged to be let down, and one old man vomited and began tumbling over and over.

The dog took it in his stride. He'd seen it all before.

Even Sander was airborne. Arms folded, and looking decidedly unimpressed, he wondered if he should counter with some of his own magic, but he knew that would only make Ragnall even more grumpy, and that's when things could get out of hand.

'Ragnall!' Sander said. 'Let us down. Gently.'

Ragnall half-opened his eyes, a twisted grin on his face. 'I can keep this up all day, y'know.'

'Yes, we're all very impressed. Come on.'

The patrons of the Jolly Cooper found themselves slowly sinking to the straw-strewn floorboards. When they landed, they shared terrified looks and the room remained silent save for the crackling fire.

Ragnall let himself descend before the red-faced man. He was coming down from the high of magic and, with the drifting, yellowed eyes of a seasoned drunk, Ragnall looked into his antagonist's face and said, 'Now piss off back to Eriworth, you pig fucker.'

The red-faced man inflated again, but Sander stepped between them and steered him towards the bar. 'Whoa, whoa, whoa, no, let's not start that again. Where are you from, friend? Let me guess, Port Byle, yes? I grew up a little way down the coast, y'know? Tell me, does the *Pride of Agrona* still dock there? A magnificent ship. Here, let me buy you a drink...' He gestured to Astrid: *Whatever he's having!* She quickly poured him a large gin, and in moments, the red-faced man's anger was quelled by the warm glow of mother's ruin. 'Let's get everyone a drink, eh? This one's on me!' Sander added quickly, aware that everyone in the tavern was glaring at him with empty tankards in their hands.

Sander had hoped for some kind of cheer for his generosity, but his fellow patrons just picked up their conversations from where they had left off and someone started playing a fiddle. *Ungrateful buggers*, Sander thought to himself.

Being a mage had taken its toll on his nerves over the decades. He was thirteen years old when Ragnall had come to his village looking for apprentices. Sander's abilities were beginning to manifest and his parents had more than enough on their hands with nine other children to feed, so they were happy to take the old man's coin and wave their middle son farewell.

Sander had excelled at the trials and his skills soon drew the attention of local guilds and landowners looking for a mage. Then he struck it lucky: the king himself was looking for a new mage (the old one, Yon Wrightly, having passed away at the grand old age of two hundred and three). Sander always walked a fine line between confidence and cockiness, but this time it worked. He impressed King Bhaltair with his grip on court politics, the state of the economy, truth-seeing and negotiation strategies – all covered in Ragnall's extensive training curriculum – but to truly demonstrate his powers, he knew he had to try something incredibly audacious. Something that would not only convince the king and queen that their citadel and people were safe from invaders, but a feat that would have everyone from the Newlands to Eru, Myrista and Rigo talking about him.

Sander had stood alone in the long grass on a sloping rise about half a league from the walls of the citadel, a solitary figure buffeted by the summer wind. He asked the king to give the order in his own time for every available trebuchet on the walls to fire the heaviest stones in his direction at once.

Repelling flying objects was a fairly standard task for a mage. Having the skill to control more than a dozen was impressive. King Bhaltair took Sander's request at his word and fired over seventy rocks and boulders at the young man.

Sander knew that merely flinging the stones to the ground wouldn't be enough.

When he heard them launch, he raised his hand, closed his eyes and drew on the power of the Lapis Moon, visualising each stone in his mind. With an instinctive magical skill that came easily to him yet impressed everyone he met, Sander was able to move them around, swirling them like apples in a barrel.

They were transformed from hurtling projectiles into satellites orbiting the citadel. Seventy miniature moons and more, all imbued with enough magical energy to keep them circling in the sky around the citadel indefinitely. They added extra power and status to the citadel, making it a must-see destination for travellers and merchants alike, and gave nervous traders, and any potential invaders, something to worry about as they approached its gates. People called them the Mage's Moons and Sander promised to keep them aloft for as long as he was the King's Mage.

Sander soon found himself working as the youngest Royal Mage since records began.

For the first thirty years or so, Sander breezed through it all, but recently things had started to go sour. The queen died in childbirth. Sander had done all he could to save her, but death is beyond even the most powerful mage's control. After that, the king's flinty persona no longer had a cheerful counterpoint, and a once happy and confident court became a place where everyone was treading on eggshells.

And then Ragnall started drinking heavily. Sander had no problem with a happy tipple in the holidays, but whenever he visited his old master these days, he found him in a state of inebriation, railing against the world in general and sometimes – in his darker moments –

muttering about a vision he'd had of a great change, the end of magic, the end of everything.

This didn't help Sander's increasing anxiety attacks one little bit. All winter, he'd found himself waking up just as he was dropping off into a deep sleep, his heart racing, convinced he was having a heart attack. He would sit up, gather his breath, lie back down to sleep and exactly the same thing would happen again.

This summer would be Sander's fiftieth. He was tired and longed for a break. He'd been looking forward to the Springtide weekend for some time and the last thing he needed was Ragnall picking a fight with everyone they met.

Satisfied that the Jolly Cooper had returned to its normal self, Sander began to move back to where Ragnall now sat cross-legged on the floor. A man slouched on a barstool, wearing the yellow robes of a Brother of the Faith, gripped Sander's arm.

'Use your magic while you can, wizard,' he slurred, with breath that could light a candle.

'Actually, if you were paying attention, my friend, I didn't use any magic.' Sander reassured him with a friendly pat on the arm. 'As my tutor used to tell me: a big man starts a fight, the bigger man walks away.'

'Your tutor was an idiot.'

'Maybe. That's him there.' He shook his arm free of the Brother's grip and thumbed towards Ragnall, who was trying to pull himself upright using a barstool. 'The one who just had you lot floating in the air.'

Ragnall lost his grip and fell back to the floor. 'Me arse!' Ragnall wailed, getting a nervous laugh from the remaining onlookers. Sander winced. Ragnall was already a joke again.

'The word is out.' The Brother leaned closer, staggering forwards off the stool onto his feet and spraying spittle into Sander's ear as he whispered, 'Your time is up. You and all magekind. It's written in the stars. Astronomers agree that the blue moon will die and the hour of the Faith is upon us.'

Sander bristled at yet another doomsayer and gently but firmly pushed the Brother away. 'Y'know, Brother, you're starting to annoy me. I don't want to use magic on you, but it would be the easiest thing for me to stop your heart for a few moments, or make your brain explode, so back off.'

'Arrogant little turd,' the Brother spat, reaching into the folds of his cloak and pulling out a knife.

Astrid was yelling as the Brother slashed at Sander's throat. Sander stepped back, instinctively reaching out, finding the irregular rhythm of the man's heart. He gave it a gentle squeeze. The pain alone was usually enough to deter any ill-wishers.

The Brother's eyes bulged as he tried to say something, but all that came out was an insensible slur ending in a gargle. He fell face first on the floorboards.

Sander closed his eyes and listened. No heartbeat. The Brother was dead.

'Oh, shit.'

Sander's own heart nearly stopped. His chest felt numb and he thought he was about to have the kind of panic attack that usually woke him in the middle of the night. He'd never killed anyone before. It was something every mage expected to happen at some time – their power often attracted the foolhardy with something to prove – and he and Ragnall had discussed at length how to deal with such an occurrence, but nothing could have prepared Sander for the sight of the dead Brother lying at his feet.

'Ah...' Sander shuffled on the spot as the crowd around him began to dissipate. Some backed away, expecting him to kill them next; others took the time to gulp down their dregs before edging towards the door, having seen enough magic for one evening. 'M-must've had a weak heart,' Sander stammered. 'You can't say I didn't warn him.'

Astrid stomped around from behind the bar and grabbed Ragnall by the scruff of the neck, pulling him to his feet. 'That's enough! Winoc, tell the Guardhouse we've got a dead'un.'

'Yes, Mum.' Winoc, Astrid's spiky-haired son, took a welcome break from washing dishes and hurtled outside.

'You two.' Astrid flung Ragnall into Sander's arms, nearly knocking him flying. 'Out and don't come back.'

'I tried, Astrid—'

'OUT! You're barred.'

Sander left a few coins for the mess and to cover funeral arrangements and carried Ragnall outside in the first blue light of dawn. The main street was empty. Those who had fled the Jolly Cooper left only dust in their wake. A Springtide chill blew between the closed stores and quiet hostelries, swinging their dying lanterns and making doors and windows clatter and creak. It sweetened the air.

The moons were bright in the night sky, and most of the windows in the white stone homes that loomed in the hills and woods surrounding the village were dark. Sander tried to sort his thoughts in the silence, but it was soon broken by the clattering armour of the village guards closing in. There would be tedious questions and Sander would have to play the King's Mage card once again. To knowingly attack a member of the King's Court was punishable by death anyway, so hopefully this would all be over swiftly.

Thoughts and ideas began to crystallise in Sander's mind. Thoughts that had been stirring for a while. Thoughts of leaving and retirement. A man had died, and Sander knew it was time for a change.

'When this is all sorted...' Ragnall kicked at the cracked and flaky mud in the street. It hadn't rained all week. 'Want to go and wind up a troll?'

Haldor Frang's Prophecy

King Torren asked Rosheen to stay and help with the negotiations as a truth-seer. He offered her more coins, her usual rate this time, and the comfort of his own yurt for the night. She took the coins but couldn't possibly shove an old man out of his bed. The power of the Lapis Moon had completely refreshed her and she would sleep under the stars with Anzu.

That's a lot of money. Anzu tipped the lid of the chest open with her beak. *Enough to go home?*

'Enough to get us there,' Rosheen replied as she brushed Anzu's coat. 'But not a place of our own.'

We could work on the way. Anzu sounded excited now. *Travel through Mylar having adventures. Earn enough for a bit of land in the northern hills?*

Rosheen smiled at Anzu's childish enthusiasm. The mage had to remind herself that Anzu missed the blue open skies of home more than Rosheen ever would. 'Sounds like a plan,' she said. 'We could make a start tomorrow, perhaps?'

Anzu hopped around on her back feet, eyes wide with excitement. *Yes! Yes, let's do that. First thing.*

'Come here, you big idiot.' Rosheen took the griffin's head in her hands, smiling brightly. Anzu's eyes were as big as apples but looked as delicate as glass, with a jet-black iris surrounded by a shining golden ring. Anzu blinked and inclined her head. She couldn't smile, but there was a happy, gentle demeanour in the way her bright white head feathers arranged themselves.

We're going home? the voice in Rosheen's head asked. The voice that only Rosheen could hear, the voice she had known since the day she had named Anzu on her sixth birthday.

'Yes. Yes, we are,' Rosheen told her.

Torren sent emissaries to the leader of the mercenaries to offer terms of peace. Haldor Frang agreed to meet at midnight but was nearly two hours late when he finally arrived.

Torren summoned Rosheen and she left Anzu happily tearing a dead boar to pieces with her beak and claws. A crowd of Torren's soldiers had gathered around her, wide-eyed in fear and admiration as the griffin's beak broke ribs like breadsticks and her talons hacked away at the hog with the skill and dexterity you'd expect from an experienced butcher with a sharp cleaver.

Frang was younger than Rosheen had expected. Not much older than her. Maybe mid-thirties, it was difficult to tell. His face was nut-brown and wrinkled by a life spent exposed to the sun. His dark beard might once have been immaculately groomed, but now it was ragged at the edges and flecked with grey and white. Tattoos of black tears dripped from his green eyes. He did not bother with the usual furs and gold of a warlord or a king, preferring a simple leather jerkin and trousers, good boots and a short blade on his belt. He was as much of a fighter as his hired swords. Haldor slouched in the chair opposite them, legs crossed, one foot dangling in the air.

'Rosheen Katell, yes?' He grinned when he saw her. 'You're a hard person to meet, young lady. Finally, the honour is mine.' He jabbed an accusing finger at Torren. 'You grabbed her first, Torren, you crafty old devil. That hardly seems fair.'

Rosheen immediately felt at a disadvantage, as if this strange, over-familiar man had been stalking her from afar. She remained silent, however, reminding herself that this was Torren's meeting, and waited for the old king to reply.

'Mages have kept the peace for three generations,' Torren said with a calm, even voice. 'Why would you be foolish enough to try and disrupt that peace?'

'Good King Torren.' Haldor's voice had a northern warmth to it, peppered with rhotic rolls of the tongue. Rosheen listened carefully, trying to pin it down. 'Peace suits you. It allows you to keep your riches, grow old in comfort, hire witches to win your battles.' He flashed Rosheen a smile and gave her a wink. 'Peace does not suit me, however. It means poverty where I come from. Scratching a living from dust and rocks and ice. You and the other kings in the New-lands, particularly the south, seem unwilling to dole out the benefits of your rule, so I have decided that the time has come to take my share.'

'Your share?' Torren coughed a laugh. 'You'll be grateful to leave with your life and passage back to wherever it is you came from.'

'Grainne,' Rosheen said, unable to resist joining in any longer. 'He's from Grainne, more specifically Dagdun on the north-east coast.'

'Very good.' Haldor was genuinely impressed. 'Magic?'

'No, just an ear for accents,' Rosheen said modestly. 'I worked with some merchant sailors from there once. They somehow managed to earn a living without killing people.'

'Sadly, the ocean and I do not make good company.' Haldor mimed vomiting over the side of a ship and laughed, clapping his hands together. 'For so long I have wanted to meet you, Rosheen Katell. *The Witch Who Thinks She's a Warlock*, they call you.'

'I've been called many things.'

'Oh no, don't worry. The stories I hear are good. Drust Krax speaks very highly of you. He warned me you might try something cunning today. I should have listened to him.'

The last time Rosheen had seen Drust Krax, the Warlord Chieftain of Arranrod, he'd tried to kill her after his wife died of an incurable pox. He said he couldn't afford to look weak and the nurse – Rosheen, in this case – would need to take the blame. He was genuinely apologetic as he drew his sword. Rosheen had escaped by the skin of her teeth using a version of the same trick she'd used on the battlefield today.

'That's nice to hear,' she said. 'How is he?'

'Fine. I had to take a couple of his fingers, but he swears loyalty to me now.' Haldor's head tilted at her reaction. 'You expected me to say he was dead, didn't you? Krax and his men are good warriors. Better on my side than dead. I'm no savage.'

'I never said you were.'

'Plenty of others do, yes?' He flashed his teeth, the swagger still there, but Rosheen saw the resentment simmering underneath. He desperately wanted to be taken seriously. 'You move around with your griffin from place to place, work for hire.'

'It makes for a more interesting career.'

'Like a warlock!' He clapped his hands together. 'That's why they call her the...' He trailed off as he looked around for a reaction from

Torren and his guards but got none. 'Oh, never mind. Why have you ignored me, girl? I wanted to hire you and your wonderful beast.' He leaned forwards, a suggestive glint in his eye.

'At the moment, we're employed by King Torren.' Rosheen gestured to the old man next to her, whom she could sense was growing impatient with their banter. Despite herself, she was enjoying this.

'Ah, an exclusive arrangement, I see.' Haldor nodded solemnly.

'No, not exclusive. Though I only work for those who can be vouched for. I asked after you, and the few who had ever heard of you said you were mad. The Dogmeat General, they called you.'

'Better a bad reputation than none at all.' Haldor pursed his lips so hard she thought for one moment he was blowing her a kiss. 'It's a shame as I was hoping today's little distraction would convince you of the seriousness of my intent.'

'I sincerely hope you didn't stage a battle where people died in order to attract my attention.'

'You should be flattered.'

'I'm horrified.'

'It's the only way people like me can get the attention of people like you. Perhaps some other time, eh?'

'Perhaps.'

'Tell me, why don't you and the beast—'

'Anzu.'

'A lovely name. Eruish?'

'Yes – well, Mylarian.'

'Of course. So why don't you and Anzu settle down with a king or a warlord like other mages?'

Most warlords or kings asked her this question sooner or later, usually as a precursor to offering her a permanent position, and she gave Haldor her usual response. 'Kings are all fine and good, but sooner or later they die and their mad son or daughter takes over, and they always start by beheading those people who were loyal to the old king.' She rested a hand on Torren's arm. 'No offence.'

'None taken, my dear,' the old king replied, resting his chin in one hand and clearly wondering when he might get a word in again.

Rosheen turned back to Haldor and continued, 'And you're always faced with the choice of stand by and watch or interfere. Neither of which interests me much.'

'What's he paying you? I'll double it.'

Torren shifted uncomfortably, but Rosheen was quick to answer. 'I follow the Mages' Code, Haldor Frang, and I do not take kindly to those who would try to usurp it.'

'Ah.' Haldor nodded. 'Principles. How's that working for you?'

'It made me the mage I am today, thank you.'

'One stuck in a rut, I hear.'

'Not at all.' Rosheen answered a little too quickly and with far too much offence.

Haldor cackled. 'Touched a nerve, eh? Yeah, I bet you're all too happy playing midwife to peasants and wiping the arses of incontinent royals, hmm? Not up for an adventure with a real warrior, then?'

'And that would be you?'

'I'm about to make things interesting around here, witchy-warlock. Join a winner while you still can.'

'I hate to disappoint you, but that's not the most tempting offer, and I must refuse.'

'Fair enough, I tried.' Haldor took a noisy, deep breath through his nostrils, and like that, he was serious again. 'I have swept through the Newlands like a fire, old man.' He turned his attention to Torren, who was a little thrown at being the focus of the warlord's gaze once more. 'You think your little mage-girl here and her glorified flying pussy will stop me?'

'They did today,' Torren said, regaining his composure, unimpressed with the warlord's sudden mood swings. He unravelled a parchment and began to read. 'These are our terms: you will surrender your arms and your banner, and your commanders will be taken into our custody. You will decamp with your host at first light, leaving our borders with immediate effect. You are henceforth banished from the Kingdom of Agrona, and any attempt to return will result in your immediate arrest, punishable by death. You—'

'Tell me, old man, what will you do when the magic has gone?'

Torren sighed. 'What in the world are you talking about, you ridiculous fool?'

27

'When magic is no more?' Haldor spoke as if this news was common knowledge. 'When the power shifts from people like you to people like me?' He turned from Torren to Rosheen. 'You. Mage. He brought you here tonight as a truth-seer, yes? Let me show you something...' He reached into his jerkin and, with clatter of steel on chainmail, the King's Guards jumped into life, levelling their swords at him.

Haldor froze for a moment.

Then he leapt to his feet and ripped open his jerkin, popping buttons and revealing his bare chest, barking at the guards like a dog. 'C'mon! Yes! C'MON! DO IT!' He pushed his chest against their sword-points. The king's men staggered back like first-year cadets.

Haldor fell into his chair in hysterics, barely able to breathe, he was laughing so hard. Torren and Rosheen shared a glance: *He's a maniac!*

Haldor cleared his throat and regained his composure, taking a scroll from within his jerkin. He flattened it out on the table between them, toppling over goblets as he did so. His tone was calm and serious again. 'After I laid waste to Drust Krax's stronghold in Arranrod, I employed the services of his astronomer. A nervous man; jittery, crazy eyes. Kept babbling on about the end of magic.' Haldor stood and leaned over the scroll. Rosheen, well versed in astronomy, joined him. It was covered in smudged and scratchy diagrams showing the movement of their world and its moons around the sun. He pointed to the blue moon. 'Lapis: the source of all your power, am I right, witchy-warlock girl?'

Rosheen said nothing, wondering where this was going.

'That's how it works, isn't it?' Haldor persisted with a mischievous grin, delighted to have befuddled the mage. 'You magical beings, the mages, trolls and dragons – your griffin companion! – you all dance around naked and worship the moon and it gives you your power, yes?'

'No, no, no.' Rosheen puffed her cheeks out and shook her head, speaking to Haldor like he was a child. 'The Lapis Moon has a field of energy. Mages have their own latent magical energy, and we use it to engage with the moon's and harness its power. There's no worshipping involved, no nudity, just years of study and hard work.'

'That's a shame about the nudity, I was rather hoping—'

'Get to the point, Haldor,' Rosheen snapped. 'We're here to discuss your surrender.'

'Of course, of course. Look at these.' Haldor's finger found what appeared to be illustrations of small suns shining in the firmament. 'These are massive rocks in the stars. Comets, he called them. And this one' – his finger jabbed at a large red circle with a long golden tail – 'this one is the biggest of all. It's coming soon. You see this line? See how it curves? Straight for the Lapis Moon. Days away, he said, and then—'

Screaming, Haldor ripped the scroll into scraps, flinging them into the air above him. The pieces fell around them like autumn leaves as he stared Rosheen square in the eyes. 'Oh, I see I have your attention now,' he said. 'This comet will collide with the Lapis Moon, shattering it into a billion pieces and taking with it the source of your magical powers. Your own latent energy will not last, magic will die, and there will follow years of chaos as each of the realms fights for control. The bloodshed you've seen today is nothing compared to the slaughter to come, and the dull peace you've grown fat on will be washed away like shit in a sewer. Nothing will ever be the same again. These are the last days of magic, Rosheen Katell. Enjoy them while you can. Now tell me, truth-girl, am I lying?'

Crosses on an Arc

As Rosheen and Anzu threaded their way out of Torren's camp, everyone around them made haste as they packed up tents and equipment for the return to Castle Agrona. The peace terms had been agreed and the warlord escorted back to his own camp.

'He was telling the truth,' Rosheen said. 'At least, he thought he was.' Rosheen's earliest gift was truth-seeing. Since she was a toddler, she had been able to tell if someone was lying, and there was no doubting the warlord's earnestness.

We've seen too many doomsayers in the past to take yet another one seriously, Anzu reminded her. *He may well believe what he's been told, but that doesn't make it the truth. Come on, Rosheen, you're not an amateur. You can spot a delusional freak, surely?*

'Gods, you sound like Torren.'

Then I'm in good company. Speaking of which ...

Anzu nodded ahead to where Torren was being helped onto his horse by a freckled stable girl. It took several attempts and some mild cursing on the king's part, but he eventually found himself in the saddle. He was surrounded by milling red-robed advisors proffering scrolls and seeking his signature.

'Rosheen, Anzu.' The king waved his advisors back and gave the mage and her griffin a jaunty salute.

'King Torren.' Rosheen smiled. 'Might I ask one last favour?'

'I am forever in your debt. Name it.'

'Could your astronomer check Frang's calculations?' she asked. 'I need to know.'

'I'd love to help, but I've not employed an astronomer for some time, my dear,' Torren told her. 'What goes on in the heavens is no business of mine – the sun and the moons still rise and set regardless of any interest I take in them. There are people I can consult in Castle Agrona if it would make you happier?'

Let's kidnap Haldor's astronomer, Anzu suggested.

'There's no one in the camp who could help?' Rosheen asked Torren.

'I'm afraid we didn't bring Natural Philosophers of any kind, my dear,' he said with a smile. 'We left in rather a hurry. But I shall ask my wisest minds when I get to Castle Agrona.'

If Haldor's prediction were true, then waiting for Torren's advisors might be too late. She had to find out for herself.

'That would be wonderful,' she replied anyway. 'Thank you.'

'Where shall I send word?' the king asked, distracted by his advisors who gathered closer around him like dogs keen for treats.

'I have lodgings at the mages' temple in Canwick,' she said.

No we don't. Anzu's voice sounded puzzled. Then she added, sounding a little disappointed, *Oh, you're lying. Are we doing the kidnapping thing? I was joking.*

'You're welcome to come with us.' The king gestured at his departing soldiers.

'Thanks, but no. We have unfinished business to attend to,' she told him.

I hate it when you do this. Anzu stamped her feet. *Just because I can't speak doesn't mean you can drag me into your lies, woman.*

'As you wish.' The king chuckled at Anzu's stamping. 'Looks like she's keen to get a move on, eh? Fare thee well, Rosheen, Anzu... Right, what the blazes do you lot want, hmm?' The king trotted away in the midst of a heated discussion with his red-robed advisors.

Rosheen pulled herself onto Anzu's saddle. 'Hey, Anzu.' The mage stroked the griffin's white feathers, which usually calmed her down, but she continued to bristle. 'What did you say about kidnapping Haldor's astronomer?'

That was a joke. A joke? You remember jokes? They're funny things that don't get us killed.

'How about a proper grooming? Feathers, talons, the works. You've not had one of those in ages.'

Are you trying to bribe me, woman?

'Yup.'

You really think I'm that shallow?

'I'll throw in a full massage and a beak polish.'

Anzu made a growling noise that came from the pit of her belly. One part deep thought, two parts desire.

You're on.

Rosheen saddled up Anzu, donned her hand-carved shell goggles and they took to the skies.

They followed the coast towards Nuddcombe Valley where Haldor was encamped, accompanied by a flock of white geese in an arrow formation over the delta where the Alar River spilled into the White Sea over glistening moonlit sandbanks. It would take a good hour's flying, and Torren's terms required that Haldor leave by dawn, so he might not be there.

He was.

Anzu was first to see it.

By the gods, Rosh…

Rosheen's view was limited by the narrow slits of her goggles and so she slipped them off for a better look as they circled high above a sprawling mass of tents in the wide valley below. Countless glowing fires sent ghostly spirals of smoke into the night sky. Dozens of horses, pigs, cattle and sheep were enclosed in makeshift stables and pens, and a well and a pump had been installed by a weir.

Even from their vantage point in the clouds, Rosheen and Anzu could hear the noise of blades chopping meat, along with the bubble and slop of vegetables, soups and broths boiling over. It was the kind of hubbub you would expect in a small town.

'He must have at least a thousand mercenaries,' Rosheen called over the whipping wind.

Some are preparing to move out, Anzu added, and Rosheen could see a dozen or so armed riders mounting horses and heading back on the road to Castle Agrona. *Not enough for a counter-attack… Sabotage? Whatever it is, they're completely ignoring Torren's terms. We should warn him.*

'We will, we will, but I want to find this astronomer first. Look, there.' Rosheen pointed down to the largest yurt in the centre. 'That must be Haldor Frang's. That's where I need to be.'

Are we dropping in unannounced or something more subtle?

'I don't want him knowing we're here.' She pointed at a clearing in a wood beyond. 'Let's put down there. I'll cast a glamour and sneak in, you be my eyes above, and if I'm not back in an hour, or if you see me getting my arse kicked, come and fetch me.'

Subtle it is, then.

Rosheen moved as silently as she could past forges busy with armourers, the rhythmic *chink-chink* of hammers shaping hot metal blades on anvils. To some, she would be a movement out of the corner of their eye; to others, nothing more than a shadow moving from one dark spot to another, mistaken for a cat or fox prowling for food.

Those going about their chores were one thing, but guards on alert were something else entirely. Many were trained to spot the signs of a moving glamour; a few even had low-level magical abilities of their own. Rosheen needed an extra pair of eyes, and they circled high above her.

Whoa, whoa, stop...

Rosheen obeyed the voice in her head and hunched down behind a small pyramid of ale barrels, not daring to peek out. She glanced up to see a dark shape move between the moonlit clouds above. Anzu.

There's a pair of guards about ten feet to your left. You could move further around the camp to maybe find another way in. Wait there a moment and let me check.

For all her other magical abilities, Rosheen had no psychic skills whatsoever and was unable to reply directly to Anzu. And so she could only listen, keeping low and still, while her griffin worked on a solution.

Okay, I've circled the camp. These fellows are part of an inner ring of security. I think beyond here it's Haldor's trusted circle only. You should be fine once you're past them. Give me a minute and I'll try and distract them. Keep your ears open...

Half a minute passed, then she heard Anzu's voice in her head. *Incoming!*

The body of a dead goose came crashing down on one of the storage tents, punching into it with a smack and folding the tent in on itself. The poor bird must have been petrified as the griffin plucked it from the air, broke its wings and dropped it from on high.

'Show yourself!' one of the guards called, running to investigate. The other stayed at his post but took two steps forward to track his comrade's movements. He had his back turned to Rosheen and that was all she needed.

She dashed past him, quick and silent as a purse-snatcher's hand.

There were more people to avoid as she wove her way to the centre of the encampment, but she moved with purpose and confidence as though she belonged there; skulking around would only burst the glamour's bubble. She strode with her head held high towards Haldor's guards and his yurt, and not one of them saw her.

Rosheen, don't bother with Haldor's tent, Anzu said. *Have a look in the one behind it. I think that's the one we need.*

Rosheen circled the big yurt, doing her best to disregard the grisly sight of half a dozen or so heads on spikes arranged outside its entrance, to discover a smaller, more ragged tent squatting in its shadow, its sagging canvas propped up with yew branches. Its roof was split open and the tip of a telescope peeked out. An astronomer's observatory. She slipped inside.

Be quick! I'll keep watch.

It was pitch black in the tent, but with a few blinks, she drew on her power to heighten her vision in the darkness. Shapeless blurs soon became a table, scrolls, optical glasses and a bed with a man sleeping face down. The astronomer. She moved to him first, wondering if she should wake him.

Rosheen saw an empty bottle of Keevan whisky in his hand and reckoned he wouldn't be much use to her anyway. She placed a hand over his head and, with a few words of incantation, sent him into an even deeper slumber.

In the centre of the room stood the telescope, a tall brass cylinder resting at an angle on a rotating stand. Reaching from the floor to the canopy, it looked like an outsized horn, but it was topped with a curved glass lens and pointed up into the heavens through the slit in the canvas. Rosheen hadn't seen one since she was a child in Eru and certainly not one as large or sophisticated as this. In the eastern desert villages, the skies were clearer and the stars brighter, one of the many things she missed about home. She ran her hand along its surface, admiring the craftwork where the various sections had been seamlessly joined together. There was a slot in its middle for sliding in different sized lenses. She levered one of the lenses out on its brass ring for a closer look. Save for a few scratches and bubbles, the grinding and polishing of the glass was near-flawless.

At the lower end was a cushioned stool facing an eyepiece. She crouched down and peered through.

It was as if the heavens were in the room with her.

The stars shone through the lens with a sparkling clarity and the darkness beyond had a depth that star-watching with the naked eye had never given her. This was an incredible work of craftsmanship, less a mere telescope and more like a portal. She fantasised about crawling up its brass tube and stepping through into the firmament. A part of her wanted desperately to turn the telescope around to see the moons, or even Anzu in flight, but any movement might attract the wrong kind of attention.

Briefly wondering how much time she had left, Rosheen tore herself away from the greater universe and instead unravelled the astronomer's scrolls on the table. There were the usual measurements and observations of the moons, stars and sun, the kind of thing that she and all mages studied as part of their apprenticeship. She was a little rusty, but as she looked at the charts and calculations, it started to come back. How the blue Lapis Moon's orbit danced around the planet in an elliptical circle, passing in front of its grey brother twice a day. Rosheen recalled a song that compared the Lapis Moon to a boastful younger sibling eager to please its parents.

She discarded that scroll and unrolled another. This looked a little more like the one that Haldor had torn to shreds earlier. It was covered with the astronomer's same spidery writing, and the smudged diagrams looked like they'd been scribbled in a mad haste.

Rosheen...

She shook her head, ignoring Anzu. She was so close. There were numbers, calculations scrawled around the edges, along with a series of small crosses all linked with a curved line.

Rosheen, there are men leaving Haldor's tent.

It was like they were plotting a course.

They're headed towards you. They're circling the tent. Get out, Rosheen, now!

She followed the curved line... and it crossed directly with another arc.

You might want to find a place to hide...

The path of the Lapis Moon. These two objects were destined to collide. Nothing could stop it.

Right now, Rosheen!

'Some time tomorrow night,' a voice behind her said.

Rosheen didn't move. She could sense Haldor standing in the entrance to the tent, his men milling behind him. There was no way out, but he was flashing his grin as he approached her with open arms.

'I knew you couldn't help yourself.' He rested an arm around her shoulders and joined her looking at the scrolls. 'You knew I was telling the truth.'

'This proves nothing.' She released her hold on the scroll and it curled back on itself. She gestured at the unconscious astronomer. 'He could be as mad as you.'

Rosheen, are you okay...? Give me a sign.

'Ah, but you can see for yourself.' He kicked the sleeping astronomer. 'Dagmar, wake up!' But he did not move.

If you're okay, move the big thing poking out of the tent.

'I put him under,' Rosheen told Haldor. 'Don't worry, I think I know how this works.'

She took the scroll with the crosses and moved to the telescope's eyepiece. With a heave, she twisted the device on its base, hoping the movement would tell Anzu that she was safe.

Was that you? Rosheen, was that you? Do it again.

She made another adjustment, now hoping that Haldor didn't pick up that she was sending a signal.

Good, I'm on standby. Do something drastic if you need me.

Examining the coordinates and making a quick calculation in her head, Rosheen reckoned she would need to rotate the telescope thirty degrees to the east. She moved it again, more precisely this time, then leaned forward and adjusted the focus.

It was exactly where it was supposed to be. Nothing more than a white dot against the endless black of space. It might have been mistaken for a star, but it didn't have a star's shine. Instead, it was dull, heavy, oddly inert and unthreatening. It didn't appear to be moving at all, but she knew that if she looked again in a few moments, it would have inched forwards. Another cross on the astronomer's arc. Imperceptibly crawling across the sky, unstoppable and as inevitable as the sun rising in the morning. And it was about to destroy her entire life.

'One more day.' Haldor's voice wasn't gleeful or triumphant, merely matter-of-fact. 'One more day of magic left. What will you do with your day, Witch Who Thinks She's a Warlock?' He swung the telescope's eyepiece away from her. 'What will you do with the rest of your life without that power? What will you do with your beast? How long will she last without the magic that sustains her?'

Her mind raced. They could run. To where? Eru? Their plans were based on a slow journey east, but they would need a place to shelter now. Tomorrow.

They could go back to Sabley, the valley village where her father was a tanner and her mother looked after her little brother Oskar. She'd spent her teens hating the place. The smell of it, the muck in the streets, the grey, lifeless faces of the people who lived their entire lives there, never venturing further than the next town, stuck in an even bigger rut than Rosheen. Oh yes, Haldor had been right about that and it had stung her, but Sabley and its dull ways might be safe. Safer than here, at least.

And Anzu. What would happen to her? Rosheen's mother had stolen the egg especially for her sixth birthday. The excited little girl had spent the next two summers feeding Anzu, imprinting herself upon the griffin until she was ready to fledge. Rosheen first heard Anzu's thoughts when she was eight years old and the griffin had been Rosheen's guardian and companion every day since. Rosheen had stuck by her, even when Anzu's young, animalistic impulses had got the better of her. Rosheen couldn't contemplate abandoning her.

Or, even worse, without her source of magical power, would Anzu die?

'When the end comes, nothing will ever be the same again.' Haldor peered through the telescope's eyepiece. 'People, *ordinary* people, resent your magic, your powers and the way mages have abused their privilege.'

'I have never—'

'Oh, yes, I'm sure you're as pure as the rain that falls from the sky.' Haldor leaned back from the eyepiece. 'But vengeful mobs rarely check their victims' credentials.' He spun on the stool to face her. 'I like you, Witch Who Thinks She's a Warlock, but if you want to survive the chaos that follows the end of magic, you will need to be on the winning side. You're welcome to join us here. You strike me as smart and resourceful.'

'That's if you're right, of course.'

'You know I'm right. You've seen it for yourself.'

'So, magic is gone, people panic, kingdoms wage war and Haldor Frang... does what, exactly?' Rosheen said, doing her best to remain defiant. 'This rabble is no match for Bhaltair's armies.'

'All I seek is an audience with King Bhaltair of Taranis. I want nothing more than his respect, an understanding between us.'

'What sort of understanding?'

'His is the most magnificent stronghold in the Newlands, he commands the greatest armies, and I want him to recognise a fellow leader of men.'

'Good grief, it always comes down to ego, doesn't it?' Rosheen shook her head. 'You'll kill hundreds of innocents, burn their homes and crops, all so that you can get into a dick-measuring contest with all the other crowned clots.'

'Greatness is measured in respect, not the size of one's genitals.'

Rosheen didn't have an answer for that one.

Rosheen, is everything all right? Anzu's voice came to her and Rosheen gently nudged the telescope with her fingers.

And Haldor saw it. 'Signalling to Anzu? Why be coy? Invite her down!'

Rosheen grimaced but did nothing more, not wanting to give him the satisfaction that he was right.

'And so, anyway, Bhaltair will not meet with me,' Haldor continued. 'He won't even receive my emissaries. Word came to me that he dismissed me as a savage.' Haldor raised a mock-offended eyebrow. 'I know. Me? How dare he?' Haldor moved over to a pile of black, jar-like cylinders stacked in a pyramid by the maps on the table. He hefted one of the objects, then hopped it from hand to hand like an amateur juggler.

'Is that... an explosive shell?' Rosheen took a step back. 'Should you be doing that?'

Haldor shook the shell and it rattled like peas in a jar. 'Flash powder from Rigo.' He grinned. 'Very rare, very expensive, very volatile. Have you ever seen one go off? Magnificent colours. And the heat! If I am to bring King Bhaltair to the negotiating table, I need to make some noise, yes? Grab his attention. And that's where you come in.'

'I won't do it.'

'You haven't even heard what it is yet.'

'I don't need to,' Rosheen said. 'I can see it in your eyes. I don't hurt people, Haldor. And this is insane. If your plan is to take advantage of the fall of magic, why not wait till it actually happens? How many men died today because of your belief in a drunk astronomer's calculations?'

'While every other warlord and king in the Newlands will be scrabbling to make sense of what has happened, I will already be seated in Castle Agrona with a battle-hardened army and a ready strategy for consolidating my power. I'm basically a genius.'

'Agrona?'

'The attack on Castle Agrona is already under way. By noon tomorrow Old King Torren will be dead, and what was his will become mine.'

'What?' Rosheen's lips went numb. While she was here playing around with astronomers and warlords, Torren's home was being overrun. Her belly sank with a sickening guilt and she knew she had to get out of this place now. Without another word, she backed away to leave.

40

'Farewell, witchy girl.' Haldor didn't move to stop her. 'Be sure to inspect the heads on your way out.'

Rosheen tried to ignore his words as she marched out of the yurt into the crisp night air. Her intent was to find Anzu and fly straight to Castle Agrona. But she couldn't fight the instinct to glance at the spikes.

As she did so, Rosheen's skin tingled and crawled, her stomach turned and she felt light-headed.

There, side-by-side, were the heads of her mother and father. Both had their eyes closed, foreheads crinkled into frowns and mouths half-open as if about to ask a question. Instinctively, she drew on her powers to restore her senses, but the heartache remained and the tears still came.

'I assure you, they felt no pain.' Haldor's voice came to her as if in a dream.

She spun to face him, ready to tear his heart from chest, but he was holding a small square of parchment up for her to see.

'Take it,' Haldor said. 'Look closely.'

Rosheen unfolded the parchment to find a charcoal sketch of a young woman. After a few moments, she realised it was her. She had a vague memory of posing for Mr Doon in Sabley for—

Her heart froze. She looked up to Haldor's unblinking eyes and the tattooed tears below them. 'How did you get this?'

'Your brother loves you very much,' Haldor said in a soft whisper. The words made Rosheen feel nauseous.

'I don't believe you,' she said, the words coming as a ragged whisper.

'The truth-seer doesn't believe me? Then find him. Use your magic.' Haldor stepped back and folded his arms in anticipation. Rosheen didn't move. A half-smile crept across Haldor's face. 'Oh no. That's right. You can't, can you? Moon children are a blind spot for you mages, hmm? You can find me, my men, King Torren, whoever, but a moon child…? Your own brother? He's like a ghost to you, isn't he? One of the great mysteries of magic and moon children. How wonderful. I could talk about it all night. The research I did, looking for a mage with such a weakness. It's no accident that I chose you,

Rosheen. I'm sorry, but I look for people I can exploit, and you were ripe as summer strawberries.'

Rosheen felt like she was in a bubble. No sound could penetrate it. Blood pounded in her ears. This couldn't be real.

Rosheen. Anzu's voice came to her. *I'm giving you two more circuits of the camp, then I'm coming down.*

'I always get what I want, Rosheen,' Haldor said quietly. 'I will do whatever it takes.'

'I could kill you right this moment.' Rosheen's mouth was dry, her voice trembling. 'You'd be dead before you hit the floor. Where is he? Where's Oskar?'

'The boy's not here, Rosheen, I'm not an idiot. He is in a safe place, a secret location that I know nothing about, so don't bother trying to squeeze it out of me. He's being looked after by a man called Yanick Heck. Yanick brings the lad food and water and sings him songs – Yanick has an uncommonly beautiful singing voice for such a brutish-looking man – and he has told Oskar that his sister Rosheen will be joining them soon. What Oskar doesn't know is that if you refuse me again, or should any harm come to me, then Yanick will move behind Oskar and silently slit his throat. His head will then join theirs.'

Rosheen didn't need her magic to tell that he wasn't lying.

'One small favour before magic is gone for ever.' Haldor stepped closer, taking her hands. 'You won't be killing anyone. One little thing for me and then you and your brother will be free to live under my good graces.'

Rosheen…? Anzu's voice came to her, cutting through the swirl of confusion in her mind. *Is everything okay? Can you hear me, Rosheen? Hello…? Hello…?*

How to Wind Up Trolls

'What is wrong with you?' Sander asked as he and Ragnall hid whispering in the rocks by the covered bridge over the River Lug. The sun wasn't high enough to bring any direct light to the valley, but Sander lay on his back and watched as daybreak stained the clouds bright pink. 'We could have enjoyed a quiet drink, put the world to rights, had a good laugh. But no, you have to insult every nutcase with a blade and I end up killing a man. I've never killed anyone before, Raggy. One minute the man's spitting his hot, boozy breath in my face, the next...' Sander's voice trailed off as the memory of the dead man on the tavern floor flooded back and his anxiety returned in the form of a numb feeling in his chest. Sander found himself rubbing his breastbone, trying to bring some feeling back as he panted like a mother in labour.

'Oh, they're idiots, boy.' Ragnall's voice wasn't as slurred now, but he was no less bitter. 'Remember how hot it was last summer? They were happy to live in their own filth and were surprised when the plague broke out, and *then* they had the nerve to be pissed off when I asked for fair coin for my troubles. Don't know why I bother. I should leave them all to rot in their defilement.'

Ragnall was what mages called 'Old Magic'. His family went all the way back to the Mage Wars over three hundred years ago. His forebears were mages to great kings and warlords, so they were dismayed when he rebelled and chose what many considered to be the lesser craft of hedge wizardry. Mages were rare enough as it was. Perhaps one in a hundred thousand people had some level of magical ability, and those with any kind of talent were even more uncommon. Kings and queens competed to tempt the finest mages into their employ. Ragnall's choice to follow the more noble, though considerably less affluent, path of hedge wizardry had probably cost him an actual king's ransom, a lavishly decorated room in a tall tower, a daily choice of the finest foods and wines and his pick of royal concubines.

'I think I've made a terrible mistake.' Ragnall took a swig from a gourd he had concealed in his robe. 'I wanted to serve these people, be of use, and not be stuck in some castle somewhere with a bunch of pompous twats. But bloody hell these people don't want to be helped, Sander, I can tell you that.'

'You've had a long winter, that's all,' Sander reassured him. 'It's Springtide. Put all that behind you.'

'Mother was right.' Ragnall swished the gourd around as he got to the dregs. 'When I left, she warned me that hedge wizardry was "of the people". I told her, *I know that*, I said, but I didn't realise she was giving me a warning. I envy you, Sander.'

This last comment threw Sander. Ragnall was short on compliments, and his stock of envy was even scarcer. 'You what?' Sander asked.

'I know the politics up there must be a nightmare, but when was the last time you had to pierce a cyst on some swineherder's scrotum, eh?' Ragnall took another slurp, smacked his lips and exhaled. 'No, I should jack it all in, go back home. Mother's dead now, and Father must be hanging on by the skin of his teeth.'

'They serve Queen Cliona in Cerwidden, is that right?'

Ragnall nodded. 'Yeah, she's what? A hundred and twelve? I'll step in and take over. How hard can it be? Yes, yes, yes.' Ragnall took a final gulp from the gourd, wiping his lips on the back of his hand. 'It's time for a change.'

'Change.' Sander pondered on the word. 'Do you think Bhaltair would give me some time off?'

'Time off?' Ragnall wrinkled his nose. 'You're not some farmhand, Sander, you're the mage to the most powerful king in the Newlands. A man whose enemies can't wait for him to slip up. He'll more likely let you have your way with his wife's corpse than give you a vacation.'

'I'm here, aren't I? He let me have this.'

'Springtide weekend is a deeply sacred festival. It's been honoured by our people for thousands of years. He *has* to let you take this weekend off or he'll incur the wrath of every mage in the Nine Kingdoms. What do you want time off for, anyway?'

'I need to think about where my life is going. I killed a man today, Ragnall.'

Ragnall nodded and placed a hand on his former pupil's shoulder. 'That's what this weekend is about. Contemplation of the mage's path and all that. Yes, you took a life, and that's a terrible thing. It's what you do next that will define you.'

'And what's that?'

'Buggered if I know, Sander. Maybe you need some time off?' Ragnall cackled and cuffed the younger mage around the head.

'Brilliant, thanks, Ragnall,' Sander said.

Ragnall peered around the rock towards the covered bridge. 'I reckon he's asleep again. Ready?'

Sander nodded as he tied his long hair back with a ribbon.

After a count of three, the pair of them jumped to their feet and ran across the wooden bridge, shouting, 'Wake up!' at the tops of their voices and stamping their boots on the rickety boards. The Springtide weekend, while acknowledged by all as a sacrosanct festival, was also a time for mages to let their hair down, and it had become something of a tradition with Sander and Ragnall to spend theirs teasing the local magic wildlife.

From below came the disgruntled groan of Cleff, the bridge's troll, who instinctively awoke and growled at any noise from the bridge above. Now the sun had risen, he was slow and groggy. He roared and waved his fist at them as he clumsily clambered up the rocks to catch them, but they were already legging it down the road, chuckling to themselves, having played the same trick on the poor troll half a dozen times this morning already.

Bored of pranking Cleff, the two of them decided to retire to Ragnall's cave. This was guarded by another troll, Gorm. They wouldn't be tormenting this troll. Ragnall and Gorm had an arrangement.

Gorm was once the terror of the Arranrod Mountains, the patriarch of a family of trolls who emerged from caves and underground rivers to regularly raid lowland farms in the dead of night for sheep and goats. Gorm was disgraced after an unfortunate incident when he got drunk on cider given to him by local shepherd boys and, in his stupor, shoved one of them over a cliff. The lad tumbled to his death on the rocks hundreds of feet below. When the villagers rose up and killed Gorm's family, he fled, banished from his beloved mountains for ever, shunned even by his own kind.

Now he lived in exile, deep in Ragnall's mushroom cave. It was an arrangement beneficial to both of them. Ragnall got an excellent guard for his secret cave, and Gorm got somewhere safe to live.

Trouble was, every now and then, Ragnall needed the troll out of the cave, and trolls aren't noted for listening to reasonable requests. It's well known than trolls are averse to sunlight and lightning; it's less well known that they also loathe the sound of church bells.

Ragnall kept a pair of Faith bells – consecrated by First Minister of the Faith Yorath Pasco himself – behind a rock near the cave's entrance. He handed one to Sander and they started ringing them directly over the sinkhole entrance to the cave.

It wasn't long before they heard low grunts, the clink of tumbling rocks and the heavy slap of large, bare feet moving about. A meaty hand with chubby fingers gripped the stones at the edge of the sink-hole, and arms thick as oak tree trunks heaved the rest of the blue-skinned giant out of the cave. He looked askance at Sander and Ragnall, perhaps considering swiping them with a gigantic backhander, but they rang their bells faster and harder.

'Come along, Gorm,' Ragnall said over the clanging. 'Off you pop, old friend. Sander and I need the cave for a while.'

Gorm slapped his hands over his ears and sloped off into the wood.

'Will he be all right?' Sander gestured up at the rising sun.

'He always finds a shady spot. He'll be fine.' Ragnall extended an arm into the dark hole in the ground. 'After you, Sander Bree.'

Sander knew the cave almost as well as Ragnall. It was where they had practised magic when he was first apprenticed to the old man, a hide-away from the village's gossips and the citadel's spies.

Drawing on their powers to adjust their eyes to see in the pitch darkness, they passed through Gorm's big chamber, a surprisingly tidy nest of hay and grass scattered with the bones and skulls of sheep and goats, all sucked dry of their meat and marrow. Another handy side-product of Ragnall's arrangement with Gorm was that Ragnall would sell the bones to passing troubadours who hollowed them out to make wind instruments. He often griped that it was better money than he made from hedge wizardry and would sometimes fantasise about opening a music shop in the village. This kind of distracted daydreaming had become all too common with Ragnall of late. His heart simply wasn't in it any more.

As they descended down a narrow, twisting tunnel, the air became stifling and the heat made their backs sweat, but it soon opened up into a larger passageway where they could stride upright without fear of banging their heads on the dripping limestone stalactites.

After a short walk, the air became cooler again and a light drew them into a larger chamber, one as big as King Bhaltair's throne room in Taranis. A beam of sunlight shone through a hole in the ceiling, giving the pool below a strange, milky glow.

'A bowl of the finest potage in the whole of the Newlands, my friend?' Ragnall asked, throwing back a sheet to reveal his old pots and pans. He grew edible fungi down here, and Sander had to admit that the old coot made the best mushroom soup he'd ever tasted.

'It's the only reason I put up with your moaning, Raggy,' he said, untying his hair, shrugging off his robes and wading into the pool. Floating on his back, the cool water washed away his perspiration, and his hair spread around him like a halo. From here, Sander could look up through the hole in the ceiling. The moons were visible, but pale in the daylight. The weeds and vines that clung to the cave's ceiling were reaching up for them, stretching to snatch a satellite in their grasp. 'What do you think he meant?'

'Who?' Ragnall assembled some dry sticks and with a flash of energy from his hand started a fire.

'The Brother in the Jolly Cooper.' Sander continued to stare up at the moons. 'He said the end was written in the stars, and that astronomers had agreed the Lapis Moon will die.'

'Oh, please. Have you ever met an astronomer? Gods, they're an excitable lot. It's a new philosophy and they're desperate for attention, that's all. If we panicked every time they said some rock was going to wipe us all out, we'd never get out of bloody bed.'

'The Brother sounded pretty convinced.'

'Oh, who knows what those gullible zealots are thinking half the time?' Ragnall dipped a pot into the water, filling it three-quarters full then hanging it over the fire. 'Brothers of the Faith both fear and covet our powers, Sander, never forget that. Awe and envy are close cousins.'

'It got me thinking, is all. I've had some odd dreams recently.'

'Prophecies?' Ragnall asked, suddenly interested. Sander had never possessed much of a skill for foresight, but dreams were often the first inkling of a tumultuous future.

'Bad dreams,' he said. 'I think my heart's going to explode. It's beating really fast, and if I don't wake up then I'm sure I'm going to die.'

'That's anxiety.' Ragnall dismissed Sander's worries with a wave. 'Perfectly normal when negotiating the slippery slope of middle age.'

'You grow out of it, then?'

'No, it generally gets worse,' the old man replied with a chuckle.

'Oh, perfect, great, wonderful.' Sander was directly under the moons now, the pool's water filling his ears. 'What if it all ended, Raggy? What if our magic left us?'

'Mages have been experiencing those kinds of dreams and visions since the beginning of time, Sander. All mages do.' Ragnall gestured with one hand and a small black cauldron came floating from its nook and across the cave to hover over the fire. 'By definition, the end of magic is our greatest fear.'

'You've had them?'

'No,' Ragnall said, answering far too quickly for Sander's liking.

'You bloody have. I can tell when you're lying.'

'Silly dreams, that's all.'

'Is that why you've been hitting the firewater so hard?' Sander joked. 'You've seen the end of the world and you want to go out high as a kite.'

Now Ragnall took far too long to reply. Staring into the flames, he said, 'Visions are not literal, Sander. They're open to interpretation. A confused message from your own mind that something is wrong and needs addressing.'

'What did you see?'

'Nothing.'

'The end of magic?'

'Magic has always been with us, Sander Bree, and it always will be. Calm yourself.' He kicked at the water, splashing Sander who jerked upright and had to paddle to stay afloat. 'Our kind might not be kings, but we rule this world.'

'We do not—' Sander started to scoff.

'Oh no?' Ragnall looked offended. Angry, even. 'There's been peace for centuries, Sander, and it's thanks to us. No king or warlord dare go on the offensive because they know the consequences. They've read about the Mage Wars, how it laid waste to the land, how the elves and goblins and other magical species were wiped out. It's a delicate balance, to be sure, but it bloody works.'

'What about that nutter from the north? The Dogmeat General.'

'Who?'

'Bhaltair's been watching him. He's been fighting other warlords, stirring up trouble. Apparently, he butchers his enemies and serves them as dog meat.'

'Or he's from Grainne.'

'What makes you say that?'

'They play a game with dice up there called "Eating Dog Meat". Maybe he's good at it? Who is he, anyway?'

'Not sure, but he keeps winning skirmishes and then fades into the night.'

Ragnall sneered and dismissed him with a wave. 'Ach, we've had his like before, and we will again. All it takes is one good mage and then *he's* dog meat.'

'Why not us?'

'Eh?'

'You and me. We could take him down. Have a bit of an adventure.'

Ragnall considered the idea for precisely three heartbeats. 'Ah, let some other mage do it. And if he ever shows his face around here, you can drop one of your rocks on him.' He scooped up a wicker basket and started peering into the dark where the mushrooms grew. 'Seriously, Sander, learn to relax. Take it from me, we've never had it so good. Now stop pissing about and help me with this soup.'

Ship Song

Oskar felt sick. Not the kind of sick where he had eaten something bad and Mother – *Oh, Mother, I miss you, I miss you, I miss you* – would comfort him, but a strange queasiness all over. His stomach turned and tumbled, his head ebbed and flowed between a pounding headache and a faint giddiness, even his lips felt numb and fat, and the thought of food brought him anguish.

The cabin lurched to one side and there were shouts from above. Oskar recognised Yanick Heck's voice, sounding like a crow with a chest infection as he coughed orders at the men on the ship's deck. These were followed by the thump of boots, more creaking of ropes and the flap of sails.

They had boarded the *Queen Mathilde* after hours stuck in a cage on a bumpy road, listening to Yanick's life story interspersed with songs that Oskar somehow knew were filthy even though he could not understand the words. There was little time for rest as Yanick drew his dagger and shoved Oskar towards the lone ship at the end of the wooden pier. It was about the size of his home at the farm – *the flames and the smoke, oh gods, I can never go back* – but before he could explore, Oskar was taken down into the hold, manacled to a post propping up sacks of rice and flour, and left alone.

The ship set sail not long after and that's when the rocking began. Oskar's father – *Oh, Father, why did you fight back? I would have gone with them peacefully and they would have let you live* – told stories of their family's journey across the Sugar Sea from Eru, how the waves had been higher than mountains, and how sea monsters had nearly bitten the ship in two, and how the ships themselves sang strange songs. Oskar had always been enthralled by these stories and desperately wanted to travel the oceans. Well, here he was, and it was by turns boring and sickening and terrifying.

The noises in the gloomy hold kept putting him on edge. Oskar could hear the *scritch-scratch* of rats moving around him, the curious *bawks?* of chickens in cages. Bottles and jars rumbled and clinked with the swell of the sea, sacks of flour puffed tiny breaths of white cloud as they shifted, and ropes creaked with the strain as they held wooden crates, barrels and water casks in place.

From all around, a new noise came. An eerie moaning, as if the ship itself was sighing sadly. *Shipsong!* So, Father wasn't making it up. He had told Oskar how Eru Oak was magical, and that shipbuilders always made the keel of a boat from Eru Oak because it would sing and keep the sea monsters away.

Up above, Yanick started to harmonise along with the ship. Oskar didn't understand the words, but this tune was sad and Yanick's voice became high and light, almost like Mother's when she sang him a lullaby. It was hard to believe it came from the same man who hacked and barked his way through a conversation.

The hatch to the deck was wrenched open with a loud rattle of lock iron that made Oskar jump. Heavy boots came clumping down as the ship's boy descended into the hold. He was about the same age as the shepherd boy in Sabley Village, and he sloped around with hunched shoulders as he lit the lanterns. He approached Oskar with a steaming bowl in one hand. The smell of fish stew wafted over Oskar and he retched, but nothing came up. The boy's freckled face twisted as he cackled at Oskar's nausea.

'Get this inside you.' He deposited the tin bowl on the deck by Oskar's feet, but Oskar could not even bring himself to look at it.

For a moment, the ship's boy stared at him, then, '*Blurgh!*' He lunged forward, making Oskar flinch. The boy laughed and stomped his boots on the deck in delight. Oskar began to think of some of the children in Sabley Village. He had seen them taunting cats and dogs, and if he had the misfortune to cross their paths, they would do the same to him. This boy had their streak of cruelty.

'Yah!' the ship's boy cried, raising a fist.

Oskar cowered, but the blow didn't come.

'Fuckwit,' the boy muttered to himself, then scooped up the bowl and spoon again. 'Eat it.' The boy shoved Oskar on the shoulder, but Oskar shook his head. 'Eat or I get a whippin'.'

Oskar shook his head again. The ship's boy grabbed Oskar's jaw, squeezed and forced the spoon into Oskar's mouth, clanking it against his teeth. The hot liquid filled Oskar's mouth and he gulped down a little of it, spluttering the rest. It burned his tongue and was far too salty, but before he could object, the ship's boy had another spoonful for him.

Though his legs were manacled to the deck, Oskar still had the use of his hands and he smacked the bowl away, spilling some of the stew over the ship's boy.

The boy jutted his lower jaw and the pale skin under his freckles reddened as he stared down at the mess on his lap. 'Oh gods. I look like I pissed meself.'

Oskar sputtered a laugh. He didn't want to but couldn't help himself.

The boy's arm was a blur as he brought it around to slap Oskar across the face. Oskar shuddered with shock. 'Ain't laughing now, are you? You bastard!' He formed a fist and began beating Oskar about the head while repeating, 'Laugh at me, will ya? Laugh at me?' again and again. Oskar curled into a ball and began screaming, but the boy kept pounding him, his hard, gnarly knuckles making Oskar see stars with every blow. One mashed Oskar's ear and he howled in pain and moaned for him to stop, but this only made the ship's boy box his ears all the more.

And then it did stop. There was a scuffling of boots on the deck and Oskar looked up to see the man with the long white hair and jagged teeth gripping the boy's scalp. Yanick Heck, Oskar's kidnapper, swung the ship's boy around, face first into a wooden post. The boy's nose broke and jerked to one side with a crack that made Oskar wince more than any punch. Yanick did it again, and this time, a yellow tooth came spinning from the boy's mouth and clattered to the deck. Yanick threw the ship's boy after it. He landed hard and pawed at his bloody nose and mouth.

'He's not to be touched.' Yanick pointed at Oskar.

'M-my nose. You broke my nose!'

'Next time, Craig, it's your bollocks. Now get back to yer chores afore I throw ye overboard.'

'I'm telling my uncle!' the ship's boy yelped as he scurried back up the steps, at the top of which he was greeted by the cruel laughter of his fellow sailors.

The deck hatch slammed shut and there was darkness once more.

Yanick crouched down by Oskar, taking the boy's head in his rough hands.

'Just a few bruises,' he muttered.

Oskar winced as Yanick brushed his fingers against his ears.

'There now. You'll be all right. You must eat, boy.' Yanick picked up the bowl and stirred a bent spoon in what remained of the oily chunks of fish and bread. 'Can't have you dead before your sister gets back. She'll be sad, Haldor'll be pissed at me, and that's when heads roll.'

He held a spoonful under Oskar's nose. Oskar hesitated. The smell made him convulse, but he knew that Yanick wouldn't take any nonsense, and so he leaned forward and took a sip.

'Good laddie.' Yanick gave him another helping, and another, then let the spoon clatter back into the bowl. Something in Oskar's belly demanded a refill and with shaking hands, he snatched up the spoon and bowl and scarfed down more. 'Away you go. We'll be here a few nights on the *Queen Mathilde*, going around in poxy circles, guided by the Ocean's Hand. Need to see if that crazy astronomer was right. We'll get you to your sister once we're back on land, then we'll go south to…' It took Oskar a moment to realise that Yanick had stopped talking. He glanced up to find the sailor giving him a familiar look. One that he saw in the faces of his old neighbours and the villagers. They didn't look at anyone else like that, only him.

'You haven't a clue what I'm on about, do you boy?'

Oskar tried to reply, but only a strange moan came out.

Yanick scruffed his hair and stood. 'Get some rest,' he told Oskar. As he rose up the steps to the deck, he added, 'And if your sister does as she's told, you'll be with her in a day or two.'

A day or two. Oskar felt the stew bubble inside him. A rolling wave made the ship lurch once more and he knew it wouldn't be long before it all came back up again. But a day or two – he could manage a day or two. He could survive for a day or two. And then he would see Rosheen again.

The ship began to sing again and Oskar hummed along with it. The lanterns swayed with the swell and sent orange light and long shadows sliding around Oskar as he ate his stew.

The Mighty Citadel of Taranis and Its Many Aromas

Sander woke up around mid-afternoon. He left Ragnall asleep in his cave and started to stroll along the Taranis Road. His every footfall made his head pound like a bass drum, and he despaired that all his headache potions were in his chambers at the citadel. He wasn't sure what Raggy put in his mushroom soup – some kind of secret ingredient that Sander suspected was nothing more than home-made hooch – but it made his mouth dry and the skin around his skull feel tight. He spent the first mile or so of his walk convincing himself that the symptoms were some kind of allergic reaction to the soup and that he would surely be dead before the end of the day.

This was a perfectly normal thought cycle for Sander. Assume the worst, wallow in pity, then shrug it off and feel better about himself. Only these days, it was getting harder to shrug off the doom and gloom.

And now he'd killed a man.

Sander had considered using magic to fly to Taranis, but flight was exhausting and dangerous, and in his state, he'd most likely end up flattened on the side of a cliff face or misjudge the distance and drown in a lake. He convinced himself that a bit of fresh air and exercise might help walk it off, but every flat, heavy footstep just made it worse and that cloud of guilt would not go away.

He'd been walking for about an hour and a half when a passing farmer offered him a lift on his horse and cart. 'Taranis? I'm going that way myself. Hop on, Mage.'

'You, sir, are a hero and my new best friend.' Sander heaved himself up onto the seat next to the farmer, who wittered on about the route he was planning to take, as if Sander cared. The farmer ponged a bit – there were remnants of recently unloaded manure in the empty cart – but Sander was willing to put up with it if it meant he could give his head a rest. He might get even get a nap out of it, if only this fellow would shut up.

'I'm Madoc,' the farmer said. 'Madoc Shay.' He was perhaps twenty years younger than Sander. Wide-eyed with hair like freshly harvested straw, the ravages of his profession had not yet taken their toll on Madoc, apart from a raw stripe of sunburn across his nose.

'A pleasure, Madoc.' Sander smiled, not offering his own name and hiding under his long hair so that only his nose poked out between the blond curtains.

'My ma always said to do favours for mages, as you never know when you'll need one from them.'

'Your mother is a very wise woman, Madoc.'

Madoc geed his horse and they began bumping along the rocky road to Taranis. 'I expect you get people doin' you favours all the time?'

'Not as many as you'd think.' Sander didn't mean to sound ungrateful, but in truth, he was rather taken for granted. Not only by the king and the court, but by pretty much everyone he met. Barely a day went by when he wasn't asked to cure some piddling ailment.

'I have this growth on my big toe—' Madoc started.

Oh, here we go. 'Garlic juice,' Sander jumped in before he was given too many unnecessary gory details. 'Rub it on the growth, cover it with a clean bandage, repeat for a couple of months.'

'You can't *magic* it away?' Madoc waggled his fingers on the word magic. Why did so many people insist on doing that? Street conjurers had a lot to answer for.

'I'm not much of a healer, to be honest,' Sander puffed. 'And magic can be rather exhausting, especially healing magic, so if there's a regular way of doing it, then we prefer—'

'You don't want to give it a try?' Madoc reached down to take off one of his boots. 'Have a gander, p'raps?'

'Thank you for the opportunity, but no.' Sander leaned back and closed his eyes, hoping that would be the end of it.

'That's a shame.' Madoc sat bolt upright, gripping the reins, his voice terse.

Sander forced himself to open one eye. 'Try the garlic option, friend. It works, I promise you.'

'I reckoned if I did you a favour, then you might do one for me, but never mind. I know you mages think you're better than us regular folks.'

'There's no need to get like that.'

'I ain't gettin' like nothin'.'

'I could turn you into ashes.' Sander clicked his fingers and Madoc tensed. 'But I choose not to, so we're even.'

'So it's threats, is it?'

'Look... uhm...' Sander gestured at the farmer, struggling to remember his name.

'Madoc.'

'Madoc, I don't mean to be rude, but if I needed... manure, or whatever is it you trade, I would pay for your services fair and square and we'd shake hands and be on our way. Now, me curing you of... whatever it is on your big toe in exchange for a ride to Taranis – where, I hasten to remind you, you're going *anyway* – hardly seems fair now, does it?'

'If you say so.'

'I do.'

The cart continued to rock gently along the road, an uncomfortable silence between the two men. Just how Sander liked it.

'We have a mage in our village,' Madoc offered.

'Well done.'

'Name's Ragnall Rokus. You know him?'

'Actually, I do.'

'He's a twat an' all.'

'I'm going to sleep now, Madoc.' Sander closed his eyes again. 'Try anything funny and I'll turn you into a frog. One that's allergic to water.'

Any traveller coming to Taranis from the south has to follow the curve of the Tarn Valley, and there comes a point when you turn a corner and the citadel is incontrovertibly *there*. A collection of jagged white shards surrounded by Sander's slowly orbiting moons. One of the truly incredible sights of the world.

It was visible from a good ten miles away. The citadel's limestone walls gleamed in the sun, making the onlooker's eyeballs throb if they gazed for too long. What had started as a simple fort town had evolved over four hundred years into a teetering pile of towers, belfries, fortifications, spires, steeples and turrets, all scattered with scaffold and cranes as parts of it were repaired or built upon. The citadel was always growing, forever climbing upwards within its walls as the Royal Engineering Corps found new ways to make towers taller and thinner, an obsession of theirs that Sander found aggravating in the extreme. The quarters at the top of these phallic compensations often housed important people that he had to deal with, and he objected to navigating narrow, endless spiral stairwells merely to doff the cap to some courtier or minor royal. Most days, he chose to glide up and down them like a ghost. Walking was far too much effort.

Madoc pulled up about half a mile outside the main gates, directly under the path of the outer ring of floating mage moons. Beneath the ever-shifting cover of their shadows, he peered up at them fretfully. Their cart was at the rear of a queue of traders moving in and out, each one paying a tithe to enter, or a tax to leave, or having their wares searched for contraband or weapons.

Despite Sander's best efforts, sleep did not come on the journey. He had hoped the hypnotic rocking of the cart might send him off, but whenever he closed his eyes, he kept seeing the dead Brother's body and he jolted awake.

Sander yawned theatrically and hopped off the cart. 'I'll walk the rest of the way, I think. Thanks for the ride... uhm... oh... er...'

'Madoc!' the farmer snapped.

'Madoc, yes, of course. Look, I'm sorry about earlier. I had a bad day yesterday, I...' Sander squinted into empty space, trying to figure out what went wrong. 'I've done it so many times, it's almost like a party trick. I never meant to hurt the man. How was I to know he had a weak heart? I'm not a killer.'

He glanced up at Madoc who was staring at him askance. The man had no clue what Sander was on about, and he now looked more than a little afraid of his passenger.

Sander apologised again, waving the thoughts away. 'Uh, why don't you show me that big toe, eh? Maybe there's something I can do?'

'I'd rather you didn't, if it's all the same,' Madoc said in haste, all too eager to be rid of his passenger. 'Garlic juice, you say? I'll give that a try instead.'

'No, really, I can help, let me—'

Madoc shook his horse's reins and the cart pulled away, catching up with the back of the queue. He clearly wanted to be anywhere but near this babbling mage.

'Good luck with the lads on the gate,' Sander called after him. 'I'll put in a word for you,' he said, knowing full well that he'd do nothing of the sort. As mage to the king, Sander had his own private entrance by Del's Gate: a small door made from Andraste oak that predated the Mage Wars, carved with ancient runes, which opened only to his command.

He entered without fuss and shuffled along Lou-Lou's Way, a narrow tunnel through the thick walls, emerging out of another small door behind a book stall in Queen Patricia's Square, the citadel's most bustling marketplace. The sudden rush of noise and aromas was overwhelming.

What set Taranis apart from every other castle, city and village in the Newlands was the smell. If there was one thing King Bhaltair had got right, one legacy that future generations would praise him for, it was the citadel's highly efficient plumbing system. He was known across the Nine Kingdoms as Bhaltair the Plumber, though never to his face. Taranis was a fragrant citadel, a walled refuge from the perils of the great outdoors.

Sander had never been particularly keen on nature. The stench of flowers got up his nose and pollen was like grit in his eyes. In Taranis, he felt at home like nowhere else. A microcosm of the world, where he could find a Tiarnan kebab at any time of the day or night, enjoy the best baths in all of Wayland, get a full-body Morven massage, or simply shut the door to his chambers and contemplate the universe.

Traders contested for customers, hollering out special offers on the vegetables, fruit or meat that had been so ripe, zesty and fresh this morning, and now had to be flogged off before they went on the turn.

It felt like the whole world came here to buy, sell or gawp at what was on display. Elegant Tiarnans sold their silks and pottery; slender-fingered Sachari women made intricate gold trinkets and delicate jewellery while you watched; serious-looking Dands did things with spices and meat that would make grown men weep; families of Gerdas from Arranrod sold anything and everything they could shove onto their already overburdened carts; and all around were the playful screams of children.

And, unlike a lot of other nations in the north or on the Rigo continent, there were no slaves. Say what you like about Bhaltair, but putting an end to that was his first act as king. Cynics said it was simply because free people could be taxed and he needed the money – and they were right – but none of those who were freed were complaining. Well, not at first. Even freed slaves would moan about the rising taxes eventually.

Scattered here and there were remnants of the ancient magical races. Tall, fair folk who might have been descended from elves, though they were all gone, of course, and a few furtive-looking goblins huddled together as they tried to sell passers-by their potions, all of which were useless to humans, and some of which were even deadly, but the gullible were also in good supply around here, too. Sander passed a pile of blue-skinned trolls, all asleep and entwined under a heavy shade, resting before they had to pull their doubledecker carts back home at the end of the day.

Sander ducked into gloomy short-cut walkways – Stickleback Way, Pisspot Lane, Fleshmarket Close – the kinds of places where only mages dared to walk alone, then he walked up the winding stairs of the Sovereign's Rise around the backs of watchtowers and rose above the lower levels of the citadel. The noise died down to a background burble up here, where some of the wealthier merchants owned impressive apartments. The richer they were, the more ridiculous and gaudy the exterior decor. The latest thing was to clad your walls in colourful mosaics depicting scenes from myth and legend. He passed one tower that had what looked like a three-legged unicorn exploding at its base. It was difficult to tell. He wasn't much of a fan of modern art.

People started to recognise him here, too. The social climbers – courtiers, advisors, liggers and royal suck-ups – would all dutifully smile and incline their heads, some even averting their gaze. That little misconception annoyed him as it was elder Brothers of the Faith, not mages, who insisted that you shouldn't look directly at them. He made a point of glaring at the Brothers' pompous faces as often as possible.

He passed several checkpoints, his boots clacking on stone steps as he approached the vast doors to the main castle. The guards acknowledged his approach by pounding their pikes on the grand marble plaza floor, alerting the doorkeepers inside. With a crack and a groan, the giant doors opened a sliver, just wide enough for Sander to stroll inside.

Now that the noise of the citadel's hustle and bustle was behind him, Sander could start to place his thoughts into some kind of order. An important decision began to feel clearer to him, like clouds parting and revealing blue skies beyond. He didn't become a mage to harm people, let alone kill anyone. And he didn't become a mage to end up as bitter as Ragnall. It was a simple and bold choice. But was he simple and bold enough to make it?

He mulled it over as he walked through the castle almost in a daydream, taking the same route to his chambers for the umpteenth time. Inside the castle was another world altogether, and one that few denizens of the lower levels would ever see, but he knew its magnificent halls and corridors all too well. How could it be that they bored him now? He had been here too long. He was numbed to its grandeur. He remembered first arriving as a young man with Ragnall and gasping at everything he saw, but since the queen died it had never been quite the same.

He crossed the main hall, bright with lots of tall, colourfully stained windows that beamed kaleidoscopic patterns on the columns, smoothly plastered walls and marble floors. King Bhaltair preferred a contemplative court, uncluttered by mosaics or tapestries and quiet as a church. Advisors conducted their business in sotto voce huddles as they scurried to meetings behind closed doors; armoured footsteps clanged about the place, echoing off the walls, and bells rang throughout the day to call the nobles to vote, eat, pray and sleep. It was a place of seriousness and purpose.

Bhaltair may have fixed the citadel's plumbing, but there wasn't much he could do for his guards' body odour after a long shift in heavy chainmail and armour. Sander had suggested more frequent and shorter shifts and an increased ration of soap, but he had been ignored.

He had been ignored.

On such a simple matter.

That happened more and more these days.

This only made his decision all the easier.

More steps spiralled up to his private chambers at the top of the east watchtower. With a gesture, Sander began to glide a few inches above the steps. Bhaltair didn't like his mage flying about in public, but this was the beginning of Sander's private domain and the mage decided that he would do what he bloody well liked here.

In the antechamber outside his room, he found someone waiting for him, a man sat bunched on a chair, his limbs in pensive knots. Roan Pheric, the king's newest and most ambitious advisor, untangled himself when he saw Sander land gently at the top of the stairs.

'Ah, Mage Bree, the king has tasked me to command that you report to him as soon as—'

'It's Springtide, Pheric.' Sander strode straight past the stooped little man and unlocked his door. 'A sacred time for mages, a time of solitude, reflection and meditation, so piss off, there's a good chap.'

'The king said it was urgent.'

'And yet he sent you.'

'He was quite adamant.'

'Pheric, I'm exhausted and I have a bastard of a headache. Give me an hour's kip, maybe two, and I'll be right with you, okay?'

'But—'

'Pheric...' Sander took a deep breath, thought about it some more, nodded and continued, 'I quit. Tell the king I'm done. I'll discuss it further with him in the morning. I'll be gone by the end of the week.'

Pheric's mouth flexed and pouted as it tried to form words, but they wouldn't come.

'Oh, and if you're heading past the market, could you grab me some soap, please? I left mine at Ragnall's. Jasmine-scented, if possible.

Lovely, thanks, bye.' Sander closed the door in Pheric's face and set the latch. Peace at last.

He took a sharp breath that stung his nostrils. His head was giddy and he found himself standing on his tiptoes, his cheeks pulled back tight in a wide smile.

He had quit. Just like that. He felt so light. He was happy again.

Of course, he would have to find the nerve to tell the king himself, but that was one showdown that could wait until tomorrow. And he would have to find some freelance work. That could wait till the day after. First, some rest.

His room was deliberately dark and gloomy – visitors expected a touch of the gothic from a mage's private chambers – with long purple drapes that billowed gently with the spring breeze. Through the large windows was a balcony where Sander could enjoy a magnificent view of the city, his orbiting moons and the valleys rising and falling and rising up again into the distant purple peaks of the Conloch Mountains. On a good day, you could see Mount Aderyn floating above them all. There was no noise but for the occasional hoot from one of the monkeys in Bhaltair's menagerie, a maze of enclosures situated almost directly below Sander's room. He was sure the king intentionally bought the loudest howler monkeys he could find to torment his mage.

Sander slipped out of his robe, kicked off his boots and left them on the floor where he knew his ever-obliging chambermaid Elke would scoop them up in the morning. He briefly wondered who would do his washing when he was a travelling warlock, but most towns had a half-decent laundry and he had no doubt they would be honoured to have the patronage of a powerful and influential mage. Yes, this was easily the best decision of his life. No longer cramped inside these walls. Free to be who he really was, he could finally fulfil his potential. His only regret was that he hadn't thought of it sooner.

Yawning, he stood before his potions cabinet. It was made of the strongest oak, covered top to bottom in carved runes and protected by his magic. No one could access it without his command. He whispered an ancient word and waved a hand, and there followed a precise series of clunks from behind the doors as various locks and bolts

slid away. After a few moments, the doors gently drew open, revealing shelves of carefully arranged bottles and gourds filled with liquids of pea-green, blood-red and lapis-blue. He reached for one bottle
in particular. It was nearly empty. He swished it around and the red
liquid clung to the glass like lamp oil. He popped the cork, risked a
quick whiff of its vinegary odour, then took the tiniest of sips. No
magic involved. Pure Parthalan dragon's blood was rare, deadly in
large doses and quite bad for you if you used it regularly over a long
period of time. But if there was a better hangover cure, then Sander
and generations of mages before him had yet to discover it. Already
he could feel the pounding begin to lessen to a slower, tide-like throb.
His eyelids were heavy. Side effects: drowsiness.

Finally, Sander would sleep. A deep, dreamless sleep.

With a gesture, he closed the potions cabinet, inhaled deeply, then
sneezed.

Elke had put fresh flowers in a vase by the door. She did this to
annoy him, he was sure of it. He snatched them from the vase and
tossed them out through the window. He didn't wait to see them finish their long descent to the terracotta-tiled roofs below, but instead
fell face first onto his bed and was snoring in moments.

Sander was roused by a nightingale's repertoire of chirps and pulsing
tweets outside his window. He opened one eye and was dismayed to
see a deep velvet night sky pinpricked with stars. He had hoped to
sleep through till morning, but he reckoned it was only early evening
at best. His head was free of the thumping, at least, but he was still
drowsy. All he needed was a little pick-me-up. Some Angarad Wolfs-
blood, perhaps? Or a dash of Cerwidden Teardrops?

The nightingale continued to twit, beep, whistle and cheep outside.

'Oh, will you shut up?' Sander yelled. There was a flapping followed by blessed silence.

He sat upright and felt a cold flush as he remembered his declaration
to quit.

Oh gods, what a terrible, terrible mistake. He imagined himself in
rags, begging by the side of the road for food, performing conjuring
tricks – or worse – for a room for the night. He shook his head clear.

No, this was absolutely the right thing to do. He would be gone in days, a free agent. It would mean leaving his beloved Taranis behind with its food and culture, but he could travel and see parts of the world he had only ever dreamed of. This was the best idea he'd ever had. He told himself to be bold and heaved himself off the bed, scratching his balls as he shuffled and yawned across the room.

He gestured at the potions cabinet and, with a series of clunks as the locking mechanism released the various bolts and bars, his protective magic was removed and the doors swung open.

And every single bottle and gourd exploded, covering him in sticky, multicoloured liquids, all instantly rendered useless.

'What the—? OW!' He'd got a drop of Sachari Lady Spice in his eye and it stung like a bastard. He staggered back, clutching at the eye, wondering what in the world had happened.

A bell began to ring outside. Then another. And another. Now all of them. An emergency. Last time this happened, a fire consumed the marketplace. He rushed to the balcony. No smoke or flames. Sander began to wonder if this was connected to the destruction of his potions.

Eye stinging, he raced from the room, spiralled down the stairs and nearly ran headlong into a guard coming the other way. 'What's going on?'

'I don't know, Mage Bree, I—' The guard hesitated, fascinated by Sander's reddening eye. 'Are you okay?'

'Yes, yes, forget about it. Wait...' Sander froze, staring into middle space. Something tugged at his mind, a presence nearby, someone familiar. They were moving across the rooftops of the citadel. 'An intruder,' he told the guard. 'Alert the king immediately – whoever it is, they're moving fast, they're... Oh, shit.'

'What?'

'The princess,' Sander said, a sudden adrenalin surge eliminating any drowsiness. 'They're headed towards her chambers. Move!'

Boosted by his magic, Sander vaulted up the stairs five at a time to the top of the tower where Princess Yvonne Mathilde Birgitta Brianna of the House of Ultan, sole heir to the Kingdom of Wayland, resided in her chambers. She had no siblings, her mother Birgitta died in child-birth and her father had not remarried.

She was six years old – nearly seven, infectiously curious about the world and yet to be soured by court gossip. She was also blissfully unaware of what her father had planned for her in the coming years. Sometimes she asked Sander to read her stories from legend, and he did so in silly voices, which made her giggle.

She was a sweet girl, but also a valuable pawn in Newlands politics. Bhaltair ensured that she was accompanied by bodyguards at all times, while still trying to give her as normal a childhood as possible. She played with the children of courtiers but was surrounded by armed men trying to look discreet and failing miserably. The only time she ever had to herself was in her chambers, and that's exactly where the intruder was headed.

Sander knew it had to be a mage. Whoever was making for the princess's chambers must be the same person who had waited patiently for him to lower his magical defences and then destroyed all his potions. Only a mage could do that, and that meant they were either trying to poison or curse the girl. But who would be foolhardy enough to try such a thing? He tried to draw up a shortlist of candidates in his mind, but the only mages he could think of with the guile, recklessness or sheer stupidity were either dead or exiled.

He could sense the acrid tang of used magic in the air. There followed a scream, suddenly silenced. He arrived in the princess's antechamber to find four guards sprawled unconscious on the floor. Rushing forward, he found Froya, the girl's nanny, and her daughter Honora, both also out cold but breathing and alive. Inside the bed-chamber itself, Brianna lay motionless atop her sheets. She looked asleep, too. There was no blood.

A movement caught Sander's eye and he spun to see a figure crouched in the open window, dressed in black, poised to leap. His eye still stung, and as he blinked away streaming tears, it took him a moment to recognise Rosheen Katell – *The Witch Who Thinks She's a Warlock* – and he half-raised a hand almost instinctively to give her a cheery hello.

It would be an understatement to say that Rosheen was the last person on the entire planet that Sander had expected to see escaping the scene of an assassination attempt. Sander knew her a bit from her work with some of the poorer villages in Wayland. She had a reputation for integrity, fairness, compassion and hard graft. This wasn't her style at all, so what in the bloody blazes was she doing here? Their eyes met, but she quickly looked away – guilt, perhaps? – and then she leapt out of the window.

Sander hesitated. Did he follow, or look after Brianna? The girl's lips were green and chapped and she began to shiver, curling herself into a ball. Sander rested a hand on her forehead to find it cold and clammy. *A merblood curse.* Lethal but slow-acting, and Sander could cure it easily with some specially prepared merblood – but his supply had just been splattered across his chamber walls. By Rosheen!

The princess shivered violently. He could stay here and comfort her, but what good would that do in the long run? There came the rhythmic clang of guards' boots up the stairs. Excellent. The guards could look after the princess while he captured her poisoner. Besides, Sander was so baffled and pissed off at Rosheen that he had to know more. He gently placed his fingers on Brianna's head. 'Sleep, Princess, sleep,' he said, sending her into a painless slumber.

Sander then bounded across the room, hurling himself through the window and into the empty air. A decision he would come to regret for the rest of his life.

A Learned Debate on the Niceties of the Mages' Code on the World-Famous Mage's Moons of Taranis

Rosheen hated Taranis. Even up here, hiding in wait on a rooftop, the city's tall white walls made her feel hemmed in, the overwhelming aromas in the streets and markets stifled her breathing, and the sheer numbers of people crammed into one place made her sweat. But she had an uneasy feeling that its success meant that citadels like this were the future. And the future was very much on her mind.

Rosheen used magic to fly herself at great speed from Haldor's camp. She was alone, tired and had to move fast. She had found it remarkably easy to inveigle her way into the citadel, but when you're doing the unthinkable, you can find yourself pushing at an open door. No one expected a mage to murder or kidnap someone these days, simply because no mage was stupid enough to attempt such a thing. The Mage Wars had shown them that using their incredible powers with such reckless abandon could only lead to chaos. Decades of magical conflict so destructive that they had nearly wiped out all life on the planet.

The end of the Mage Wars brought with it a magical stalemate that had lasted generations, all of it dictated by the Mages' Code.

The Code was simple:

Never use magic for personal gain, always in the service of others.

Never use magic to kill, except in self-defence, or in the defence of others.

Never use magic to deceive. A mage must always speak the truth.

To say that these rules had been bent in the past was the understatement of the age, but a good mage knew where to draw the line. *We take care of our own*, was a mage's response whenever someone started to get ideas above their station, and if they acted on them, the consequences could be gruesome.

Anzu, for one, refused to have anything to do with this mission. They argued long and hard after the confrontation with Haldor, the griffin taking the moral high ground. 'Easy to do when it's not your brother with a blade at his neck,' Rosheen recalled yelling at her with more childish petulance than she had wanted. She was angry. Angry at herself for falling into Haldor's trap and angry that so much suffering had already been caused by her stupidity.

Her mother and father. Their agonised faces came to her once more and she was overwhelmed with a guilt so sickening that she felt woozy, and for a moment she worried that she might pass out and topple off the roof. She shook it away. She had a job to do.

And Haldor was right about Oskar. Rosheen wouldn't be able to find him because moon children had no magical aura, which meant that no mage could sense them. It was one of the reasons why mages were so fascinated and threatened by them.

Anzu had suggested waiting to see if this prophecy would actually come true. *Making it the first crackpot theory to do so*, she added. Rosheen tried to convince her of what she'd seen in Dagmar's charts, but Anzu wouldn't have it, reminding her of the story of Cillin of Arranrod.

Cillin was a mage from Eriworth who took it upon himself to challenge the kings of the Newlands about a century ago. After he slaughtered his own king and royal family and took the throne, the local mages united against Cillin, defeated him in combat and, over the course of a month, slowly turned the mage inside out. The story was told in vivid detail in songs and verse by troubadours and mummers across the land, and Rosheen found herself singing a grisly chorus recounting Cillin's agonising death as she watched Princess Brianna's chambers from her hiding place on the roof opposite.

Dear gods, she was actually doing this. She was actually going to do Haldor's dirty work. She told herself again and again that the girl would not be permanently harmed. Merblood poisoning was so easy to cure. It didn't even require magic. Once Rosheen had her brother back, she would do whatever was necessary to help the girl. Rosheen had been outmanoeuvred by Haldor once; she would not let it happen again. She would get this over with and tidy up the mess she had made. And then she and Anzu and Oskar would fly as far away from here as possible.

Rosheen had been loitering on the roof for at least half an hour while she waited for Sander Bree to wake from his Springtide hangover. She was gambling that he would then open his infamous potions cabinet, a device more impregnable than most fortresses, which would be her cue to get started.

Destroying Sanders' store of potions would alert him to her presence, but for the plan to work, she had to ensure that he wouldn't be able to effect a cure anytime soon.

She could sense him moving about. *Finally!* Scratching himself, he sauntered over to his potions cabinet. With a gesture, he opened it and removed its magical defences.

Without a moment's hesitation, Rosheen reached out and smashed every bottle into tiny pieces.

The sound of breaking glass was Rosheen's cue. Taking a deep breath, she hurtled through the air from Sander's tower to Brianna's. Rosheen gently stepped off the roof – making herself visible to lookouts, who immediately began to ring alarm bells – then slowed her descent and glided through the open window into the room. She had only moments to get the job done.

Rosheen interrupted a quiet scene. The princess was sitting at a table with an older woman – her tutor, perhaps? – and reading aloud a bedtime story about dragons when she sensed a presence in the room. They both looked up, eyes wide, uncertain if they should run or scream. To her credit, the woman immediately placed herself between the girl and Rosheen.

'Sleep,' Rosheen said gently, and the two of them slumped to the ground. There was no time to lose. Rosheen took the vial of Connal merblood from a small pouch tucked away in her jerkin and kneeled by the princess's motionless body.

'Are you a mage?'

Rosheen froze. The voice was behind her, and she pivoted around on her knee to find another girl peering out from the door of the privy. Outside, the alarm bells were still ringing, just as one went off in her own head.

Rosheen instantly realised her mistake. The girl on the floor was not her intended target. This girl looking at her now, standing in her linen nightgown with pretty flowers embroidered around the neck and missing three front teeth – that was Princess Brianna. Rosheen recognised her from likenesses she'd seen all over Wayland.

'I saw you fly through the window,' she said, impressed and excited by Rosheen's skills. 'You must be a mage.'

'Sleep,' Rosheen said, but the girl remained defiantly standing and awake. Sander must have cast some kind of protective spell over her. Or, like many children her age, Brianna was particularly resistant to the concept of an early night. Rosheen would have to do this the hard way.

'I'm not sleepy. Is it true you have dragon's blood in you?' the princess continued in a sweet, inquisitive voice.

Rosheen wanted her to shut up. The more the girl spoke, the harder it became for Rosheen to do what she had to do, but she instinctively found herself responding to this old wives' tale about mages with an annoyed, '*What?* No.'

'So you *are* a mage!'

'Yes, I am, so be quiet or I'll set your hair on fire.' Rosheen thought of her brother, alone and afraid, waiting for her to come and take him away, as she slowly inched closer to the girl. Rushing her would only make things harder. Keep her talking, keep her occupied, get closer.

'That's not nice.' The girl pouted. 'You won't really, will you?'

'Only one way to find out.' Rosheen raised an eyebrow, moving closer, closer. 'I'd suggest keeping your gob shut.'

'Daddy says that mages are...' – the girl pursed her lips as she recalled – '"a bane on all society and they think they blimming run the place". Daddy used a swear word instead of "blimming". I'm not allowed to swear.'

'Well, I am, so shut the fuck up.'

The girl gave an astonished, throaty gasp. 'I'm telling!'

The princess was almost in reach when the door crashed open and four of the royal guard came tumbling into the room, nearly tripping over the slumbering bodies of the woman and child.

Rosheen spun on her heels, reached out and, summoning waves of magic energy, sent them flying through the air, slamming them into the wall, cracking the plaster and knocking them out.

The princess screamed and Rosheen wheeled back around, grabbed the girl's jaw and, in one smooth movement, flipped open the vial and released two drops of Connal merblood into the girl's open mouth. Her lips turned green and shrivelled dry.

'Gods forgive me,' Rosheen whispered. 'Sleep, little princess. Everything will be fine, I promise.'

The princess's eyes rolled back and she was unconscious in moments. Rosheen checked the girl's breathing. Deep and regular. Good. Job done.

There were more footsteps coming up the stairs and the alarm bells continued to clang. Time was running out. Rosheen gently laid the girl on the bed, then rushed to the window just as the king's mage, Sander Bree, arrived on the scene.

They'd met a few times, not that he'd remember her, the arrogant dick. Rosheen couldn't help but enjoy the look of utter bafflement in his eyes – one of which was startlingly red and sore – as he took in the scene. But she wasn't here to gloat, and so she threw herself out of the window and tumbled through the empty night air over the rooftops of Taranis.

As the terracotta tiles loomed closer, she reached out with her magic and slowed her descent, landing with little more than a *clink*. There came a flapping noise from above and she looked up to see Sander leaping head first out of the tower window, his clothes and ridiculous long, blond hair billowing as he hurtled after her. Rosheen had hoped he would choose to look after the girl, but he clearly considered her welfare less important than catching the interloper. Stupid, but Rosheen should have realised that he would favour mage pride over the safety of a little girl. *We take care of our own*, indeed.

She raised her arms, sending dozens of the roof tiles around her spinning through the air towards Sander. He weaved skilfully through many of them, but a handful found their target, one cutting a gash across his forehead. With a cry of, 'Ow! What the fff—?' he lost control and spun into the roof, tumbling towards its edge.

Rosheen was already running in the opposite direction, ready to fly. She risked a glance back to see Sander was already on his feet, arms extended, a bright glow emanating from his hands. A fireball. *Shit, he's not playing about, is he?* So much for not using magic to kill.

Rosheen was barely airborne as the flaming orb arced after her, crackling in the air as it closed in, detonating with a thunderous roar that made her ears ring. The shock wave sent her spiralling over the citadel walls towards the Mage's Moons orbiting the city.

She landed hard on one of the bigger floating rocks, rolling across its rough surface with flailing limbs like a rowdy drunk ejected from a tavern. With a flick of her feet and considerably more grace, she flipped head over heels, spinning in the air to face Sander and sending her own fireball in his direction.

Sander dodged, rose above her and immediately returned fire. His next fireball punched a new crater in the moon, and the sudden squall of debris sprayed sharp chips of stone and dust into Rosheen's eyes and mouth.

They leapt from rock to rock on the slowly rotating moons that orbited the citadel. Two mages frantically exchanging blows of roiling orange flame, black smoke and blinding blue flashes of pure magical energy as each tried to get the upper hand.

Rosheen enhanced her eyesight and could see in the darkness that folk were watching them from the citadel's walls and higher towers, leaning out of their windows and pointing and shouting. She doubted that any of them had seen a display of magic like this for quite some time and were determined to enjoy the show.

As Rosheen kicked away from one of the smaller satellites, she twisted herself in the air and, with a sweeping gesture, sent the rock hurtling straight at Sander. He darted out of the way like a swift in flight, and it cannoned into a bigger rock with a crack that split the air and rattled windows in the distant citadel. Both mini-moons were smashed into smithereens. One giant shard spun erratically at Rosheen, and in her hurry to evade it, she flew backwards, slamming her body into an adjacent rock. She rolled over, shook her head, picked herself up and started running around the tiny globe and out of Sander's sight.

Rosheen doubled-back around her little moon, letting herself fall in the narrow gap between it and a smaller stone that was so close they were almost touching. She slowed her descent, then wedged herself into place, her back against one floating rock, feet pressed against the other, hidden in their shadows.

Rosheen closed her eyes, sending a projection of herself onto a nearby moon in the hope that Sander would be duped by the illusion and give chase long enough for her to lose him completely.

There was a flash and a boom from above. Sander had taken the bait and aimed a fireball at her projected doppelgänger. Time to move. But where? Go straight up and she'd be an easy target for Sander. Rosheen decided she had to fly out of there under the cover of those floating rocks.

There was a drop of about a hundred feet below. Rosheen waited a few moments for a space to open up between the ever-shifting orbiting rocks then plunged between them, arms by her sides as she concentrated on slowing her fall.

As she landed on the grass with a tuck and roll, she prepared to launch herself again, but a shadow swept overhead. Sander. Damn, the old bastard was quick, and he clearly hadn't been fooled for long. Rosheen felt an agonising pain in her chest, like someone was grinding a stiletto into her heart. She fell to her knees, pressing her hand against her sternum.

'Undo your curse.' Sander moved forward, his fingers flexing as he took a tighter grip on her heart. Despite the incredible pain, she knew he was being gentle. One squeeze and her heart would be crushed. She took a little comfort knowing that he needed her more alive than dead right now.

'He has my brother,' she managed to rasp.

'Who?'

Sander released his grip a little and she could speak more freely. 'Haldor Frang,' she said. 'It doesn't matter anyway, it all ends tomorrow.'

'Wait, what did you say? What ends tomorrow?'

'Magic,' she said. 'The Lapis Moon will be destroyed, and—'

Sander's head twitched with sudden curiosity. 'You're the second person to tell me that.'

'Who? Who else told you?'

'Some loon in a tavern, a… a Brother of the Faith, but…' He shook his head, determined to stick to the matter at hand. 'It doesn't matter. By the gods, Rosheen, what has happened to you? I never pegged you as some mad, apocalyptic soothsayer. Stop talking bollocks and undo the curse on that poor girl up there.'

'I will, as soon as my brother is safe, I—'

'No, now!' Sander tightened his grip on her heart again. Rosheen's arms felt light, numb, and her vision started to blur and tunnel. She only had moments left.

'I can't,' she gasped. 'Nothing will stop Haldor… my parents are gone… Oskar is all I have left, I… please…'

A wave of displaced air swept across the long grass, throwing dust and dirt into their mouths and eyes. Rosheen shut hers, sure that death was imminent.

Then she heard a familiar caw, a scuffling and a thump, followed by a calm voice in her head.

Brace yourself.

Sander's grip on Rosheen's heart was released, then she felt the firm hold of Anzu's front talons around her arms before her stomach fell away as they both lurched skywards at an incredible speed. The sudden acceleration nearly made her black out and the rush of air stole what little breath she had left, but when they came thumping to the ground on a hillside three miles away from Taranis, she gave thanks to whatever gods were listening that she had a friend like Anzu.

The Blame Game

Sander lay in the dirt, tittering inanely to himself, his mind giddy as he recovered from the griffin's attack. He hadn't used magic that intensely for years and had forgotten quite how ridiculous he felt afterwards. He couldn't stay like this. It was undignified and he was vulnerable. He took a few sharp breaths, slapped himself into sobriety and got to his feet.

The animal had pinned him to the ground with its talons and roared into his face, drenching him in its spittle as he recoiled from its rank breath. He kicked himself for not seeing it coming. Those two always travelled as a pair, though quite what he would have done to the animal, he wasn't sure. He would have had no choice but to try to kill it, but the creature's beak or claws would probably have finished him off first. The story went that Rosheen's family had been exiled from Eru after the griffin killed a shepherd boy. Make no mistake, that griffin could be a vicious bitch.

And now they were gone. He tried to sense their presence as he flew the mile or so back to the citadel wall, but Rosheen's glamour skills were unrivalled in the Newlands. If she didn't want to be found, there was nothing more he could do.

The bell summoning all members of the king's counsel to an emergency meeting in the throne room began to ring. Sander spat and cursed at his recklessness in chasing after Rosheen and felt a cold dread as he wondered how he was going to explain this to the king.

In the throne room, the blame game had already begun among the few early arrivals as they waited for the king. One of their number was human bagpipe General Kentigern, his voice wheezing as he laid the foundations for his defence. 'We're prepared for a full-frontal assault, not this kind of backhanded subterfuge.'

Sander, splattered with the contents of his spell cabinet and griffin saliva, slipped in through a side door, hoping to idle at the back of the crowd as usual, but found himself standing next to Roan Pheric. The little creep had grabbed Sander's customary spot and was lurking in the shadows, looking on as the warriors blustered.

'Something in your eye, Mage Bree?' Pheric leaned forward to inspect Sander's red eye.

'Sachari Lady Spice, Pheric. You want some?' Sander sneered, trying to figure out if Pheric had told the king of his decision to quit or not.

Kentigern had a hunter's keen ears, and on hearing Sander's name, he spun on his heels with a surprising lightness of foot.

'The mages' insistence on a stalemate has come to this,' the general said, jabbing a finger in Sander's direction. 'Allowing our enemies to make the first move, leaving us on the back foot.' There were *harrumphs* of agreement from some of the still-gathering members of the King's Counsel. 'I shall demand of the king that we retaliate immediately.' The general punched the air to more cheers.

Sander saw movement out of the corner of his eye. Pheric sidling away from him, not wanting to be associated with this recipient of the dreaded blame.

'Don't be ridiculous,' Sander scolded the general. He enjoyed playing with Kentigern. He was so easy to wind up. A few well-placed words would burst blood vessels on the old warrior's nose and turn his cheeks a violent shade of purple. 'What you call a stalemate, the rest of us call peace, and we'd like it to stay that way. So put your toys away, stop stamping your feet like a child and act like a leader.'

And there it was. Like the chameleons in the king's menagerie, the general's face blushed from red to purple.

'This can be fixed,' Sander said with a confidence that had seen him through decades of service with the king. A service he had hoped was about to come to an end, but events were somewhat overtaking him. 'Fixed with magic,' he continued. 'We take care of our own.'

'A pox on all magicians and their kind,' General Kentigern muttered. 'I wish we could do away with you for once and—'

'Sharp, sharp! The king!' voices cried from the other side of the throne room doors.

They crashed open and the king entered flanked by his personal guard, followed by First Minister of the Faith Yorath Pasco and the king's Principal Secretary Bevin Arne. All others in the room bowed their heads.

'I want to know how this happened, who is responsible and how we remedy it.'

King Bhaltair was many things: shorter than average, fit and trim, well presented with a tidy grey beard and, considering he was ten years older than Sander, very few wrinkles on his pale face. And he was not a screamer. In times of crisis, his voice would almost be reduced to a mutter, while his movements became so small and slight that one wondered if he was breathing at all. It was a well-practised façade designed to project an image of calm authority, but Sander knew the man was raging underneath. However, there was always protocol to observe and the king couldn't be seen to panic.

His Majesty Steffen Henning Mathias Bhaltair of the House of Ultan sat on his simple throne of oak, a modest seat for a thrifty monarch, his back bolt upright, hands gripping the armrests and knees together like a modest court debutant. He looked utterly uncomfortable, but it was how Bhaltair thought a king should present himself: stoic, immovable, impassive.

The courtiers and advisors scattered around the throne room adjusted their posture to mirror their ruler's perpendicular bearing, not wanting to appear weak or slovenly.

Sander leaned against a column near the back. From there he could see the terrified glances shared by those assembled. They were all silently building a defence, a barricade of excuses, for when the king inevitably turned to them for explanations.

Sander was no exception. This was a magical attack, something he should have somehow foreseen and prevented. He was worried that he was going to be fired before he had the opportunity to quit.

'Well?' the king demanded.

And so it made sense for Sander to chip in before the finger was pointed at him. 'Her name is Rosheen Katell, Your Highness. She said she was working for someone called Haldor Frang, I—'

'We'll come to you in a minute.' The king silenced Sander with a single finger.

The mage felt an unfamiliar tingle on his cheeks. He was blushing.

So often in this room, he had carried himself with a knowing swagger bolstered by the lofty confidence of a mage, but this time, he had been shut up like a naughty schoolboy in class. It didn't bode well at all. The king must already know of Sander's plans to quit and, from his aura of smugness, Pheric had been the bearer of the news.

Yorath Pasco was next to speak. As First Minister of the Faith, his duties were supposed to be confined to guiding the king on spiritual matters, but Sander had noticed that this slender, crook-shaped man was increasingly poking his nose into pretty much everything these days. Barely thirty, he was relatively young, ambitious and sly. He gave Sander the willies more than any army or mage.

'We have received an increasing number of threats on the princess's person, Your Highness,' Yorath said, his voice deliberately pitched low so that everyone else in the room had to move closer and pay particular attention in order to hear him. 'High-born women and children should be kept from sight and guarded well from the influx of foreigners, my King. They come in the guise of traders but bring with them loose morals and false gods. Is it any wonder that a heathen would attempt to take the life of a child? They—'

The king silenced him with a wave of his hand. 'Not now, Yorath, please.' Yorath backed away from the king with a respectful, if reluctant, bow.

Bevin Arne stepped forward to speak. A gaunt, elderly woman, Bevin was officially Bhaltair's principal secretary, but everyone knew she was the king's spymaster, a cunning old trickster with eyes in every village between here and Dagdun.

'Our mage may well be correct.' Bevin's voice was sharper and her words more to the point, as she often imparted the most crucial information and hated any kind of uncertainty. She always sounded like she was correcting your mistakes for you. She was always right. You were often wrong. 'My eyes and ears in the field suggest that a warlord named Haldor Frang is the main culprit. Until now, he's been a mere annoyance, raiding towns and villages until he provokes a military response.'

'Why haven't their mages taken care of him?' the king asked.

'He only attacks fiefdoms unable to afford a permanent mage. He catches them on the back foot, and when they find themselves at his mercy, he usually gives them the opportunity to join his forces, which they often do. If he meets a superior force, he's quick to surrender, and then in the negotiations he will accept some small payment to go away.'

'Payment?' The baffled king's eyes narrowed. 'Why don't they hang him and be done with it?'

'He's terribly charming, apparently.' Bevin pulled an *I don't understand it, either* face. 'This has allowed him to amass a considerable war chest over the last two years while quietly building his own private army of mercenaries.'

'How many?'

'Torren estimated a thousand blades on the battlefield,' Bevin said. 'Not a vast army by any account, but they're fiercely loyal. They call him the "Three Don't Knows".'

'Why? And be warned that *I don't know* is not an acceptable answer.'

'When people ask him how many men, concubines and gold pieces he has, he always answers, "Don't know." It's arrogant self-mythologizing, Majesty, nothing more.'

'And the mage?' Bhaltair finally turned his gaze to his own magician.

Here we go. Sander tried to put aside the king's earlier dismissal. He drew himself up, knowing that Bhaltair loathed a cringer in these situations. Those who grovelled and apologised would get short shrift. Bhaltair liked someone who gave as good as they got.

'As I was saying, Your Highness, her name is Rosheen Katell.' Sander strode with youthful confidence through the old men scattered around the room like badly carved chess pieces. Youthful compared to these crusty old goats, anyway. Truth be told, he wasn't much younger than the average general, but his magic kept him *looking* young, and they resented that most of all. He hopped up the steps to the throne and flicked his long hair back, something he knew particularly annoyed the balder soldiers. 'She's never been any kind of threat before. I've met her briefly once or twice; specialises in mediating disputes, negotiations – she's a truth-seer, I believe, originally from a village in the Mylar Mountains in Eru. She rides a griffin, but she's not the type to—'

'*I don't care about her fucking pets!*' The king rose up from his throne, the skin on his face pulled tight over his round cheekbones, tendons protruding from his neck, his larynx bobbing with every word as he screamed in Sander's face. '*I want to know how she go in here, what she poisoned my daughter with and why I bother with a mage if he can't prevent this.*'

Sander stumbled back on the steps, falling to the cold flagstones. His hands were trembling. He had never seen the king like this before, not even after the queen died.

Bhaltair shuddered a cleansing breath, composing himself once more. Behind him, the others peered down at Sander. At the epicentre were Pheric and General Kentigern, sharing a glow of gratification which quickly spread around the room now that the blame had found a home.

'She did the unthinkable,' Sander said, his voice now softer than Yorath's. 'No one in their right mind would do this – it's suicide. And she's a good mage, sticks to the Code. She said… she said something about Haldor holding her brother as hostage.'

Bevin hummed and nodded. 'It's a common ploy to try to compromise a mage, but few get away with it.'

Sander saw the king raise an eyebrow, as if filing that little titbit of information away for later use.

Sander decided to steer the conversation back to the most important matter. 'Majesty, your daughter is cursed with merblood. A couple of drops are lethal. I've put her into a deep sleep so that she feels no pain, but soon she'll slip further into a stupor and then…' He hesitated, anticipating another royal outburst. 'Death.'

The king was back on his throne, looking askance at Sander, barely tolerating his existence. 'How long?'

'Two weeks. Perhaps sooner,' Sander said, then added quickly, 'But the cure is simple. A small solution of merblood properly prepared will undo this completely. Just a few drops. That's what's so baffling – so much effort for something that can be cured so easily, I—'

'You have this cure to hand?' The king leaned forward.

'I did, but Katell destroyed my stores moments before the attack.'

'You can get more?'

'There's a settlement of merpeople at Connal Lake.' Sander did a quick mental calculation, his dreams of early retirement becoming increasingly unlikely with each passing word. 'I need a rest now, but I can fly there tomorrow.'

'Why not fly now?' asked the king.

'It's exhausting,' Sander said, reluctant to admit that he was also terrible at flying. The lack of breathable air made him giddy, the cold made his eyes stream and his sense of direction was diabolical. 'And it's too easy to get lost in the dark. I need few hours to rest and time to plan my journey. I can leave at noon tomorrow.'

'You'll leave at first light,' King Bhaltair said in a voice that would clearly brook no argument.

Sander was puzzled. 'Why the hurry? We have time to—'

'Clear the room.' The king gave the order to Bevin, who gestured at the doors to those assembled. They were only too happy to withdraw in a hurry, leaving Sander, Yorath, Bevin and the king in the throne room.

No one spoke until the final click of a door closing signified that they were alone.

'Your Highness.' Sander got in first. 'I should explain: as I'm sure you've heard, I do wish to retire from your service, but rest assured that I will not cease until your daughter is—'

'We'll discuss your plans later,' the king said, then gave Bevin her cue.

'Her Highness Princess Brianna is betrothed to Prince Aeden, son of King Jerrik, ruler of Parthalan,' the old woman said.

'The betrothal ceremony is to take place in three weeks,' Yorath added. Sander now understood the king's hurry for a cure. He blanched briefly on realising that he had not been included in the negotiations, but now was not the time for petty gripes.

Bevin continued, 'The joining of our two nations will create an alliance unparalleled in the Newlands, if not the world. Our armies' blades will be double those of even our most powerful enemies, and our economic reserves will allow us to dictate terms of trade. The continued peace that we have enjoyed in the Newlands for over three hundred years depends entirely on this union.' Bevin's tone hardened. 'It is crucial that she lives.'

'That's an awful lot of pressure for a six-year-old girl,' Sander puffed, immediately regretting it as the king bared his teeth.

'The princess is well prepared for her part in this,' the king said, descending from his throne, his hand on the pommel of his sword. 'As is the First Minister and my Principal Secretary. The question is, King's Mage, are you?'

Sander's mouth was dry, a sudden weight pressing on his shoulders. 'I am, my King.'

'Do this and we'll discuss favourable terms for your release from my service. Fail and you'll never work for any noble, landowner or gentleman ever again. By the time I'm done with you, you'll be shovelling mer-shit back at that farm on the coast where we found you. Do you understand?'

Sander nodded.

'You'll leave at first light and be back with a cure before nightfall.'

Sander was given permission to visit the princess in her chambers. As he floated towards the top of the winding stairs, he could hear a wordless sobbing from inside the room. The guards on the door opened up for him and Princess Brianna's nanny Froya and her daughter Honora stumbled out, arm-in-arm. They looked up at Sander, wailed some more and began their descent on foot.

Sander stepped inside. In a classic display of closing the gate after the horse had bolted, there was a guard at every window and two on either side of the girl's bed. He wasn't sure now why he had come. He thought back to when he first found the princess, playing the scene over and over again in his mind. He should have stayed behind and helped her instead of hurtling after Rosheen, but without his potions, there was nothing he could have done even had he stayed.

She looked peaceful now, as though she were in a deep sleep, but after a couple of days, those few drops of merblood would start to take effect. Her breath would become rasping as her lungs filled with fluid and she began to drown. Sander knew a few Natural Philosophers who spoke of methods of draining the fluid from the lungs, but their techniques were crude and untested. Why poke holes in the human body when a potion can fix the patient in moments? Sander shivered at the idea that ordinary people would be at the mercy of these quacks if magic were to disappear.

Sander kneeled by the girl's bed, pretending to pray. He had no doubt that Yorath had eyes in the Royal Guard and it would serve Sander well to appear humble before the new Goddess. He was really thinking about the journey ahead, south along the Taranis Road, then following the Jade River to Connal Lake. Then he had to handle the merpeople, a psychotic bunch at the best of times, hiding in the craggy rocks on an island in the middle of the lake.

There was some talk of Sander taking the girl with him and curing her on the spot, but as he finished his fake prayer and glanced up at the little girl's face, he knew she was in no condition to be moved, especially in flight.

Even now, in her comatose state, there was a hint of a smile on her face.

'You've only ever shown me kindness, young lady,' he said in a voice loud enough for the guards to overhear. He needed them to report back that he was upset and sincere. 'Your father and I may not see eye to eye, but you're an innocent and do not deserve to die so young. I promise, I swear to you by the Lapis Moon, that I will do whatever it takes to make you well again.' He wasn't sure if he should reach out and pat her on the head or something. He wasn't terribly good around children. He decided against it.

He got to his feet, catching a glimpse of the Lapis Moon through the window. Hanging silently below Greystone's all-seeing eye, it looked like a blue teardrop. Sander could not possibly have known, but this was the last time he would ever set eyes on it.

The Dogmeat General

Anzu dropped Rosheen on the side of a hill from a considerable height. Rosheen's landing was hard and kicked all the air out of her. She writhed on that green hillside for what felt like an eternity, thrashing her legs helplessly, flapping her arms, shaking her head from side to side, anything that might will her lungs to work again. When they eventually did, she could only lie there taking deeper and deeper breaths as her still-reeling mind recovered from the giddy delirium of intense magic use.

You deserved that, said a righteous voice in her head.

'What's done is done. You don't have to be happy about it.' Rosheen tried standing, groaned as the world pivoted and fell back to the ground. 'Frang said he was going to attack Torren at Agrona. We need to move.'

The attack will fail and Frang will turn out to be yet another maniacal loon. What's the hurry?

'That loon has my brother.' Rosheen pushed herself up on her elbows. 'It's a good three hours' flight to the coast, and I want to get to Frang and find out where my brother is before our warlord friend ends up with his skull skewered on a spike on Torren's traitors' wall. Let's go.' Rosheen puffed to her feet, waving the griffin down.

Anzu landed with a heavy thud, giving Rosheen a squinty, sidelong glance before offering her saddle to the mage.

The first hour of the ride took them east of the Conloch Mountains from Wayland into Agrona, after which they followed the Taranis Road south for another two hours, slowed by relentless bad weather, until they reached the River Alar.

The first sign that something was wrong came with the trickle of refugees heading the other way. A few tried to flag them down, begging for help. Some were bandaged and bloody, others wide-eyed and terrified by what they had fled. Rosheen and Anzu flew low for a better look but couldn't loiter to hear their stories. Any other day and

Rosheen would have stopped to do what she could to help, but she had to free her brother first.

Anzu began to flag, her breath ragged, steaming in the night air. The rhythm of her wings became more erratic as she struggled with the final climb over Drudd Hill. That's when they saw the smoke.

By the gods. Anzu's voice came to Rosheen's mind. *What have they done?*

Rosheen had always been impressed by Castle Agrona. It stood tall on limestone cliffs, facing the ocean as if defying it to do its worst. Its outer walls were low but incredibly thick, impregnable to conventional attack, and towering over the castle stood Torren's Beacon, a lighthouse that had saved many a sailor from certain doom on the rocks around the harbour.

Only now the lighthouse wasn't there. And the once-jutting cliffs were crumbled like a child's sandcastle, with freshly exposed limestone glowing bright in the moons' light.

Once again, Haldor Frang had done the unthinkable. He had somehow tipped a vast portion of the cliffs onto the shore below, taking almost half of the castle with it.

As they circled above, they could see huge fragments of Castle Agrona scattered about the shore, leaving great gaping holes in the defences. Some of the lower levels were now exposed to the night sky. Here and there, slain bodies sprawled in the labyrinth of zigzagging stairwells, servants' quarters and prison cells.

How in the gods has he done this?

'Rigo flash powder.' Rosheen thought back to the shells Haldor showed her in his tent. 'Bombs to bring down the walls.'

He's insane. The other kingdoms will crush him.

'Maybe,' Rosheen said. 'Or maybe he's betting that they'll be too busy fighting each other when the Lapis Moon's gone?'

Remind me never to play cards with him.

Smoke rose from within the castle's inner bailey. Frang's men must have rushed the gaps in the wall, taking Torren's men completely by surprise. As a fortification, the castle was now useless, but the tents Rosheen and Anzu had seen only yesterday were now being raised again as Frang's men made camp inside the shattered walls. Gods, they were fast. And walls or no walls, they now had the confidence to stake a claim to whatever bit of land they occupied.

Despite her hurry, Rosheen had to take a moment to comprehend what she was seeing. She thought of all the times she had approached this castle, knowing that she would be completely safe and welcome once inside. But now it looked like an ancient ruin from the Ceezan Empire.

Her stupor was broken by the sound of pounding hooves below. Two riders approached from the castle road bearing Frang's banners.

'Rosheen Katell,' one of the riders called to her. Anzu flexed her wings, gliding down to a spot on the final approach to the castle. Anzu bowed her head, ribs expanding and contracting heavily. If Rosheen was exhausted, Anzu was on the verge of collapsing.

'My Lord Haldor Frang welcomes you to Castle Agrona,' the rider said. Rosheen recognised him as one of Torren's men and marvelled at how quickly loyalty changed hands in the aftermath of battle. 'Word of your good work has reached us,' the rider continued. 'He awaits you in the castle square.'

The castle road arced in a graceful curve along the cliff's edge, the night air fresh with sea spray. As they approached the castle gates, Anzu's head began to twitch as her keen senses were the first to encounter a new collection of odours: the stench of rotting flesh, vomit and shit.

The scent of war. Anzu's voice sounded grave and her head began to sweep from side to side, scanning for potential danger.

Torchlit bodies were strung up over the portcullis, some on flagpoles. All were skinned, their once-red muscles exposed to the elements, turning brown and black as the rot set in. Flies buzzed around them and crows pecked at their eyes. One wore a crown and, seeing its wispy beard, Rosheen realised with a sinking heart that she was looking at her old friend King Torren.

By the gods, who are we dealing with, Rosheen? These people are butchers.

Rosheen didn't reply as she and Anzu were led to the castle's main square. Surrounded on all sides by sheer walls, Rosheen remembered it as a bustling marketplace, but now it was a charnel house with the bodies of soldiers lying frozen in twisted tableaux of their final moments.

Torren's men moved about the corpses, robbing them of the rings on their fingers, jabbing with their swords those they thought might still be alive. Many of the dead were in their night things, completely taken by surprise. The battle hadn't been over long and Rosheen was quietly grateful that they hadn't arrived here sooner to see the carnage. Would she have intervened and saved Torren? Or would she have stood by, hoping for a quick end so that she might see her brother sooner? It was a choice she was grateful she'd been saved from making.

On a dais in the centre of the square was Haldor Frang. Now shirtless, his face and torso were covered in the blue woad paint traditionally worn by Grainne warriors in battle. There were streaks under his eyes where the woad had run, covering his own tattoo tears, but Haldor had not been crying. His teeth flashed a manic grin as he loosely gripped a broadsword in one hand, its point dragging on the floor of the stone dais. Smiling, he looked down at the two men kneeling before him. Rosheen recognised them as a pair of Torren's commanders, men of battle and courage, though they looked utterly lost and despondent now.

Frang noticed Rosheen and Anzu approaching and his face lit up. 'My witch and her griffin! How wonderful to see you both. I'll be with you in a moment.'

His face darkened again and he hoisted the broadsword to his shoulder with both hands. He looked ridiculously small for such a big weapon, but no one was laughing as he addressed the men on their knees.

'Gentlemen, you have a choice,' he said, his voice light, conversational. 'Execution, swift and merciful, or you can swear loyalty to me and keep your rank and privilege. What is it to be?' On this last, he crouched down to better hear their voices.

The first commander, a broad man with a bright snow-white beard, kept his eyes on the ground as he muttered something.

'I'm sorry.' Frang leaned closer, cupping his ear. 'What was that?'

'I swear loyalty to you,' the white-beard said, voice trembling. 'I am my lord's servant.'

'Very good.' Frang grinned, patting the man on the back. He kneeled by the next commander, a balding man with a grey beard who proudly raised his chin high before speaking clearly.

'I choose death,' he said simply.

Frang gripped the man's shoulder in a brotherly fashion, stood back, raised the broadsword in both hands and brought it down.

On the white-bearded commander's neck.

It took Rosheen a few moments to comprehend what she had seen. Even Anzu stepped back a few paces, stunned. *If I weren't so exhausted, I might suggest that now would be a good time to run.*

Rosheen's heart was beating fast and she felt a wave of disgust wash over her. Though not at what she had just seen, but at what she had felt.

It thrilled her.

The foul reek of bloodshed, the bodies, the life and death of it all, the danger. This was not an ordinary day. She had poisoned a princess, escaped the clutches of a powerful mage and seen a man beheaded before her. She was no longer stuck in a rut. She had finally broken the routine of her regular life and, in doing so, encountered death and chaos, and she had to admit that they excited her. She shook the thought away.

As the man's head rolled off the dais and across the main square's cobbles, Frang helped the balding man to his feet. 'That was a coward,' Frang told him. 'Go with my friends here. Get cleaned up, fill your belly, rest, and we'll talk in the morning.'

Frang gestured at a pair of nearby guards who took the still-quivering commander and led him away.

With a grin, Frang dropped the sword, which clattered like discarded cutlery as he hopped off the dais. He welcomed Rosheen with open arms. 'Young lady, you are extraordinary,' he said, gripping her shoulders and kissing her on both cheeks. He took a moment to bow his head to Anzu. 'I thank you both for your excellent work. I—'

'My brother.' Rosheen's tone was as direct and stern as she could make it, but there was a brief vibrato of fear and she knew Haldor would hear it. 'We had a deal, Haldor.'

'Your brother is safe and well, and I keep my promises,' he said, soft and sincere. 'Tonight's the night. Take my advice: find a spot on the cliff with a good view and watch the world change. Few of us will have that opportunity and it would be a shame for you to waste it. Go and see your time of power come to an end.' He squeezed her arm. 'We'll talk again in the morning. You, your brother and your pet here will be free to go.'

He left Rosheen rooted to the spot. She could feel the world turning under her feet. A world that might be considerably different in the morning.

The Day the Moon Died

It was the single most important event in the known history of the world. A disaster, a revolution or a revelation, depending on who you were. It changed everything. Across the world and over time, the destruction of the tiny Lapis Moon was directly or indirectly responsible for tidal waves, raging storms, floods, forest fires, famine, the extinction of entire species of flora and fauna, the evolution and bloom of new species, and the fall and rise of countless kingdoms. Tides and horoscopes would never be the same.

It was the middle of the day in the western continent of Rigo when it happened, and in the blink of an eye the sky flushed from blue to a blinding white. The people of that vast land had no explanation for what had occurred until full moonrise, when the first scattering of what would become known as the Great Ring appeared in their night sky. Countless tiny, glittering rocks dashed across the firmament in a narrow band.

In eastern Myrista, it came with the dawn, and most people there were awakened to the change by the frantic clang of monks' bells. The scribes and philosophers there called it the Moonfall and, in a culture where prophecy was valued highly, there was a scrabble among them to be the first to declare that they had seen it coming all along.

In Eru, where storytellers had travelled from town to village entertaining people with the same myths and legends for generations, a new story now presented itself, but they were unsure of its middle or end. They only knew they were at its beginning.

Rosheen and Anzu saw it all for themselves. They took Haldor's advice and found a quiet spot on the cliffs overlooking the sea. Anzu lay flat, tail lopping idly from side to side as Rosheen took off her reins and saddle and sat next to her, gently stroking the feathers around her head. It was a clear night and Rosheen could see every ridge and valley on the Lapis Moon's surface. She felt as if she could stand on her tiptoes, reach up and touch it. It wasn't big. Tiny when compared to its brother, probably no bigger than the Newlands continent itself, but its low orbit gave it the illusion of magnitude.

There's a Natural Philosopher in Arranrod who talks about going up there. Anzu's voice broke into Rosheen's silent contemplation.

'Where did you hear that?'

Remember our little expedition to Parthalan last year? Heard those two guides arguing about it on the way. Been trying for years, they said.

'And how would they get up there?'

Some sort of enormous flying machine, apparently. Giant bags of gas, or something.

'You're a giant bag of gas.' Rosheen reached over and ruffled Anzu's feathers. Her smile didn't last. 'They'll have to find something new to do tomorrow, won't they?'

Think of all those great minds who've studied it. All for nothing, Anzu said. *They say it's a fragment from a much bigger planet, broken apart during the birth of the universe.*

'Mother called it the All-Seeing Eye.'

Hmm, in Parthalan it's the Trickster, in Sachari it's the Lover, and in Trertos they call it Greystone's More Interesting Sister. I forget the actual word they use, but it's much more poetic and loses something in translation.

'Think they'll still sing songs about it?'

Of course. More so when it's gone.

'I thought you said this was all nonsense?' Rosheen frowned at Anzu's fresh pessimism. 'It hasn't happened yet. Haldor's a fool.'

Anzu didn't answer. There was no point in arguing. They would both know for sure soon. For a while, they said nothing at all, simply looked up at it like never before, trying to store its image in their minds in anticipation for when it was gone.

'The Faith say it was put there by the Goddess to ward off a terrible, ancient evil,' Rosheen said.

Oh, what would they bloody know?

'Not much, but it doesn't stop them from banging on about it.'

They're going to be a nightmare after this, aren't they?

'Can you blame them?' Rosheen kicked a stone over the cliff's edge and listened to it *clack-clack* as it bounced against the rock wall. 'With us out of the way, the stage is all theirs.'

We won't be out of the way entirely, will we? A shudder rippled up

Anzu's body, starting with her tail, then her haunches, and finally she shook her wings and head. She did this when she was cross sometimes. *We'll have our own magic, won't we? The… the magic inside us… I mean, no one knows how long that will last, do they? Could be days. Weeks. Years, even. It's… it's… it's been lying dormant inside us all our lives, hasn't it? I'm not saying it's an endless well of energy, but there has to be something there. Maybe… maybe we don't need the moon at all!*

Rosheen could hear the tension crack the voice in her head. She had never seen her friend so agitated. 'Take it easy, Anzu, we'll make it work.'

That's easy for you to say. You'll still be you. I'm a magical creature. I can only talk to you like this because of that bloody moon. Oh gods, what will I become without magic? She circled frantically, then scratched her beak on the rocks at the cliff's edge. *I'll change. Or die.*

'You won't.' Rosheen sat by Anzu and held her tightly. 'You're my conscience, for gods' sakes. I won't allow it.'

You won't be able to do a thing. Anzu stopped the scratching and craned her neck up to look at the Lapis Moon once more. *Promise me something.*

'Anything.'

Don't let me hurt you.

'What do you mean?'

If I become wild. An animal acting on instinct. I'll—

'You're being ridiculous. How could you possibly know what'll happen?'

I know because it's there inside me. That… animal rage, that need to hunt and kill. And you know it, too.

Rosheen cast her eyes down, unhappy to be reminded of why her family were exiled from Eru in the first place. A young Anzu, not fully trained, taunted by the butcher's son with a stick. Anzu lashing out, the boy screaming in a pool of blood and a whole village turning against them.

'That was a long time ago,' she said.

Doesn't matter. It's there all the time. I can keep it in, push it down… I can't promise the same after we change.

'Anzu, I won't hurt you,' Rosheen said. 'And you won't hurt me.'

But a griffin was a griffin, a troll a troll, a dragon a dragon. Magical through and through. Faeries, elves, merpeople, wyverns, sea monsters – all were given some kind of enhanced strength or power via their link to the moon.

Likewise, mages, those rare humans with some kind of innate magical ability, had always relied on the moon's power, which waxed and waned with its elliptical orbit.

What about Oskar? How will he change?

'That's an old myth,' Rosheen said.

The Goddess put the moon there to vanquish an ancient race of demigods who threatened the world. Maybe he's a demigod?

'Do you even hear yourself? He's a child, Anzu.'

Sorry. But Alby Clim said Oskar was affected by the moon, so its destruction might cause some change in the boy?

'Can we not talk about this now?'

Of course. All I'm saying is a demigod brother might be handy in the coming chaos. Stay open to the idea, because the truth is no one really knows how that thing works.

Anzu was right. No one knew the source of the moon's energy. Perhaps some invisible force, yet to be comprehended? Natural Philosophers spoke of waves of light and energy beyond the sight of humans, and invisible sources of power like the magnetic poles, but mages weren't too keen on investigating further. They revelled in the mystery and, like their street-conjuror counterparts, they knew that the explanation would probably be terribly banal and a disappointment to everyone. They thought of the Lapis Moon as a respected friend, a partner in the business of magic. Oh, they took it for granted, but every now and then, they would look up and give quiet thanks for its power and imagine it was smiling back at them, happy to continue endowing them with the strength that made them so remarkable.

If the Lapis Moon had any clue about the catastrophic change it was about to undergo, it showed no sign of it now.

Anzu, whose eyes were always better in the dark, saw it first.

There!

'Where?' Rosheen's gaze darted across the sky, unsure what she was even looking for. She half-expected a fireball of some kind. A star with a blazing tail.

Moving through Petra's Belt. Bloody hell, it's a size.

Rosheen found the constellation, and her eyes were drawn to a patch of the sky where the stars briefly blinked out of existence, only to reappear a moment later. The meteor was a vast shadow of darkness against the field of stars, almost half the size of the Lapis Moon and moving eerily slowly. Sometimes its edges glistened as it caught the light of the sun and she could see stellar debris swirling around its tail like sea spray.

She didn't know how long they stood there watching in silence, but it eventually moved behind the Lapis Moon.

And then nothing happened.

'It missed?' Rosheen dared to whisper. 'Oh, thank the gods, it—'

She was startled by a sudden cacophony of snapping wings and throaty *caws* as a flock of gulls broke free from their nests on the cliff face and flew over and around Rosheen and Anzu in a blind panic. They both ducked down, arms and legs raised to protect their eyes from the swarm.

Somewhere in the distant hills, wolves began to howl, insects that should have been asleep began to chitter, and Anzu's feathers and fur bristled in anticipation.

I don't think so.

The gulls were gone and the bugs and wolves fell silent as a pulsating and dazzling flash came from the far side of the Lapis Moon, momentarily flooding the night sky with bright white light and throwing long shadows that swept across the ground, creating an eclipse that faded as quickly as it appeared.

For a moment, the moon glowed from the inside like a lantern.

Its surface became riddled with tiny glowing cracks, reminding Rosheen of the famous giant stained-glass window in Keevan Abbey. Then, in complete silence, the Lapis Moon broke into a billion pieces that spiralled away in every direction, colliding with one another, tumbling, crashing and turning themselves into dust in a frenzied tarantella. For a heartbeat, Rosheen and Anzu could see the moon's core, which flared white-hot, enraged at its exposure, but then snuffed out like a candle, first cooling to orange, then black, until finally it, too, was smashed to smithereens. Of the meteor, there was nothing to be seen, reduced to powder drifting in orbit.

The Lapis Moon, the Trickster, the Lover, the All-Seeing Eye, the Mages' Moon that had been the cornerstone of Rosheen's life and the life of every mage who ever lived, was now scattered in the void like so many grains of sand.

Rosheen felt listless and struggled to keep her eyes open. She staggered back, her knees buckling, and slumped against Anzu's side, holding her tight.

I love you, Rosheen, Anzu told her. *Whatever happens, never forget that. Love, forgiveness, mercy… none of these need magic to feel real.*

'I know, I know,' Rosheen whispered back in Anzu's ear, wondering how to reassure her. Anzu trembled at her touch, staring at the distant horizon, somehow calm in the knowledge that she might lose her mind soon. 'I'll watch over you,' Rosheen promised. 'I won't let anything happen to you.'

It's going to be fine, Anzu told her. *Don't fuss. I'll be all right.*

They stayed together in an exhausted embrace, taking turns to weep until sunrise.

Sleep came easily to Sander that night. He had a plan of action: a quick trip south, get the blood, save the girl, retire on a high, then live as a free agent for the rest of his days. With this roadmap in his head, he was able to sink into the pillow and a deep slumber.

Waking wasn't so easy. His chambermaid Elke, an elderly Morven woman whose blonde hair was bound into impressive and intricate rope-like plaits, was used to working around him, so he was surprised to find her shaking him into consciousness. 'Mage Bree, my lord, wake up!'

'Elke, please,' he begged, ducking under the covers, 'I had a long day yesterday, so—'

'No, no, you must see this, Mage Bree.' She threw back the sheets and pulled on his arm, her surprisingly strong grip yanking him upright.

'Ow, that really… ow.' Sander winced at a new pain. Not only in his arm but all over his body. His neck, his shoulder blades, the base of his back, they all ached. He made more noises of discomfort and Elke hurried back from the window and made to grab him again. 'No, please, I'm perfectly capable... Ow, bugger.'

'What is it? Are you injured, Mage Bree?' she said, her voice impatient.

'I ache all over. My arms, my legs, my...' He felt his forehead. 'I'm burning up. What is wrong with me?'

'Sounds like a cold, Mage Bree, or a fever, but please, come and see—'

'Mages don't get colds,' he said as she lunged to grab him again. 'All right, all right, I'm up, I'm up, where's the fire, woman?'

Clutching his back and moving like a much, much older man, Sander followed Elke to the balcony and was astonished by what he saw.

'Elke, it's still dark! Why the bloody hell are you waking me up in the middle of the night?'

'Look, Mage Bree.' She pointed to the sky. 'It's gone.'

'What's gone?' From here, Sander could see the first light of dawn glowing behind the zigzag peaks of the Conloch Mountains. Bright above them was Greystone and...

Sander had heard the expression 'my heart skipped a beat', but it was something else entirely to actually experience the sensation of a microscopic near-death experience.

The Lapis Moon was not where it should have been.

In its place was a strange blue glow, like a mist in the stars. Billions of tiny particles streaming across the cloudless sky, shifting as they were positioned in orbit by the gravitational pull of the world below them.

The Lapis Moon was gone.

No, this didn't make sense. Sander shook his head. Feverish and groggy, he staggered across the room to the cupboard where he kept his charts. He had learned the orbits and phases of the moons by rote when he was apprenticed; he knew exactly where it should be and it wasn't there, but he had been under a lot of pressure recently and he could be completely wrong. Of course, he was overworked and struggled to remember what day of the week it was, so it was an understandable mistake.

Elke, a recent convert to the Faith, nevertheless began babbling about her old gods and their astrological counterparts. The Morvens were sailors and the stars and moons meant everything to them. Every Morven child knew how to navigate by sight, but she must be wrong, too, surely. They both had to be wrong. The blue moon would no doubt peek over the horizon any moment now.

Sander threw the cupboard doors open and his charts tumbled out onto the floor. He fell to his knees, snatching them up one by one, inspecting the names on the scrolls and tossing them away until he found what he was looking for. He tugged on the scroll's red ribbon and it sprang open. He spread it out on the floor, smoothing the parchment with his hands.

There was no mistake.

'It's gone, hasn't it?' Elke stood over him, peering down at the chart. She could read it as well as he.

'It... uh...' Sander's mind felt like a child's puzzle, its pieces scattered across the floor. 'It looks that way.'

'How?' Elke moved back to the balcony, staring into the mess in the sky above her.

'I... I don't know.' What did this mean? This, and the pain he now felt?

No magic?

He had to try some magic right here and now, even though his fevered brow and churning stomach told him that it wouldn't work. But he had to try, a quick experiment, and with something that Elke wouldn't notice, just in case the unthinkable happened and he failed. He would read her thoughts. Yes. He briefly closed his eyes, reaching out with his mind. Clairvoyance was never his speciality, but it was something he could test without making a fool of himself.

Nothing. It was like being unable to hear, see or smell.

Okay, no telepathy, so maybe some light levitation?

Nothing. He remained firmly stuck to the floor.

Telekinesis?

He glared at the scrolls scattered around his room. It should have been the work of a moment to send them floating back into the cupboard, but they were defiantly motionless.

Oh Gods, oh Gods, oh Gods.

It was gone. There was no doubt. His magic was gone.

A plan. Sander always had a plan, a way out of any fix, but it usually involved magic, and if he didn't have that…

He glanced over at Elke by the window and wondered how to play this. How long would it take people to realise he was powerless? He had to bluff it out. Leave the city fast and make a run for it. He had plenty of time, surely? And people had bigger things to worry about than some mage, didn't they? A moon had been destroyed!

Yes, he had time, not much, but enough, and if he used it wisely, he would be free before anyone got any stupid ideas.

Elke's voice broke his train of thought. 'What will you do now, Sander?'

Sander. Not Mage Bree, not my lord, nor my master.

Sander.

He was ready to make a pithy comment, but then he saw something happen to Elke's face and it terrified him. That façade of respect she wore for him, the arrangement of deference that she bore every day simply faded away.

She knew.

And if she knew, then the king knew. And Yorath. Everyone.

He was *ordinary* now. The thing that had made him special, that made strangers avert their gaze, that prompted guards to swing castle doors open for him, that won him private audiences with kings, was gone.

'I don't know,' he muttered, when he eventually answered Elke's question. Still on his knees, he fell forward on both hands, panting for breath.

'You're going to be sick? I'll get the bucket.'

'No, Elke, I'm fine, we…' He managed to get up on one knee, a nervous suitor pleading for a final chance. 'We have to keep this a secret.'

'People will notice there's only one moon, Sander.'

'Just for this morning, please, I beg you. I… I need to get my head around this. What it means. This can't be it, this can't be the way it ends… Oh gods, the wars this will cause. Without mages, so many people will die, this can't be real.'

He stumbled upright, wriggling his arms into his jerkin.

'Where are you going?' Elke watched him as he tugged on his boots.

'I'm going to…' He stopped himself. Now that veil of deference was gone, he realised with a cold jolt that he couldn't trust this woman. 'I must speak to the king,' he lied. 'You're right. People will notice before sunup, but we must make plans. There will be chaos otherwise.'

'And what use are you to the king without your magic?'

And there it was. The question everyone would be asking this morning. And Sander did not have an answer.

Yorath Pasco joined His Highness the King on the open-air landing of the Royal Observatory, an uncommonly thin tower, even by Taranis standards, on the south side of the citadel, topped with an onion-like dome through which poked an impressive brass telescope.

Bevin and Pheric were already with the king on the landing. They were all looking at the same thing: the new constellation in the sky, the shattered remains of the Lapis Moon.

Yorath had been woken by Orren Nels, one of his more enthusiastic apprentices. She had been studying the scrolls in the library when she saw a flash of light through the stained glass. Thinking it was the End Times, she joyously prepared for death, but lying prostate on the flagstones of the library floor for a while without any kind of revelation, she realised it was something almost as momentous and ran to inform the First Minister.

The end of magic.

'It is a sign from the Goddess, my King,' Yorath said, raising his arms high.

'No, Yorath. A cow birthing a two-headed calf is a sign,' the king said, not taking his eyes off the incredible sight in the sky. 'This is something a great deal more substantial.'

'The people will panic, my King,' Bevin said. 'We must prepare for rioting. We need to prepare a speech to calm them.'

'I'm not sure a *business-as-usual* message will win them over, Bevin. We need a better demonstration of our take on this new world.' For the first time, the king glanced around him. 'Where is Mage Bree?'

Pheric raised a finger, like a schoolchild with the answer. 'He wasn't in his chambers when I went to fetch him, Your Highness. I fear he has fled.'

'And you wait till now to tell me this?' the king said, lowering his voice, and Pheric quivered under his glare.

'Of course he has fled.' Yorath knew this was his moment. 'He knows the truth: this is the end of magic. His powers, fed by the moon, will fade and die. As will all magical creatures.'

'The moon's still there, Yorath.' The king gestured at the wide streak of blue in the sky. 'It's just in little bits.'

'Indeed, my King, but if you will indulge me: Natural Philosophers tell us of a mysterious field of power around the Lapis Moon, much like our own magnetic fields at the poles. That, surely, is now scattered into the abyss of the firmament. You need only—'

Yorath was interrupted by a prolonged rumble as deep and booming as the most powerful thunderstorm, and the tower they stood on began to sway. The Newlands were not prone to earthquakes, but Yorath had been in Trertos as a boy when one had crumbled the city to dust and this felt exactly like that. The king, Bevin and Yorath only had time to share puzzled looks before it was over. There was a brief silence before cries of panic began to echo from the citizens far below.

'What in the gods was that?' the king demanded.

'Majesty.' Bevin Arne narrowed her eyes as she looked beyond the citadel's walls. 'I believe our celebrated Mage's Moons have fallen to the ground.'

She was right. Whatever latent magic was keeping them aloft was already exhausted, and now they were scattered around the citadel like an ancient henge, sacrificing themselves as if to prove Yorath's theory. Surely this was another sign from the Goddess? Yorath chose not to press his point as he saw a flicker of fear on His Majesty's face. He knew what the absence of magic would mean. A new world where war was a certainty, where an alliance with Parthalan would be more important than ever.

'Find Mage Bree,' the king said, his voice quiet. 'Find him and bring him before me immediately.'

'I think I can help with that.'

Yorath turned back to the stairs that led to the landing. 'Step forward, my dear. It's quite all right.'

Guided by Orren, a Morven lady shuffled out of the shadows. She kneeled before the king.

'Who is this?' the king asked.

'Mage Bree's chambermaid, Your Majesty.' Yorath smiled. 'She has some information that may help us.'

Shouts throughout the *Queen Mathilde* woke Oskar with a jolt. Cries of, 'Wake the captain!' cut through the mess of curses, prayers and cheers. Yanick's voice silenced them and nothing was said for so long that, despite the sting of the manacles chafing his ankles, the incessant clucking of the caged chickens and the rough swell of the Ocean's Hand sending the ship up and down, Oskar was able to drift back to sleep.

When Craig woke him with a kick, there was sunlight leaking in through the deck planks above. The ship's boy, silent and bruised after their last encounter, laid a plate of hard biscuits and brackish water by Oskar's feet.

'Thank you,' Oskar said.

Oskar.

Said.

The ship's boy looked at him for a moment, surprised at the utterance but not enough to be curious. It had been made clear that his interaction with Oskar should be kept to a minimum. He wasn't paid enough to be curious. And so he loped back up the steps to the deck.

Oskar waited until he was absolutely sure Craig had gone before trying again. 'Thank... you. Thank you. Thank you, thank you, thank you.'

Oskar slapped a hand over his mouth, his smile so wide it threatened to split his face. The words were clear. The words came straight from his mind to his mouth with no effort at all. Tears welled up in his eyes. He blinked them away, and that's when he noticed something else.

He looked intently around the murky deck. The words stencilled on the crates, once vague and fuzzy, were now so clear he could make out the woodgrain beneath the black ink. He couldn't actually read the words, but Oskar recognised the shapes of the letters, and memories of his mother and Alby Clim and Rosheen trying to teach him to read came flooding back. He could see particles of dust slowly drifting through the shafts of light, the tiny grains of flour strewn around the flour sacks on the deck.

The sloshing of the waves against the hull, the chatter and burble on deck, the gentle ripple of the sails caught by the wind – noises that were once woolly and muffled were all distinct to him now. The ship wasn't singing, but perhaps it would start again soon?

And Oskar's thoughts, always so jumbled and confused, now fell into place like the neat pieces of a puzzle. Somehow, as if the gods had lit a candle in his brain, he could think, speak, see and hear like never before.

And then one thought, one far more important than any other, came to him with such simple clarity, it made the hairs on his head stand on end.

He could escape.

He could escape and go home!

He did not have to stay here. He did not have to be a prisoner. He *had* to escape.

He was on a ship in the middle of the sea, so now was not the time. But when? And where would he go? Home? To find Rosheen? To Mother? She might still be alive – he had a son's duty to go to her. The possibilities whirled around his mind. He buried his head in his hands, wanting the flood of thoughts to slow for a moment so that he could make sense of them. First things first: he knew he had to conceal his newfound abilities from Yanick and the crew. If they got any whiff of this change, they would treat him differently. Especially Yanick. Oskar knew he had to be that younger brother for Yanick again and play the fool. The only others who knew were the chickens and the rats, and he intended to keep it that way.

Oh gods, he hoped this feeling would last. He pinched himself, bit his lip until he drew blood. This was no dream, it was really happening, and the world was new to him now. And a terrible realisation chilled him: every day, every minute until this moment had been a dreadful waste, a poor excuse for a life, and he did not wish to waste a second more. He couldn't wait for them to dock. Despite Yanick's promises that he would see his sister soon, Oskar knew from the chickens and the piles of provisions around him that this ship was ready to stay at sea for weeks. He had to get back on land as soon as possible and find his sister and mother. And anyway, he was fed up with other people telling him what to do. It was time to take control of his life.

He glanced again at the flour sacks, wooden barrels, crates and water casks stored around him. He might not know the words painted on their sides, but he'd seen the ship's cook raid them for grain, rice, flour, water and rum. And, in a moment, he knew exactly what he had to do.

Anzu

The dawn firmament crackled. Orange and white streaks of light and smoke moved across the sky, stretching like skeletal fingers, colouring the clouds they pierced, making them shift like ink in water.

The noise woke Rosheen. With a series of groans, she unfolded herself from her foetal sleeping position, then stood and stretched as she looked out over the misty sea, its waves slopping and churning on the rocks below the cliff as they reflected the light show above. She was exhausted even though she had not moved all night. Her head ached, her shoulder blades protested whenever she moved her arms, and standing and moving about had her grunting and gasping in a manner not unlike her late grandfather when he got up early to milk the cows.

She hadn't meant to sleep, and with a flush of panic, she remembered her promise to watch over Anzu.

Rosheen spun on her heels to find her griffin asleep by the cliff's edge. *Anzu's alive!*

Rosheen was so happy and relieved that she wanted to wake the griffin, but knew she'd be just as tired, if not more so. Sleep had come in peaks and troughs of deep, intense dream states followed by sudden jolts back to consciousness. And then she was roused by a new sound in the sky.

A shower of Lapis Moon fragments moved over the water in a hazy band, like a distant storm. They were an impossibly long way off, but at the same time, she felt like she could reach out and send the tiny particles spinning away with a brush of her fingers.

She looked around in a full circle: none were making landfall. Those that fell would be lost in the vastness of the cold White Sea that stretched from here to the pole. Rosheen wondered what she would do with a fragment of the moon if she found one. What effect would it have? Could she draw on its power in the same way she could draw on the Lapis Moon's? She began to wonder about the effect a missing moon would have on the tides, and then felt another wave of exhaustion wash over her. She needed a proper sleep.

There came a low purr behind her.

'Oh, thank the gods, you're okay, Anzu. I was beginning to think—'

Anzu was awake, alert and frozen about ten yards from Rosheen. The griffin's haunches were up, the fur on her back bristling, front paws stretched, claws extended as she watched Rosheen, unblinking. Anzu had moved around Rosheen so that the mage was trapped, with only the long drop of the cliff behind her. And Anzu looked like she was about to pounce.

'Speak to me, Anzu.' Rosheen kept her tone as calm and steady as possible, even though she knew Anzu could probably smell her sudden fear. 'Let me hear your voice.'

It didn't come. The griffin's eyes stayed on her, her breathing becoming more ragged as mucus began to drip from her beak. Rosheen kept eye contact while slowly backing away, careful not to get too close to the cliff edge.

'Fight it, Anzu.' Rosheen thought she saw something – a glimmer of Anzu's old self in her beautiful golden eyes as her pupils dilated. 'I know you're in there, I know you can hear me. Please don't give in.'

The griffin shook her head and Anzu was gone. What looked up at Rosheen now was a wild animal inspecting its prey.

Rosheen had seen the untamed half of Anzu come to the fore many times in the past – in fights, when she was in heat, and of course that time back home in Eru. Rosheen had never dreamed she would be on the receiving end. The attack was imminent and it would be sudden and ferocious. There was no point in running; all she could do was remain still, stay calm and wait.

For a long moment, there was only the gentle buffeting of the wind and Rosheen's heart pounding in her ears.

Rosheen saw the muscles in Anzu's legs jerk, then her wings flapped open as she jumped. Rosheen was ready to flip over and out of the way, but she discovered that the strength she could usually count on wasn't there. She floundered, landing badly in a heap, face down. She felt the dead weight of Anzu's claws press on her back, pinning her to the ground. Next would come the blade-like stab of a beak at her neck if she didn't move fast.

Gritting her teeth and letting out a cry, she twisted around, grabbing Anzu's beak and holding it shut. The griffin shook her head to break free, but Rosheen's grip was firm, so Anzu pushed away, skittering back and slipping out of the hold.

Breathless, Rosheen also backed away, one of her boots slipping on the cliff's edge. A few stones broke loose and clattered as they bounced off rocky protrusions before dropping into the foaming sea. 'Please, Anzu. It's me, Rosheen!'

The griffin bounded towards her again and Rosheen had no choice but to leap straight at her, gripping her head feathers and swinging her legs over Anzu's back, cursing herself for removing the reins and saddle earlier. Rosheen clamped her legs tight around Anzu as they tumbled over the cliff's edge into the empty air.

They spiralled down towards the rocks below and for a moment, Rosheen was sure they would crash there in a bloody mess. But Anzu spread her wings and Rosheen thanked the gods the griffin could still fly.

Anzu flapped hard to gain height and Rosheen clung on, anticipating that she would next try to flip her off her back. She did exactly that, twisting in the air, bucking and jerking as they hurtled past the cliff face. Rosheen gripped a wing with one hand, digging her fingers into Anzu's fur with the other.

The griffin went into a steep dive, coming perilously close to the cliff wall, as if she was going to scrape Rosheen on the cliff face. Rosheen tried to plead with Anzu, but the rushing wind took her breath away. In moments, she would be dashed against the granite and dead before she hit the rocks below.

So she did something that only a few hours ago would have been unthinkable. She gripped the humerus bone that connected Anzu's body to her wings and twisted hard. The bone was hollow and light and broke easily. Anzu cawed in pain and they both began to drop like a stone.

They plunged into the sea. Before either could surface for breath, the push and undertow of the breaking waves swept them out, then, almost as suddenly, propelled them back towards the rocky shore. Rosheen lost her grip on Anzu and was shoved against a smooth boulder, banging her head and seeing stars before being dragged under the surface. Anzu, never a great swimmer, swirled away with the waves, her bad wing hanging limp as she tried to paddle.

Rosheen kicked to the surface, hands flailing for anything to hold. Her knuckles grazed against rocks as she fumbled for a grip, coughing and spitting the brine from her mouth. She pulled herself out of the sea, collapsing onto a jagged black rock edged with green, slippy moss. Rosheen discovered that the waves that had looked so languid from the clifftop were pounding against the rocks, filling the air around her with foaming sea spray.

Before Rosheen could get to her knees, Anzu burst from the waves. The griffin planted her feet on Rosheen's chest, shook the water from her fur and, with a jerk of her head, clamped her beak around Rosheen's face. Robbed of breath, Rosheen began to panic. Her feet kicked, her arms pounded Anzu's head, but the griffin only bit down harder.

As the beak pierced the skin around her temples, Rosheen's hand found a loose rock. She gripped it and brought it smashing against the side of Anzu's skull. Anzu bit harder still, her pungent breath blowing into Rosheen's eyes, her thick saliva spraying on the mage's face. Anzu leaned her full weight on Rosheen's chest, pushing all the air from her. Terrified, Rosheen gave a primal roar that could be heard over the tumult of the crashing waves and bashed the rock against the griffin's head as hard as her failing strength would let her. And then her world faded to black.

Rosheen dreamed of home. Of the Mylar Mountains, red and barren in the setting sun. Of her mother bringing home an egg for her birthday. Feeding the hatchling. Naming her. Imprinting herself upon her. Watching her fly for the first time.

And then giant, grey waves came crashing over the mountains, washing everything away.

Rosheen's eyes stung and she coughed salt water from her mouth as the dream was snatched away from her. The tide was in, the sea had calmed.

The grey water was diluted with red clouds. Through her blurred vision, she saw a shape. A body half-on, half-off the rocks, pushed and pulled by the eddies.

Anzu.

The griffin's eyes were closed in peace. The line of her beak was such that she looked like she was pouting, and Rosheen half-expected to hear some withering comment from her old friend, but none came.

Rosheen was empty. Drained. She crawled to the moss at the edge of the rock and rested a hand on Anzu's head, her fingers moving through the feathers covering the now unfamiliar shape of the griffin's skull where her rock had caved it in. Rosheen found her body convulsing as the sobs came.

She could not recall how long she spent cradling Anzu's body, nor how she found herself wading out into the waves. All Rosheen knew was that she could see no future. However much she loved Oskar, she knew that Frang would double-cross her. The boy was a good as dead. Anzu was dead. Torren was dead. Her mother and father were dead. Magic was gone. Her world had ended.

The waves took her further out, and she lay on her back, gazing up at the sky.

The shower of Lapis stones had moved across the water while she was unconscious. It was closer now, and as the sea washed in and out of her ears, she could hear distant splashes as the stones impacted on the water, sinking to its bed.

Something made her look directly up. She saw one coming straight for her. There was no mistake. The tiny dot was getting bigger and bigger, spinning like a drill bit. She closed her eyes and opened her arms wide, ready for it to plough into her, to take her down into the depths.

And then she thought of Oskar.

A Village Hanging

Sander found Ragnall in his shack on the edge of Lugham. The old man was throwing stuff into a knapsack. Nothing useful like maps or rations. Instead, his priorities were a bag of his dried mushrooms and a gourd of Keevan whisky.

At the sound of the shack door opening, Ragnall had spun on his heels, a knife gripped in his gnarled hand. He sagged with relief when he saw it was only Sander. 'You got out. Good one. Well done.'

'What do we do, Raggy?' Sander almost fell into the shack, exhausted from his half-run, half-walk from Taranis to Lugham. He had left when it was still dark, missing breakfast, and his belly rumbled in anticipation of elevenses. His body complained whenever he moved now. He wasn't running away. He told himself that again and again on the way. He was seeking the advice of a fellow mage. That's what he would say if he ran into any of the King's Guard. 'What do we do?'

'I'm going north.' Ragnall tied up his bag and hoisted it over his back. 'Cerwidden. Finding Father and then disappearing for ever. It's not much of a plan, but you're welcome to join me.'

'I can't, I...' Sander thought back to that little girl and how she would start to suffer over the next few days. 'I made a promise. You heard about Princess Brianna? Rosheen Katell told me this would happen. Oh gods, oh gods.'

'A promise? To a girl who'll be dead before the month is out, or to a king who will soon realise you're about as much use to him as rocking horse shit?'

'No, no, he needs me—'

'For what? A cure? You'd need merblood from one of the clans.'

'Have you got any?'

'What would I be needing merblood for?'

'I'll go south. The Nolwen Clan at Connal Lake.'

'And how will you get there? Fly? No, all bets are off, Sander. The world has changed. We're now the lowest of the low, my friend. From top dog to dog shit in moments. Did you see it happen? By the

113

gods, it was beautiful. I actually pissed myself, I'm not ashamed to say it.'

Sander's mind was addled. A life of certainty had been usurped by disorder. When he spoke, his voice trembled. 'I was tested, Ragnall. I was tested and I failed. I keep thinking back to how I should have—'

'There'll be plenty of time for regrets later. For now, just do.'

'We're running. We're actually running away. Okay, okay.' Sander took a breath. 'What's the plan?'

'There are King's Guards on every road, and a few patrolling the woods, I imagine. Some might look the other way for a few coins. You got any money?'

Sander patted the pockets of his jerkin. Nothing. He never needed the stuff, usually. Most folk were happy to oblige him with complimentary food and drink in the citadel, and he never thought to take any when he left his chambers. *Stupid, stupid!* He would need to start thinking differently now. About money, food, shelter, everything.

'That's okay.' Ragnall slapped his former apprentice on the shoulder. 'We'll manage. Put that hat on and stuff your hair into it – you'll stand out otherwise.'

Sander did as he was told, folding and tucking his hair into a grey, woollen hat that stank of pipe smoke. He would have to wash the pong out of his hair on the move, he supposed.

Ragnall looked him and up and down. 'I've seen better-dressed scarecrows. Perfect. Let's go.'

They wound their way along a narrow path that ran around the edge of the village. Brambles tugged at their clothes as they hurried over the uneven ground, their hoods up.

'Raggy,' Sander called after his old tutor. 'Are you... aching at all? Muscle pain, that sort of thing?'

'Like you've gone twelve rounds with a troll?'

'Yeah.'

'Our bodies readjusting to the lack of magic, perhaps? Who knows? I bet we'll learn more about magic in its absence than when it was—'

Ragnall stopped in his tracks, raising his palm. Sander stumbled to a halt. He looked around Ragnall to see a pair of King's Guards loitering by a stile at a crossroads. He and Ragnall crouched down out of sight among the ferns that lined the path.

'Wait here,' Ragnall said as he weighed a small leather pouch of coins in his palm. 'I'll sound them out. I think I recognise one of them. Owes me a favour or two, so we should be okay.'

'He's not going to let us walk by, surely?'

'No, but a few coins might buy us some temporary memory loss. A delay of half an hour or so before they report in. Not much, but gives us a chance to be somewhere else.'

He started to move, but Sander clutched his arm. 'And what if it doesn't?'

'Run like a demon with the gods at your tail, boy.' He winked. 'We'll be fine. In the meantime, do not budge an inch until I say so.'

Sander watched as Ragnall made his way down to the main track where he hallooed the waiting guards. There was a clatter of armour as they readied their swords, but Ragnall raised his arms in surrender and continued to walk towards them. Sander couldn't quite hear what the older mage was saying, but it was clear from the tone of his muffled words that he was turning on the charm.

He lowered his arms as he got closer to them, then turned his back on Sander as he spoke. He rested a friendly hand on one guard's shoulder as they huddled together. Sander saw Ragnall reveal the money pouch. The guards exchanged glances. Honest men, oath swearers, aware of the consequences of taking a bribe, but also poor men on a meagre soldier's wage and in need of a few extra coppers – and who would know, after all?

Sander shifted on his aching haunches. Something was wrong. This was taking too long, and there was something a bit too chummy about their little conference. He desperately wanted to creep closer to hear their conversation, but Ragnall had told him to wait right here and Sander knew he wasn't stealthy enough to evade the King's Guard. Then something happened that gave Sander the chills. One of the guards looked directly at where Sander was hiding. Merely a glance. Less than a second.

It was like he'd just been told where to find him.

By Ragnall.

And it was Ragnall's reaction, a gesture snapping the guard's attention back to him – *Don't look!* – that confirmed it for Sander. The old bastard was selling him out. Not only bribing the guards but offering them a sweetener: the king's own mage on the run. He's hiding in the ferns over there, don't you know? *Stupid, Sander. Stupid, stupid! Why did I trust the wily old sod?*

Sander wanted to run, then hesitated as he tried to think of a way out of this that didn't involve magic. So many spells or incantations could have finished this in moments: sending the guards to sleep, a glamour to sneak around them, a projection or noise in the woods to distract them. All gone.

In the end, Sander realised that he couldn't run, and hiding was no longer an option. He was buggered if he was going to allow Ragnall to benefit from turning him in.

'Er... Morning,' Sander said as he found himself standing, visible to all as he gave a little wave. 'Hello? Yes, over here. Well, I guess you knew anyway, and I figured I'd save you the trouble of all this pretence. So. Here I am. Come and get me.'

The startled guards raised their weapons once more, barking at him to surrender. Ragnall first looked annoyed that his plan had been scuppered, then followed a flash of pride that his protégé had taken the initiative. He inclined and shook his head and smiled in a way that offered an apology. *Sorry, son, I had no choice.*

As the first guard shoved Ragnall to his knees, declaring him under arrest, the second guard started to make his way up the path towards Sander.

And that's when the younger mage found his feet and ran.

Despite his aching limbs, Sander discovered that he could run a great deal faster than he had expected, so much so that the woollen hat Raggy had loaned him came flying off as he vaulted a gate at the edge of the village. Of course, having an armed King's Guard on your tail added an extra something, and Sander easily lost his pursuer when he slipped between the lean-to buildings of Lugham.

Sander's chest burned and his back dripped with sweat as he clambered over a small pyramid of barrels and found himself in a dark alley.

He recognised it as the back entrance of the Jolly Cooper. Normally, it would be bustling with activity first thing in the morning as barrels of ale were rolled off carts and into the tavern, but he was alone save for a couple of rats foraging in the shade. For a moment, he wondered where everyone was, then heard jeering voices coming from the main square.

He sidled up to the corner of the tavern, dropped to his hands and knees and dared to peer around the corner.

The street was heaving with people. Everyone in Lugham was here, plus whatever travellers were passing through when the Lapis Moon was destroyed. Some in the crowd looked afraid, children huddled with parents, the elderly and infirm were jostled, but others cheered like it was Year's End. A few were silent, motionless, smiling quietly with hands on sword hilts. Experience had taught Sander that those were the ones to watch.

Another low roar. This wasn't a human noise, but a more mournful sound. The crowd parted, revealing the blue hulk of Cleff the bridge troll, roped and bound, being led into the square by his captors whose cries of victory were matched by the villagers' cheers.

Cleff was naked, pathetic and grotesque, his belly wobbling with each staggered step and his sorry-looking, saggy testicles swinging around between his legs. He fell to his knees but roared more defiantly this time and the crowd instinctively backed away. A troll would normally defend himself easily against this rabble with a swipe of his mighty arm, but Cleff was tired and listless without his magic strength. His blue skin was dry and cracked after so much exposure to the morning sun. He bared his teeth to warn the crowd off, but a couple of people Sander recognised as local farmers ran forwards and jabbed him in the buttocks with their pitchforks before scurrying away. Their cowardly attack was greeted with more cheers of approval as blood seeped from the wounds. As Cleff tried to reach around and stem the flow of blood, another farmer clambered onto the troll's back. He raised his machete into the air, crying, 'Shall I? Shall I?' and the crowd's fervour reached a frantic peak as they gave their assent.

The farmer swung the machete with a well-practised stroke and it sliced through the skin at the back of Cleff's neck. The troll hadn't seen the blade coming and his eyes widened in shock at the sudden pain. He howled in terror as his skin split, revealing purple flesh and muscle.

The clamouring of the gathered mob became a deafening white noise and Sander clapped his hands over his ears. For a moment, Cleff's eyes met his. Two doomed creatures from a dying age. Sander found himself wiping tears from his cheeks, partly for Cleff, but mostly because he knew he might be next. He had to leave this place now, or at least find somewhere to hide.

More blades hacked into the troll's body. His eyes went dim and rolled back and his tongue lolled from his mouth as the villagers butchered him in their village square with whoops of laughter and song.

There came a new noise.

'Unhand me, you ungrateful bastards!'

Ragnall, his hands tied behind his back, was shoved into the square by two heavies armed with daggers. He must have given the King's Guards the slip but been captured by something even more dangerous: men with vengeance on their minds. Sander recognised one of them as the red-faced man from the other night at the Jolly Cooper. The one Ragnall had accused of interfering with a pig.

They shoved Ragnall to the ground and the old man cursed their mothers and their fathers before showing them a little of his old fire. 'Back off. Untie me now or I'll kill you all before you can blink.'

A few of the crowd moved away, but the red-faced man and his companion stood their ground. 'Is that so?' he said. 'I'd like to see you try.'

'Careful, son,' a voice from the crowd said. 'He might still have a bit of the magic in him.'

There were murmurs of worried agreement and Ragnall got to his feet again. 'Let me go and we'll pretend this never happened. You don't like me and the feeling is largely mutual. There's no need for any more bloodletting.' Sander saw Ragnall glance at poor Cleff's body nearby. 'I'm going to walk away and—' But the red-faced man's blade was pressed to his chest and he could go no further. 'I have no quarrel with you, sir.'

'"Sir", is it?' the man said. 'The other night I was a pig fucker.'

'The other night I'd had too much to drink. So shall we let bygones be—'

The red-faced man raised the blade to Ragnall's neck. 'No, let's play a game. It's called Move and I Kill You.'

'I, uhm, I'm not familiar with the rules of that particular—'

'There'll be no more blood!' A new voice, close to Sander, made him jolt with shock. He backed a little further into the alley's shadows as Astrid, with her son Winoc in tow, strode out of the Jolly Cooper and across the square. 'Not in front of the children.'

Sander could see Ragnall start to relax. 'How very wise, Astrid. And the gentleman who spoke out is indeed correct. The Lapis Moon may be gone, but I still have a little of the old magic in me. I'd hate to use it in anger and have held off from doing so because I am not a vindictive man. Indeed, I am willing to forgive and forget this entire—'

'Do that trick again.' Winoc's voice shattered Ragnall's little moment. Sander could see that Ragnall knew precisely what was coming next and that there was nothing he could do to stop it. 'The other night you levitated up to the ceiling, then you levitated everyone else. If you've got a bit of the old magic in you, then show us.'

'Young man, I... am no street conjurer. I do not do requests.'

Without warning, the red-faced man drew his dagger blade across Ragnall's cheek. A thin line of crimson buds appeared, followed by a stream that began to trickle down his cheek. 'He bleeds. We can kill him, magic or no.'

'What did I say about blood?' Astrid barked, and once again, Sander could see Ragnall's face briefly light up at the thought of freedom. For one glorious moment, he had a saviour in the unlikely form of Astrid. 'We'll hang him instead,' she said, eliciting a huge cheer from the crowd. Before he could react, Ragnall was carried away, borne on the arms of the throng. And that's when he caught Sander's eye.

'Sander! Help me! Help me, please!' He reached out to where Sander was hiding and faces turned to find him.

'Oh, not again,' Sander said, rising on his trembling legs. 'Cheers, Ragnall. Thanks very bloody much.'

'There! This one's mate,' someone cried.

'I saw him kill a Brother of the Faith!' said another.

'Murderer!'

Once more, Sander was on the run.

Sander scrambled out of the village and into the woods, cutting through brambles and ferns. He stayed off the path, kept clear of Ragnall's shack and found himself sprinting headlong towards the cave, the only place he could think of where he might possibly be safe from the pursuing mob. Not daring to look back, he could hear their wordless baying bouncing off the trees around him, along with a new noise: the incessant *huff-huff-huff* of a hound that surely had his scent and would be on him in moments. Sander rushed past the boulder that blocked the main entrance to the cave. There was no way he could shift that on his own and Gorm the troll was nowhere to be seen – *probably dead, too*, he thought – so he kept going. Running full pelt, Sander nearly missed the sinkhole entrance and was in such a state of panic that he hurled himself into it, not thinking about the drop into the gloom below.

He landed awkwardly in the shallow water and saw flashes of light as a jolt of pain shot up from his ankle. He'd twisted it and putting any weight on it only brought more lightning stabs of agony and curses through gritted teeth.

He flicked his hair back, waded to the shore and armed himself with one of Ragnall's old frying pans then found a dark corner in which to hide.

Oh, Ragnall! Despite the betrayal, Sander found himself shedding a tear for the silly fool and tried not to think of what they would do to his old master. He hoped it would be quick and painless, and that they would extend the same mercy to Sander.

The hound's barking came echoing through the hole in the cave's ceiling. 'Ralf's got a scent, this way!' called one voice. Ralf was the dog who slept by the fire in the Jolly Cooper. His nose would find Sander in no time. Sander gripped the frying pan more tightly now, wonder-

ing if he could bring himself to kill a dog, particularly one he was on
first-name terms with.

Sander tried not to breathe too loudly. The cave amplified his every
noise. From somewhere in the dark came a deep moaning noise and
the sweat on his back turned ice-cold. Sander scanned the shadows,
but there was no one else here with him.

Another moan reverberated around him. It made Sander think of
Myristan monks who summoned their gods with enormous horns
made from mammoth tusks. It was both mournful and threatening,
and there was only one other resident of the cave that could be making that sort of noise.

'Gorm?' Sander called. 'That you, old friend?'

The creature's lamentation was joined by clinking and splashing.

Clink. Splash.

'Gorm, if that is you, could you keep it down, please?'

Clink. Splash.

'Seriously, Gorm, there's a mob with a hound, please…'

Clink. Splash.

'Stop it.'

Clink. Splash. Clink. Splash.

'Shush!'

It was coming from the far end of the cave. Another chamber. A
place he'd never bothered to explore before. Was there was another
way out of here? He got to his feet, ignoring the pain in his ankle, and
waded through the pool towards the noise.

Clink. Splash.

Ralf was barking for his master. It boomed around the walls like a
dragon's roar and made the hair on Sander's arms stand on end. The
hound must be at the cave entrance, waiting for someone to move the
boulder. Not much time.

Sander hurried through the water, every step sending bolts of
agony from his ankle.

Then came the distant echo of stone grinding on stone, accompanied by a chorus of *Heave! Heave!* as the mob struggled to move the
boulder at the cave's entrance.

Sander tripped on an unseen rock in the pool and fell face first into the water, dropping the frying pan and losing it. As he pulled himself out and clawed his way onto the shore, he saw a narrow crawl space between the rocks.

And Gorm the troll.

Clink. Splash.

The blue-skinned creature had his back to Sander as he methodically moved a rock half his size from one side of the flooded cave and dropped it on a pile of others nearby.

Clink. Splash.

Gorm heaved one more boulder aside, revealing a maze of amber stalactites hanging above placid, cloudy green water. An underground river, thank the gods! Sander had no idea where it might lead, but anywhere was better than here.

Sander heard a distant rumble then a cheer. The boulder had been moved by the mob. 'Go get him, Ralfy!' A drumbeat began to resonate throughout the cave – *thud-a-dum-thud-a-dum-thud-a-dum-thud-a-dum* – the relentless rhythm of the hound's paws, his heavy panting getting louder and closer.

Gorm's hole was now big enough for him to squeeze through, and he stretched one leg into the darkness.

'Gorm!' Sander cried, and the troll froze. Listless, Gorm turned his head to the mage and snarled. The troll's magic might have gone, but he was big enough to break Sander's face with a single punch. 'Please...?' Sander gestured to himself and the river. 'Me too...? Can... can I come?'

Ralf entered the main chamber of the cave with a bark. A clarion call to his masters: *I've found him!*

Startled, Gorm flung himself into the water and splashed away between the amber stones, fading into the darkness.

Sander made to scrabble after Gorm, but Ralf had spotted the mage and bolted across the cave at an incredible speed, knocking him to the rocky ground.

It was all Sander could do to raise his hands over his face as the hound bit into his forearm, nothing vicious, more a firm grip to make clear who was in charge now. Sander didn't bother to struggle. He was too exhausted, and when the mob's hands grabbed him, he didn't resist.

They dragged him like a sack of potatoes over the cracked and dusty ground through the square. Whenever he looked up, he could see the silhouetted shapes of his bearers, the bright sun behind them making his eyes throb. Every now and then, one of them punched him in the face for daring to make eye contact. Then someone in the surrounding mob would barge to the front, kick him the ribs and receive a cheer for their efforts before melting back into the crowd. Sander settled on looking down at the ground rolling beneath him, spitting the dust from his mouth and blinking the grit from his eyes.

When they finally propped him upright, he immediately wished that he were face down again. They were at the silver oak by the crossroads on the edge of the village. The hanging tree.

Sander let slip an involuntary moan when he saw that the tree had already borne fruit.

Ragnall's body twisted slowly in the morning breeze. A thick rope around his neck, a grimace of agony frozen on his bloated dead face.

Sander jumped, startled, as someone tugged a rope over his head, the rough hemp biting into his skin and tugging on his hair. 'No, no, please.' He found himself kicking and lashing out as they dragged him towards the tree. 'I didn't mean to hurt anyone, please let me go, please. I wasn't running away, I was seeking advice from a fellow mage. I'm the King's Mage, let me go, I'm the *King's Mage*!'

He watched as one villager hurled the other end of the rope over the hanging branch of the tree. Sander knew the face from somewhere but couldn't quite place it. It took him a few moments before the penny dropped.

'Madoc!' he called to the dung farmer who had given him a ride to Taranis only a couple of days ago. 'Madoc Shay. See, I remember you. Please, Madoc, please tell them this is all a terrible mistake.'

There was a moment, a brief, blissful moment, where Sander saw Madoc's face soften as he thought about what he was doing. It was Sander's last glimmer of hope.

'He's a murderer, Madoc!' one man cried.

'Killed a Brother of the Faith in cold blood!' yelled another.

Sander saw the change in Madoc's eyes, from light to dark as if someone had pulled a shade across the sun. 'No, please, that wasn't me, Madoc, no!'

Madoc, the dung delivery man with the growth on his big toe, took a firm grip on the rope and pulled hard, hoisting Sander into the air.

Immediately, Sander's head felt heavy. His tongue was forced against the roof of his mouth as the rope tightened around his neck. There was a hissing noise in his ears and flashes of light at the periphery of his vision. He pawed helplessly at the rope, but his fingers felt fat and useless and the world around him began to fade to darkness.

The last thing Sander saw was a glint of sunlight on metal as someone barged through the crowd. Someone from the King's Guard, wielding a sword.

The Power of the Stone

Rosheen's plan had come together in the few moments it took for her to dive down after the fragment of the Lapis Moon that splashed into the sea next to her. A sudden change of heart, an impulsive will to live, a desire for revenge, all fired up by the sensation of magic returning as the stone plunged into the waves.

She felt its power.

This stone, this tiny fragment of the shattered Lapis Moon, reeked of magic.

Rosheen could use its power. She would have magic again.

Glowing bright blue, the stone began its descent to the seabed. Rosheen took a breath and swam after it. The sea salt stung her eyes and the push and pull of the waves tossed them both around. She kept on kicking, her hands reaching out as the sensation of magic – like waking from a deep, refreshing sleep – grew stronger.

And then she had it. Clasping it in both hands, she cradled the Lapis stone to her breast like a newborn then drifted to the surface, its power easing her pain and awakening her own latent magic from its slumber. It was hers, and for a moment she basked in the joy and hope it gave her.

Breaking the surface, Rosheen looked around for Anzu's body. Perhaps she wasn't beyond healing? Maybe the stone could mend Anzu's wounds, suppress the animal inside and bring back Rosheen's friend? It was a big ask, but Rosheen wasn't about to give up on her yet. All she could see were choppy waves. Anzu was gone. Slipped under the surface. Rosheen dived down to find her, the stone's glow a tiny lamp in the vast sea, giving her the strength to swim like a fish, managing her breath and blood flow so that she could stay under for ten times as long as normal. She did not know how long she spent searching for Anzu, searching for any glimmer of her friend's presence, but the sun was high when she finally gave in. Anzu was nowhere to be seen, and Rosheen knew that she might spend the rest of her life swimming these depths and never find her. With a broken heart, she allowed herself to rise to the surface once more. There was some pain that magic could never heal. And so, blinking away tears, she swam for the shore.

Shivering and soaking wet, Rosheen tucked the stone into her jerkin and, using its power, began a slow levitation up the cliff face to where she could see a gaping wound in the castle's walls.

The sun's light became a diffused bright white as it passed through the band of Lapis shards in orbit. Everything around her was drained of colour. She landed gently on the clifftop, feeling heavy. Her knees buckled and she collapsed on grass that was more white than green in this new light. She lay there for a moment, catching her breath, her head spinning. The stone was giving her power, but it wasn't the same as the strength the moon once provided. It was the difference between Eru tea and Keevan whisky: one made her perky, but the other put a fire in her belly that made her feel invincible. Those days of invulnerability were over.

At least she was dry now, apart from those spots where her clothes bunched at the backs of her knees and other joints. Her hair was straw-like, smelling of stale sea salt, and she caught a whiff of her own body odour wafting up through her jerkin. Even with a good glamour, any half-decent guard would smell her a mile off.

Fighting an impatient inner voice that wanted to rush in, screaming and snapping the bones of everyone in sight, Rosheen painstakingly made her way past the broken outer walls of Castle Agrona, across the exposed outer bailey and into the main keep.

Still unsure of the strength of her power, Rosheen waited for guards to turn away then glamoured past them, stealthily making her way to Torren's throne room, where she was sure she would find Haldor Frang.

He wasn't there. Plenty of his men were milling about, sharpening weapons and cleaning their boots. One was even taking his ease squatting over an empty fireplace, but the warlord was nowhere to be seen.

A distant howl of anguish froze everyone in the room for a moment. Some fearful looks were exchanged, followed by resigned shrugs from those who had been with Haldor for some time and become used to unexpected caterwauling.

Another cry. It was coming from the cells beneath the castle.

Silently, Rosheen backed into the shadows and began a descent through the twisting stairwells. A new noise gradually became louder and clearer. A hammering. Wood on nails.

Rosheen discovered Haldor Frang in a torchlit cellar. Around him were alcoves housing wooden wine barrels in neat stacks. He was bare-chested and standing atop a ladder propped up against a huge cask more than twice as big as the others. He was hammering its lid firmly into place and whistling a tune that Rosheen recognised as an old Grainne sea shanty.

'Become a vintner, have we, Haldor?' Rosheen took some pleasure from the warlord's startled look when he saw her at the cellar door.

'Rosheen Katell.' He recovered quickly, lowered the hammer and gave her his usual wide grin: half genuine pleasure, half manic. 'Ah, but where is your friend? The griffin,' he asked, hopping off the ladder and clapping the dust from his hands. Then a flicker of sadness. 'Oh, no. Became a beast again, did she? Perhaps she's better off that way. Creatures who speak with the mind... hardly seems fair on the rest of us, does it?'

Rosheen felt her face blush and kicked herself as Haldor saw it, too.

'How sad. How very sad. That's why you're exiled, yes? From Mylar? She killed a child, I hear.'

Rosheen said nothing, but Haldor once again knew he was right. 'Don't be ashamed. The divide between our civilised selves and the beast within is a small one.'

Thump.

The noise came from within the large barrel.

Rosheen looked startled, but Haldor said nothing.

Thump, thump.

'What's in the barrel, Haldor?'

The thumping became frantic, as if something inside was struggling to get out. Haldor had to raise his voice to be heard over the clamour. 'Let me show you something... Now, where is it?' He glanced around the cellar in the manner of a gaoler who had lost his keys while the desperate thumping from inside the barrel continued. 'Ah, there it is.' He strode over to a small pyramid of beer barrels, reached behind them and retrieved a severed human head.

Rosheen shivered at the sight of the head and the blood that drip-dripped from the neck, and it took every fibre of self-control she had left not to scream in shock. The poor soul was open-mouthed and staring into eternity with wide eyes. He had good teeth and a well-groomed beard. Probably from Taranis, Rosheen guessed.

Thump, thump, thump!

'Bhaltair sends me this.' Haldor gripped the head by its long, blood-soaked hair, shaking it like an unwanted bill. 'A messenger, a herald of the mighty King Bhaltair of Taranis with word that the king does not negotiate with savages. Even now, when his daughter is at death's door, they won't meet with me. What does it take, Rosheen? What must I do next?'

Haldor tossed the head across the room into a darkened corner where it hit the flagstones with a sickening crack. Meanwhile, the thumping in the barrel was becoming feebler.

Thump… thump… thump…

'Call *me* a savage? They let their children die rather than negotiate.' He whirled around to where the poor herald's head had landed and spat. 'Bastards.'

The thumping in the barrel stopped and Haldor raised a finger. 'If you'll excuse me…?' He scooped up an axe from the flagstones and brought it cracking down on the large barrel, just above one of its iron hoops. Water began to gush from the split, but the axe was lodged firmly, and so Haldor used its leverage to tip the oak cask over. It landed with a crash, its lid breaking open, spilling the cask's contents across the floor: dozens of gallons of water and the body of a merman.

He landed with a heavy slap and Rosheen staggered back in shock as the water splashed around her boots.

She crouched by the merman's body, turning him over. He was dead. His face frozen in contorted agony, all his skin was shrivelled and desiccated, dry as parchment, his veins black tributaries now that the blood inside him was nothing but a thick glue.

128

Rosheen dipped the tip of her finger in the water and tasted it. 'Dand salt,' she said. 'You bastard.'

'My ma told me how her grandma used it when fighting the mer-people in the Mage Wars. Quite rare, and toxic to merfolk. I took this fishy fellow from a colony we encountered in Eriworth.'

'Encountered? Or wiped out?' Rosheen asked, unsure if she really wanted to know the answer.

'I do what needs to be done,' Haldor said. 'He was to be my insurance policy. A ready cure for the princess. All they needed were a few drops of his blood. I'm not unreasonable, Rosheen, I don't want to hurt a little girl, but now they've forced my hand.'

Without the merblood, the princess was as good as dead. Rosheen felt the bile rise in her stomach as she remembered what a pivotal role she had played in this game. And why she had done so.

'Where is my brother, Haldor?' She kept her voice even and calm. 'I did what you asked.'

He looked at her again, though now as if seeing her for the first time. 'How did you get in here?'

'Bring me my brother, Haldor, and I'll leave in peace.'

'Magic,' he whispered in happy awe as he put two and two together. 'You still have magic. Guards!' he called, and immediately Rosheen could hear the clatter of armour as the guards in the corridor outside approached.

'Haldor, we had a deal.'

He waved dismissively at her. 'Calm yourself, woman. The boy is safe. How do you have magic?' He trailed off as his eyes fell on the bulge in her jerkin. 'You have a stone? A piece of the moon! Oh, I *am* impressed. May I see it?'

Rosheen took a step back, a hand half-raised, ready to act. 'My brother.'

Six guards came rattling through the door behind her, another three through the one behind Haldor. They levelled their swords at her.

Haldor barely noticed them, fascinated by Rosheen. 'I wonder: are you in the market for some mage work? Half of this lot fear me, the other half want to kill me, but you have a little integrity and, of course, you have magic.'

Then why not use it? Rosheen thought to herself. *Because there's a part of you that's almost certain it won't work.* And from the look on Haldor Frang's face, he was thinking this, too.

She closed her eyes and reached out, finding the soldiers' minds in the dark. There they were – yes, yes, yes! She had magic! – and they were already exhausted. Time to do them a favour and send them to sleep. There was a crash of armour and Rosheen opened her eyes.

One guard lay face down on the bloodstained flagstones. The others remained standing, albeit with heavy eyelids and slack jaws.

'Ha! It worked.' Frang clapped his hands together. 'After your trick on the battlefield at Canwick Tor, I told my men to mentally prepare themselves for another one of your little mind invasions. They know when they're being attacked now, and they know to fight and not give in. And you're weaker than before! You'll have to do better than—'

Haldor Frang fell to his knees, clutching his chest as Rosheen took control of his heart.

'I won't ask again,' she said.

Haldor looked to his guards with a pained *What are you waiting for?* expression on his face.

Those still standing shook themselves awake and rushed at Rosheen, swords raised. She released her grip on Haldor's heart, deftly stepped around the first guard's blade, grasped his arm and sent him spinning until the point found a gap in the armour of the second guard. With a yelp, he ran headlong into the sharp steel, a surprised look on his face as the blood began to gush from his belly, spreading down his leg armour.

Rosheen kicked him away then brought her elbow up sharply, connecting with the first guard's nose and sending him stumbling back. Six guards remained and their blades were moments away from impaling her.

She used those few moments to summon the power of the Lapis stone and sent a burst of blue and white energy blasting in a bright radius around her. Haldor and the guards were thrown back, crashing

into wine barrels, alcoves and the ceiling before tumbling unconscious to the floor.

Rosheen scooped up a discarded sword, spun on her heels and in
one swift movement swung it around until the point found Haldor's
neck. He was still on his backside, one hand massaging his chest as his
heart found its rhythm again.

The melee took only a few moments. Rosheen's heart was racing.
She had forsworn violence as part of her work. She had some rudimentary combat training, of course, but she hated it and would never
normally resort to using it, yet here she was discovering that not only
was she quite good at it, but it stirred feelings of excitement in her
that she wasn't entirely comfortable with.

She was appalled to see the impressed grin on Haldor's face. 'I blink
and suddenly everybody's dead. I don't mind telling you, Rosheen
Katell, but I am aroused right now. Very impressive.'

'Not dead. I'm no murderer.'

'Tell *him* that.' Haldor nodded at the wounded guard, who clutched his
bleeding belly, his heels kicking around the blood pooled on the floor as
if he could run away from the pain. Rosheen, sickened by the sight of his
agony, wanted to help him, but couldn't take her eyes off Haldor.

'Where is my brother?'

'I honestly don't know.'

'A lie.'

'A choice.' He batted the blade away from his throat. 'I prefer not to
know, lest some mage or torturer tries to pluck it from my mind.' He
got to his feet. 'When word of my death reaches Yanick, then your
brother dies. He could be here in the castle, he could be on the other
side of the Newlands by now. I don't know and I don't care. But I
need your power and I will do whatever is necessary to harness it.'

'Kill my brother and I kill you.'

'I thought you just said you're not a murderer.'

'In your case, I'll make an exception. I will do whatever it takes to
avenge my—'

'Oh, I'm sure, yes, yes. I welcome death, Rosheen, but think of your
poor, unsuspecting brother. Imagine him happily playing as Yanick
silently moves behind him and brings the blade across your brother's

neck. Or perhaps he sees Yanick draw his dagger? Think of how terrifying and confusing those last few moments would be. How helpless
the boy must feel.'

No one felt more helpless than Rosheen in that moment. She went
numb. Even with her magic, there was nothing she could do against
a determined maniac like Haldor Frang.

'None of us wants it to come to that, do we?' He smiled as he patted
Rosheen's arm then gestured at the wounded guard writhing on the
floor. 'You can help him? Please do, poor fellow. Go, go.'

Rosheen nodded, got to her knees and placed a hand over his
wound. Closing her eyes, she could sense a bright light in his gut,
where the blade cut into him. Once again, she summoned the power
of the stone and the light in his belly began to fade as the wound
healed. The man twitched and spasmed, but she sent him to sleep then
opened her eyes.

Haldor nudged him with his boot. 'He's dead?'

'No, he should be fine. He's lost a lot of blood. He needs rest and
water.'

'Remarkable. Simply remarkable,' he said softly, then Rosheen saw
something flash by her head. A blade came slashing down, hacking
into the guard's face, cutting into his open mouth and almost splitting
his head in two at the jaw. His mandible flopped loosely. More blood
flecked Rosheen's face as she jumped back.

Haldor's eyelids hung heavy and his lower jaw jutted out. Bloody sword
in hand, he looked more savage than ever. 'Just in case you doubted my
ambition,' he said softly. 'I would ask you to assassinate the king, but your
compassion would stay your hand, hmm? Even with your brother's life
at stake. Pathetic, really. But I do have a job for you. I've received word
that Bhaltair is sending a band of men south to find merblood. Most likely,
they'll take it from the Nolwen Clan at Connal Lake. All I want you to do
is find them. My men will do the rest. Then, and only then, will you be
reunited with your brother.'

Rosheen found herself nodding. Agreeing to work for this madman
again. He was giving her more details on the mission, but she couldn't listen. All she could think of was how much longer the power of the Lapis
stone would last. And whether it would give her the strength to kill him.

Shave and a Haircut

It might be easier, Sander thought, to list the parts of him that didn't hurt.

He tried not to think of the pain, but the throbbing in his head, the raw skin around his neck, the stabbing agony from his twisted ankle, the cracked ribs, his swollen tongue, the tender bruises around his eyes, the dog's toothmarks on his arms and the general aching of all his muscles made too much noise combined for him to block them out.

His fingers. Yes, the fingers on his right hand were in pretty good shape. He flexed them now, appreciating those few digits and taking some small joy from the fact that they didn't send spasming jolts of agony through his body when they moved. And his hair was in good shape, though in dire need of a wash. He could really do with that bar of jasmine-scented soap right now.

They entered Taranis through the South Gate. Sander was manacled to the floor of a prison wagon, the only light coming through the bars of a tiny hatch in the door, but he knew he was home once he caught scent of the Tiarnan kebabs and heard the baying of the crowd. The people of Taranis could throw a good riot when they put their minds to it and the destruction of the Lapis Moon was all the excuse they needed to start looting and smashing things up.

The wagon came to a stop. A key turned in the lock and the door swung open. Sander was greeted by the sight of Enok, the king's own executioner.

'Oh gods.' Sander's belly sank. The wagon had pulled up in the south square, where various guild chambers surrounded a row of gallows and an executioner's block. He didn't understand why the king's men would save him from one public execution only to drag him here, but Enok was pathologically good at his job and Sander knew he only had moments left to live.

Enok fussed with the manacles, keeping Sander's hands bound while releasing him from the chains. He dragged Sander from the wagon and across the glistening flagstones of the citadel's south square. It must have rained overnight, Sander mused, noting the depth of the puddles and that such heavy rain was unusual this time of year.

Dear gods, the things you think of as you're being dragged to your execution.

Daylight reflected off the water, making Sander's eyes throb. Knowing that he was about to die gave the mage a new appreciation for all things around him. The fresh scent of the moist air. Even the weeds between the flagstones emitted a rosy aroma. He admired the remarkable craftsmanship of the colonnades around the square, the tiny stone gargoyles dripping rainwater from their gullets and the splendid acoustics that enabled Sander to clearly hear every curse the baying crowd spat at him.

At first, Sander's ego was bolstered by the thought that so many people had turned out at such short notice for his demise, but then he saw more corpses hanging from gibbets and gallows around the square and he realised that he was merely the latest attraction. Men, women and children from every nook in the citadel had gathered here to curse the last vestiges of the magical world, their faces contorted with hatred delivered with the absolute certainty of the ignorant.

Guards held the mob back as Enok hauled Sander through the square. They passed a chicken run draped in wire. Inside, Sander saw the tiny bodies of faerie folk within, torn to pieces, their little limbs strewn about their torsos on the scattered straw. Sander looked on aghast as a man with a thick beard and shiny bald head emptied a wooden bucket into the hutch. Half a dozen captured faeries tumbled onto the ground. Their wings were limp, and he was shocked to see their skin almost translucently pale, not the vibrant greens and blues he was used to. The crowd's sudden vitriol for them was as chilling as the change in the air before a storm. Faeries were close to extinction anyway. Centuries of luring humans into the woods with promises of gold and sex only to then assault or kill them led to regular culls. And now the crowd wanted them gone for good. The bearded man lifted a door in the run's side and a fighting dog, pink-eyed and foaming at the mouth, dashed in. The faeries ran to the chicken wire, pulling desperately at it, trying to squeeze through and escape, but one by one they were snatched up in the dog's jaws, shaken till their spines broke and torn to pieces. The mob roared its approval.

Looking up, Sander recognised the bodies of a few of his fellow former mages displayed in gibbets or dangling from ropes. Old Fedelma Dewart from Nuddcombe rotated slowly at the end of her hanging rope, her eyes bulging in eternal surprise. She had dedicated her entire life to healing. Why kill her?

'Shut up.' Enok broke his stride to kick his boot into Sander's gut. The mage, unaware that he had actually said anything, convulsed and felt bile rise in his stomach.

Sander thought of all the ways that magic could have saved him: an incantation to burn the rope around his wrists or melt the chains around his ankles, a gesture stopping Enok's heart, then a glamour to steal away into the shadows as he slipped through the crowd—

'I said shut up!' Enok kicked him again.

Again, Sander hadn't realised he was muttering aloud.

'Magic won't help you now, trickster.' Enok grabbed the long tail of Sander's hair and yanked him up some slippery steps, then shoved him onto the dais where the executioner's block waited, its wood freshly chipped by the criss-cross marks from a deep-cutting blade. It took a moment for Sander to realise that the black tar-like substance congealed around its base was blood from the block's previous victims.

Released from Enok's tugging, Sander was finally able to stand. The square was heaving with people. From up here, he caught a glimpse of the bloated corpses of a couple of young giants lying among the throng, purple gashes in their necks where their throats had been cut.

Enok pulled an executioner's leather mask over his head.

Sander couldn't help but laugh. 'Why bother, Enok? Everyone knows who you are now.'

'Tradition.' Enok's muffled voice came through the mask's small rectangular mouth hole. 'On your knees.' He didn't wait for Sander to comply and kicked the back of the mage's calves. Sander winced as his knees crunched on the gritty dais.

'Not that I'm complaining,' Sander said as Enok shoved his head on the block and brushed aside the mage's long, blond hair, 'but why aren't I being hanged like everyone else?'

'Variety,' Enok said, raising the axe high and getting a cheer from the crowd.

Sander felt the blade of the axe rest on the back of his neck as Enok lined it up for the killing blow. Sander was astonished at how calm he felt. As someone who panicked when his laundry hadn't been done, he could not believe how sanguine he was about this whole situation. The crowd fell quiet. Sander dared to glance up to see a flap of yellow robes cutting a swathe through the crowd.

'Mage Sander Bree,' Yorath bellowed in his church voice, the one he used when preaching the Faith to the masses. 'I come with His Majesty's authority. He, in his infinite wisdom and good grace, offers you one last chance for forgiveness.'

Ah, so that was why he was so calm: he knew all along that they were playing him. They couldn't possibly kill him. He might not have magic any more, but he was still useful to them.

The crowd didn't like this one little bit and a few began to boo Yorath, but he carried on regardless. 'Mage Sander Bree: do you denounce the ways of magic?'

Sander sighed at the idea of playing along with this silly charade, but if it got him off this block... 'I do,' he said.

'Will you accept the love of the Goddess and embrace the Faith?'

'I will.'

'Do you beg forgiveness for your sins against the Goddess, your king and your people?'

'Oh, I do. Most sincerely.'

'Very well.' Yorath turned to the crowd and raised his arms high. 'With the authority of his majesty King Steffen Henning Mathias Bhaltair of the House of Ultan, and with the blessing of the Goddess, I forgive you your sins, Sander Bree.'

There followed a chorus of boos and jeers from the crowd, upset that they might be denied a beheading.

Sander smiled and was about to ask Enok to remove the blade from his neck when he saw Yorath give the axeman a nod.

'Carry on with the execution,' he said, to rapturous cheers from the relieved crowd, then turned to descend the dais.

'Wait? What?' Sander screeched. Now the real panic kicked in, backdated to when he first saw the Lapis Moon shatter. His heart threatened to burst through his chest, blood rushed to his head and a new reality became apparent to him. He was going to die and nothing was going to stop it. 'You said you'd let me go.'

'I said you would be forgiven. Absolved of your sins, the Goddess will now welcome you into the afterlife. I've granted you an eternity in her blissful embrace. You could at least be grateful.'

'What about the princess? You're going to let her die?'

'His Majesty will be sending his best men. You are not needed.'

'I am,' Sander blurted, without thinking of a way that he could qualify it. 'I can... *congress* with merpeople, influence their thoughts.'

'Not without your magic.' Yorath, bored of the conversation, turned and made his way back through the crowd.

Sander shouted after him, 'No one knows merpeople as well as me!' That wasn't strictly true, but there was no one in Bhaltair's employ who had the first clue. 'Their behaviour, their culture – I grew up on the Andraste Coast, I know them. My... my first magic was with merpeople. When I was a boy, a mermaid called Effie tried to lure me into the sea, but I was able to send her to sleep. The villagers and the Kelish used to pay me to patrol the coastline. I know them!'

Someone in the crowd started a slow clap. Others joined in. They wanted a decapitated head and they wanted it now. Sander looked around desperately and his eyes fell on the congealed blood at the base of the executioner's block.

'How do you keep the blood from going black after you've extracted it from a merperson?' Sander said so fast he was nearly babbling. 'It needs to stay warm and fresh and only I know how to do that!'

'Others will know.'

'Who? Show them to me!'

Yorath wasn't listening and Sander began to tremble as he watched the yellow cloak slip behind the temple door.

The blade came off Sander's neck as Enok readied the axe.

'What do you want? To hire a mercenary with this knowledge who will hold you to ransom, or a desperate man who will do anything to live? Anything!'

Sander heard Enok's feet shift as he leaned back, raising the axe for the final blow.

'HALT!' a voice called across the square.

All heads turned.

To find King Bhaltair watching from a high balcony.

'You are now a Son of the Goddess,' Yorath intoned as Enok shoved Sander through the doors of a small Faith chapel, not much more than a ramshackle hut tucked down a shady cul-de-sac in the artisans' quarter of the citadel. 'And we shall begin your initiation.'

Sander didn't like the sound of that, but it had to be better than a beheading.

The doors creaked shut behind them and Sander's eyes began to adjust. He had expected to find a small, dusty nave with rows of empty pews, but instead he had stumbled into what felt like a busy factory. Dozens of yellow-robed acolytes of the Goddess bustled around rows of wooden printing presses, arranging plates of letters, carefully aligning papers, cautiously applying ink, leaning on levers, turning screws and hurrying away with reams of pamphlets and chapbooks with titles like 'The Evils of Magic' and 'Healing Through the Power of the Goddess'.

'Not wasting any time, are you?' Sander muttered.

'One of the things you learn as a Minister of the Faith is that people desperately crave direction,' Yorath said as he led the way through the industrious brethren, through the chancel, then down spiralling steps to the dormitories. 'There's a whole underclass extremely unhappy with their lot. Sooner or later, they decide that whoever is in charge is to blame and their frustration can lead to revolt and a dead monarch. Much better for us to steer that... *energy* towards a more viable scapegoat.'

'You're blaming mages for this?'

'The king is responding to the concerns of his people.' Yorath flashed a rare smile. 'Now that magic has failed, we cannot afford any kind of insurgency. You understand, of course?'

'I am at the king's disposal, as always,' Sander said with little real enthusiasm, conserving all his energy for staying alive.

Wooden bunks lined the edges of the room and bald-headed novices sat silently on benches running through the middle. They were supping some kind of runny gruel from wooden bowls. A few dared to glance up at Sander as he was herded through the hall. Yorath snapped his fingers and one acolyte got to his feet and scurried behind them, a three-legged stool in his grip.

Yorath took them through another smaller torchlit corridor and Enok threw Sander into the baths, a chilly room, perfectly square and lined with cracked tiles. A thin mist of ice-cold condensation hung in the air. Sander stumbled down the slippy steps into the freezing water, yelping in shock as his skin tightened.

A large man dressed only in red and white striped baggy pantaloons with a leather pouch slapping at his crotch entered the room. 'Clothes off,' he commanded as he scratched at the patchy abundance of black curly hair strewn across his bare torso. Sander, befuddled yet happy to be alive, did as he was told.

The large man shoved Sander head first into blisteringly cold water, held him there until Sander's lungs began to burn in protest, then brought him up again. He gripped a brick of grey soap in one hand, smacked it against Sander's head and began to lather it into his long, blond hair. *Finally, a hair wash!*

As Yorath prepared to sit on empty air, the acolyte behind him positioned the stool under the First Minister's backside. That took some confidence. Surrendering to gravity, knowing that someone was always on standby to break your fall.

'A Son of the Goddess is pious, does not ask questions, speaks when he is spoken to and obeys every command.'

'Yorath, I'm sure you're enjoying every minute of this, but I am not—'

A backhander across the mouth from the large man shut Sander up. Pain shot to Sander's lips and he could feel warm blood trickling down his face. The large man unravelled a rolled-up set of razor blades and knives from his leather pouch. He tugged Sander's hair and began sawing at it with one of the knives.

'No! Please, not the hair!' Sander cried, but another smack across the face silenced him.

The tonsorial butchery continued and clumps of his blond locks fell into the cloudy bathwater and began to separate into drifting strands.

'Your confession on the block,' Yorath continued, 'is why you are here. It made you a noviciate of the Faith. Had you been executed, the Goddess would have welcomed you, the sinful confessor, into her warm embrace. By the king's mercy, you live, and so in life you are apprenticed to our order. You will wear the robes of the novice, you will learn the Word by rote, you will relinquish your hair and you will call me Master.'

Countless sarcastic responses came to Sander but, not wanting another slapping from his barber, he chose not to reply. Another clump of hair drifted down into the bathwater.

'Sharp, sharp! The king!' cried voices from outside the bathroom.

Enok, the acolyte and the barber all bowed for their king. Sander did so, too, his hands covering his modesty. He couldn't recall when anyone had last seen him naked, let alone a king, and he began to feel inadequate.

Yorath rose slowly, not taking his eyes off Sander.

The king, no-nonsense as always, strode in and got right to the point. 'Angarad is mobilising, the patrols on their border report that Eriworth is unusually quiet, which immediately raises my suspicions, Old King Torren of Agrona is dead, his castle fallen to a warlord, and we are days away from a full-scale war. And then I received this...' Bhaltair took a scroll from within his robes. 'A message from Haldor Frang, offering to meet to discuss the terms of my daughter's recovery. I have to say, I admire his nerve. Most political assassinations are done with a little more subterfuge, but at least he has the decency to be blunt.'

'You'll meet him?' Sander asked.

'Don't be ridiculous. We do not commune with mercenaries, nor pander to their demands. My daughter's union with Parthalan must go ahead if we are to meet this threat. You will travel to the settlement at Connal Lake, retrieve the merblood from the Nolwen Clan, return here and cure my daughter in a week. Is that understood?'

Sander managed an astonished nod, grateful for a sliver of hope. 'Yes, yes, of course. And my eternal gratitude for your mercy, Your Majesty.'

'Majesty.' Yorath lowered his heavy eyelids in a well-practised imitation of solemn thought and wisdom. 'Forgive my impudence, but this simply cannot be done.'

Sander broke free of his barber's grip. 'Yes, yes it can. I can do it, Your Majesty, I can!'

'Indeed, the desperate promise of a condemned man is always a cast-iron guarantee of success,' Yorath mused. 'Let us be truthful: this journey would be difficult enough *with* magic. It's simply impossible without it. Forgive me, Your Majesty, but I can't see what this man can possibly contribute.'

'No, wait, please listen, I can do this, I can!' Sander insisted. 'It's only merblood. Merpeople are magical, yes, but merblood remedies aren't dependent on magic to work. They simply need to be prepared properly, and I know how. Please!'

'Majesty.' Yorath sidled closer to his king. 'Let us be frank, Sander Bree has been the beneficiary of Your Majesty's good graces for most of his life, and what have we received in return? Complaints, opinion, arrogance. He is a luxury we can no longer afford. The people need to know that we have control and their best interests at heart. Better to keep him here under my supervision, and instead send your best men to retrieve the cure.'

'I need to prepare the blood the moment is it drawn,' Sander blurted.

'How is it prepared? Tell us,' the king demanded.

Sander took a breath, steeling himself. 'Forgive me, Majesty, but this is complicated potion work. It's not simply a matter of—'

'He lies!' Yorath's seething anger boiled over. 'You would dare to use the cure for the king's dying daughter as bargaining chip?'

'No, no!' Sander insisted. 'Look, I could write a list of instructions, yes, but without my skills and experience, it would be all too easy to make a mistake, and that alone would be enough to seal the poor girl's fate. Let me do this for her, then I will return and submit myself to Your Majesty's mercy.'

'Majesty, I must protest—'

King Bhaltair raised a hand, silencing Yorath. 'Leave us,' he commanded, and Enok, the barber and the acolyte left the bathroom. 'You, too,' the king told Yorath, who hesitated for half a heartbeat, then backed out in a graceful exit.

The king beckoned Sander closer. Sander waded to the bath's steps to kneel at the king's feet.

'I love my daughter,' the king said, his voice soft as he addressed Sander. 'I'm aware that you and others in the court think me to be cold and heartless, but I reserve my affections for those who are worthy of it. You believe that, don't you, Bree?'

Sander nodded.

'I've never told anyone this before, but every time I look at the princess, I see her mother. The most difficult thing I have ever done' – the king took a deep, cleansing breath – 'is watch that woman die. Something of myself died with her that day. And now my daughter faces a similar fate, and I discover that I have little choice but to put her future in the hands of...' Bhaltair looked Sander up and down. 'You.'

It wasn't disgust or loathing that Sander saw on the king's face. It was fear. Here was a man used to having control over everything in his domain, and now the life of his daughter and the fate of his kingdom were in the hands of a naked, shivering and powerless mage. Sander himself was terrified at the prospect, so he could only imagine what it was like for Bhaltair.

'I will not fail you, my King,' Sander promised.

'You had better not.' Bhaltair found his voice again. 'If she dies, I'll kill you myself. Slowly. With the most agonising poison available over the longest period of time possible. Do we have an understanding?'

'We do, Majesty.'

'Good. You leave immediately.'

An Ordinary Man

The sun was sinking between the clouds as Sander was frogmarched through the castle by three King's Guards and deposited in a courtyard by the South Gate, essentially the back door to the citadel. They took position on either side of the main gate, looking dead ahead but somehow also keeping their eyes on him.

Sander fidgeted in his white noviciate woollen robes which itched like a bastard. His freshly bald head was tender, the skin over his skull covered in dozens of nicks and cuts. He kept prodding it, feeling the odd clammy heat of his pate, discovering moles, lumps and bumps that he had never even known were there.

'Noviciate Bree?' It took Sander a moment to realise that someone was addressing him. He spun on his ill-fitting sandals to find an all-too-young captain of the King's Guard striding across the courtyard towards him. The man's shoulder-length blond hair bounced in time with the red cloak that billowed behind him and his freshly polished armour shone. 'I am Gunnar Jarl, captain of the King's Guard.'

'Yes, I know.' Sander extended a hand that was ignored. He let it hang there for a moment before reluctantly withdrawing it. 'We've met several times.'

The captain looked at him askance, as if there couldn't possibly ever be any kind of circumstance where they might ever have met.

'I was at your passing-out ceremony only a few weeks ago,' Sander said. 'You came top of your class, if I recall.'

Gunnar made an odd noise, a long, drawn-out *mnnyeah* like a door creaking, as he acknowledged some vague memory of the event. 'Forgive me, Noviciate Bree. The celebrations went on for some time and my memory is hazy.'

'Sander.'

'Beg pardon?'

'I'm Sander, not this Noviciate Bree bollocks. Call me Sander.'

'I'm afraid I'm under strict instructions not to.'

'Yorath's instructions?'

'I couldn't possibly say.'

'I'll take that as a yes. So what's happening?'

'Our orders are to accompany you to the Nolwen Clan at Connal Lake, ensure that you correctly retrieve the merblood as necessary and see you safely back again.'

Sander did some quick sums in his head. 'That's going to be tight,' he said. 'If we hit any bad weather, or bandits… It could take a week just to get there.'

'You will have her cured within a week, no longer,' Gunnar said. 'The king was quite insistent.'

'I'll be quicker on my own. Give me your fastest horse,' he said.

'Definitely not. King's orders.'

'Okay, so why are we wasting our time chatting? We're off straight away, are we?'

'Very soon. We have half a dozen cavalry ready to accompany us at the barracks by the Lugham River, we're waiting for—'

'Good. Quicker we start, quicker we get back. I reckon we should take the Taranis Road, follow it south to the Jade River, then—'

'Noviciate Bree, let me make this absolutely clear,' Gunnar Jarl said as he rested a hand on Sander's shoulder, silencing him. 'I have my orders and they do not involve listening to you. We will travel to Connal Lake, which is few days' ride south from here, along a route of my devising. We will then obtain the merblood using whatever methods I deem necessary and we will return. It will be quick, uneventful and a model of King's Guard strategy. Am I clear?'

Sander knew he had little choice but to work with this golden-haired buffoon. It was this quest or a slow death at the king's own hand. Well, there was a good chance that both options would end in death, but at least on the quest there might be opportunities for escape once it was all over.

If it wasn't for that bloody Lapis Moon, he would have quit by now and become a roaming warlock, answerable to no one. He allowed himself to wallow in the thought for a few moments.

'May the Goddess bestow her blessings upon you this fine evening.'

Another voice, bright, perky and a little too loud for comfort, bounced around the courtyard and burst Sander's bubble. A young woman in yellow Minister's robes came towards them with open arms. She was as bald as Sander but her skull so perfectly smooth, shiny and pale, it was almost white. 'My Brother.' She kissed Sander on both cheeks. 'The soil, the sun and the sea,' she said, reciting the standard greeting between Faith brethren, then stood back expectantly.

Sander's eyes darted to Gunnar, who gestured at the young woman. 'This is Junior Minister Orren Nels. She will be joining us on the journey, offering, uh, spiritual guidance... I believe you're supposed to kiss her back.'

'Oh, sorry.' Sander pulled a face, embarrassed. 'I'm new.' He leaned forward and pecked her on the cheeks like she was an elderly aunt. 'The soil, the sun and the, er, sea.'

Orren smiled with half-closed eyes. 'The death of magic has brought us together, Brother. Allow me to teach you the ways of the Goddess and we shall convert the entire world.'

'No chance of supper first?'

'Sarcasm is the refuge of the unholy scoundrel, Brother.' Her smile disappeared as she turned to Gunnar. 'You will deny my Brother a day's rations. He must learn that levity has no place in the Goddess's plan.'

Sander's hunger multiplied. 'She can do that?' he said.

Gunnar shrugged. 'Where you're concerned, yes.'

'I am here on the First Minister's orders to ensure the purity of your body and mind, Brother.' Orren took Sander's hand as she spoke, looking at him with sincere eyes that made him feel like he was back on the execution block once more. 'Heed my words and you shall be enlightened. Defy me and you will know only misery.'

Sander drew breath, ready to unleash a little more defiance in her direction, but then it occurred to him that she would merely deny him another day's rations, too.

'Shall we get a move on, then?' he said, in as cheery a voice as he could manage.

The South Gates cracked open, revealing a skinny stable boy holding the reins of three beautifully groomed horses with shining black coats. Beyond those, Sander could see the shattered remains of some of his once-celebrated Mage's Moons, now nothing more than peculiar standing stones surrounding the citadel. A sad remnant of his power.

Sander had briefly imagined that they might leave amid a parade with cheering onlookers, conquering heroes off to save the princess, but their mission had to remain a secret. And so the three of them stepped out of the citadel into the setting sun, mounted their horses and set off with only the clip-clop of hooves to herald their departure.

After an hour's riding, they were met by half a dozen of the King's Cavalry at the tiny barracks where the Taranis Road crossed the Lugham River. They looked a shambolic lot, but, unlike most of the men wearing armour in Taranis, some of these old soldiers had actually seen a bit of action. Sander even recognised one of them from the Chronicles, a grizzled old warrior, with the complexion of a walnut, named Malachy Nye. He was the lone survivor of the Siege of Fourfoot and the first soldier to storm the walls at Ragomar. Minor skirmishes compared to the Mage Wars, but stuff worthy of story and song all the same. Sander was reassured that these battle-hardened warriors would act as bodyguards for the journey, but he was also dismayed that their presence would make any kind of escape all the more difficult.

Gunnar was trying a little too hard to be unimpressed with Malachy's military experience and greeted the old soldier by ordering him to remove the woollen hat that was pulled tight over his head. 'It's not regulation,' Gunnar said.

Malachy said nothing. He lit his pipe. Two other cavalry riders, named Bent and Wob, chimed in.

'All due respect, Captain, he don't remove the hat for no one, sir,' said Bent, a man whose head was an almost perfectly rounded cone that didn't bother with a neck and instead funnelled out directly to his bulging shoulders.

'Got special dispensation from the king, he reckons,' said the thin-faced Wob, whose nose was so large and pointy that it might be mistaken for a beak.

'On account of him being a war hero and that,' finished Bent.

Gunnar made that door-creaking noise again. 'Very well,' he said, unconvinced but reluctant to take it any further. 'Let's get a move on.'

Sander realised with a creeping dread that he would be outside the walls of the citadel for some time. The fields on either side of the road reeked of manure, the night air was filled with pollen and he was sneezing constantly and blinking grit out of his eyes. As a mage, he could have conjured up remedies to improve his humour, but now he was stuck with the symptoms. Just like everyone else. Just like all ordinary people.

Oh gods, I'm one of them. That terrible realisation kept coming back. *You're ordinary now. No magic, no position, no power, merely a demoted mage who can suffer colds and diseases and pain like the rest of them.*

'Wassat?' barked Wob.

'Wassat what?' replied Bent.

'Not you,' Wob said before gesturing at Sander. 'Him! Talking to himself. Fella's a loon. Bit wrong in the head, are we, matey?'

Sander blanched, realising he had been thinking out loud again. He had to bury these thoughts and concentrate on the moment.

'Nothing,' he replied, shaking his head. 'Thinking aloud.'

'You were a mage and all that, right?' Bent asked, one eye squinting.

'That's right.'

'And you've consorted with merpeople in the past, right?'

'I have.'

'Is it true…' Bent hesitated and glanced over to Wob, who urged him on with an encouraging nod. 'Is it true that they're so aggressive on account of having the sexual urges of a human and the private parts of a fish?'

For a moment, Sander didn't know quite how to respond. He might have expected this kind of ill-informed prejudice from an une-ducated villager out in the sticks, but Bent and Wob were soldiers. They were men of the world, allegedly. Or not. For they had just confirmed that they were both as thick as pig shit.

'Bent…' Sander took a cleansing breath. 'It is Bent, isn't it?'

Bent nodded, eager that he was finally going to get the definitive word on this burning issue.

'Bent, will you do me a favour and piss off and never speak to me again? Thanks ever so.'

'Oh, charming.' Bent pouted before steering his horse away.

Wob's head had turned a livid pink with suppressed anger and he leaned in close to Sander. 'There's no need for that, fella.' He scowled as he nodded ahead to Bent, who sat sulking in his saddle. 'We might only be cavalry, but some of us have feelings, too, so have a smidgen of consideration, eh?'

He galloped off, soon catching up with Bent and placing a consoling hand on his shoulder.

Sander despaired at his inability to make friends. Those two were supposed to protect him on this trek, but he doubted they would throw themselves in the path of an arrow now. He resolved to remain as silent as possible for the rest of the journey.

It was pretty enough out here, with gently swaying fields of corn and hedgerows bustling with nocturnal wildlife, but in Sander's experience, it was best observed from a distance. The grass on the verge might look a lush place to rest your head for the night, but its blades would always find bare skin to prick, the air and the earth were teeming with insects looking for something to bite, and there was shit from every animal, large or small, everywhere.

Sander's horse tripped, tipping him forwards in his saddle and nearly sending him tumbling off. It was making a habit of this and he was convinced that even his horse had it in for him.

A pair of nightingales exchanged gossip in the trees around them. Their song was often lost in the cacophony of the citadel even at night, but out here, each trill and cheep rang out loud and clear.

Again.

And again.

And again.

'Oh, shut up!' Sander blurted, then blushed at the stupidity of his anger. Bent and Wob turned their heads to see what the fuss was, but when they saw it was only the mad mage, they whispered insults and jokes, had a good laugh and continued riding on.

'The birdsong troubles you, Brother?' Orren insisted on riding beside him. Inexperienced, she allowed her horse to meander and often had to trot to catch up with him, but she never flagged and rarely stopped talking. 'I have wondered if birdsong is the voice of the Goddess speaking to us in a tongue that we might never understand.'

'Why would she bother?' Sander grumbled. 'Why doesn't she tell us what she wants us to hear instead of all this pissing about?'

'Mystery.' Orren brightened, her fingers grasping at some unseen object floating in front of her. Sander realised he had made a mistake in replying as she clearly now saw this as an opportunity to become engaged in a religious debate. Those only ever ended in his getting wound up. 'The inscrutability of the Goddess is the key to her wisdom. Her ineffability, her *mystery*, is what keeps us enthralled. To have the answers would be both a blessing and a sadness. The Word says that the truth will only be revealed to us in the afterlife.'

'Convenient.'

'First Minister Pasco said you would be a challenge. That's why he chose me. You are a test of my faith.'

'No, Orren, you're a test of mine. All my faith in humanity goes out of the window when I hear you babbling this nonsense. There is no Goddess, just a set of rules that people like Yorath use to dupe the simple and needy.'

'And magic was no different?'

'Magic worked, Orren. It wasn't based on a load of wishy-washy promises from an imaginary friend. It actually did stuff, helped people, and it kept things in check.'

'It kept a status quo for a few hundred years.' Orren spoke like she was reciting a well-rehearsed verse, but Sander was pleased to finally hear a bit of bite in her voice. 'It kept our world, our society, stagnant, stifling progress in Natural Philosophy and the study of the mind. The thoughts of the Faithful were ridiculed, but now our time has come. The destruction of the Lapis Moon was a clear sign from the Goddess.'

'Of what?'

'Of two big rocks smashing together.' A new voice, soaked in tobacco and gin, cut into the conversation. Malachy Nye sat waiting for them on a jet-black horse that looked as solid and chunky as he was thin and wiry. The old soldier had a white clay pipe puffing between his lips and an immovable woollen hat on his head. Sander and Orren had fallen behind the rest of the party and Malachy had been sent to retrieve them. 'Cap'n says to shift your arses, so get a move on.' He jabbed a thumb further up the path. Orren, obedient as ever, shook her reins and shuffled along.

Sander looked the old man in the eye. Malachy's face was a tapestry of nicks and cuts, white and pink against his light brown skin, but his eyes had a youthful glint in them. The sharp aroma of his pipe smoke made Sander's nostrils tingle and he was reminded of his grandmother, who also enjoyed a clay pipe. Sander instinctively knew he was in the presence of someone who wouldn't take any shit and that made him feel more relaxed than since before the fall of the Lapis Moon.

'You saw it?' Sander asked him.

Malachy moved his horse to the rear of Sander's and encouraged it to get a move on with a *chk-chk* noise and a slap on the arse. Soon, all three were trotting along the path, catching up with the others.

'Lads on the night watch seen it,' Malachy said, eventually. 'Gave us a shout in the barracks and we all ran outside. Stood there looking like lemons as the moon broke up, and young Vilmar here...' Malachy gestured forward at a fresh-faced rider keeping pace alongside Gunnar Jarl. 'He's got good night vision, has Vilmar. Well, he was the one on watch and he said he saw this big old rock, moving as slow as you like, slip behind the Lapis Moon then... wallop.' Malachy punched a fist into his palm with a smack. 'Small mercies, sunshine: if it hadn't hit the moon, then it might've done us all in.'

'A rock,' Sander whispered. 'All this for a bloody rock.'

Malachy gave a deep, throaty cackle. 'Don't take much to change the world, do it?'

Sander recalled his astronomy lessons with Ragnall back in the day. 'We knew there were planets and other objects moving around the firmament,' he said. 'Y'know – shooting stars and meteor showers, but... we'd never imagined anything like this.'

'Even if you had, you wouldn't've been able to stop it, would ya?'

Sander thought about it. Was there any kind of magic that might have shifted something that big? How could something so unknowable, so random, change so much?

'It was guided by the Goddess's hand,' Orren chirped. 'Nothing could have stopped it.'

Sander and Malachy shared a weary look. They were both already sick to the teeth of her unwavering certainty. Sander knew that Orren was only the beginning. The Faith's time had come and nothing would stop it.

The Queen Mathilde's Rats

'I had a brother like you.' Yanick lifted the spoon to Oskar's mouth. 'A moon child.' Oskar took a sip, slurping loudly and making sure that some of it dribbled out of the side of his mouth and down his chin. Appearances had to be kept up, after all, even though a pain burned inside as it began to dawn on him how much he had been patronised his whole life. Oskar was technically an adult now, but everyone had treated him like a toddler. His mother, father, Rosheen, Alby Clim – they had all spoken to him in the soft tones reserved for timid children, they had stroked his hair and cheeks and looked at him with those sickening pitying eyes. By the gods, he never wanted to see that expression again, but even as he glanced up, he could see Yanick doing exactly that.

Yanick gently caught the dribbled fish stew and scooped it back up into Oskar's mouth. 'He didn't live to be as old as you, but his mind was... feeble, had the same look about him. Dull eyes. Spoke in moans and grunts.'

Poor bastard, Oskar thought. If only he had lived long enough, he might have changed like Oskar had. Though the cause of his change baffled him. Something strange had definitely happened the other night, some kind of trigger. He caught snippets of conversation from the crew as they worked on the deck above: something to do with lights in the sky, the Lapis Moon. Oskar couldn't quite piece together the whole story, but they kept babbling on about how they had never seen anything like it, how it was going to change everything, and how there was a war coming. Oskar had heard about lights near the poles where the gods were supposed to dance, but how could they start a war? None of it made any sense. And the ship had stopped singing. He had come to enjoy its mournful song, but since last night, it had been silent, and that worried Oskar. Of course, he desperately wanted to call out, *What's happening?* but to suddenly speak clearly would only be asking for trouble. And he didn't want anything to jeopardise his escape plan.

THE END OF MAGIC

'Y'know what they say about moon children?' Yanick paused the spoon by Oskar's lips as if expecting the boy to answer. 'Cursed, they are. Wicked creatures. The last remnants of demons who came from the Underworld and brought evil into our lives. All they had to do was blink and entire armies would fall on their swords. No magic could stop them, so the Goddess struck them dumb and put the blue moon up there to watch over them all.' He slipped the spoon between Oskar's lips. 'Total shite, of course, you poor fuckers are just wrong in the head, but people love a scapegoat.'

Oskar had not heard this tale before, as if Alby Clim would ever tell him this as a bedtime story, but he had been called 'demon' and 'devil' by some of the children in Sabley. He had thought it was part of their everyday wickedness, though now it seemed there was a bigger mythology.

'I called the wee fella names,' Yanick continued, swirling the fish stew thoughtlessly in the tin bowl. 'My brother. I took the piss all the time. I shoulda stuck up for him, but instead...' Yanick's shoulders shook and Oskar realised the big man was fighting back sobs.

Staying in character, Oskar moaned and reached up for Yanick's long white hair, stroking it gently in sympathy.

'Away with ye.' Yanick shook him off, rubbing at his eyes. 'Soft bastard. Tell anyone and I'll rip your lungs out.'

Oskar didn't react, just kept up his blank look. Yanick sniffed away the tears and laughed. 'Like you'd ever... Dozy lackwit.'

The deck hatch clattered open and the noise made Yanick jump like a child caught stealing biscuits. He dropped the bowl and spoon and clipped Oskar around the ear. 'Eat, you daft bugger!'

Yanick got to his feet to greet the man descending the steps. He was dressed in a dull white apron smeared with brown and red streaks where, in what passed for hygiene on a privateer ship, the ship's cook habitually wiped his hands clean. 'Cap'n.' The man nodded back to Yanick.

'I'm sick to the tits of the fish stew, Glaw. How about we shake up the menu and wring a few of the chickens' necks?'

As one, the chickens turned their heads up at their captain with

154

accusing looks, and Oskar wondered if they had also been released from a fug of feeble-mindedness.

'Those scrawny buggers? No, we need their eggs, Cap'n,' Glaw said as he moved among the food crates and barrels, looking for something specific. 'Got us some salted pork here somewhere. How d'you fancy that?'

'I'd commit acts of depravity with livestock, Glaw.'

'I'll take that as a…' Glaw's face went slack, then he said in a horrified whisper, 'Oh, what the buggery bollocks?'

Oskar couldn't quite see, but he knew what was coming. He kept his head down, eyes fixed on a knot in the wooden deck.

'You're supposed to make sure these stay sealed,' Yanick growled.

'I'm no idiot, Cap'n. I did…'

This morning, Oskar had discovered that his manacles weren't locked, merely pinned. After all, the lad is simple: why bother with a lock?

'Aw, gods, this one, too.'

When he was sure that the coast was clear, Oskar had slipped out of his manacles.

'All of them?' Yanick's voice threatened to crack.

Oskar's first task was to remove the brass cocks from each of the water casks. They were tight, but he found the strength to unscrew them, then tossed them away into the murk of the hold.

Next, Oskar went hunting. He found his first rat, left headless by the ship's cat, behind a rum barrel. Rats had never bothered Oskar. They were always scurrying around the tannery back home, and one of his regular chores was to set and clear the traps.

The second rat he grabbed by the tail as it gnawed on a rope and slammed its head against the deck. The third rat was already sniffing around one of the open casks. Oskar grabbed it and tipped it inside. Rats were good swimmers, but it would get tired and drown eventually.

Oskar had returned silently to his manacles as if nothing had happened and waited.

'Rats in every single one, Glaw!'

A dead rat in every water cask. No one on board ever drank the water – they stuck to beer and rum – but Glaw came down every day and filled a bucket for the galley.

'Dead rats and shite!' Yanick cried. 'Oh, fuck, and there's two of the bastards drowned in the rum.'

Oskar couldn't take credit for that but smirked all the same.

'What are you playing at, Glaw?'

The ship's cook remained silent, his eyes darting as he thought.

Yanick came to his own conclusion. 'It's Craig, isn't it? Bloody Craig. I shoulda known. He's not got the wit to look after the provisions, I told you.'

'Forgive me, Cap'n. I thought he was ready.'

'Clearly not. *Devin, get down here!*'

The hatch swung open and the *Queen Mathilde*'s first mate Devin came stomping down the steps, his muscle weight alone threatening to crack each one as he did so. He was a brawny man with Sachari tattoos curling around his arms. Oskar had never heard him speak and he greeted his captain with a quick bow of his head.

'Craig. Here. Now,' Yanick ordered and Devin nodded and ran back the way he had come.

'Don't kill the boy, Cap'n,' Glaw said. 'He's kin. My sister's lad. Not quite the full complement of wits, if y'know what I mean?'

'Maybe I'll hang *you* instead?' Yanick growled.

'Just teach the boy a lesson, eh?'

Moments later, the ship's boy was hauled down the steps by Devin and hurled at Yanick's feet. Accusations flew back and forth, curses were exchanged, denials made and mothers' lives sworn upon, but Craig was soon found guilty of negligence in the court of Yanick.

'Tie him to the mast. Give him the lash,' Yanick ordered.

'Please, Cap'n, no!' Craig pleaded, his nose still bent and purple from their encounter yesterday. 'Uncle Glaw, do something!'

'I'll straighten it with your ma, laddie.' Glaw shrugged sheepishly. 'Lessons must be learned. I always said it would be tough.'

'Oh gods, please, no.' He was sobbing now, on his knees with tears streaming down his cheeks and bubbles of snot at his nostrils.

Oskar couldn't help himself as his lip curled into a smile.

And Craig saw it.

'It's him!' Craig pointed and Oskar got back into character, the smile gone as he cowered beneath shaking hands. 'The lackwit, he did it.'

'You low bastard.' Yanick shook his head. 'You'd pin the blame on that poor bugger? He's manacled to the sodding deck, you moron! Who's the lackwit now? *Two* lashes.'

'No, please!' Devin was already dragging Craig away.

'Two, Cap'n?' Glaw sucked air through the gaps in his teeth. 'Is that not a wee bit—?'

'You want some, too?'

'Two it is, and he'll be grateful for your mercy, Cap'n.'

Then Oskar heard the words he had been longing to hear.

'We'll set sail, make for Port Byle and restock,' Yanick said. 'And it's coming out of your share, Glaw.'

'Cap'n, yes, Cap'n. Sorry, Cap'n.'

'And get that bastard cat down here to earn his bloody keep.'

Yanick assembled the crew on the deck of the *Queen Mathilde* and Oskar heard him give sentence. 'Two lashes with salt rubbed into the wounds in between. And that will be the end of it. A man will learn from his punishment and there will be no reprisals, is that understood?'

There followed a disgruntled wave of 'Aye, Cap'ns' from the crew. They were philosophical about the water, but there had been earnest vows of Craig's disembowelment when they learned about the rum.

Then came the whip-smack of the cat o'nine tails and Craig's first screams.

The journey to Port Byle dragged long into the night as the *Queen Mathilde* struggled to find favour with the swell of the Ocean's Hand, or any puff of wind for its sails. The ship didn't sing, but the voyage was instead interspersed with Craig's agonised wailing. Oskar felt a pang of pity, but then he remembered that these people had kidnapped him and killed his father. He didn't want to think about what they might have done to his mother, so the feeling didn't last long and dissolved into one thought.

One word.

Good.

Alby Clim had always taught Oskar to forgive those who wronged him, to turn the other cheek to aggression and anger, and Oskar had always done so. He never had much of a choice, to be fair, but this new feeling of satisfaction at Craig's pain and suffering fed something inside Oskar that grew and grew. A calm kind of wickedness that made him happy.

Oskar nodded off at some point and, somewhere between sleep and waking, he thought he could see the sailors on the deck above. In his mind, he saw them as pinpricks of light as they hurried about their business. The dream, if it was a dream, faded as he was awoken by the irregular bumping of the *Queen Mathilde*'s hull against a pier. They were docked. It was dark, but footsteps scuffled across the deck above and Yanick barked orders.

Oskar thought about waiting but, for all he knew, they had been here for hours and were preparing to leave again. This was his only chance. He looked around. The lamps had long since guttered and died but, even in the dark, he could still see sandbags, tattered sails awaiting repair and coils of rope lying about. He hefted one of the coils onto his shoulder and, watched only by an envious clutch of chickens from their wooden cage, crept up the stairs to the hatch.

He cracked the hatch open a little, enough to see Yanick had his back to him, hollering orders from the ship's forecastle as crates of fresh food and barrels of rat-free rum were hoisted aboard. Oskar took a deep breath, swung open the hatch, positioned the rope so that no one could see his face and strode up onto the deck.

His heart was in his mouth as he wove through the bustling crew. There were at least two dozen of them and everyone was heads down and busy as Yanick continued to yell at them.

Oskar wove between them on knees of jelly. He couldn't make for the gangplank, that was far too risky, but he might be able to clamber off the back of the ship. Yes, none of the crew was working there and he could shimmy down one of the ropes tied to the dock. As he formulated his plan, he stumbled on the corner of a canvas sail, causing the two crew members who were folding it to look up. Directly at him.

Oskar looked right back at them, overcome with a tingling, oddly calming sensory numbness. He didn't drop his rope, or run, but an earnest wish kept racing through his mind.

Don't see me, don't see me, don't see me, don't see me, don't see me.

The words looped again and again, and he stood there, rooted to the spot. Then something extraordinary happened.

The men's eyes glazed over and they returned to folding their sail. It was as if they had looked straight through him.

Oskar found he could breathe again. Not chancing his luck by stopping to ponder what had just happened, he shifted the rope on his shoulder and kept moving, eventually finding himself where the quarterdeck met the aftcastle. The night was cloudy, the light was poor and he was hidden in the shadows, but it would only take one head to turn, see him and raise the alarm.

Oskar dropped the rope, casually swung his legs over the side and clambered onto one of the mooring ropes. He planned to shimmy along the rope to the pier and then run headlong for the bustling town beyond.

Oskar's mind, vision and hearing might have improved, but he was still physically feeble. After only a few moments of shimmying, he slipped, his stomach lurching as he fell forwards. Hands flailing, he found the rope again, clinging on with his chubby fingers, his feet dangling. He was helpless, like a fly trapped on a web as the rope bounced up and down, weakening his grip, and then, finally, springing him into the water.

He slipped under with barely a splash, but the water stung his eyes, and when it got into his mouth it was salty, and the taste reminded Oskar of a foul medicine that Alby Clim used to give him when he had a fever.

He was so distracted by this that it took him a few heartbeats to realise he was drowning. As the weight of his sodden clothes pulled him down, he flapped his arms and kicked his legs as he had seen other children do in the Sabley River in summers past, but all it did was make him spin in ever-descending circles.

He brushed against one of the pier's pillars before hitting the bottom, kicking up a cloud of sand around him in the murk. His lungs burning, Oskar clung on to the pillar and pulled himself up, his fingers slipping on algae and seaweed as he desperately fought every instinct to take a deep breath.

He broke the surface, spat the foul water from his mouth with a croak and gasped in lungfuls of air as quietly as possible. He found himself on the other side of the pier, now facing the front of the ship. The *Queen Mathilde* looked so big from here, its stem arcing out of reach to a bowsprit that stretched up, almost touching the clouds in the overcast night sky. Oskar couldn't reboard now even if he wanted to. There was no going back. There were no alarms or shouts. They didn't appear to be looking for him. In fact, everyone was disembarking. Bootsteps clattered on the gangway and the sailors laughed and joshed. Oskar heard the words 'shore leave' more than once.

Oskar waited, wrapping his arms and legs around the pillar and shivering so hard he began to wonder if he might make the whole structure rattle. Eventually, the noise of the crew melted away towards the orange torchlights of the town beyond.

Flexing his fingers to bring some semblance of life into them, Oskar pushed himself from one pillar to another, trying desperately to keep his splashing and sloshing to a minimum.

He had two more pillars to go when, behind him, someone hopped off the ship's gangplank and onto the pier. It was Devin, the ship's first mate. Oskar froze. Devin glanced up and down the length of the pier, the curving harbour wall and the black water gently swirling below. Oskar was convinced that the tattooed man looked directly at him, but instead of raising the alarm, he unravelled his breeches and a silver arc of steaming piss curved through the air into the water, followed by Devin's loud exhalation.

Oskar kept completely still, waiting for Devin to finish. The first mate took several shakes to empty his bladder, tucked his bits away, then idly picked his nose and wandered back up the gangplank to the ship.

Oskar pushed himself through the lapping waves to where the final pillar met the harbour wall and a flight of stone steps rose out of the water. He flailed blindly for the steps, finding one and fumbling with cold, fat fingers and losing his grip, scratching his knuckles. His hands were trembling when he eventually got on the steps. He heaved himself up, pushing with his knees, and finally he was out of the water.

He took a moment to catch his breath and clambered on all fours up the steps to the top of the harbour wall.

He was free.

His chest shook and he found himself sobbing with convulsive gasps of pure joy. He stretched to his full height, extending his arms as far as they would go, flexing his fingers and standing on tiptoes. He could see better, hear the gentle slosh of water in the harbour, smell the salt in the sea air. He felt more liberated now than at any time in his life so far, and the happiness that surged through him made him feel like he could fly.

And, gods, he was hungry for something other than fish stew.

He looked around to find a parade of lean-to buildings facing the harbour, all glowing yellow and orange with torches and firelight. Roars of laughter and cackles of delight came from within. Oskar couldn't understand the writing on the hoardings, but each one boasted a painted sign: red lions, green dragons, white unicorns. Taverns. With food.

A door clattered open under a sign with a likeness of the late Queen Birgitta smiling enigmatically. A sailor staggered out, fell to his knees and vomited vigorously onto the flagstones. The man righted himself, spat out the last chunks of his spew then wavered back inside.

Yes, taverns had food, but they were also havens for trouble, and for all he knew, Yanick's crew could be in any or all of them.

Oskar started shivering again. He needed dry clothes, food and money to buy them with, but he daren't risk looking for any of them here. He had to find a part of town where he wouldn't be spotted by one of Yanick's men. Tucking his hands into his armpits for warmth, he scurried along the harbour wall, away from the taverns.

And that's when a line broke in the clouds, parting them gently like someone turning the page of a book. Oskar glanced up at the new light and stopped in his tracks. He looked up again and couldn't believe what he was seeing. Greystone was hanging as bright as always, but the Lapis Moon was gone, replaced by a bright blue band draped across the stars like a veil.

It rose from the far horizon of the sea and arced directly overhead, disappearing into the hills behind the town. Oskar wondered if it was some kind of crack in the sky, but with his new eyes he could make out individual chunks in the band. Like particles of dust, they were slowly turning in a kind of dance with their companions, countless fragments of stone all swirling and somehow held in place in the night sky. They looked so bright and clear that Oskar thought he could rise up on his toes and reach out to touch them. If he did, he wondered, would they make some kind of tinkling sound like broken glass?

That's when it dawned on Oskar that he was looking at what remained of the Lapis Moon. The world slowed around him as he tried to make sense of what he was seeing. The shining blue moon that had captivated him so much as a child had somehow gone, smashed to pieces and scattered across the sky. Bards in the village sang songs about it, and children learned rhymes all about its magic and power. Some said that gods lived on the moon, that it brought luck and curses and a good harvest.

And now it was gone... and Oskar had changed.

A jumble of thoughts came all at once. Could Oskar's clear mind somehow be connected to this change? Yanick told him that the Goddess put the Lapis Moon there to watch over the moon children and now it was gone... This was too much of a coincidence, surely? Had the moon kept Oskar's mind in a kind of fog all his life? And now, what if that fog was gone and—

'Hey, lackwit.'

Oskar spun on his heels to find Craig propped up by two women. They were about the same age as Oskar's mother, but their cheeks and lips were red, and their eyelids were painted blue, and they appeared to be wearing only frilly underwear. Oskar didn't quite know where to look and so found himself gazing straight at Craig's scowling face.

Oskar thought back to the strange encounter with Yanick's men on the *Queen Mathilde*'s deck and blurted, 'Don't see me, don't see me, don't see me!'

Craig knotted his brow as he tried to figure out what Oskar was babbling on about, then shrugged the two women away, stepped forward, raised a fist and hit Oskar so hard that he broke three of his own fingers.

Border Crossing

'Manipulating the weather?'

'No.'

'Mind control.'

'No.'

'The power of suggestion, surely?'

'No more than you lot.'

'Metamorphosis.'

'Oh, don't be so bloody ridiculous.'

'Time travel.'

'Shut up, Orren.'

Orren was so annoyingly exuberant that Sander had wanted to shove her off her horse for the last five miles. Maybe it was his hunger from a lack of rations that made him yearn to wipe the bright smile from her face? Or that he had been ordered to start the fire when they had breakfast, but he couldn't and they all laughed? Or that he had to do the washing up while they ate? Or that his horse kept threatening to tip him off? Or that a bird had shat on his shoulder? Or that everything out here made him sneeze or cough?

Orren had started the conversation innocently enough by asking what Sander missed the most about magic, and then proceeded to reel off a list of things that mages simply couldn't do.

'Curdling milk?'

'Why in the world would I want to do that?'

'We hear many stories of mages spoiling foods and crops to bring petty disputes to an end that satisfies their needs.'

'Propaganda spread by your lot.'

'*Our* lot.'

'Eh?'

'You're one of us now, Brother.'

'Oh yes, of course. Sorry, that had somehow slipped my mind.'

'Curing diseases.'

'Nnn— Oh, actually, yes, we do have a few healing skills. Some mages are better at it than others.'

'*Did have*,' Orren corrected Sander, flashing teeth made yellow by the sugary porridge that was the mainstay of the Faith's diet. 'And *were*.'

Sander's hand folded into a fist and he took a calming breath. He knew she wasn't doing this out of any kind of deliberate spite. The joy she found in his misery came from a profound sense of righteousness. A shining certainty that she was right about everything. That didn't make it any less teeth-grindingly annoying.

'I forgive you, Brother,' she said with a smile. 'It will take you some time to adjust to the new truth of the fall of the mages and the time of the Faith.'

'Hmm, you're not wrong there.'

'"Do not crave power, my children, and be wary of greed. The soil, the sun and the sea will provide all you ever need,"' Orren quoted. 'The Book of Fountainhead, chapter one, verse one.'

'Right,' Sander said with all the enthusiasm he could muster. 'Gotcha.'

They were still heading south on the Taranis Road, and more peaks of the Conloch Mountains were becoming visible through the haze. Another day away, at least. Sander was saddle sore and didn't have the riding skills to keep up with Gunnar's men, and so ended up trailing behind with Orren stuck to him like a limpet. Malachy stayed with them, too, having drawn the short straw to be Sander's personal bodyguard. As Sander rode, Malachy and his nag circled around him, watching the woods and fields on either side as they moved, idly twirling his trusty halberd as he did so. When Sander asked what he was looking for, all he got in reply was, 'No idea, son. Cap'n told me to watch for ambushes, but he was vague on who might be doin' the ambushin'. That and you're as slow as arseholes, so I have orders to poke you up the jacksy if you fall behind too far.'

'Thanks, Malachy. I feel so much safer now.'

They found Gunnar and the rest of the cavalry clustered on the prow of a hill by a stile. In the distance rose impressive cone-shaped hills draped in lush vegetation, but the men were all gazing down into the valley below with a mixture of excitement and hesitancy. Sander knew what they were looking at. He had been this way many times before, but it never failed to take his breath away.

The Jade River curved around the conical hills below them, its deceptively still surface the same colour as the pea soup they served in the Jolly Cooper. A few barges and skiffs left triangular wakes behind them as they negotiated the bends and, where the river narrowed, there stood a covered wooden bridge wide enough for trolls to pull fully laden carts across from one side to the other.

Sander noted the swollen river was lapping at the underside of the bridge. 'That's not right,' he said.

'Tides are all screwed up,' Malachy said, stuffing tobacco into his pipe. 'Only one moon, now. Pity the poor bugger who has to rewrite the tide charts, eh?'

And then everything changed as the sun passed behind the Lapis ring. Sander expected everything to turn blue or green, but instead it all grew strangely brighter and washed out, details becoming more indistinct, as if their eyes were struggling to register these new hues.

Sander glanced over at Wob and Bent as they exchanged nervous glances. It clearly troubled them, but these were soldiers trained not to ask questions. No one remarked on it, but conversation in the group dropped to a low burble. Even the birds in the trees went quiet. This was the norm now, and somehow everyone had subconsciously decided to accept it and move on. *How quickly these things happen,* Sander thought ruefully.

The rhythmic thump of hooves grew louder and Sander looked over to see one of Gunnar's riders cresting the hill at the at the top of the path that zigzagged down the hillside to the covered bridge. As well as being a crossing, the bridge also marked the border control between the realms of Andraste and Wayland. They would need to pass through it to reach the merpeople's lake.

'The word?' Gunnar called to the rider as he reached the top.

'Forgive me, Captain, but the word is no.' The rider was Rasmus Anund, another vaguely familiar face to Sander. One of the more ambitious social climbers in the military from one of the richer families in the court, and yet another clueless yes-man with no grip on how the real world worked. He was, naturally, Gunnar's second-in-command. 'They say that until the crisis with the Lapis Moon is put into some kind of context, the border is closed: no trade in or out, and they made it clear that any transgression will be seen as an act of war.'

Gunnar's Adam's apple bobbed up and down as he mulled his options and made the strange creaking noise that signified he was thinking. 'For the sake of good ongoing relations between Andraste and Wayland, I shall take a party to the border crossing and negotiate our passage myself.'

'*Negotiate?* Oh, you're joking, aren't you?' Sander said. 'Throw your weight about, man. Puff your chest out, tell them who you are and threaten to cut their balls off if they give you any grief.'

'That is not how we do things in the King's Guard.'

'It's how we did things as mages.'

'And look how that turned out for you.' For a moment, Gunnar's voice cracked and he sounded like a petulant teen in a classroom debate. He drew himself upright once more. 'We do not want to risk any acts of aggression. We shall—'

'There's a young girl dying back home, Captain, a princess, and we have a week to save her. If the king were here, he'd tell you to draw your sword and do your negotiating with the sharp end.'

'My orders from the king are clear, and they stipulate that we shall not antagonise any of our neighbours. I am confident that the negotiations will be short and—'

'Aye-aye. Baldie's up to somethin'.' Malachy nodded back down the zigzag. All heads turned to find Orren steering her horse along the path. She was already halfway down.

'Lieutenant, intercept the Sister and bring her back here,' Gunnar ordered.

'Sir!' Rasmus replied, then gestured at the two closest riders. Vilmar was by far the youngest of the group, all elbows and wide eyes. Norrey was their cook and looked lost without a ladle in his hand. 'Vilmar, Norrey – you're with me!'

They all pulled on their reins and turned their horses onto the zigzag path. It was not only narrow but perilously steep and eroded by decades of abuse from over-laden carts. Sander and the others watched as the slowest horse chase in history unfolded.

'Sister Orren, stop! I order you to stop!'

To her credit, Orren ignored all of Rasmus's pleas and once she was on a flat path, she leaned forward in her saddle, kicked at her horse's haunches and rocketed towards the border at breakneck speed. Rasmus and his riders didn't stand a chance of catching her.

'Where did that come from?' Sander wondered.

'What's that?' Gunnar said with a sidelong glance.

'She could barely stay on the bloody thing earlier and now she's off like the wind.'

Malachy cackled. 'P'raps it's magic?'

'Or she's a devious bugger who can't be trusted?' Sander returned Gunnar's glance, but the captain of the King's Guard said nothing. Instead, he quietly fumed, pretending to study maps while they waited in silence.

Sander dismounted, massaged his sore buttocks and lay on his back in the tall grass. He let the blades wrap around him and found himself calmed by the gentle rustle of the leaves in the breeze, the renewed tweeting of birds in the air and the scurry of unseen insects in the undergrowth. He breathed in the air, wondering if he might actually like it out here in the fields and grass after all, and if he lay here long enough, perhaps he would be forgotten and left behind. Indulging in this simple fantasy, he allowed himself to let down his guard and closed his eyes. Before he fell into a slumber, the pale face of Princess Brianna came to him and his belly knotted with shame.

A boot connected with his backside, snapping him out of it. Malachy stood over him, now tapping spent tobacco from his pipe. 'Looks like our girl got a result,' he said.

Sander couldn't be sure how much time had passed, but the sun had moved beyond the Lapis ring. The sky was blue once more and lush greens had returned to the hills beyond the Jade River.

As he creaked to his feet, he could see Orren, Rasmus, Vilmar and Norrey trotting down the hill path side-by-side and smiling. They came to a halt at the bottom of the zigzag and beckoned for the rest of the party to join them.

Sander went to run a hand through his hair – often messy after a sleep – then remembered with a sinking feeling that he was newly bald. As Gunnar started barking orders, Sander heaved himself onto his horse's saddle and began the perilous ride down the zigzags.

Orren's self-satisfied smile was unbearable to behold.

Rasmus was clearly smitten. 'Our passage through Andraste is guaranteed,' he said, his voice rising almost half an octave with excitement. 'And all thanks to Sister Orren.'

'That's simply splendid,' Gunnar said, a wavering grin on his face. 'Though I must insist that in future, you come to me first before you go haring off on—'

'I felt that time was of the essence.' Orren's smile grew with her defiance. 'Standing and talking will not achieve our goal. The Word of the Faith says—'

'That's all very well, but we have a chain of command here and I will strenuously insist that it be observed.'

'*Strenuously insist?*' Sander knew he should be quiet, but he couldn't help himself. 'She ran off without permission. Give her a bollocking. You would me.'

'The Sister used her initiative and got results.' Gunnar ground his teeth. 'All we've had from you is insolence. I will choose who is to be punished and when, and I will not have my authority questioned by a disgraced conjuror.'

'Tell me, Captain, would you strenuously insist that any bandits we meet along the road be on their way and leave us alone? If we encounter the massed hordes of Haldor Frang's men, will we politely contend that they lay down their weapons and surrender? Gods wept, man, what sort of commander are you?'

Gunnar's nostrils flared, but he kept his cool. 'When I want your opinion, Noviciate Bree, I shall ask for it. In the meantime, I order you to be silent.'

Sander gave him a few moments of contemptuous quiet before turning to Orren. 'So how did you do it?'

'I found a fellow Sister at the crossing. Our shared love of the Goddess brought us this blessing.'

'Handy.'

'The Faith offers succour to weary travellers and merchants, and my siblings post themselves at key positions on the main trading routes.'

'You mean you prey on the tired and needy and pounce on them at border crossings in order to boost your numbers and the coins in your coffers?'

'We selflessly give compassion and offer sanctuary.'

'And do each other favours, like letting one another cross closed borders while customs officials look the other way?'

'Do you wish to cross the border or no, my Brother?'

'Hey, I get it. We did the same thing as mages, we just didn't dress it up in a load of flowery bollocks.' Sander shrugged, knowing full well that they did precisely that: giving a noble code to what were nothing more than elaborate privileges. Free pints and meals in taverns to 'honour my Lord Mage'. Oh, those were the days.

'Such cynicism will be your downfall, my Brother.' Orren's smile widened as she turned to Gunnar and Sander knew what was coming next. 'A day's rations, Captain?'

'Let's make it two.' Gunnar's lip curled and his eyelids drooped in glee. 'You wanted to know what kind of commander I am, Noviciate?'

'Yeah, whatever. I need to lose weight anyway,' Sander muttered.

'What was that?'

'Nothing.' Sander turned his back on Gunnar and geed his horse.

Soon Sander was leading the procession to the crossing with Malachy cackling next to him. 'What's so funny?'

'If there's one thing I've learned that's kept me alive, Brother, it's to roll with the punches.' Malachy gently twirled his halberd around, bringing it to rest on his shoulder. 'If them in charge want you to kiss some new king's arse, or bow and scrape to some new god, then what's the harm in that? Keeps them happy, keeps me alive.'

'What if you find their god a bloody great sham? A huge lie to stay in power?'

'If you don't believe in it, then there's even less reason to worry about praying. None of it'll mean nothin', so your prayin' means nothin'... Except to them. Don't fret on it. Gods and kings come and go, but there's always some new dickhead around the corner.'

'Sorry, Malachy, but I'd like to scrape a little dignity out of this whole exercise.'

'Dignity?' Malachy twisted his face like he'd bitten down on a lemon. 'You know what your trouble is?'

'I reckon I'm about to hear it.'

'You think you're sitting at the top table, mate. You're so used to feasting with kings that you don't know nothin' else.'

'Oh, don't give me that noble peasant rubbish, Malachy. I've pissed alongside lepers, just as you've kissed the captain's ring. I don't care who you are – we all deserve to hold our heads up high and be who we are, and I won't have any idiot in a robe tell me otherwise.'

'Don't say I didn't warn ya.'

'I appreciate the advice.'

'And if you're hungry and you ever want a share of my rations...'

'Oh, thank you, Malachy, that's—'

'You can go fuck yourself.'

Oskar Sweats

Oskar fought to keep his eyes shut.

The glare of the sun not only beamed from the sky, but reflected even more brightly off the sea and bloomed into an utterly blinding white when it passed behind the band of Lapis stones in the sky. Even the briefest glimpse made his eyeballs pulse with a lightning stab.

That was the least of his worries.

Craig's punch had knocked him out, but when he awoke on the *Queen Mathilde*'s deck, the pain in his ribs, back and head told him he'd been given a good kicking while he was unconscious.

Oskar was tied to the middle mast of the ship. They were back at sea, riding in the Ocean's Hand, with the full blaze of the sun bearing down on him. He could feel his dark skin tenderising, blistering with each passing minute.

And then, at the ringing of the hour bell, Devin would whip him. Three lashes. The whip's knotted cotton cords were tipped with fish-hooks that slapped against his skin so hard, he thought he would split in two. Craig, whose broken fingers precluded him from administering the whipping, was given the honour of rubbing salt and vinegar into the wounds for good measure, which he did with vigour, spitting every possible curse into Oskar's ears.

Oskar's screams did nothing to ease the pain, which came in forms that varied from a general ongoing ache in his every muscle, to an incredible jolt through his entire body that made him see stars as he writhed and spasmed uncontrollably against the mast. He often passed out, and the last thing he saw were the rotting teeth in the mouths of the grinning crew, all too eager to make him pay for his deception.

All except for Yanick. His blank face betrayed no emotion. He watched, silent and motionless, his long white hair fluttering in the sea breeze as Oskar slipped into unconsciousness.

Oskar drifted in and out of the blackness, unsure of how much time had passed. He was lying on his side on the deck, free of the mast.

173

As his skin blazed and pulsed with the ebb and flow of pain, Oskar's mind tried to piece together what he had seen on the dock. The broken Lapis Moon, its pieces scattered across the night sky, and his sudden transformation from a simpleton into... Well, what was he now?

Yanick woke him by chucking a bucket full of warm water into his face.

No, not water. Too late, Oskar recognised the ammonia stench of piss as he instinctively gulped a mouthful down.

Oskar tried to beg for mercy, but all that came out were slurred moans, much like his old self. Yanick pulled Oskar to his feet and shoved him back toward the mast.

'How about a sweat, boys?' Yanick called to the crew, and the reply was instant and deafening. Oskar flinched at the noise, noticing with a sudden numbing flush that the captain was holding a noose of rough rope in his hand.

Yanick yanked the noose around Oskar's neck. The rope felt heavy, the new weight making Oskar's knees buckle. It was rough and rubbed at the soft flesh under his chin. A strange sensation of calm filled Oskar. Soon it would be over. He had seen a hanging once in Sabley. Oskar didn't know the man's crime, but the villagers had been certain of his guilt. They cheered much like Yanick's crew as they draped a similar length of rope over a high branch of an oak tree. The noise grew even louder as they hauled the man into the air. A dark patch appeared on his breeches as he pissed himself, then his feet kicked for a few moments before going still. Oskar would endure this final humiliation and the pain would end and his miserable life would be done. It had played a final cruel trick on him by briefly opening a door to a new world where he wasn't the butt of everyone's jokes. Oskar wondered what chance he would have stood out there in the world, anyway. His father was dead, he had no idea what had happened to his mother, or where his sister was, and he had not a single friend in the world.

Yanick did not swing the rope over the yardarm as Oskar expected. Instead, he handed it to Craig and Glaw, who both tied it around the mast, tethering Oskar to it like a dog.

By now, the crew were chanting, 'Sweat! Sweat! Sweat!' and one of them produced a fiddle and began to play a jig. Oskar wondered if he was required to dance.

'If it were up to me, I'd hang you.'

It took Oskar a moment to realise that Yanick was talking to him.

'But Haldor wants you alive for as long as your bitch sister does his dirty work.'

Oskar took some little hope in hearing that Rosheen was alive, imagining her sweeping out of the sky with Anzu and taking him away from this living hell.

'So until the last mage in the Newlands is done for, I have to keep you alive.' Yanick spat on the deck. 'Take it from me, sonny – you'll wish you were dead.'

The crew had formed a circle around Oskar then drawn their blades and begun jabbing them at him. He jumped back to avoid a cutlass, then yelped in agony as he felt the sting of a blade cut into the fat of his buttocks. He spun on his heels to find more blades poking at him. Those who didn't have a sword were clapping in time with the fiddle's jaunty rhythm and Oskar found himself dancing. He soon realised why they were chanting 'sweat': it poured off him in the midday sun as he hopped about, dodging the sharp blades, not always successfully.

As he staggered around, using all his remaining energy and wits to evade being skewered, one thought kept vying for his attention. Something Yanick had said about 'the last mage'. Did that mean all the mages were gone? Or dead? It didn't make any sense.

He winced as the point of a sword glanced across his shin. Blood seeped from the cut, a warm trickle down his leg.

Oskar remembered Alby Clim telling him stories of the first mages and how they had worshipped the Lapis Moon, convinced that it was the source of all their power. So, if the moon had been destroyed, did it follow that their power had, too?

Oskar's vision flashed and he felt like he was falling down a tunnel as his whole body contorted in pain. Someone had slapped the whip wounds on his back with the flat of their sword, and for a brief moment he felt as if he were on fire. Another blade slashed across his chest, a new pain to momentarily distract from the old one.

Oskar desperately tried to keep his thoughts on track. If magic had gone, how was Rosheen the last mage? That didn't matter, he told himself. She wasn't here and wasn't coming.

He slipped and fell to his knees. A pool of blood had formed around him, the cuts in his body feeding it more and more with each passing moment. Crawling now to avoid the blades, he added bloody hand-prints to the red footprints already smudged across the deck.

Concentrate! He shook his head to stay alert, spraying pink droplets of sweat and blood.

So... so... so... If magic was gone, and he was no longer a fool... were the two things connected? Had the Lapis Moon and the power of magic fogged his mind since birth? Had its removal freed him?

Something odd happened then. The world turned sideways. The ship's deck and the surface of the sea were reaching up into the sky. Oskar realised he was sprawled face down on the boards, his ragged breath creating ripples in the blood lapping around his face.

The fiddler had stopped playing and Yanick was saying something to the crew, who jeered and booed. Oskar hoped it was over, that death would come and the pain would go. Instead, he was hauled to his feet and dragged back down into the hold, and it was some tiny relief that he would no longer be in the sun's unflinching glare. The darkness beckoned and welcomed him like a brother.

Rosheen's horse panted and puffed clouds of vapour into the dappled light of the wood, its ribs shuddering as they grew and shrank like a bellows under her legs. She'd pushed him too hard on the road from Agrona all night and all day, but they had left later than she wanted and needed to make up the time.

Of course, if Anzu were here...

Rosheen missed Anzu so much that it ached. She would be fine for a short while, maybe hours at a time, and then some trivial thing would remind Rosheen of her friend and the pain would return, washing over her like the waves on the rocks where she killed her. More than Anzu's wings, she missed her wisdom. She would almost certainly be talking Rosheen out of this insane mission. Gods, she should have lis-tened to her before. There must have been some other way out of this.

She glanced at the eight men on horseback that Haldor had chosen for her. She thought she recognised one as a former commander of Torren's, but most were long-standing members of Haldor's militia, and she even recalled a couple from the battle with King Torren's men. She had asked for their names, but Haldor told her that none would be forthcoming. 'Dead men walking have no names,' he added, somewhat cryptically. 'They will be led by Bowden. That is all you need to know.'

Every one of them had the dead-eyed stare of a killer. Drawing a sword and taking a life were nothing more to them than snapping a chicken's neck for dinner. There was no mirth in their laughter; their words were few and simple and spoken with little urgency. And even though they ate, pissed and shat like any other human, there was something so hollow and empty about them that Rosheen realised that when folk spoke of undead demons, they were most likely referring to men like these cold-blooded killers.

They were perfect. They would do what she would not.

Bowden, a man whose face bore all the wear and tear of the business end of a wooden mallet, drew his horse level with hers. Haldor had ordered him to watch over Rosheen. 'Don't trust her for one second.' She had been right there when he gave the order. You could at least admire Haldor's candour. He simply told it as it was and informed Rosheen that if she tried to run then Bowden would kill her at the first instance, and her beloved Oskar's death would be slow and agonising.

As an added security measure, eight birdcages dangled from Bowden's saddle. Each day, he would send a homing pigeon back to Haldor with a coded message assuring him that all was going well. If a bird failed to return then Haldor made it clear that poor Oskar would be dead before the day was done.

'That it?' Bowden said, nodding at a lake below.

Shaped like a crooked finger, the lake stretched away to the horizon and, were it not for the distant backdrop of misty mountains, the casual traveller might think they had reached the sea. At its deepest, the water was still, but by the shore, weed-infested waves slopped lazily, soaking the air with the scent of damp stagnation.

The gnarled knuckle of a densely wooded island rose in the centre of the lake. Thick with wild foliage, it was riddled with tiny inlets, rocky fjords and caves where white gulls nested and circled looking for food. There were no homes, no warm glow of hearth fires burning, no pontoons or docks. Just a dark, tangled, unwelcoming mess of overgrowth.

This was Connal Lake. The island was a reservation for exiled merpeople. Refugees from some ancient clan blood feud, they had been relocated here by the Council of Regents and left to fester and brood, and so the rest of the Newlands let them be.

Rosheen didn't even know for certain if Sander and his entourage were coming here, but it's where she would have headed were she in his boots. Yesterday, she would have consulted with Anzu and come to a more informed decision, but there were no certainties any more. Only hunches. Gods, Rosheen missed her so much.

'Have your men assemble the boat,' she told Bowden.

At Bowden's nod, his men clambered down from their horses and began untying sections of a boat that had been brought in pieces from Agrona.

Rosheen scanned the island. There was no sign of any merpeople, only a pebbled shore lined with boulders where a boat might land. Of course, no one ever dared visit the island. The merfolk were rightly feared. Some would patrol the shallow waters of the lake shore and try to tempt the more gullible humans, but few adults fell for that any more, and naive children not only made for poor eating, but killing and eating one tended to enrage the local human community and resulted in braying mobs and bloodshed. And so they kept themselves to themselves, swimming in the deep, staying in the shadows, squabbling with each other.

Tonight, Rosheen and her men would need to draw them out.

No human would ever get close to the island without the merpeople sensing their splashing or paddling, but Rosheen was, for the moment, no mere human.

She unwrapped the calfskin bag hanging from her saddle. The blue glow of the light from the Lapis stone drew the attention of Bowden's men. They had probably all suffered at the whim of magic at some point and were happy to see the end of it. Their dull eyes briefly flared with the stone's refracted light, and a few of them even took half a step back.

Rosheen relished its power. Having lost magic once already, she didn't want to see it go again. The stone's light was dimmer than when she first found it. How long would it last? She knew that Haldor, Bowden and all their men would be wondering the same thing. Biding their time for the right moment to pounce. But for now, it worked.

Rosheen had carved a rudimentary staff before setting off, and she reached around to untie it from her saddle. Using her magic, she made a gesture with her free hand and the acorn-like cup she had fashioned at one end of the staff opened like the petals of a flower. Rosheen placed the stone inside and closed the cup tight around it, then twirled the staff around gracefully, its motion leaving a pleasing blue streak on her retinas.

Then she remembered why she was here. And what a terrible thing they must do next. If Sander and his companions came to Connal Lake – and she was sure they would – it had to be a dead end, and that meant doing something unthinkable. She reassured herself that she was just a guide and that Bowden and his men would be the ones to get their hands dirty.

She also knew that she was fooling only herself.

Rosheen thought of Oskar. Alone, confused, orphaned and desperately frightened, sharing a cell with one of Haldor's killers who was simply waiting for the word to cut the boy's throat. She recalled Anzu's mad idea that the boy might have become a demigod, his powers unleashed by the destruction of the moon. If he was, she could really use his help now.

'The glamour will only work if they're not looking for us,' she told Bowden. 'Stay silent, and when we paddle, keep the splashing to a minimum. We'll move slowly, stealthily and with purpose. Understood?'

'We know what we're doing, witch.' He didn't even look at her as he spoke. 'Get us to the island and keep your magic rock out of my face.'

Just a guide, Rosheen told herself. *Just a guide*. She set her jaw, raised the staff and motioned Bowden's men forward.

The Mountain and the Dwarf

Breakfast ended unexpectedly with a mountain falling from the sky.

Orren was shaving Sander's head at the time.

'Keep still.' She slapped his shiny pink pate. 'I'm nearly done.'

Around them, Gunnar's men repacked their gear as they prepared for the day's journey. They had made camp overnight at the edge of a cluster of limestone shards known as the Stone Forest, on a bare outcrop with a breathtaking view of the Conloch Mountains, their purple peaks stretching away as far as the eye could see.

But the eye would always be drawn to Mount Aderyn. The floating mountain.

Hanging in the air like a loose fragment of the planet, Aderyn was one of a handful of known floating mountains around the world. Each one was a remnant of the Mage Wars, put there by mages so powerful that their magic soaked into the rocks and kept them aloft for hundreds of years. Sander could only wonder in awe at the immense magic energy it must have taken to put it there in the first place. His own floating stones had only lasted a few hours without magic, and he reckoned it could only be a matter of time before Aderyn and its kind came crashing down. He just didn't expect to be there when it happened.

Aderyn was considered a sacred place by the Salm People who lived on it and visitors were discouraged, the only access provided by long, ragged rope bridges that could be cut if uninvited guests ignored the warnings to turn back. There were several thriving mining communities in the mountain's shadow and Sander had argued that they should stop by the dwarf villages that nestled in Aderyn's shade and warn them to evacuate, but Gunnar was giving it a wide berth, preferring the Stone Forest route instead.

The viewpoint was a popular spot for travellers to rest and enjoy the magnificent sight of the mysterious mountain. It was littered with the remnants of fires, burned pans, broken tent pegs and cracked clay pipes. It was also rumoured to be a nook frequented by bandits, but they preferred their victims to travel in small numbers; traders laden with goods and money, not a half-dozen well-armed and -trained cavalry from the court of King Bhaltair.

Vilmar, the youngest of their group, saw to the horses' food and water, then sang old Wayland folk songs to himself in a breathy falsetto as he brushed their coats. The ever-cheerful cook, Norrey, whistled his own tune in an entirely different key as he prepared a breakfast of fried eggs and corn, occasionally pausing to add herbs after first running his hands through his jet-black, greasy hair. Orren was always pestering him with suggestions for changes to his recipes and he bore her intrusions with a weary grin.

Bent and Wob, a couple so inseparable that Sander wondered if they were married, were debating the best way to fold a ground-sheet, and Gunnar Jarl stood with his second-in-command, Rasmus, studying maps with a frown that made Sander think of schoolchildren when first confronted with algebra. Sander wasn't much encouraged when he saw a flicker of realisation on Gunnar's face, followed by Rasmus helpfully turning the map forty-five degrees. Malachy, paranoid as always, had his back to the floating mountain and was peering into the Stone Forest ahead of them. Between the oaks, beeches and box trees were great shards of limestone that jutted out of the ground at odd angles, creating a maze from which bandits could easily pounce on an unwitting traveller.

'I am perfectly capable of doing this myself,' Sander snapped at Orren as her blade nicked his head again, but she just applied more soap to his scalp, making it sting and tighten.

'That misses the point entirely,' she said as she massaged his head vigorously. 'This is a shared experience between siblings of the Faith. With blade and bare hands, we learn of trust and kinship.'

'Do I get to do you next?' Sander asked.

Orren ignored him. 'The Goddess says when we take away our vanity, we are all revealed to be one and the—'

Orren fell silent, her head cocked bird-like to one side. Sander heard it, too. Everyone did, and they all stopped what they were doing to listen.

A delicate cracking like distant thunder was followed by what sounded like the whole world caving in on itself.

Mount Aderyn was breaking in two and falling out of the sky.

Sander and his companions all watched in astonishment as great shards of it tumbled down into the shadowy valleys where hundreds of dwarvish miners and their families lived in villages clustered along the Connal River. They felt the impacts moments later, deep rumbles that shook the ground beneath their feet, rattled loose pebbles and toppled over a few of the limestone shards in the Forest. The horses whinnied and reared up, and Vilmar, Bent and Wob hurried to calm them. Slate-grey dust came billowing next, puffing and expanding, filling every inch of the valleys.

'Even the rocks are succumbing to the new world order,' Orren said, with a little too much glee in her voice for Sander's liking. The cloud of dust was beginning to clear, revealing a pair of jagged, flint-like fins of rock resting lopsided in the valleys.

'For gods' sakes, Orren, give it a rest. There were families living in those valleys.' Sander found his voice trembling. 'Children. All dead.'

'The path the Goddess chooses for us is a mystery, and those who fall will be welcomed into her embrace,' Orren said with all sincerity.

'Oh, fuck the Goddess!' Sander kicked at a frying pan, causing poor Norrey to duck for cover from flying eggs, corn and hot fat.

'That just cost you today's rations,' Gunnar barked.

Sander was about to remind him that today's rations were already off limits to him but thought better of it, clambering onto his horse and geeing him back onto the path into the Stone Forest.

A gentle but incessant rain of mountain dust continued to fall for the rest of the day. It drifted softly through the sunlight that cut between the canopy above and the shards of limestone, settling in their hair, and on their clothes, lips and tongues. This meant more frequent stops for water to swirl and spit the stuff from their mouths, but even the river was cloudy with billions of tiny particles and none of them much fancied filling their gourds with it.

Sander wiped the powdery matter from his bald head, briefly inspecting the chalky grains on his palm before smearing them on his robe. His stomach gurgled. He usually staved off his hunger by nib-bling on nuts and watercress as they rode, but the Stone Forest around them had become a pale, ghostlike afterworld. The leaves, nuts, and fungi were all dusted with the remains of Mount Aderyn. He continued to pick nuts and stuff them into his pockets, though, in the hope of finding a clean stream or pool to wash them in.

A squirrel skittered across the path in front of them, leaving a trail of powder in the air behind it. Sander's horse whinnied, rearing a little. He gave the beast a reassuring pat, sending puffs of dust into the air.

'What did you say?' Orren pulled her horse alongside his.

'What?'

'Something about a squirrel,' she said, her eyes darting from side to side as she looked for it in the undergrowth.

Sander exhaled wearily. He was thinking aloud again and he had no clue that he was doing it. 'It's nothing,' he said. 'I'm tired. Go away.'

They came to a fork in the path through the Stone Forest, and Gunnar and Rasmus consulted the map again. The choice was between a trail running along the top of a chalky rise, where they would be exposed for all to see, or a steep decline into the clustered limestone fingers that mixed with dense knotweed and willow trees. After a while, Gunnar pointed downwards and they began their descent. Sander was almost certain they were lost. His thoughts of escape, so strong when they first embarked on this farce, were fading fast. This maze of stone and wood with its polluted food and water was no place to attempt any kind of a runner.

'What was that?' Orren asked again.

Oh gods, was he still thinking aloud? 'Nothing!' he said.

'No, not you.' She leaned forward in her saddle. 'A noise from down there. Captain, stop!'

Gunnar raised his hand and the cavalry train came to a halt before it had even got on its way again. Rasmus galloped back to ask what Orren had found.

'There! Do you see it?'

Sander and Rasmus followed her guiding finger to a painted caravan crashed in a bed of bluebells at the bottom of a bowl-like dip between the standing stones. One of the caravan's axles was broken, as were the spokes in its wheels. Its rear door was hanging from a single hinge and pots, pans and broken crockery spilled down its steps into the bluebells.

Something moved inside. A leg. A small leg clad in a lilac boot decorated with bows and bells. There came a whimper, too.

'There's someone inside!' Orren cried. 'A child.'

'Captain.' Rasmus waved Gunnar over. 'Civilian in need of assistance.'

Gunnar gestured at Bent and Wob as he rode back up the path. 'You two: fetch the water and see what we can do to—'

'This is bandit country, Captain,' Sander said, looking at the labyrinth of trees and stones around them. 'Could be a trap.'

To his credit, Gunnar didn't retort with his usual outright dismissal of anything Sander said. 'Wait!' Gunnar called, and Bent and Wob stopped in their tracks. He rubbed his eyes and made that nasal creaking noise. There were dark shadows underneath them and his lips looked dry, caked with mountain dust. Sander wondered how much sleep the captain was getting. 'Rasmus – have the men take positions around the bowl.'

Rasmus saluted and led Vilmar, Norrey, Bent and Wob scurrying around the perimeter of the dip.

'Sister Orren, Noviciate Bree – you're with me. Malachy: watch our backs and stick to these two like glue.' Gunnar nodded at Sander and Orren as he dismounted.

'Yessir.' Malachy straightened to attention, before getting off his own horse.

'Down there?' Sander nodded towards the cart. 'Get stuffed.'

Gunnar extended a hand and helped Orren down from her horse. 'If we're attacked, you'll be safe with Malachy and me by your side. Plus you both have experience in healing, and there's a child down there who's hurt and needs our help.'

'Have faith, Brother.' Orren gently took his arm. 'There is no shame in fear, but we must be brave in the face of—'

'I'm not bloody scared— Well, yes, actually I am. This is so clearly a trap.'

Gunnar set his jaw. 'If it's a trap, then—'

'No.' Sander extended a warning finger. 'You're about to say, *Then let us spring it!* or some other heroic cobblers. No, no, no. Those are always the last words of a valiant fool.'

Gunnar made that creaking noise through his nose again, annoyed that his moment had been ruined. He drew his sword and began to make his way down the steep incline. 'Just get on with it.'

Orren followed obediently. Gunnar, unbalanced by his sword, slipped on some loose rocks. With his free hand, he steadied himself on one of the limestone shards, then sheathed his sword and resumed his descent.

Sander turned to Malachy, who was leaning on his halberd with the demeanour of a man at ease, but his eyes were flitting from side to side as he looked for any potential attackers. 'I'm with you, mate,' the old warrior said in a low voice. 'This stinks to the skies, but… if there's anyone out there, I don't reckon I can see 'em.' He gestured towards the bowl with his halberd. 'Come on. Down y'go.' It wasn't threatening, but it was clear that Malachy had orders to follow and Sander, one way or another, was to follow Gunnar and Orren.

Sander descended into the bowl by stumbling from one spiky bush of weeds to another. His feet slipped and he found himself running vertically downwards with heavy, slapping footfalls. He scythed through the bluebells then crashed into the canvas roof of the overturned caravan, bouncing back off it and falling on his arse in a cloud of grey dust.

As it cleared, he found Gunnar and Orren looking at him like the disappointed parents of an excitable, clumsy child.

'What? I slipped.' Sander pouted.

'Dickhead,' muttered Malachy, who had somehow arrived behind him without making a single noise.

Sander looked up to where Vilmar, Rasmus, Norrey, Bent and Wob were standing on the perimeter of the bowl, though from down here, it looked less like a bowl and more like the bottom of a well. Getting out again would mean clambering up the steep slope on all fours like the apes Bhaltair kept in his menagerie.

Gunnar drew his sword again, positioned himself by the caravan's broken door and peered in. 'It's a child. A little girl,' he said, sheathing the sword and ducking inside.

As Sander got to his feet, brushing the grey dust from his robes, Gunnar pulled the unconscious body of a small girl from the caravan.

'Brother, quickly.' Orren beckoned Sander over.

From her build, the girl appeared to be about the same age as Princess Brianna. She wore a pink, frilly dress that looked two sizes too big for her, her face was obscured by a hood and her hands were bound behind her back. They were odd hands for a child, Sander thought. The palms were calloused and red, the fingers gnarled and stubby. As Sander moved closer, he felt a chill, a dreamlike sense of inevitability that something was about to go horribly wrong.

And he was proven right as Gunnar and Orren pulled back the hood to reveal not a child but a bearded dwarf with a gag tied around his mouth.

The dwarf began to panic, kicking and struggling against the ropes and the gag and uttering something urgent but incomprehensible.

'Gunnar, we should go. We should go *right now!*' Sander began to back away and ended up walking into Malachy who placed a hand on his shoulder. *Not yet.*

Gunnar tugged the gag free and the dwarf found his breath before crying the words that Sander didn't want to hear. 'It's a trap, you idiots! Run!'

Whistling noises came from the Stone Forest. At first, Sander thought it was some strange birdsong, but then something tumbled into the dusty bluebells by his feet. Sander snatched it up: a long, feathered shaft ending in a deadly point.

'Archers!' Malachy shouted. 'Take cover!'

Sander heard a sound from above like someone trying to dislodge phlegm from their throat. He looked up to see an arrow had hit Vilmar in the back of the neck, its point bursting through his gullet with a spurt of crimson. He fell forwards, coughing and choking on the blood gushing from his mouth, trying to reach around for the arrow before tumbling down into the bowl.

Rasmus, Norrey, Bent and Wob ducked for cover as more arrows came, followed by the war-cries of their attackers.

Gunnar began shouting orders, but his men had disappeared. More arrows spiralled aimlessly into the bowl. Their hidden attackers were firing blindly, but it was enough to send Sander and the others scurrying for cover. Orren dashed inside the caravan as the dwarf took an arrow in his leg. He howled in pain, thrashing about in his dress.

'Get behind here!' Malachy grabbed Sander and pulled him behind the upturned caravan as another salvo of arrows rained down, their points digging into the ground around them or hammering on the wood of the caravan.

There came another noise, a low rumble like the collapse of Mount Aderyn but much closer to home. Sander dared to glimpse out from behind the cover of the caravan to see a dark shape moving through the Stone Forest above.

A troll, bereft of magic, listless and slow, came swaying to the edge of the bowl. Somehow, these clowns had trapped it and were using it as muscle. Sander saw more movement behind it as a trio of hooded bandits rushed up and shoved it over the edge. Snapping bushes and smashing rocks to dust, it came rolling down, almost comically, into the base of the bowl where it flailed to a halt, honking in pain and flapping its arms and legs like a giant baby having a tantrum.

Sander whinnied a laugh at the ridiculousness of it all, but then realised that they were stuck in a bowl with an angry troll and no easy escape route.

'This way!' Gunnar waved them away from the troll to a steep incline behind the caravan, but before they could take two steps, another hail of arrows came and they scurried back to their shelters.

And the movement brought them to the attention of the troll. He may have been sluggish, but he was also pissed off. He thundered at them, one huge hand swiping at the caravan, flipping it over.

Orren came flying out, finding herself at the troll's feet.

She reached down and drew something from her boot. A dagger.

'Full of surprises, that one,' Malachy said in genuine admiration as they watched Orren stab the troll in the calf. It howled in pain and staggered back, giving Orren the chance to crab away from immediate danger.

'How come she gets a knife?' Sander whined. 'I want a knife. Give me a knife!'

Gunnar charged the troll next, swinging his sword, which bit into the creature's forearm, where it became stuck. Gunnar pulled at it but it wouldn't budge, and the troll lashed out, sending Gunnar flying, now swordless.

More arrows came and Gunnar ran back to the caravan for cover, but the troll followed him and, with the sword still stuck in his arm, began to tear the vehicle to pieces.

Sander, Malachy, Orren and Gunnar ran in four different directions and the bowl became a storm of wood, canvas, wheels, pots, pans, bedding and clothes as the troll continued to smash and pound anything that moved.

Another cry came from above, some kind of signal between the bandits. The troll turned instinctively at the sound, unknowingly treading on the dwarf's legs and breaking both of them with a sickening snap.

'Oh gods, what a day!' the dwarf wailed in despair.

The bandits came running down into the bowl. Their moment had arrived: their prey was unarmed and had no cover. It was time to attack.

Malachy raised his halberd and Orren gripped her dagger, but that was it for weapons. Sander snatched up an iron kettle that had landed by his feet during the troll's demolition of the caravan. It wasn't much, but it was heavy and had a good handle. Gunnar was unarmed.

'Rasmus! Attack! Now! Rasmus!' The captain's voice became louder and more desperate, as if shouting at a greater volume could make hope a reality. 'Rasmus, where are you?'

There were eight bandits in all and they came from all directions at once, six men, two women. One of the women continued to fire arrows as she closed in; the others all had swords. Malachy swept one of the flying arrows aside with his halberd and stuck the closest bandit in the belly. The man died spitting blood as he fell to the ground.

The woman without the bow came at Orren with her sword swinging down, but the Sister of the Faith didn't hesitate to step inside the clumsy blow and stab her attacker in the neck. Blood came spurting from the wound as the bandit slumped face first into the bluebells.

Gunnar took on three of them without his sword. They piled onto him, and he fought with a frightened, scrabbling desperation. He looked inexperienced, fumbling for a grip or misjudging punches, but then he twisted and broke the arm of one of his assailants over his knee. In the blink of an eye, he had that man's sword and was fighting back with renewed confidence. This was the kind of fighting he knew, that he had trained for, and he was soon parrying blows and slashing at their heads. They backed away immediately.

Malachy swung his halberd at the others, who also kept a safe distance, while a couple ran around the back of the troll for cover.

Sander panicked and threw the kettle at the red-haired bandit who approached him. The bandit dodged it, still coming at Sander, sword raised. Sander ducked under the sword and hurled himself at the man, grabbing him around the waist. They fell to the ground in an embrace, the bandit's sword arm held down by Sander. They were face to face as they rolled around, the man's beard scratching against Sander's cheek. Sander hadn't needed to fight since he was a child. Magic had always done the job for him, but this bandit lived for a scrap, and he was clearly enjoying every moment because he knew that he would soon wriggle free of the grip of this weakling Noviciate of the Faith and stick him in the belly.

Sander kneed the bandit between his legs, but his kneecap merely hit a solid codpiece. The bandit cackled and wriggled his sword arm free. He raised it for the killer blow.

There was a flash of metal as a blade flew by and the bandit's weapon arm was spinning through the air, quite separate from its body, almost waving a fond farewell as it landed with a thud in the bluebells. Malachy twirled his halberd and brought it down, puncturing the red-haired bandit's chest and killing him instantly. Malachy kicked the corpse aside and pulled Sander to his feet, then almost instantly shoved him to one side again as the troll lumbered towards them.

With a swipe of its arm, the troll sent Malachy spinning through the air, crashing into the wreckage of the caravan. For a brief moment, Malachy's woollen hat slipped from his head, revealing white, wispy hair and long, pointy ears.

Elvish ears.

Sander was the only one who saw them. Malachy threw him a

quick *Don't-you-say-a-bloody-word* glare and tugged his hat back on as the troll raised a meaty fist to crush him.

In the blink of an eye, Malachy snatched up his halberd, jabbing it under the troll's chin, and the creature choked with a surprisingly high-pitched scream. Malachy pushed the blade in further, piercing the brain, and the creature's eyes rolled back in their sockets. It crashed down on its bottom, first resting in a sitting position, then slumping into a pile by the remains of the caravan.

Hearing more war-cries, Sander feared that bandit reinforcements had arrived, but then he recognised Rasmus, Norrey, Bent and Wob as they came charging down into the bowl with their swords drawn. The remaining bandits took one look, decided that the jig was up and ran back up the bowl to dart between the jagged limestone fingers as quickly as they had appeared.

Orren ran to the centre of the bowl. 'We must help the wounded,' she said.

Rasmus saluted Gunnar and got a half-hearted one back. Gunnar said nothing, but he was clearly disappointed in his lieutenant for running away when he was needed the most. Rasmus sensed it, too.

'We regrouped a short distance from the bowl, sir,' Rasmus explained. 'We were outnumbered and felt that attacking from the enemy's rear would prove to be a more successful strategy, as indeed it did.'

Norrey, Bent and Wob nodded with the guilty, wide-eyed enthusiasm of men who had all just agreed to tell the same lie.

'Vilmar.' Gunnar's eyes lost focus and he bunched his hands into a fist to stop them shaking. Sander wondered if this was his first real taste of combat. 'Where's Vilmar?'

Norrey found the boy face down in the bluebells, the arrow stuck in his neck. There was nothing they could do now but bury him.

Sander kneeled down by the poor dwarf, who had stopped thrashing in pain and was now breathing in short, irregular bursts. His legs had been pulverised by the troll. He was dying and he knew it.

'I left the village for help.' The dwarf's voice was faint and rasping as he struggled for breath between words. 'I was grabbed by these bandits as I entered the forest. I tried to explain, I'm going for help, I said, I'm going for help, but they wouldn't listen.'

'What's your name, friend?' Sander asked.

'Lowri.' He winced and clutched at the remains of the arrow in his crushed leg. 'Gods, the pain.'

'Someone find a willow tree,' Sander snapped at the others. 'Find a willow tree, cut a few slivers of bark and bring them to me.'

Malachy, Norrey, Bent and Wob shuffled in circles, looking at the Stone Forest around them as if trying to recall when they last saw a willow tree.

'Now, people!' Sander shouted. Gunnar jabbed a thumb and his men ran off in different directions.

'Left for help?' Sander turned back to Lowri. 'Where from? What help?'

'Rynley, that's my village, it was... Oh gods, you've never seen anything like it. Completely destroyed by the mountain. So many dead, but there are a few left on the other side of the river. I told them I would bring someone. I told them help would come...' Lowri coughed and grabbed Sander's arm. 'Have you come to help?'

Sander hesitated, wondering what to say, leaving a gap for Gunnar to blunder in.

'I'm afraid not,' the captain said. 'We are on a mission and cannot allow—'

'Yes! Yes, we are, we're here to help.' Sander nodded, taking Lowri's head in his hands. 'Don't listen to him, he's an idiot. We're the first and more will come. We have food, water and blankets for your friends, your family. They'll be fine. The village will be rebuilt before the winter.'

'You promise?' The dwarf smiled, his eyelids heavy.

'Absolutely, my friend. I look forward to sharing a pint with you in the new tavern.'

'That would... that would be nice...' Lowri's head slumped back and a last breath left his body with a sigh.

Malachy was first to return with the willow bark. 'Got it,' he panted.

'Don't worry,' Sander said quietly. 'He's not in pain any more.' He looked up at Malachy, who was reprising his *Don't-you-say-a-thing* expression, his Elvish ears safely tucked under his hat. Sander gave him a microscopic shake of the head: *Your-secret-is-safe-with-me.*

'I don't much care for being called an idiot, Noviciate Bree,' Gunnar pouted.

'A person's final moments are precious, Captain,' Sander said as he lowered the dwarf's body into the bluebells. 'Why make them more difficult than they need to be?'

Norrey, Wob and Bent arrived next, all empty-handed. 'Don't we have to put a stake through his heart or something?' Bent asked.

'That's vampires.' Wob rolled his eyes. 'Dwarves you bury with gold or they come back from the dead.'

'He's not magical, you morons, he's just short,' Sander snapped. 'Dragons, merpeople, mages, trolls – all magical, yes? Poor Lowri was a dwarf. A race of people a little below average height. You knew that, right? Please tell me you knew that.' Sander ground his teeth as he got to his feet and looked at the sorry crew before him. 'Gods wept. The King's Cavalry, eh? The best there is? I despair that my life is in your hands.' He turned on Gunnar. 'You, Captain, gave up the high ground and led us into what was clearly a trap, and when we had to fight, half your men ran off and all your shouting couldn't bring them back. You might not care for being called an idiot, Gunnar, but your actions tell their own story.' Sander strode past the captain and started climbing up the side of the bowl.

'Where do you think you're going?' Gunnar asked.

'I'm going to Connal Lake,' Sander said, not even looking back. 'You can follow me. Unlike any of you lot, I actually know the bloody way.'

Oskar's Questions

Pain was a fact of life now for Oskar. He understood that it would always be there, like the weather and the mountains and the sea. Even lying completely still, his body burned. He was permanently taut, his muscles and tendons frozen in tension, his whole being clenched tight like a fist. The smallest movement broke his scabbed skin and left him gasping. Worst of all, it was so exhausting that he could barely think straight. All night he had tried to comprehend what had happened to the world – to him – but there were too many unanswered questions. The only witness to his pain was a solitary chicken in its cage, its companions having been served up in lieu of the soiled rations before they picked up fresh supplies in Port Byle. She was, no doubt, the most prolific egg layer of the lot. Oskar reflected mournfully that she perhaps served a greater purpose in the world than he ever would.

Yanick came down into the hold. Instinctively, Oskar backed away, hissing in pain. He was manacled to the deck. And not with a mere pin this time.

'That's an iron lock from Sachari, laddie.' Yanick carried a bucket and a ladle, which he set down by Oskar. 'And I have the only key. No chance for you to go sneaking around in the middle of the night, spoiling our food, drowning rats in the rum.'

He grinned yellow teeth, then reached back to tie his long white hair in a pony-tail. With a graceful swoop, he sat cross-legged before Oskar, then swirled the ladle in the bucket a little before taking it out and proffering it to the boy.

Oskar hesitated, eyes flitting between the ladle and Yanick's face, trying to read for any kind of duplicity.

'Don't worry. I'm under orders to keep you alive, son.' Yanick took a sip of the rum himself. 'If you die, I die.'

He offered the ladle again and the boy leaned forward and lapped it up like a kitten.

'Why the act?' Yanick asked. 'From the moment we found you,

you played the fool. Even around your mother. You *lied* to your *mother*?' Yanick's face wrinkled in disgust at that.

Oskar fought back a smile. This man was a cold-blooded murderer who led a vicious gang of cutthroats who revelled in torture and torment, and yet lying to your mother was apparently the worst crime in the world.

'It wasn't...' Oskar coughed and choked on his words. It was the first time he had spoken without screaming since he was brought back on board. Words didn't come easily. Yanick fed him the ladle of rum again, and the liquid felt syrupy and warm in his throat. 'It wasn't an act.' His tongue felt thick in his swollen mouth and his words were slow and clumsy, but merely speaking his mind aloud was almost as liberating as having his chains removed. 'I don't know what happened. I woke up one morning... and my mind was clear.'

'That easy, was it?' Yanick's heavy-lidded eyes remained unimpressed.

'I know it sounds ridiculous, but it's true. You hear of miracles, of the blind being able to see, of the lame walking. Perhaps it was a miracle?'

'Ach, you're not one of those Faith converts, are you? Had one of them on me ship last year. Had to keel-haul the cunt just to shut him up.'

Oskar tried to speak but could only croak, so he shook his head instead.

Yanick gave him more rum and he drank it greedily, the warmth of it washing over him. Even the ever-present pain was subsiding a little.

'I think it was the moon,' Oskar said finally. Since that night, his hearing, sight and strength had only become stronger, his mind sharper. 'That night... something changed.'

'Aye, you're not wrong there.' Yanick cackled.

'What happened?'

'The Lapis Moon. It's gone, lad. Destroyed.'

'How?'

'Buggered if I know. Some say it was old and crumbled into dust and that our world is next. Others reckon it was hit by a star or another moon. Some say it was the wrath of the Goddess, but if I hear any more of that nonsense on my ship, I'll feed them to the sharks.' Yanick gave Oskar another sip of rum. 'It's gone and for good, and now my tide charts don't make a lick of sense, and it took magic with it. All except your sister's, o' course.'

'She's alive?'

'She was a couple of days ago.'

'You saw her?'

'I have eyes and ears in Port Byle. They get word from Haldor to me. She's doing as she's told, and she's the only reason you're alive.'

'I'm a hostage?'

'That you are, laddie. And you should be grateful. That lot on deck want to flay you alive and I'm telling you now, that's not an exaggeration.'

'She does magic for you – she still has magic, yes? – and all the time, she's worried that I'm in a prison somewhere?'

Yanick's hand moved so fast that Oskar didn't have time to dodge the heavy slap across his cheek. A new pain. Just what he needed.

'Too many questions, boy.'

'I'm sorry.' Oskar bowed his head. 'I'm sorry for everything I've done. I only want to go home. To be with my sister. You can understand that, can't—'

Another slap, harder, stinging around the ear this time. Oskar shut up and kept his head down.

'Do you have any idea how many of those bastards up there want this ship?' Yanick spittled into Oskar's ear. His voice was low. He didn't want to be heard, and for the first time, Oskar detected something like fear in the captain's voice. 'Every last one of them thinks they can do a better job than me, and there isn't one who wouldn't cut my throat in my sleep if they thought they could get away with it.' Yanick grabbed Oskar's jaw and yanked the boy's head up so their eyes met. 'You have made me look a fool, boy. I have to show them what happens to anyone who tries that. The punishment is brutal and will continue to be brutal. I have to show them who's in charge. You will suffer. And you will go on suffering until I am satisfied that the job is done.'

Yanick seized Oskar's hair and pulled him to his feet. The boy yelped as his knees buckled, but Yanick gripped his neck to keep him upright.

'You can stand, yes?' Yanick nodded, releasing his hold. Oskar wavered but stayed upright.

'Where...' Oskar found himself breathless merely standing on two feet. 'Where are we going?'

'You're going nowhere.' Yanick rapped the ceiling with the ladle. Some kind of signal. There were cheers of approval from above and the clatter of boots rushing across the deck as the crew gathered.

'What's happening?'

'The next stage of your penance, boy.' Above Yanick, the *Queen Mathilde*'s deck split in two as the crew opened the hold doors. A gust of sea breeze billowed around the hold, blowing out the lamps and stirring up little eddies of flour. Bright sunlight stabbed Oskar's eyes. He blinked them shut.

'If you can stand, you can fight. You ready to fight?' the captain asked.

'F-fight? What?' Oskar dared to squint open his eyes to see a chubby dark-skinned boy descend the steps, pass Yanick and walk with a steady pace straight to where Oskar was chained. Oskar didn't know his name but recognised him as a cabin boy. Bottom of the ship's food chain, lower even than Craig, tormented by the rest of the crew and someone with a lot to prove.

As the boy got closer to Oskar, he shuffled his feet like the Sabley Village Springtide Dancers, and then, very much *unlike* the Sabley Village Springtide Dancers, he punched Oskar right on the nose.

It was a weak hit, fumbling and uncertain, but Oskar saw stars and a roar of approval came from the crew gathered on the deck above. As Oskar clutched his throbbing nose and learned to cope with this new pain, he glanced up to see the cabin boy circling the hold, arms held high in triumph.

'Again, Padrig!' the cries came from above. 'Do him!'

Compared to the first punch, the second was more confident. Oskar heard a crack come from somewhere inside his face, then an incredibly sharp pain right below his eye. The boy had broken his cheek-bone.

'You want this to end?' Yanick's voice came from the deck. Oskar twisted his head up to see the man with the long white hair, now untied again and whipped about by the sea breeze, looking down into the fight pit with his crew slavering behind him like a pack of ravenous dogs. 'You want this to finish?'

Oskar nodded, his head trembling.

'Then fight!' Yanick bellowed, and the noise from the crew was unlike anything Oskar had heard before. A guttural lust for blood that started in their bellies and came out of their slack, drooling mouths like a dragon's roar.

'Fight me! Fight me!' the cabin boy screeched as he rained down blows on Oskar.

Oskar fell to the deck and curled into a ball and, as one rib cracked, he caught the gaze of the sole surviving chicken in her cage. She watched him impassively, her head tilted to one side, flapping her wings when startled by the yelling. Oskar realised that he and the chicken shared the same fate: caged until dead. The only way out of here was to die. It would ease his pain and free his sister.

If he had to die, there had to be some way to take all of these bastards with him.

Daffin

Rosheen and Bowden had stayed with the boat on the rocky shore of the merclan island from the dead of night, all through the morning, then on till the late afternoon. He kept an eye on her to ensure she wouldn't escape, pausing only to snort phlegm into his mouth and hock it into the water.

The lake changed from green, to grey, to blue, then to white when the sun moved behind the Lapis ring. Its shimmering sent Rosheen into a stupor. And all the while, she was trying not to listen to the distant screams that sporadically broke the gentle hiss of waves on shingle, trying to convince herself that she had nothing to do with this, that the bloodshed would have happened sooner or later even without her help.

Most of the merclan were slaughtered in their sleep. There was a nest by a weir at the centre of the island where they all gathered at night, and that's where Bowden's crew headed. They were big men but moved like cats through the thick woodland, stepping so softly that the grass sprang back upright after they had trodden on it.

The first few screams startled those left alive and a handful slipped away into the river that led to the lake, and that's what took the time: hunting them down, blocking their only escape and making sure they were all dead.

Not long after sunup, there was an earthquake.

The pebbles on the beach rattled like a tambourine and the surface of the water briefly retreated then came rushing over the shore, breaking beyond the treeline and settling in puddles in the wood. Bowden and Rosheen said nothing, but shared confused looks as they wrung out their soaked boots.

Only seven of Bowden's men returned to the boat, cleaning the scarlet merblood from their blades and carrying three heavy hessian sacks. One had been killed by a merman described by the returning survivors as a 'complete psychopath', which Rosheen thought was either high praise, a complete absence of irony or a combination of both.

None of them was particularly concerned by the death of their companion. Indeed, Bowden asked three times if they were sure that all the 'fishes' were dead. He was ready to send them back again until they emptied the hessian sacks. Twenty-seven heads rolled onto the rocks. Twenty-seven merpeople as per the last census of the island a year ago. Rosheen's heart turned to ice when she saw that three of them were children, their eyes closed in eternal sleep.

Rosheen found herself convulsing and vomiting into the waves, where her bile mingled with Bowden's phlegm. Some of Bowden's men laughed. Or, rather, they made that humourless, guttural bark that passed for laughter in their ranks.

'C'mon, back on the boat,' Bowden ordered.

Rosheen gestured to the heads. 'You're just leaving them there?'

'Too many to take with us,' Bowden said, scratching the stubble on his chin.

'Won't your master want some kind of proof?' Rosheen tried to put a sneer in her voice, but it broke a little and she had to choke back another sob.

'He's not my master.' Bowden fixed her with a murderous look. 'And he trusts my word. Now get on the fucking boat.'

Leaving the heads on the shore, they rowed back to the mainland. The chill wind bit Rosheen's skin, but she was beyond caring about the cold. She felt hollow inside, and a sickness gnawed at her stomach that she knew would never leave her.

Arriving on the mainland, they were interrupted by a ragged group of dwarvish miners and their families – refugees heading south on the Emerwick Road. Bowden and his men ignored them, moving off the road and back into the wood, but Rosheen stayed to speak with a few, grateful for the distraction of conversation. And that was how she learned that the earthquake had been caused by Mount Aderyn falling from the sky, destroying entire villages. The refugees begged for food, the warmth of a fire, but Bowden had returned, looking for Rosheen. He drew his sword and told them to keep moving.

Later that night, Bowden released a pigeon into the sky. It veered left, then went flapping up over the grey Connal Lake, eventually fading into the dust-specked sky. It would home its way to Haldor Frang, carrying a coded message reassuring him that all was well, and so Rosheen's brother Oskar would live another day.

Rosheen had noticed that this was always when Bowden's men were at their most twitchy. They knew that if she were to attack or flee now, it gave her the longest time to rush back to Agrona and try to save her brother.

Rosheen's truth-seeing skills were still strong and she knew that Haldor genuinely had no clue where her brother was. There was no point in escape. Not yet. He was a clever bastard and appeared to have considered every possible eventuality. Her job was to think up something he hadn't foreseen, but it hadn't come to her yet.

Rosheen watched the pigeon disappear into the distance. Night was falling and a bitter wind swept in from the lake. She and Bowden returned to the shelter of the camp, not a word exchanged between them. The plan was to wait here for the night and see if Sander's group came this way. They would give them till morning, and if Sander didn't show, they would move south to the Andraste Coast where the last surviving merclan were settled in a coral sinkhole.

Bowden joined his remaining men, inspecting the salmon smoking on their fire. Rosheen stoked her own fire, a smaller one away from the others', and reflected on a day that would haunt her for the rest of her life. Her staff was in its calfskin bag. The power of the Lapis stone was still feeding her, but what use was that if she couldn't stop more killings? If she couldn't help refugees desperate for food and shelter?

She began to wonder if Oskar really was alive. If all this wasn't some sick deception on Haldor's part. No, she had seen the truth in his eyes. Oskar was alive. And she would find him. She had to keep believing that.

After a meal that tasted of nothing and a drink of gritty water, Rosheen was ready for sleep. She stood, shouldered the calfskin bag with her staff inside and headed into the dark of the wood.

'Where are you going, witch?' Bowden said, his mouth full of wet, pink salmon flesh.

The rest of the group stopped talking and turned to look at her, their leather jerkins creaking as they did so.

'A piss, then sleep,' she said. *Or as much sleep as I can get around you murdering bastards*, she thought.

'Be quick,' he warned her.

'I'll be as long as it takes, okay?' she snapped back with weary bravado.

She found a spot by a creek, rested the staff beside her, scanned the bank for wiping leaves, and squatted.

After a few moments, she heard footsteps swishing through the long grass towards her. The noise came from the south, so it wasn't one of Bowden's men, and as the hooded traveller stepped into the moonlight, she could make out the features of an older man with a wispy beard and a nose and cheeks reddened by what she suspected was a lifetime of excessive indulgence in wines and spirits.

He carried a pack on his back that was almost as large as he was. He hefted it onto the creek's bank and it landed with the tinkle of bottles jostling for position inside. He undid his breeches and began to pee.

'When you're done, be on your way,' Rosheen whispered and the man jumped, sending his urine splashing on his boots.

'Good lady, do forgive me,' he said in a refined voice more at home in a royal court than a ditch. 'I had no idea you were there. I shall do my business and be gone before—'

'Be quiet!' she hissed. 'Seriously. Go now, you're in danger here.'

'Danger, you say?' He immediately began tucking his bits away in his breeches. 'Then I shall wish you a good night and...' He reached for his pack, and hesitated. 'Does that put you in danger, too? Can I help at all?'

'No, just—'

'Who's this tosser?' Another voice came out of the darkness. One of Bowden's men arrived behind Rosheen, the Tiarnan with the white tattoos scored across his black skin. She looked around, pulling up her leggings as she did so. That would have to wait till later.

'He's no one,' she said. 'Some pedlar having a piss.'

'You were talking to him,' the Tiarnan said.

'Yes, I was telling him to sod off.'

'And I am happy to oblige.' The pedlar smiled, doffing his hat and reaching for his pack. 'A splendid evening to you both.'

'You're coming with me,' the Tiarnan said, beckoning him over.

'He's done nothing wrong,' Rosheen said, picking up her calfskin bag containing the staff. 'Let him go.'

The Tiarnan shoved past her and grabbed the pedlar and his pack before he could move.

And so they found themselves standing around Bowden's fire, and now that Rosheen could see the pedlar close-up, she swore that she knew him from somewhere.

'My name is Daffin.' He bowed low before Bowden. 'I am a vendor of cures and herbal remedies, purveyor of ancient and mythological relics and consultant to three of the kings and queens of the Nine Kingdoms, and many more princes, dukes and duchesses besides.'

'Why did you bring him here?' Bowden said to the Tiarnan, glowering at him from under heavy and disapproving eyelids. 'What did I say? What were my orders?'

The Tiarnan bristled, knowing he had made a mistake, yet inhaling deeply and expanding his chest in a defiant, animalistic display. Bowden, unimpressed, turned his attention to Daffin.

'Why were you spying on us?' Bowden was a great believer in getting straight to the point. He sharpened his hunting knife on a leather strap as he spoke, its *scritch-scritch* noise accompanying the conversation like a lion scratching its claws.

'Spying?' Daffin splayed an innocent hand over his heart. 'Good sir, I was simply taking my ease en route to an urgent appointment tomorrow morning with a man in Emerwick. Experience has taught me to stay out of other people's business. I shall bother you no longer and we shall pretend this never happened. I wish you well on your journey.'

'What's in the bag?' Bowden nodded at Daffin's pack.

'My wares: natural restoratives and panaceas for every eventuality.'

'Business must be booming,' Bowden said. 'Now magic's out the window.'

Rosheen saw Daffin's face tremble, almost as if he were trying not to burst into tears, as if he were trying to bury a deep sadness. *Oh gods, he's a mage,* she thought. *He has to be, and if I saw that, then so did Bowden.*

'Indeed it is, sir.' Daffin sniffed himself upright again, back in character. 'Why, only today, I was attending to the people of Rynley, who were cursed terribly with a plague. Were it not for my services, many more would have died. You would do well to avoid it for a few days, at least. Poor, wretched folk.'

'Rynley?' Bowden stopped sharpening his blade, looked up and smiled.

Rosheen knew what was coming. 'Bowden, let him go. He hasn't done anything.'

Bowden ignored her and kept his gaze on Daffin, looking for tells. 'What's your name again?'

Daffin bowed once more. 'Daffin, sir, I—'

'Daffin what?'

'Daffin Ogham.'

Rosheen couldn't place the name but, damn it, she knew him from somewhere and she wished he would shut up and go.

'Where you from?' Bowden asked.

'Originally? Uhm, I was born in Taranis. Of course, it wasn't the magnificent citadel we all know now. Back then—'

'No, where'd you come from today?'

'Rynley, as I said.' Daffin dared to briefly glance at Rosheen, perhaps searching to see if he was saying the right thing. He surely knew that the mercenary was on to him.

'Bowden, what is the point of this?' she said. 'Let him go.'

'Rynley?' Bowden continued. 'Dwarf mining village? In the shadow of Mount Aderyn?'

'Ye-es.' Daffin nodded with a smile.

'Which fell from the sky this morning destroying everything beneath it.'

Daffin stumbled on that. 'It... what?'

'The mountain.' Bowden started sharpening his knife once more. A faster rhythm now, as if he was going to need it soon. 'Dropped like a stone on Rynley this morning. Wiped it out.'

'My... goodness,' Daffin said, genuinely shocked. 'Those poor people.'

'They was all cursed with the plague a minute ago.'

'Well, yes, but one must have sympathy,' Daffin said hurriedly. 'I surely just missed it.'

'No.' Bowden shook his head. 'There's no way you'd miss a sodding mountain tumbling out of the sky. So, do you want to have another go at your bullshit story?'

'I... beg your pardon?' Daffin said, with a flash of anger.

And that's when something clicked into place in Rosheen's mind and she finally recognised him.

His name was Jago Rees, a good man, a warlock who roamed the south offering his services to kings and peasants alike, with a particular skill for healing. They had never met, but she had heard him speak at gatherings of mages and once saw him attending to the wounded after a skirmish in the fields of Arranrod. And now he was reduced to masquerading as a pedlar of placebos.

'What's your name again?' Bowden's voice was flat, almost bored.

'Daffin. Now look, I'm in something of a hurry, and—'

'What's in the bag?'

'I told you – my wares.'

'Where you from?'

'I think I've made myself quite clear.'

'Where you from?'

'Rynley, and before that—'

'And where you going?'

'Eriworth. Now, if you're done—'

'No, mate, no.' A gravelly laugh worked its way up from Bowden's belly as he slowly shook his head. 'You said you had an urgent appointment tomorrow morning with a man in Emerwick.'

Rosheen saw Jago's eyes dart as he reran the conversation in his mind.

'Emerwick,' Bowden said again. 'Not Eriworth.'

Jago stammered for a response, 'Yes... uh, yes, that's what I meant. I... was mistaken.'

'What's your name?'

'Daffin.'

'Where you from?'

'Rynley.'

'Where you going?'

'… Eriworth.'

'You alone?'

'Am I what?'

'That's enough.' Rosheen pulled her staff from its calfskin bag, revealing the glowing blue Lapis stone. A few of the men took an involuntary step back, but Bowden stood his ground, while Jago's eyes lit up like a child gazing at a birthday cake. He was completely entranced by the stone.

'I knew it, I bloody knew it,' Jago said, dropping the educated accent and babbling with excitement. 'I thought I could feel the old power again. There were rumours that stones fell in the White Sea… It works, yes? You have the power again?'

'Shut up!' Bowden backhanded Jago across the face and the old warlock yelped like a child.

'Let him go,' Rosheen said, the bloodlust in her rising, the same desire to lash out that had saved her in Haldor's wine cellar.

Bowden stepped forward. 'Or what? You'll kill us? Do that and you know what happens to your brother.'

'Unlike you, I don't make murder my first resort,' she said, trying to resist the ugly desire to strike out and kill him. 'I could blind you, cripple you, hurt you just enough so you can still send those messages back to Haldor.' She could, and she knew it would be easy.

'Then do it.'

The blink of an eye passed, and Rosheen realised that she had hesitated too long.

'Come on, girl.' Bowden took a step closer to her. His grin was gone and he was deadly serious and sincere, almost begging for death. 'What you waiting for?'

'Yes!' Jago screeched. 'What are you waiting for? Do it!'

Bowden looked annoyed by Jago, as if he'd forgotten he was there. Bowden gave a tiny nod to the Tiarnan who drew a dagger and stabbed Jago three times in the neck. The old mage's eyes bulged in astonishment as he fell dead into a patch of snowdrops, spraying a fine mist of blood onto their white petals.

Rosheen felt numb as she watched Jago's blood stain the white flowers. All the pent-up anger in her had nowhere to go and now only made her hands tremble, and she hated herself for it.

'What you don't understand, girl, is we all signed up for a suicide mission.' Bowden scratched lazily at his unshaven chin and gestured at the Tiarnan, who stepped forward. 'C'mere.'

'Boss?'

'You fucked up bringing the old mage here,' Bowden said. 'I made it clear no one was to come close to the camp.'

The Tiarnan looked to the others for help, but no one came forward. 'Yeah, but I thought he was a spy, I thought—'

Bowden gave another signal and the man behind the Tiarnan drew a knife and slit his throat. The Tiarnan's head was pulled back at an unnatural angle, making the wound yawn open and sending a shower of blood flooding from his neck. He fell into a deathly embrace with Jago.

Rosheen's heart was racing now, unsure who would die next.

'Those birds I send back ain't only for you, they're for all of us,' Bowden told her. 'We're dead men walking. Haldor has our families, too, y'see. If we come back alive but empty-handed, they die.' He gestured towards the men at his side. 'This one's sister, this one's missus... my old pa, all of us. If we do a runner, they all die. If we don't kill the king's mage, they die. Only our success or our deaths will guarantee their lives. And as far as we're concerned, there won't be many of us coming back from this alive.'

'That's sick,' Rosheen said.

'That's Haldor Frang,' Bowden said, nodding in agreement. 'He will do whatever is necessary to win, but he also sticks to his word. So do us all a favour and kill us where we stand. Our families will be freed. The next bird I send will report that our Tiarnan here died in the field. Haldor will know that he fulfilled his obligation and his wife and daughter will be released. The only ones who can lose are you and your brother. So kill us. Please.'

Rosheen lowered the staff.

'Thought not,' Bowden said, disappointed. He snapped his fingers at his men. 'Dump these two in the lake. I don't reckon the mage is coming this way. Even if he does, there's nothing here for him. He'll head south for the coast. And we'll be waiting for him.'

Oskar's Final Fight

Oskar watched Craig light the lamps with his one good hand, his broken fingers swaddled in a bandage stained brown with lamp oil. Every time Craig reached up to light a lamp, he winced. *It hurts*, Oskar thought, and Craig's pain made him feel good. He couldn't be sure if he liked this new feeling. He thought back to living in Sabley, when he never had a bad thought about anyone, not even for those who were cruel to him. Alby Clim talked of how the best way to win a fight was never to start one, but Oskar was fairly sure that the mage had never been kidnapped, had his father murdered and endured unspeakable torture at the hands of ruthless pirates. Or, if he had, his magic would have seen him through the ordeal. It was easy to spout homilies when you could summon enough energy to kill someone on the spot. Oskar wondered what Alby Clim was doing now. How he was coping without his powers to keep everyone in line. The old mage must have made enemies in the past and they would now be looking to exact their revenge. Would he even still be alive?

Craig winced and swore again, gently flexing his broken fingers. Like a boy with a sore tooth, he couldn't leave them alone.

In a strange way, Oskar's own constant pain had become more bearable. It was part of him now, like an extra arm or leg. It wore him down, bent his back, but he was slowly learning to cope with it, and pain meant he was alive, at least.

Craig kicked him in the ribs and it all came back in a white-hot burst of agony. The ship's boy grabbed Oskar's hair with his good hand. 'I'll be the one fighting you later.' Craig spat into Oskar's face, panting like an excited dog. 'I gave the captain my rum ration for the honour.' Then his voice became a whisper as he moved closer, his words puffing into Oskar's ear, making the hairs on Oskar's neck stand on end. 'He expects me to give you a beating like all the others, but y'know what? I'm going to kill you. He doesn't think I can do it with a broken hand, but all I need to do is get you down on the deck and step on your throat. I'll crack it with the heel of my boot, and

I'll watch as you choke to death. You'll be dead before the sun goes down. How does it feel knowing that, eh? Oh, I'll get a flogging, but it'll be worth it. Some of the crew says if the captain does flog me, then they'll string the old bastard up, too. That's how much they all hate you, you little shit. Think on that.'

Craig released Oskar's hair with a jerk and stomped back up the steps to the deck without another word.

Oskar didn't doubt for one heartbeat that Craig meant what he said. Death had preoccupied most of Oskar's thoughts since the fights began, but Yanick wouldn't let him die. He always stopped the fights before any real damage was done. He somehow knew exactly how much pain Oskar could endure. Oskar had made attempts to fight back in the hope that this would impress Yanick and bring the fights to an end, but the boy didn't have it in him. His half-hearted swings and weak punches were no match for the anger and bloodlust that simmered in every member of the crew. Their constant need to fight and inflict harm felt alien to Oskar. And yet he burned with a desire to see them all die. He knew he had to act now, with this next fight.

He was exhausted. Every part of him was in pain, and that drained him of every ounce of energy. He wanted to sleep now. He thought back to when he was a boy and broke his wrist falling from a tree. He ran crying to Mother, who called for Rosheen. His sister, only vaguely aware of her magic skills back then, had been tending to Anzu at the time but still rushed to help him. She took Oskar's broken wrist in her hands, closed her eyes and repeated the same word again and again: *Heal... Heal...*

A similar exhaustion had overcome him then and he fell into the deepest, most comforting slumber he could ever recall. And when he woke, his wrist was in one piece again. As Oskar tried to sleep, he muttered that same word to himself again and again in the vain hope that saying it would take some of the pain away. 'Heal... Heal...'

The fight was due to start at sundown, after the crew had dropped anchor and lowered the *Queen Mathilde*'s sails for the night, leaving it to rise and fall and sway in the Ocean's Hand.

Oskar had a short, deep and comforting sleep unlike any he had known before and, as the remnants of strange dreams faded away, he was woken by raised voices on deck. Yanick arguing with Glaw and Craig. Apparently, Craig's cast-iron certainty that he would be fighting tonight was anything but. More angry voices followed from the crew. Oskar had no doubt that this was a fight they all wanted to see and he knew exactly why.

Oskar prayed to whatever gods might be listening to give the captain the strength he needed to stick to his guns, but those angry voices became louder and more mutinous, and soon Yanick caved in to popular opinion.

The hold doors were hauled back to rapturous cheers from the crew, oil lamps dancing with the sudden movement of air. The Greystone Moon was bright tonight and gave Craig a ghostly glow as he descended the steps, raising his bandaged hand high. He was shirtless, revealing a few toned muscles under the puppy fat. A crude tattoo of a dagger stabbing into his chest shuddered as he jumped the last few steps.

Oskar got to his feet, the manacle and chains tugging at his ankle. He winced, but only from habit. Any movement was usually accompanied by stabs of blistering agony from all over his body, but now... nothing.

No pain.

He flexed his hands, his arms, rotated his shoulders. Not even a twinge of discomfort. If anything, after his refreshing sleep he felt as if he could leap overboard and swim all the way home. What had happened?

He reached under his tattered shirt, around to his back where Yanick's whip had split his flesh.

No scars, no blisters. Nothing but smooth skin.

Heal... Heal...

'Against my better judgement,' Yanick shouted above the crew's hubbub, 'I am allowing Craig a fight for retribution.' The crew roared their approval and Yanick waved them back to a low rumble. 'Craig – you've been warned. Keep it short and no permanent damage. Oskar...'

Oskar looked up to Yanick's pitying face.

'Keep telling yourself that it'll soon be over, lad.' Yanick raised an arm then brought it swinging down. 'Fight!'

Before Oskar could move, Craig was on him, his good fist finding Oskar's head in a flurry of jabs that sent Oskar reeling. Had this happened before his healing sleep, it might have knocked Oskar out, but with his renewed energy, he stayed upright

A brief look of confusion crossed Craig's face as he danced back on hopping feet. Setting his jaw, he sprinted forwards, aiming a kick at Oskar's face. Oskar's hand was a blur as it found Craig's ankle. He twisted it, sending the ship's boy crashing into the chicken's cage, smashing it to pieces. The chicken celebrated its newfound freedom by flapping its wings and dashing around in circles.

With Craig's fall there came a bigger, pleasantly surprised roar from the crew – *finally, a real fight!* – and with their enthusiasm came a surge of energy in Oskar. He pinned the ship's boy down. But, having got him where he wanted him, Oskar didn't know what to do next.

Craig did, and his knee connected with Oskar's groin, followed by a kick that sent him spiralling across the hold deck, tripping over his chains and tumbling into a sack of rice. Before Oskar could get his breath back, Craig was leaning a knee on his belly and grasping Oskar's skull, his thumbs pushing down on Oskar's eyes.

'No, no, please!' Oskar began to panic, his legs kicking helplessly, his arms flailing. His hands found Craig's head, then his ears. Oskar gripped both ears, pulled Craig closer and bit down hard on the boy's nose. There was a crunch. Something gave way. Oskar couldn't be sure if it was one of his teeth or Craig's nose, but then the ship's boy screamed and staggered back, clutching his face, blood streaming through his fingers. The crew jeered again, enjoying Oskar's newfound violent streak.

Craig looked at his palm, the blood from his broken nose filling the lines on his hands like the red veins on a chard leaf. 'You fuggin' barf-dud!' he cried as he flicked the excess blood away.

Oskar kicked out before Craig could hit him again.

To everyone's astonishment, not least his own, Craig flew through the air. He slumped into a pile of flour sacks the same way Oskar's father would fall into his rocking chair at the end of a long day. From the tops of the sacks came little puffs of flour dust, shooting straight up then slowing into tiny whirling eddies which danced around in the warm air near the oil lamps.

Next came a *whoomph* like a sail catching the wind. There was a blinding light and Oskar instinctively closed his eyes, feeling an intense heat warm his cheeks. He opened his eyes again to find that Craig now wore flames around his head like a bright hood, which fluttered up his waving arms as he tried to pat them out. All the while, he was screaming, calling for his Uncle Glaw. Oskar saw the flour dust around Craig shimmer and ripple. In an instant, the ship's boy was burning from head to foot, his body a writhing black silhouette shrouded in orange and blue fury. The ship's hull was alight now, too, and out of the corner of his eye, Oskar saw Yanick leap down from the deck into the hold, pulling off his shirt to help put out the fire.

Craig's flaming body was too hot for Yanick to get close. The boy ran blindly, bumping into the steps leading up to the deck, spinning clumsily, losing any sense of direction as he continued running through a bulkhead door into the aft hold compartment.

Oskar did not know that was where they stored the gunpowder. Oskar didn't even know there was gunpowder on the ship. So he was completely unprepared for deafening crack of thunder that now sent him flying through the air and smashing into the hull. Countless splinters of wood sprayed around him and the ship lurched as it broke in two.

Ice-cold seawater flooded the hold as the *Queen Mathilde* rolled and tumbled on the tide. Oskar watched as the aft half of the ship, a burning carcass that briefly made him think of the walnut shells his father cracked at Year's End, broke apart into a scattered mass of burning debris. The startled crew disappeared beneath the rolling waves, dragged under by the Ocean's Hand. Oskar shut his eyes against the stinging water as it lashed at his face. In his mind, he thought for a moment that he could see the crew as pinpricks of light, flailing in the water as they sank, snuffed out one by one as they drowned. Oskar shook his head clear and opened his eyes as his shattered half of the ship rolled again then pitched forwards, making his stomach turn.

Yanick was thrown against the steps and they broke like twigs. Oskar gripped his chains and took a deep breath as what remained of the *Queen Mathilde* was consumed by the deep, sighing the last note of its song as it slipped beneath the surface.

Trapped in the sinking hold, water sloshed into Oskar's ears, salty brine filled his mouth and everything went dark as he was tugged further down, his manacles bolted to the wreckage of the hull. He kicked and thrashed about in a hopeless attempt to wriggle free, but the Sachari iron held him in a grip that it would never surrender. Just as Oskar began to lose hope, he felt something brush against him, then a hand grabbing his ankle, the manacle twisting and chafing against his skin, then breaking open.

He was free!

A pair of hands then reached under his armpits, clasped across his chest and he felt legs kick them both towards the surface.

In moments, Oskar found himself gasping for air, a wave splashing into his face as Yanick pulled him towards a floating piece of debris.

'Get on, boy!' Yanick gripped the wreckage with one hand while trying to shove Oskar onto it with the other. It was a hold door, big enough for one person to lie flat. Oskar clambered on, pulling himself up using a length of charred rope lashed to the door's handle. He coughed water, some coming back up through his nostrils making him sneeze, and looked around. The moon was bright, the sea calm, but there were no other survivors.

It had all happened so quickly. Where a few moments ago there had been a ship with a crew, now there was nothing more than scraps of wood rocking back and forth on the black waves.

He and Yanick said nothing for a long time, allowing themselves to be swayed by the sea. They were at the mercy of the Ocean's Hand and it felt like the respectful thing to do.

Oskar looked to Yanick for guidance, for leadership, but all he found was a man in shock, as befuddled as he was by this sudden change in fortune. The captain kept turning in the water, looking in every direction as if he'd find his ship rising up behind a rolling wave.

'We should head for shore,' Oskar said when he found his voice.

Yanick said nothing, but coiled the charred rope around his arm and, shivering, rested his head and arms on the hold door and closed his eyes, his body and legs in the sea. It wasn't long before he fell asleep. Oskar was astonished: *How can he sleep?* But soon his own eyelids began to feel heavy as the gentle sway of the Ocean's Hand rocked him to slumber.

Oskar was woken by an unexpected noise: a familiar *bawk?* among all the loud caws from the circling gulls. He opened one eye to see a chicken, his fellow prisoner in the hold, standing on a scrap of the ship's wreckage, riding the swell and heading off for a new life. Oskar wished her well.

The morning sun's light reflected brightly off the sea, making Oskar's eyes pulse, and he squinted as he got his bearings. More and more gulls circled overhead. Did this mean they were near land?

There it was: a thin line of black on the horizon. Too far away to swim. He could only hope that the tide would take him in.

Yanick was still asleep, but it wouldn't be long before he awoke.

What would happen then? Yanick had saved Oskar's life, but for purely selfish reasons: *If you die, I die.* When they reached land, Yanick would protect him, but Oskar would still be his prisoner.

The thought came hard and clear: if he was ever truly going to be free, he had to be rid of Yanick and try to find Rosheen.

It would be simple. He could uncoil the rope around Yanick's arm while he slept and let him slip under the surface, and he would drown as he sank.

Of course, that was simple enough in his head, but the rope was so tightly wound around Yanick's arm that the slightest movement might wake him. And the gulls' cries became increasingly loud as the sun rose higher; any one of them could snap him out of his slumber.

Oskar didn't dare touch the rope but inspected it closely, looking for a spot where he could grip and release it quickly.

'If you're going to do it, *do it*.' Yanick's voice sent a cold flush of fear through Oskar's body. He couldn't tell how long Yanick had been watching him, but Oskar's hesitation had cost him the element of surprise.

He said nothing as they bobbed on the waves.

Yanick shifted, stretching his limbs and yawning. 'The trouble with you, boy, is you—'

With fast but fumbling hands, Oskar unravelled the rope from Yanick's arm and wound it around the captain's neck, pulling as hard as he possibly could. Yanick reached up and pawed at Oskar's head and they both fell into the water.

They tumbled down in a deathly embrace, Yanick punching blindly, biting into Oskar's arm. Oskar pulled the rope tighter, remembering every lash of the whip, every minute spent burning in the sun's glare on the ship's deck, every beating, every drop of piss thrown in his face.

Strength... he thought to himself. *Give me strength.*

There came a pain, as if the muscles in Oskar's arms had torn, followed by a warm feeling as they flexed, and he was able to apply increased pressure around Yanick's neck.

Yanick stopped struggling. A last burst of air slipped from his mouth, his eyes went still and his long white hair drifted gently like palm leaves in a breeze.

Oskar let him go and watched as his captor and tormentor drifted down into the murk. For a moment, Oskar wondered if he should follow him, but that word came to him again. The word he thought of when Craig got the whip: *Good.* He was glad Yanick was dead. He was happy to have killed him. It was good that he was free.

With his renewed strength, Oskar kicked for the surface.

Haldor Frang raised his fist high, bringing his marching army to a halt.

Reports of Bhaltair's Wayland forces combining with the volunteer militias of Andraste had been pouring in for the last two days, and rather than wait to be cornered in the ruins of Castle Agrona with the sea at his back, Haldor was determined to meet them head-on.

Leaving a skeleton force at Agrona, he took his banners and six thousand swords on the Taranis Road to the one place where a large army like Bhaltair's could move from Andraste to Agrona: the Ceezan bridges at the River Alar.

Only to discover that Bhaltair was already waiting for him.

The crafty bastard had already stationed troops on the east bank, blocking his way, and his camp was a well-established sea of tents on a nearby hill. *Good*, thought Haldor, who hated to be idle. *Let's get this over with.*

'Gather the Rigo flash-powder shells,' Haldor told the generals flanking him on horseback. 'We'll start by blowing the bridges, cutting off their supplies and reinforcements. We'll wipe out the troops on the east bank, then we move to the hill and finish off Bhaltair for good.'

There were barks of assent from the generals, who began passing on orders.

'Lord Frang, Lord Frang!' A young messenger came sprinting towards him with a wicker basket. Haldor beckoned the girl forward, took the basket and rewarded her with a coin. She saluted and stood waiting.

Haldor reached inside and retrieved one of his messenger pigeons. They had proven to be less than reliable since the destruction of the Lapis Moon and news from Bowden often came later than expected. For the first few days, Haldor was convinced that Rosheen had been foolish enough to betray him, but when the first two pigeons arrived together with two days' worth of messages, it soon became apparent that it was just the stupid bloody birds. Haldor's astronomer Dagmar had waffled on at length about magnetic fields changing and confusing the birds, but Haldor didn't have time for excuses. He wanted his birds to do what they were trained to do. He unravelled the scroll on the pigeon's leg and read, the smile on his face widening as he did so.

'Good news, my lord?' the messenger girl asked.

Haldor's smile disappeared. 'You're a little eager, lassie. Are you a spy? Should I have you whipped and crucified as a warning to others?'

'N-no, my lord. I only wish to serve.'

'I bet you do. Now piss off before you feel my boot on the back of your head.'

'My lord.' The girl bowed then started to run off.

'Say, girl?' he called after her, and she dashed back to the same spot, bowing once more. 'You know what? You can do me a favour.' He held up the message. 'Make sure word gets back to Bhaltair. The merclan is wiped out and his little expedition will be next. His daughter is as good as dead. Can you do that?'

'I… I'll try, my lord.'

'Repeat it back to me.'

'The merclan is dead. Wiped out. His expedition is next. His daughter…' The messenger girl hesitated, wrestling with the grim news, wondering about this man who celebrated a girl's impending death and weighing it against the value of her own life.

'C'mon, you can say it, they're only words.'

'His daughter is as good as dead!' She snapped another salute. 'All of Bhaltair's camp will know by sunrise, my lord.'

'Make sure of it.' He dismissed her with a jerk of his head and the messenger girl ran off, leaving a trail of dust behind her. Haldor returned his attention to the green pastures before him and as he began to imagine the carnage to come, he felt a familiar warm thrill of excitement in his belly. War was here. His war. On his terms. And he couldn't be happier.

Bodies in the Water

Sander guided Gunnar and his men around the Stone Forest, following the Connal River now, and as the sun began to rise behind the mountains, they finally reached the foot of the Connal Steps, a magnificent array of waterfalls tumbling into bright, aquamarine limestone pools that towered above them.

It was here that the belt of lapis–blue stones draped across the sky looked the most spectacular. A constellation of countless sapphires mingled with the watercolour blushes of the sunset's crimson and purple clouds.

Sander took a moment to admire its magnificence and then defiantly raised his middle finger at it.

He led his horse to the pools, and it lapped up the first clean water they had seen since the collapse of Mount Aderyn. He buried his head in the water, rinsing the dust from his eyes and face. When he came up for air, he found Malachy next to him doing the same and, for once, Orren wasn't stuck to them like a limpet. Finally, Sander had the opportunity to ask the questions that had been bouncing around his head ever since he saw Malachy's ears.

'Who else knows?' Sander asked quietly as he shook his hands dry.

Malachy was more precise in his washing, splashing water on his face, scrubbing vigorously, always keeping his hat on. 'Bent and Wob figured it out, but they know to keep their gobs shut,' he said.

'No one else? Not Gunnar?'

'That chinless wonder?' Malachy snorted. 'No chance.'

'I thought the elves were all dead.'

'Yeah, we might well be.'

'Really? You don't know any others?'

'Humans slaughtered us in the Mage Wars, mate. Would you stick your head over the parapet if you were me?'

'I guess not.' Sander frowned. 'Hang on, the Mage Wars? Just how old are you?'

'Bit personal, that.'

'I'm curious. Elves live for hundreds of years, and you look ancient for a human, so—'

'No idea. You stop counting after the first five hundred, but yeah, I fought in the Mage Wars.'

'You're over five hundred years old?' Sander could barely stop his voice from screeching.

'Tell the whole bloody world, why don't ya?'

'How is that even possible?'

'Magic extends our lifespan,' Malachy said. 'Well, it did till a few days ago.'

'So… you're dying?'

'We're all dying, mate. Some quicker than others. I'm a survivor. I've lasted this long, I'm sure I can manage a while longer. Now shut it. The subject is closed.'

'Isn't this majestic?' Orren's joyful voice broke through the constant rumble of the falls and Sander turned to find her at the bottom of the Steps, her arms reaching upwards. None of her companions replied, but Sander had to concede that the Connal Steps were a sight he would never tire of. 'The hand of the Goddess is more sublime than any artist's,' she declared, making Sander wince. 'How far are we from the lake?' she asked.

'We, uh…' Gunnar stammered as he began unfolding his map.

'This water comes directly from Connal Lake,' Sander said, pointing at the water gushing down the Steps. 'See there? Those paths? They're steep and narrow, but we can lead the horses up and around the pools and terraces. It'll take a few hours, then once we're at the top, it's a short ride to the lake and the Nolwen reservation.'

'We should eat and rest,' Gunnar said, fumbling as he tried to fold the map back on itself. 'We'll make camp and begin our ascent after lunch.'

'Good. We'll get the blood tonight and make for Taranis straight away. If we can avoid any more bandit raids and mountains falling out of the sky, we could be home in two days.'

'You'll kill the horses,' Rasmus said, distressed.

'I'm sorry, but there's more at stake than our four-legged friends,' Sander said. 'We can't afford to waste any more time.'

'And that's *if* we get the blood,' Gunnar sneered. 'How well do you know the Nolwen Clan, Bree? How aggressive are they?'

'They're not aggressive.' Sander despaired at the captain's ignorance. 'Not unless you provoke them. They like to keep themselves to themselves. I was here last summer. We did a bit of trading and I left on good terms. We'll be fine.' He had brought a cart full of tuna, swordfish, bass and bream and they begrudgingly gave him scales, unfertilised eggs and fresh blood, all essential ingredients for a number of key potions. They had said few words, and there were fewer smiles. Crucially, however, they hadn't tried to kill him.

'Of course, you had your magic to mollify them then,' Orren pointed out.

'They didn't need mollifying,' Sander said. 'They're good people and I've always been fair with them. They'll give us what we need, I'm sure of it.'

'Indeed,' Gunnar creaked. 'Let's hope your personal connections and charm compensate for your lack of magical ability. Men, I want you all on alert when we engage the merpeople tomorrow. Be ready for anything.'

It began to dawn on Sander how a rash promise made on an executioner's block was beginning to look like a very tall order. He didn't want to confirm anyone's prejudices, but the merpeople were unpredictable and could be savage when they wanted to be. He thought back to when he was a child growing up on the Andraste Coast. Sander and his father had been out walking their dog, Pike, on the windswept beach; Father was clumsily explaining why Sander's sister Faylen was going away when they heard a voice singing, carried on the sea breeze over the sand. It was innocent, childlike, and yet soared with such power that it stopped them in their tracks. Pike ran away, but Sander's father found himself mesmerised and walking slowly towards it.

They would later disagree on what they saw, but they could at least concur that they found the mermaid resting on a rock. Sander's father was convinced he was looking at a beauty like no other, with glowing skin, shiny blonde hair and eyes that twinkled like sapphires. Sander saw an old hag with blotchy skin that hung off her bones.

His father was completely beguiled and began to lurch towards her with open arms. Sander had heard all the stories about what merpeople did with the humans they captured. They seduced them, drowned them and feasted on their flesh. He'd even seen the body of a fisherman who had been killed by them the previous summer. The poor man had lost both his arms simply by reaching out to a mermaid in the water and had died before the boat could return to port.

Sander stood between his father and the mermaid and somehow found a connection between his mind and the mermaid's. He sent her back into the waves, breaking the spell.

That was the first time he had used his magic in front of his father. In front of anyone. News of his feat spread quickly and he was hired by the local villagers to patrol the coast, sending the merfolk back into the sea or their caves. Soon after that, Ragnall apprenticed him and he left Andraste for good.

That particular mermaid was called Helfina Glenna Grizel of the Jeltse Merclan. She taught Sander filthy jokes and shanties and, in spite of her attempt to kill Sander's father, they became friends. He hadn't thought of her in years and now the memories returned in vivid colour. It all felt so easy back then, and now it was gone for good.

Sander's belly twisted with hunger at the fatty aroma of eggs frying in a pan as they soaked up Norrey's secret recipe of grease, lard and more grease.

As Malachy stoked the fire, Gunnar and his men gathered around in anticipation. In among all the chatter and gushing water from the falls, Sander heard a new noise: a tent flap opening, followed by the gentle pad of feet on the forest floor.

Orren.

She had the same routine before every meal. She washed her hands in the nearest stream, then went searching for herbs. That's what she told them, anyway.

Sander decided that a good walk was what he needed to distract his stomach from its enforced starvation, and he took it upon himself to follow her.

Ever since the encounter with the bandits, Captain Gunnar Jarl had been acting in an increasingly erratic manner. He dithered over every decision, stammered like a nervous child when giving orders and collapsed into his tent in an exhausted heap at the end of the day.

Rasmus was too much of a by-the-book yes-man to complain about his captain's behaviour, and while Norrey, Bent, Wob and Malachy were all clearly wary of their commander's mental state, they were too far down the pecking order to question his orders. Though Sander had noticed a change in them since Vilmar's death. They were edgy, constantly looking over their shoulders, worried where the next attack might come from and who might be next to die. Rather than thinking as a team, they were thinking of themselves, and that could prove fatal when they ran into trouble again, which they surely would. The only one who didn't appear at all concerned was Orren. It was left to Sander to investigate and he had a theory.

He followed Orren at a distance through the wood. He watched as she picked some wild basil and rosemary, which she stuffed into a pouch on the front of her robes. Sander hadn't noticed the pouch before and was disappointed to find that he didn't have one. Probably a perk of advanced Sisterhood. As he looked down to double-check that he was definitely pouchless, he briefly lost sight of her and began to panic as he realised he couldn't quite remember the way back to camp.

His eye was caught by the flap of her yellow robes gliding between the trees and the hunt was back on. He found her crouching in the middle of a bright and lush clearing, the morning sun glowing on an overgrown patch festooned with white flowers, their leaves fluted out and tinged with purple edges. Some had small, spiky pods at the base of the stem, which Orren picked and put in her pouch. Sander recognised them immediately. Any mage would. The flowers were known as Angel's Trumpets; their seed pods were called the Patient Demon, a mild toxin, but prolonged use caused delirium, hallucinations and even death.

It would also explain the captain's erratic behaviour. Norrey wasn't the most attentive cook, and it would be easy for Orren to dissolve a few pods into the captain's meals or water.

Sander could confront her now, but it would be too easy for her to deny everything. He began to quietly edge away. Now that he knew what to watch for, catching her in the act would be so much easier.

He dashed through the wood, following the sound of the falls back to the camp, determined to get there before Orren. He was torn: should he warn the captain? No, he'd insist on some sort of reckoning and it would be too easy for her to deny. Maybe Norrey? Yes, he would have a quiet word with their alleged chef and see if she'd been up to anything unusual.

Sander spotted movement through the trees – Norrey, Bent and Wob, distant stick men rushing out of sight. Mightily relieved, Sander raced through the bluebells to return to the camp.

'Where the blazes have you been?' Captain Gunnar Jarl stood at the edge of the camp, hands on his hips. His eyes were baggy, watery and tinged with pink.

'Call of nature,' Sander said, jabbing a thumb back into the woods.

Gunnar shook his head, weary, like he knew it was a lie but couldn't be bothered to argue, and waved vaguely towards the nearest of the pools where the river tumbled over into the falls. 'Come and look at this,' he said.

Sander followed him to a break in the mossy rocks that lined the pool, where the rest of Gunnar's men had gathered. They were crouched over something bobbing in a calm eddy, something large, grey and glistening.

Norrey, Bent and Wob stood back when they saw Sander and Gunnar approach, revealing Rasmus and Malachy pulling the thing closer to the edge of the pool, then turning it over.

It was a merman. Most of one, anyway. His head was missing and clouds of black blood drifted from the neck stump into the slate-grey water.

'The blood – can we use it?' Gunnar asked with weary hope. 'Are we done?'

'No.' Sander found his mouth was dry and his stomach was turning.

All the death since the destruction of the Lapis Moon felt both so unreal and yet so everyday. And there was a part of him that worried he was getting used to it.

The bottom half of the merman was a pale green, his scales having lost their usual aquamarine vibrancy in death; the top half was a chalky white, his hands clenched into fists. 'It needs to be fresh,' Sander said. 'Preferably from a live donor. Then I can preserve it. This has turned black, so it's no good.'

Gunnar gave Rasmus and Malachy a signal and they shoved the body back into the turmoil of rushing white water that tumbled down into another pool. The body slowly swirled before inevitably tumbling into the pool below. And so it went, flopping from one pool to another. Eventually, it would reach the lower half of the Connal River below.

'Nothing like a healthy respect for the dead,' Sander muttered as the body rolled out of sight. 'Have you seen any others like this?'

'No. Must be some kind of tribal vendetta. I know the merclans are violent buggers,' Gunnar said with all the confidence of someone who hadn't the first clue what he was on about. 'But this is extreme, even for them.'

'Don't be stupid, this isn't the work of the merclan,' Sander said. 'That was a clean cut. Someone did that with a sword. Merfolk bite. These falls wash down from Connal Lake. Someone's beaten us to the clan. I fear we may be seeing more of these before—'

'Cap'n!' Norrey was pointing at one of the higher falls where two more pale, headless bodies fell clumsily over green boulders and came to a slowly spinning stop in a pool. And then another tumbled over. And another. Each with a heavy wet slap on the water. Soon the falls were thick with the flopping, headless corpses of the Connal Lake Merclan. Men, women and even children.

'Dear gods,' Sander whispered. 'It's a bloody massacre.'

'Who would do this?' Gunnar's voice was a whisper.

Sander noticed the captain was frowning, the Patient Demon already in his system making it increasingly difficult for him to concentrate. 'Who wants to stop us, hmm?' Sander asked. 'A warlord. One who would poison a child to score points. Haldor Frang is a singularly determined man.' What Sander couldn't bring himself to add was that Frang couldn't have done this without help. It wasn't Rosheen's style to massacre innocents, but then neither was poisoning princesses. What in the name of all the gods had become of her? There had to be some other explanation.

'Bright blessings to you, my travelling companions.' Orren arrived on the scene with an innocent smile, reminding Sander that he had probably just missed the opportunity to catch her poisoning Gunnar's lunch. He mentally kicked himself for that, but at least he couldn't blame her for this. Gunnar falteringly explained the situation to her as Rasmus sent Norrey, Bent, Wob and Malachy into the water to round up the other bodies.

'Then we have failed.' Orren's tone suggested they should pack up and head home immediately.

'Not yet, we haven't.' Sander shook his head and turned back to the camp. 'We head south for the Jeltse Clan on the Andraste Coast. Whoever did this could still be on the island waiting for us, or even in these woods. We shouldn't hang around here – we're not safe.'

'We should investigate the island.' Gunnar pulled his braces over his shoulders. 'See if there are any left alive.'

'There isn't time, Gunnar, and besides, just *look* at this.' Sander turned and gestured back at the water where Norrey, Bent, Wob and Malachy were pushing the decapitated bodies around like grisly bath toys. 'Does this look like the work of the kind of people who leave a job half-cocked?'

'Cap'n!' Bent's voice called from further up the falls. They all spun to find him up to his chest in a limestone pool, surrounded by beautiful pink water lilies that gathered in clusters on the bright blue water. He was pointing at a merman's body about six feet away from him. 'This one still has a head!'

As last words go, they weren't the greatest. Perhaps Bent should have given the situation more thought and got himself out of the water before making such a declaration?

The body sprang to life and dived down, sending its tail flipping through the air. It disappeared from sight for a moment, long enough for Bent to realise his error and start frantically paddling for shore, but then the merman broke the surface, sending the pink water lilies spiralling through the air. He attacked, dislocating his jaw like a shark and pulling back his lips to reveal razor-sharp teeth three rows deep that bit down on Bent's neck. Poor Bent screamed and gurgled as the water began to foam red and he was dragged under.

Gunnar started screaming orders as he reached for a sword at his belt that wasn't there. 'Kill it!'

Norrey, Rasmus and Wob began clambering out of their pools, then up over rocks, wading into the deep pool with the merman.

'No!' Sander shouted. 'Get out, we need him alive, get out—'

Wob was next, pulled under then dragged from side to side, screaming the whole time. His blood began to lap over the edge of the pool and the last they saw of him was a hand clawing at thin air.

Gunnar rushed back to the camp. Orren went with him.

'Hey!' Sander said. 'Where are you going?'

'My sword,' the captain cried. 'My sword!'

Poor Wob's demise had given Rasmus and Norrey time to scrabble up the mossy rocks onto the shore. Meanwhile, Malachy had moved with a deft agility up into the trees, where he balanced on a high branch above the merman's pool. He readied his halberd just as the merman leapt out of the water, arms outstretched to grab the branch that Malachy stood on. It snapped and they both cartwheeled back into the pool. Moments later, they came rolling together over the falls and plunged headlong into the pool below.

The merman again rose out of the water for the kill. Malachy had lost his halberd and floundered in the swirling water. As the merman bore down on him, teeth bared, Malachy drew a hunting knife from somewhere in his jerkin and dug it into the merman's belly. With arms that were more bone and tendon than muscle, the ancient Elvish soldier pivoted the merman out of their pool, hurling him through the air into the one below them. Malachy submerged briefly and found his halberd, took it in both hands, stood on the rocks... then lost his footing and fell in with the wounded merman.

As the pair struggled, Sander finally got a good look at their assailant and was shocked to see that it was Afon Kresten of the Nolwen Merclan. He was one of the more peaceful and reasonable members of the clan, often acting as a liaison whenever Sander came to them for blood, eggs or scales, but the merman he saw now was maniacal, biting and slashing in a blind rage, driven mad by grief and vengeance.

And he was flagging. He flopped over the edge of the pool, trying to heave himself out, but Malachy raised the halberd for the kill.

'Malachy, no!' Sander yelled. 'Let me talk to him.'

Malachy hesitated, then glanced beyond Sander to where Gunnar came rushing back with his sword drawn.

'Kill him!' the captain screeched as he ran splashing into the water. 'Kill him now!'

Malachy, who lived or died by orders, plunged the point of the halberd into the soft flesh where the back of the merman's neck met his skull. He lost his footing again and they both came sliding down with the white water rushing over the rocks.

Gunnar reached out and grabbed Malachy. Rasmus and Norrey splashed to his side and helped him back to shore as the body of Afon Kresten of the Nolwen Merclan was carried away on a cloud of pink water.

'The blood. We can still use his blood if we're quick enough!' Sander began to dash after the corpse, but something tripped him and he tumbled to the ground.

Orren stood over him, extending her hand.

'Forgive me, Brother,' she said, her voice oddly flat. 'How clumsy of me.' She took his wrist with such a firm grip that he feared his arm might snap and pulled him to his feet. She stared into his eyes, unblinking, resolute and absolutely batshit crazy.

Sander looked to Gunnar and Rasmus, hoping they had seen her trip him up, but they were too busy pulling Malachy – whose woollen hat remained defiantly on his head – from the pool. Sander spun, looking for Afon Kresten's body, but there was no sign of it. Swept away by the falls. Sander turned back to Orren, whose eyes were wide, her pupils fixed.

'Why do you want us to fail?' he asked her.

Orren released her hold on him and put a finger to her lips – *shh* – then ran to the aid of the others. 'Brothers, let me help!'

Sander was left standing breathless and alone by the rushing water, and he began to wonder what point there was in going any further.

Blood Oranges

Oskar washed up shivering, barefoot and dripping wet on a deserted shingle shore as the noon sun reached its peak. Whatever energy he had summoned to kill Yanick and swim to land had long left him. He found a nook in the cliffs where smooth amber rocks eroded by the sea had created a hollow, and he curled into a trembling ball.

Heal. Heal.

His sleep was deep. Once again, when his eyes were shut, he found that he could see life as pinpricks of light in his mind's eye, and further down the coast were more lights than he ever imagined possible. A hive of bustling bodies massed together into dazzling clusters.

Port Byle. It had to be. Were these lights in his head some kind of magic? A vision? How could they be? Magic was dead.

He awoke, shaking all silly thoughts of magic from his head, to find the sun on its downward arc. Reinvigorated, he strode along the coast, keeping to the wet sand where possible to save his bare soles, then finally vaulting over a jumble of rocks and boulders, where he found something that had him rushing to the lapping waves and vomiting what little food he had in his stomach into the sea.

Three bloated corpses were manacled to iron stakes in the sand. One was a woman with black hair; two were men, one old and one about Oskar's age. At some point, the tide had come in and drowned them all, and now black birds were pecking at their soft flesh. Slate boards hung from strings around their necks. The sea had faded the chalk words written on them, and Oskar couldn't read them anyway, but there was something about the jagged arrangement of words and letters that was entirely hateful. They all wore silk-lined robes like Alby Clim's and Oskar wondered who would do this to mages, and why.

Confused, distressed and robbed of all his energy, he continued to trudge until he could see a cluster of masts swaying on the northern horizon.

Oskar had found Port Byle once more, but no longer was it the sleepy dockside with its candlelit taverns. It was in full flow now, and he had never seen anything like it. Nothing kept still. Dockers loaded and unloaded crates as if they had just stolen them and were making a getaway. In the marketplace, vendors and buyers crammed themselves under red, blue and yellow awnings selling more fish than could possibly be in the sea. In the streets, everyone knew exactly where they were going, and if that meant shoving people like Oskar into the horse shit peppered over the cobblestones or crushing his toes with their boots as they passed, then so be it. And the noise: why talk when you can yell everything? Oskar could only conclude that shouting until you were hoarse over the constant caw of gulls must be complying to some kind of local by-law.

'Stroll up, stroll up!' a voice hollered over the hubbub, and Oskar spun to find a barker in a red cloak holding a box of mouldy fruit and vegetables. Behind him was an elderly man bent forward and locked into a pillory, his head and hands stuck through holes in the wooden board. 'Last chance to pelt the treacherous mage before tonight's drowning. Three throws for a penny and I can't say fairer than that.'

Oskar watched as an elderly woman put down her basket of shopping, paid the barker, took two tomatoes and an egg and hurled them with astonishing vigour at the elderly mage, who could only wriggle his head in vain as the projectiles splashed their putrid juices across his face.

'That's for my Ernest,' she spat at him cryptically, before picking up her basket and going on her way once more.

Oskar was baffled by the entire exchange, and after that he could only wander the market aimlessly, trying to piece together a world that made no sense to him whatsoever.

It was the smells that finally broke him. Food vendors fried sausages, eggs and bacon, bakers piled fresh loaves high on their stalls, and the warm waft of beer, tinged with the sting of pipe smoke, drifted out of tavern doors. Oskar's stomach tightened and bubbled with hunger. He couldn't remember when he had last eaten and began to feel light-headed.

While floating at sea, his plan was simple – swim to shore, hitch a ride to Sabley, find Alby Clim, and together they would find Rosheen

– but this place completely befuddled him. No one was in charge, everyone was doing their own thing and briskly told him to piss off if he so much as squeaked at them. There was no one ready to help him here.

He would make them help.

Standing in the centre of the market, it whirled around him, people whooshing by like blood in arteries. Oskar took the time to become still and not be swept up by the chaos, and it wasn't long before he saw what he needed. An oasis of tranquillity under a red and white awning played host to a colourful array of fruits and vegetables. Andraste blood oranges were in season and the vendor had piles of them on her stall, each one as big as Oskar's fist. He would only take one, or maybe a couple to keep him going. Once he had eaten, he would be able to think straight and formulate a plan.

He had no money. He thought about asking the vendor for a free orange. One of her bruised ones, perhaps? She was a Morven woman with plaited hair twisted like the pretzels on the baker's stall next to hers. Oskar had a met a Morven woman once, a travelling friend of Alby's, and she was a kind soul who gave him candy on a stick.

At that moment, a passing child reached for one of the oranges and the stallholder yelled at him, waving his hand away and turning her flinty eyes on the boy's mother, silently castigating her for not being a better parent.

Clearly, not all Morven women were like the kind soul Oskar had encountered.

Oskar had one trick up his sleeve, however. He couldn't be certain that it would work, but he guessed the worst that could happen was that she would snap at him, too.

On cut and bruised feet and moving with a slight limp, he walked calmly and purposefully over the smooth cobblestones towards the stall. His voice a whisper, he repeated the words, 'Don't see me, don't see me, don't see me.'

A short man in saffron-coloured robes approached the stall. He pointed at some large grey mushrooms and purple-skinned onions, and the stallholder obliged by plucking them from the display and dropping them into a paper bag. She weighed them on a scale and there was an exchange of coins. By the time the man in the saffron robes left, Oskar found himself standing directly in front of the oranges, and the stallholder hadn't so much as glanced in his direction.

'Don't see me, don't see me, don't see me.' Oskar was overcome with a tingling sensation. Like having a fever without the pain.

Oskar slowly reached for the oranges, never taking his eyes off the stallholder. She gazed into the distance, pursing her lips, her mind elsewhere.

Oskar took one orange. Two.

With his heart threatening to pop through his chest, he turned away from the stall.

'Hey!'

A man's voice.

'Ingrid. Thief! He's taking your oranges!'

Ingrid the stallholder took a stunned, rasping breath as she discovered this ragged, barefoot boy standing frozen by her stall with an orange in each hand. As far as she was concerned, Oskar had appeared out of nowhere.

The voice belonged to the red-bearded baker on the next stall along. Oskar had been so focused on the woman that he hadn't thought about those around her.

'Call the Watch.' The baker reached into his tabard and produced a whistle with one hand while pointing at Oskar with the other. 'Thief! Constable! Come quickly.'

The baker blew an insistent series of *pheeps* and the marketplace crowd began to part as two club-wielding constables came running towards them. Ingrid the stallholder had recovered from her astonishment at Oskar's sudden appearance and her pudgy hands were reaching out for him.

Oskar ran.

He dodged the red-bearded baker who lunged at him, then weaved through the crowded stalls with an orange in each hand. All he wanted to do was pause for a moment to eat them, but the two constables were at his heels and any hesitation would end in Oskar's capture.

He noticed that the awnings in this part of the market were less bright. The stalls here sold broken necklaces, strange-looking pipes and swords and daggers with dull, chipped blades, and the tables were decorated with animal skulls. It was less crowded here, meaning Oskar could run faster, and these less-reputable stallholders didn't look as enthusiastic to reach out and grab him as he fled.

From up ahead came more whistling. Another two constables of the Watch, overweight men in ill-fitting woollen uniforms bunched into shape with belts and braces, were headed straight for him, armed with wooden clubs.

Instinctively, Oskar darted out of the marketplace, turning left by a stall selling sandals, boots and shoes that he so desperately needed, then dashed down a narrow alley. After a few blind twists and turns, he found himself in a more labyrinthine quarter of Port Byle where women in scanty clothing stood in doorways trying to look as alluring as possible, and grimacing sailors sat under patchwork awnings getting tattoos with blackened needles as they tried not to show their pain. In this part of town, the jewellers displayed their wares behind barred windows.

This quarter was a jumble of lean-to timber buildings and sandy adobe structures, with temporary stalls in between. The shiny cobbles had become dull flagstones under his feet. They were gritty, uneven, and each turn took Oskar deeper and deeper into a maze that felt like it had no way out. More whistles sounded. More clod-hopping footsteps were closing in.

There came a stab of pain from his big toe as he stubbed it on a stone step. Oskar tumbled forward, his ribs hitting the cobbles hard.

The oranges fell from his hands, rolling across the filthy ground.

Oskar shook his head and tried to right himself as the bellowing voices of the constables called, 'This way! He's here!' and grew louder.

With the pain in his toes and head throbbing, he groaned up into something between a crouch and all fours. And then he saw her.

The girl was about Oskar's age, rounder, pear-shaped, and her skin was darker than his. She wore black leggings, leather boots and a brown tunic edged with an intricate pattern of yellow flowers. Her head had been shaved recently, and she held his oranges one-handed in skinny fingers with well-chewed nails. Her other hand held a small box. It was inlaid with intricately carved ivory patterns that looked like a tiny game board.

She was half-crouched, ready to spring into action and make her escape, but her bright green eyes were locked on Oskar and she kept muttering the same three words again and again.

'Don't see me, don't see me, don't see me.'

The Girl with the Bright Green Eyes

She dropped the oranges and fled like a scalded cat when she realised that Oskar could see her as plain as day, leaving the confused boy on all fours in the middle of the alley.

The flatfooted crescendo of clattering boots told Oskar that the constables were just around the corner. He knew he should follow her, but she was nimble where he was clumsy. She leapt onto a nearby window ledge and pounced to another one opposite. Still gripping the ivory-patterned box, she grabbed the barred windows of a jeweller's with her free hand to hoik herself up, before scrambling onto a thatched roof and scuttling out of sight completely.

Oskar, still coping with the pulsing throbs of pain from his stubbed toes, could only hobble out of sight and duck into the shadows as the constables closed in.

'Don't see me, don't see me, don't see me,' he muttered quietly, all too aware that if recent experience was anything to go by, this trick would have zero-to-little effectiveness.

Most of the constables clattered by, oblivious, but one had fallen behind. Burdened by a keen beer drinker's belly and out of breath, this lawman had little enthusiasm for the chase. He puffed to a stop, his cheeks flushed red as he leaned against the wall opposite the alley where Oskar was pressing himself back into the shade.

'Don't see me, don't see me, don't see me.'

The constable looked straight at him with watery eyes.

'Don't see me, don't see me, don't see me.'

The constable sniffed, cleared a considerable blockage of phlegm from his nose, spat on the flagstones, took a deep breath and staggered off to rejoin the pursuit.

Oskar let himself slide down the wall. Not only was he hungry and footsore, but he was now a fugitive, and more confused than ever.

That girl. Had she been a moon child like him? So many questions, and all the answers had just leapt over a rooftop.

Muttering, 'Heal, heal,' he got to his feet again. A sudden drowsiness came over him. The healing. It would send him into a deep sleep

237

like before. He had to be alert, so he stopped the chanting, choosing to endure the pain in his feet a little longer.

He slapped some life back into his face, then hopped across the alley and began climbing up the side of the jeweller's over which she had disappeared. After earning more cuts and bruises and stubbed toes for his trouble, he found himself tentatively crawling up the thatched roof.

Oskar rose out of the dank alleyway and up into the daylight above the rooftops. It was so bright that at first he could barely keep his eyes open, but once they adjusted, he was able to take in the jumble of red slate and soot-stained thatched roofs laid out before him. The sawtooth skyline of Port Byle. Pale smoke drifted lazily from countless chimneys up into the clouds above and there was a constant burble of movement below – shuffling feet, clopping hooves, rumbling cartwheels – all mingled with the cries and catcalls of the traders and punters unseen in the maze of streets and alleys. In a blue haze in the distance loomed the grey silhouettes of stone watchtowers that marked the boundary of the outer walls and gates. Beyond that, Oskar could only guess. A road to home, he hoped.

Oskar struggled to take it all in. This was by far the biggest place he had ever visited. How in the gods was he ever supposed to find that girl again?

The sun drifted out from behind the clouds and Oskar winced his eyes shut once more.

And then he saw her in his mind's eye.

In his head, the people of Port Byle appeared to him as floating pinpricks of yellow light drifting on a black void. It reminded him of Year's End in Sabley, when the villagers placed candles on the river at night, each one a wish for the coming year, bobbing aimlessly across the dark water. But this was no half-remembered dream, no delusion. This was some kind of power within him, like his vision, hearing and strength, and he would use it.

He saw a pair come together and could hear the mumble of their voices, each bob of the lights tallying with an element of their conversation – a nod of the head, a bellowing laugh.

Another light zipped by them. Was that her? No. A delivery girl on an errand – *Excuse me, coming through* – weaving in and out of the crowd like a glow-worm.

There, high above all the others and darting around the rooftops like a grasshopper, was the girl with the bright green eyes.

Oskar knew it had to be her. She was so much more intense than everyone else. A dazzling light, her movement leaving little blue streaks on the inside of Oskar's eyelids.

He would follow her.

He took a running jump across to the next building, the thatched roofing putting a spring in his step that the flagstones below lacked. He vaulted three buildings this way, closing in fast on the unsuspecting girl.

She dipped out of sight and Oskar closed his eyes again. There were more lights milling about here. She had taken him back to the edge of the crowded market, but she still stood out from the throng, bright as the northern star. She was walking now. Alone and descending in a spiral. Down some steps, perhaps? She was inside one of the larger buildings. Some kind of workshop, maybe? A cylindrical structure with a conical thatched roof that was frayed at the edges and had begun the slow process of unravelling.

Oskar peered down over the edge of the roof he was on. Quite a leap, and one hell of a drop, especially for his battered feet. He moved back for a longer run-up, summoned what little energy he had and ran full pelt, pushing away from the roof and arcing through the air, arms and legs flailing as he muttered, 'Jump, jump, jump,' again and again.

He was going to make it. Just. He reached out, ready for what promised to be a clumsy landing on the conical thatched roof.

He fell straight through it.

Oskar's body punched a hole in the thatch, then slammed into one of the supporting timber rafters underneath. Bouncing off it, he fell twenty feet, landing with a splash in large wooden tank full of fish.

Dead fish. All piled on top of one another in a pungent brine.

Croaking for breath, he broke the surface, reached up for the tank's lip and heaved himself over the top to tumble onto the dusty straw below like a damp load of washing.

As he rolled onto his back, he found himself once more looking into the girl's bright green eyes.

She wasn't alone. She was halfway to handing the ivory-patterned box to a young man with a round, pink face, furnished with a thin moustache shaped like a gull's wings. He wore a tight leather jerkin and pantaloons with narrow blue and white stripes that reminded Oskar of the drapes in the Sabley Village Hall. There was a rip across one of the knees.

The man also wore an expression of astonishment. Open-mouthed, wide-eyed, yet with a grin that suggested he had just wished for a skinny boy to come crashing through the roof, and the wish had immediately been granted.

The girl looked at Oskar differently than she had earlier. Her face was slack, much like his own had once been before he changed, but her bright green eyes couldn't hide a combination of surprise and venomous hatred.

'My dear boy, most people use the door,' the man said, stepping forward with his arms open. The girl stayed put. 'Are you hurt? Let me help you. What in the name of the gods were you doing up there?' He glanced up at the hole in the thatch. 'I always said we should have a skylight, didn't I, Gudrun?'

Oskar's legs kicked helplessly in the pool of brine surrounding him as he struggled to stand upright. 'I was, uhm, lost,' he said, finally getting his breath back.

'I should say so.' The man turned to the girl. 'Gudrun, help me with the lad. Come along, girl, he won't bite. You don't bite, do you, boy? Ha! Of course not. Look at him. All ribs and elbows.'

Gudrun remained thin-lipped and glowering, but she joined the man in grabbing Oskar's arms and pulling him free from the mess of briny straw and dead fish. Oskar was soaked through and stank of fish, which conjured thoughts of his torture aboard the *Queen Mathilde*. He shook the bad memories away and, still uncertain on his feet, looked up to see the hole in the straw roof that he had created.

'Oh gods, I'm... I'm so sorry!' he said.

The man saw the boy's expression of horror and flapped a dismissive hand. 'Fret not, my boy. It was in need of some extensive repairs, anyway,' he said, his winged moustache twitching. 'No harm done. I am Captain Bingham.' He extended his hand for shaking and Oskar took it, finding Bingham's grip to be near bone-breaking. 'My companion here is Gudrun. A simple soul, bereft of speech and wit and hard of hearing, but she understands well enough. And you are…?'

Oskar glanced at Gudrun. Bereft of speech? She had spoken to him clearly enough when he encountered her in the alley. He was about to say something when he registered the look on her face. It said, very clearly, *Don't you dare say a word or I'll kill you where you stand.* At least, he thought he was reading her expression. A part of him wondered if she was using her magic to put the words directly into his mind.

There was no doubt she was a moon child like him.

And for reasons he didn't know but perfectly understood, she wanted to keep that to herself. He gave her the tiniest of nods. He would say nothing. For now.

'Your name, lad, name?' Bingham steered Oskar to a chair where he sat the boy down.

'Oskar. Oskar Katell.'

'Oskar, plucky Oskar, Oskar, explorer of roofs and survivor of splash-landings. What were you doing up there?'

Oskar's eyes must have flicked to Gudrun because Bingham grinned as he put two and two together.

'Aha! Yes, she is beguiling, isn't she? She's a pretty thing. A niece of a cousin. I have made many promises regarding her welfare, so temper your passions, young man.' Bingham hooted when he saw Oskar's offended expression. 'You don't look like a rake to me. No, I take care of her and she helps me around the stables. So, brave Oskar, tell me your story and we'll share a pipe.'

'I… I don't really have the time. I must—' Oskar stammered as he took in the rest of the room. More large water tanks were positioned around them in stable stalls and the vinegary stench in the air was starting to make his eyes water. 'These are stables?'

Bingham smiled as he lit his pipe. 'Once upon a time. Now it's host to a different kind of creature.'

'So… not horses?' Oskar frowned.

Gods, you're dim.

Gudrun hadn't spoken, but when Oskar turned his head to see if she had, it was clear from her unimpressed expression that the words had come from her. How did she do that?

'Oh, there are no horses here, my young friend,' Bingham said, oblivious to Gudrun's interjection. 'A couple out the back, actually, but this place is for something special. Tell me, have you ever flown?'

No. Tell him you're not interested and leave. Now.

'I... er...' Oskar was about to describe one flight on Anzu's back when he was a child that had utterly terrified him, but the look on Gudrun's face made him decide against it. 'No,' he muttered.

Oskar had gone chasing after this girl with little idea of what he would do if he caught up with her. And now that he had found her, she wanted him gone on pain of death. He had countless questions for her, but it was crystal clear that she wouldn't give him any answers. It was good enough for him to know that he, at least, wasn't alone. There was nothing for him here, and it was time to go home.

'Mr Bingham—'

'*Captain* Bingham, if you please,' he said, the pipe clenched between his teeth. 'You may have heard of me?'

Oskar's blank face told him he had not.

'What am I thinking? Of course you haven't. I am a flyer of some note, if I say so myself.'

'Captain Bingham, I must get to a village called Sabley, do you know how—?'

'Sabley, Sabley...' Bingham narrowed his eyes and puffed on his pipe again, and Oskar was reminded of when the village children played at being grown-ups. 'Can't say I've heard of it. Not local, is it? Which of the realms might it be in?'

Oskar faltered. He didn't know. Of course he didn't. Why would a collector of pisspots and dung know about realms or maps or politics? By the gods, he didn't even know where he was going.

Andraste, you fool, said Gudrun's voice in his head.

'Uh... Andraste.'

'Ahh, I see. You're in Agrona now, boy. Next kingdom along. Tell me – how does a young lad from Sabley in Andraste get lost in Port Byle in Agrona?'

'I was...' Oskar hesitated. How much should he tell him? How much was even believable? 'I was kidnapped. I was taken from my farm after my father was killed.'

'Oh my goodness. Gudrun, did you hear that?' Bingham jolted upright in a puff of white smoke.

Gudrun remained slack-jawed, but her mind said, *Boo-bloody-hoo. We've all got a sob story.*

'How terrible for you, boy. But you're free of your captors, yes? You've vanquished your foes?'

'I... Yes, I have.' Oskar smiled proudly. He hadn't thought of it like that.

'A true hero. You've survived a kidnapping, incarceration, a terrible ordeal. No small amount of mental and physical abuse, I imagine, hmm?'

'Er... yes.'

'You are fortunate to find me, boy. We will return you to this Sabley place. That much I promise.'

'Thank you very much.'

Seriously. Leave now. Walk out through that door and go.

'By the gods, you poor soul, I expect you're famished, aren't you?' Bingham spun on his heels and clapped his hands at Gudrun. 'Some food for our friend, Gudrun, please.'

Gudrun, playing the part of simple servant, clumped inelegantly between the water tanks and shuffled out through a door, but Oskar could still sense her presence. *I hate you*, she told him.

'I'm sorry, I don't have any money for food, Captain Bingham.'

'Money? The curse of our times, don't apologise, my friend. I remember an age when a man's word was his currency, his promise a guarantee of trade. I am a man of honour, and I will get you home. However, I have a task that I must complete first, and then...' Bingham paused and chewed on his pipe. 'Would you like to see something incredible?'

Oskar felt obliged to nod, though the last thing his day needed was any further surprises.

Bingham clapped his hands with excitement and ran over to a pair of doors as high as the stable's ceiling. Beside them hung a leather riding whip, which he snatched up with one hand while pulling open the doors with the other.

'Behold!' He spun to face Oskar, whip and arms aloft.

'Uhm...' Oskar glanced around an empty exercise corral. Circular, dusty and bereft of anything remotely incredible, unless he counted the collection of colourful pantaloons hanging on a washing line. 'There's nothing to see.'

'What? Oh.' Bingham turned back, shook his head, then crouched down, jiggling the whip to beckon something or someone unseen. 'Come on, sweetie, this is no time to be timid.'

A lizard-like head with a long snout, mournful black eyes and a downturned mouth peered around the doors and inclined towards Bingham. The head was almost as big as the captain and it was on the end of a long, smooth-skinned neck that came winding into the barn. It was followed by two leathery wings the size of the sails on the *Queen Mathilde*, a round body the colour, texture and shape of a lime, two muscular legs and a coiled tail that ended in a fork. It unfolded itself and filled the barn, its head rising to investigate the hole Oskar had created in the roof.

'Observe,' Bingham said, cracking the whip in the air.

The creature's head turned to Bingham, who led it over to the fish tank that Oskar had landed in. The creature became so excited at the sight of the fish that it began to drool at the mouth, but Bingham cracked the whip again.

'Petra, hold!' he commanded, and the creature paused, obviously desperate to get its fill but obedient to its master. Bingham slowly raised the whip, watched eagerly by the animal, then cracked it again. 'Petra, eat!'

Petra immediately plunged her head into the tankful of dead fish with enthusiasm.

'A... a dragon?' Oskar said when he finally managed to speak.

'A wyvern, dear boy, a wyvern,' Bingham corrected him. 'Two legs, a forked tail, smoother skin, only eats fish and, crucially, doesn't breathe fire. Beautiful, isn't she? I call her Petra, after my late mother. She liked fish, too.'

'How did you... how is she even here?'

'You, young Oskar the bold and curious, are looking at the first tame wyvern in all the Newlands. And I, Captain Bingham, am her master and pilot.'

That last word rattled in his mind. A pilot was what Rosheen sometimes called herself when she rode Anzu. 'You fly on her?'

'The tests have been somewhat hair-raising so far.' Bingham winced a little through his smile. 'But without magic, this creature has become somewhat more open to discipline and training, and we're ready for our first real mission tomorrow.'

'We?'

'Gudrun and myself. Oh, that girl may look simple but she has uncanny vision. Can spot a target a mile off. Almost like she's psychic!'

I bet, Oskar thought.

'So, dear boy,' Bingham said, slapping Oskar on the back, 'while we're away, could you look after the stables? Sweep the floor, scare the rats, fix the roof, that sort of thing?'

I spat on the bread.

Oskar spun to find Gudrun standing behind him holding a tin plate with some bread and cheese. Her emotionless face betrayed none of the spite that came directly to Oskar's mind. Remembering how famished he was, he cautiously took the plate from her and bit into the yellow cheese.

And I wiped my arse with the cheese.

Oskar stopped chewing. Gudrun kept her face still, and he had no way of knowing if she was lying. He didn't care. He was hungry and resumed chewing.

'Can't I come with you?' he asked Bingham between munches.

No. Definitely not.

'It will be dangerous, my lad. We have been commissioned to serve with the brave army of King Bhaltair in his fight against the encroaching mercenary forces of the renegade warlord Haldor Frang. Now that magic is no longer with us, Petra is an essential component of His Majesty's battle strategy. We are proud to serve the king by providing him with aerial reconnaissance, the only force in the Newlands to have such eyes in the sky.'

Oskar understood about one word in three. 'So… you're not actually fighting in the battles?'

'Oh gods, no. Simply flying above the action and reporting back on what we see. Perfectly safe.'

'She's very big,' Oskar persisted. 'Can't I sit at the back?'

'Every passenger must earn their place, my boy. What would you do?'

Petra's head emerged from the fish tank as she extended her neck to gulp down her lunch, then she flapped open those incredible wings with a snap that hurt his ears. They all took an involuntary step back, buffeted by displaced air.

'Please, Captain Bingham,' Oskar said, imagining climbing on Petra's back, soaring over the outer walls of Port Byle and swooping down into Sabley Village where his mother, Alby Clim or Rosheen would be waiting for him. A naive dream, perhaps, but Sabley was his home and he knew the people there, and the warmth of the fire in the tavern and the comfy cushions of his favourite chair called to him. 'I… I probably shouldn't tell you this, but the constables want me for stealing oranges, I know it's wrong, but I was hungry, I can't leave the port without being spotted, so your wyvern is my best chance of escaping and getting home. I know Gudrun's strong, but I'm strong, too.'

Back off. You're not the only one who needs to get out of this dump.

'What I need is an experienced hand,' Bingham said, narrowing his eyes.

'I served on a ship,' Oskar found himself saying, his desperation giving the truth a slight twist. 'The *Queen Mathilde*. I worked hard, I followed orders, I'm quick to learn and I will do absolutely anything to leave this place and go home. Please, Captain. Let me come.'

'Well, well.' Bingham smiled and took the boy's arms. 'Oskar the unbowed. Oskar the unflappable. After such an impassioned plea, how can I possibly refuse? And it can't hurt to have another pair of eyes up there. What do you say, Gudrun? Can he come along?'

Bingham turned to the girl, who remained outwardly silent and impassive.

Only if I can throw him off over the Sugar Sea.

'Look at her.' Bingham grinned. 'As if she cares. Of course you can join us, Oskar. You can take turns as lookout with Gudrun. I shall navigate. And then, once we return triumphant, we will fly you home. I promise.'

'Thank you, Captain.' Oskar shook the man's hand, but over his shoulder he could see Gudrun glaring at him with her bright green eyes.

Congratulations, moron. You've just signed up with a cold-blooded murderer.

Wolves with Swords

Open fields did little for Sander's nerves.

'Pretty, in't it?' Norrey nodded at the wide expanses of corn around them, slowly swaying in the breeze. After Vilmar's death, Norrey had been tasked with the care of the horses, and he led them in a line behind his own ride, which was overburdened with clanking pots and pans.

'We're too visible,' Sander complained, fidgeting in his saddle. 'And you look like a horse thief with a crockery fetish with that lot behind you. You're making a hell of a racket, Norrey. Can't you muffle them at all?'

'Why?'

'Because if we really want to draw attention to ourselves, we should do it properly. I was planning on ringing a bell and screaming, *Come and get us! Here we are! We're tired, desperate and a bit shit at defending ourselves!*'

Norrey gave him a blank stare.

'That was a joke,' Sander said. 'It's dangerous out here and that racket isn't helping.'

Their encounters with the bandits and Afon Kresten, last of the Nolwen Merclan, had only confirmed every prejudice Sander had against their glorious Captain Gunnar Jarl. Their depleted and ragged band was noisy, visible and vulnerable and needed to get off the main path before they were noticed, and he had said as much to Gunnar. The young captain dithered, made that weird noise through his nose and said he would make a decision when the time was right.

'All we see is traders and farmers.' Norrey curled his lip and half-closed his eyes, something he only usually did when he was concentrating on his cooking. 'What's dangerous about that?'

'The enemy has eyes everywhere,' Sander said. 'Someone'll report us soon enough.'

'Andraste ain't our enemy.' Norrey's eyes were almost shut now. 'Are they?'

'Andraste and Wayland have a kind of begrudging mutual respect based on trade,' Sander conceded with a shrug. 'But the fact is, we're not supposed to be here and any incidents could have serious political repercussions. If a passing Andraste guard decides to stop us, our only choices will be to surrender or fight.' Sander glanced at Gunnar riding behind him, his eyes red in a scowling face. After losing so many of his men, Sander couldn't be sure if the captain would be ready for a scrap or capitulate instantly.

'Or Sister Orren could talk to them?' Norrey said, brightly. 'She has a way with words, that one.'

'Doesn't she just.' Sander couldn't bring himself to look back at her. She knew she was being observed, though she remained as wincingly cheerful as ever. Sander hoped his scrutiny would be enough to stop her from poisoning Gunnar's food and drink with more seeds of the Patient Demon.

The heroes who left Taranis with their heads held high were a sorry-looking lot now. After four days on the road, they were hunched in their saddles. They all knew that they should have been heading home in triumph by now. Instead, Sander was leading them further south on what they all suspected was a fool's errand, but the alternative was to return empty-handed and condemn a little girl to death.

'Rasmus.' Gunnar spoke rarely now and only then with a resigned weariness. 'Ride ahead, will you? See... see if you can find a spot to camp for the night.'

Rasmus murmured a reply and pulled on his reins, galloping away. Even the noble lieutenant who could recite entire chunks of the King's Guard Handbook had lost all faith in his golden captain. Only Malachy was unchanged, but then he was always strung as tight as the strings on a fiddle.

Gunnar may have led from the front, but this was now Sander's mission. After verbally bollocking Gunnar for giving the order to kill the only live merperson they had seen so far, Sander declared that they would head south, through the farmlands of Andraste, along the coast and to the sandbanks and corals where the clans he knew from his childhood resided.

He was going home.

'Home?' Malachy echoed, riding alongside him, and Sander realised he'd been thinking aloud again. 'You from around here, then?'

'Andraste. A village on the coast, or thereabouts.'

'Can't you remember?'

'There are times I prefer not to.'

'Family troubles? Run away from home, did ya?'

'Shut up, Malachy.'

As the sun went down, the clouds moved in and it began to rain, which was when Sander discovered that his robes were extra water-absorbent. Quickly losing their shape, they clung to his thighs, back and arms and he began to shiver. Orren's were cut from better cloth, keeping her warm and dry.

She caught him staring and smiled. 'Do not cower in the rain, my Brother. Hold your head up high and welcome the Goddess's tears.'

Sander replied with a low grumble. Out of the corner of his eye, he saw Malachy twirl his halberd from its resting place on his shoulder into a two-handed attacking grip. Through the drumbeat of rain on his hood, Sander began to pick out the distinct sound of hoofbeats up ahead. Norrey and Gunnar slowly moved their hands to their swords.

It was Rasmus. He came galloping back down the road and every-one relaxed as he brought his horse to a stop by Gunnar's. 'I've found a farmhouse two miles south, Captain.'

'What about the residents?' Gunnar asked.

'It's abandoned, sir. And with good reason,' Rasmus said, with a peculiar look on his face. He struggled to string the words together. 'It's been... well... *flattened*, sir.'

'Flattened?'

'Yes. Squashed, if you like.'

'By what?'

The dragon was draped over the remains of the house like an unmade bed sheet. Its lower teeth jutted pathetically out of its enormous jaw, the rain battered its wings with a rhythmic pitter-patter, and its scaly body, once a vibrant crimson, now a muted burgundy, lay broken over the rubble of a white stone farmhouse.

'A sorry end to a glorious beast.' Sander rested a hand on the tip of its horned nose.

'It's definitely dead, right?' Norrey stayed on his horse, ready to bolt, while the others dismounted.

Sander opened the dragon's eyelid to find only rolled-back whites. 'I'm no expert, but she looks pretty dead to me.'

'No expert?' Norrey quivered. 'I thought you was a mage. Weren't you lot always consorting with dragons and such?'

'How do you know it's a she?' Rasmus asked, then snorted, signalling to the world that he was about to make the funniest quip that anyone had ever heard. 'You looked up its skirts?'

No one laughed as Sander gently closed the dragon's eyelid. 'I know it's a she because only the females can fly. Males are smaller, more aggressive and guard the nests while the female hunts. And no, Norrey, I've not consorted with dragons, but I did once see whole flights of them soaring over the Western Mountains. They nest on the rocky coasts at the edge of Parthalan and, contrary to all the nonsense you might have heard from tavern storytellers, they keep away from humans – they're not interested in gold or virgins. They live mainly on fish.'

'Ungodly vermin.' Orren, for once, wasn't smiling. She looked genuinely repulsed and stood back from the animal's body, as if being near it might taint her. '"Spurn the scaly beasts that nest in their own filth, for they are vile and wretched and have no place in the divine plan."'

'I'm sure she spoke very highly of you, too.'

'It is from the Book of Beasts, chapter five, verse—'

'Yeah, yeah, I know.'

'We will rejoice in its passing, Brother. The end of magic also sees the end of dragons. Join me in prayer.'

'No, I don't think I will, thanks.' Sander ran his hands across the beast's scales, which were rough as sandpaper and cold as stone. 'Me and this beauty have far too much in common.'

'There's a body here,' Gunnar called from around the other side of the creature's corpse. 'And another.'

Sander, relieved for the interruption, rushed from Orren to join Gunnar.

The captain had found the crushed remains of a husband and wife, surrounded by shattered crockery, an iron frying pan and a splintered table and chairs. The front of the farmhouse had been completely destroyed by the impact of the crashing dragon, but the back half still stood, as did a handful of empty stables and barns.

'Poor sods,' Sander muttered, then he looked up and scanned the yellow rapeseed that surrounded the farm buildings. 'There's no damage to the field around us, so the thing must have just dropped out of the air. Of all the places it could have landed... "More eggs for breakfast, my love?" "Yes please, my darling, oh, what's that noise?" Wallop.'

'You're talking to yourself again,' Malachy muttered in Sander's ear. 'Shut up, Malachy.'

'It's getting dark. We'll camp here tonight,' Gunnar declared, with Orren at his side, and Sander found himself wondering if it was his idea or hers.

'You're joking, right?' Sander gestured at the dead creature. 'There's a bloody great dead dragon lying here. It won't be long before it starts to attract the curious, and in these parts, curious people come with swords and pitchforks.'

'We'll post a guard.' Gunnar waved vaguely at Rasmus, who saluted with little enthusiasm. 'Norrey – prepare supper.'

Night had fallen by the time Norrey dished up their ration of day-old salmon. Sander had watched him from the moment the cook first lit the fire and skewered the fish to serving it up now. It was Sander's first proper meal after all his ration punishments and his belly groaned in anticipation as he shovelled the food into his mouth. Chewy, overcooked salmon had never tasted so good.

Orren had stayed away.

That gave him a deep satisfaction. It was tiring to constantly watch over the food, but if that was the price he had to pay to keep Gunnar from delirium and to scupper Orren's plan, then so be it. She would know that the Patient Demon only worked with regular doses, and already Gunnar was recovering, his sense of purpose returning as he and Rasmus reviewed the map of their journey so far.

'By the gods, we should be halfway home by now,' Gunnar said, like a man awakening from a deep sleep.

Rasmus tapped a finger on the map. 'These marshlands lie between us and the merpeople colony. The terrain will slow us down, but the Kelish who live there are friendly enough and we should arrive by nightfall tomorrow.'

Tomorrow. The end was in sight. Soon they would have what they needed, and Sander would be back in Taranis by the end of the week. And then what? He would have to get out of the bloody Order of the Faith, that's what. He would be patient. Plan his escape carefully. Maybe he could leave them some written instructions with the merblood and flee on the journey home? That way, the princess would be cured and he would be away before Orren, Yorath and the king had him thrown back into the citadel's dungeons. Oh, he knew that he and the king had a deal, but Sander was no fool. He had no doubt whatsoever that Yorath would be poisoning the king's mind in his own way. All that waited for Sander back at Taranis was a cell or a death sentence. He had to run. He'd be a fugitive, but what other choice did he have? They'd be fighting a war, anyway. They had bigger things to worry about than some former mage doing a runner. Tomorrow. Yes, tomorrow was when Sander's life would be under his control again.

'Water, Captain?' Orren was standing next to Gunnar with his tin cup and tomorrow suddenly felt a long way off.

Where the blazes did she get that from?

'Fresh from a well on the other side of the farm buildings,' she said, answering Sander's unspoken question and placing it by the captain's plate.

'Oh, thank you very much.' Gunnar reached for the cup and Sander began to panic.

'Ah! A spider!' Sander didn't have time to think, just leapt to his feet and kicked over the cup. The water splashed on the captain's breeches. 'Did... did you see that? Huge, it was. Where's it gone?'

Gunnar's mind might have been foggy but he wasn't an idiot. He knew Sander's little act was no accident, and he saw the brief flash of hostility shared by Orren and Sander.

'What is going on?' he demanded.

Sander's mind rushed as he tried to calculate what effect it would have when he said what he was about to say.

'She's poisoning you.' There. He said it.

Orren remained unmoved, her face remaining in its constant state of passive judgement.

'What?' Gunnar blinked.

'How's your mind, Captain? Bit fuzzy? Headaches, blurred vision? She's been putting Patient Demon in your food and drink,' Sander continued. 'I can't prove it. If I could, I would have said something sooner, but I did see her picking the seeds earlier. Search her. Check her little pouch-thing.'

He was doing so well up to that moment. Sander instantly knew he shouldn't have said it, and he blushed as he watched Orren silently turn her robe's pouch inside out. Nothing.

'Of course, there's nothing in there *now*,' Sander said with a shrug. 'She knew this moment was going to come. They're probably… stuffed up her backside or something.'

'Noviciate Bree.' Gunnar got to his feet, wiping at the wet patch on his breeches. 'Listen to yourself. Since we set out, you've done nothing but complain or mutter gibberish to yourself. Your contribution to this mission has been precisely zero.'

'Hey, I got us here, didn't I? You want to know why we've been wandering all over the place? It's her. With or without the poison, she's been messing with your mind, and believe me, there's precious little to play with there.'

'Oh, I see, I'm an idiot, am I?'

'The man who led us into a blatantly obvious bandits' trap? Who gave the order to kill the only live merman we've met on this poxy journey? I'm not sure, let's ask someone else. Vilmar? Bent? Wob? Oh, wait, we can't, they're dead.'

Sander instantly knew he'd crossed a line, but he was beyond caring now. Gunnar looked like a toddler about to throw a tantrum, but he somehow bottled it up.

'Malachy.' Gunnar's voice choked as he spoke. 'Take Noviciate Bree, gag him and tie him up in one of the outbuildings. I don't care where, but I do not wish to speak to him for the remainder of this journey.'

'Sir.' Malachy nodded and undid one of the ropes around his breeches that he used for a belt. He began to bind Sander's hands behind his back.

'He is not to be untied until we need him to attend to the merblood, is that understood?'

'Yessir.'

'Another classic Gunnar command,' Sander called as he was pulled away. 'All you're doing is condemning a girl to death because of your arrogance!'

Malachy took Sander past the farm's stables where the horses had settled for a comfortable night's sleep and around to a derelict wattle-and-daub outhouse riddled with weeds and nettles. Inside, they found a large pile of horse manure rotting in one corner.

'Couldn't keep your gob shut, could you? What did I tell you, eh?' Malachy pushed the mage down by his shoulders onto the cold stone floor and produced a grey, stained handkerchief from inside his jerkin.

'What in the gods is that thing and where do you intend to put it?' Sander asked, dreading the answer.

Malachy shoved a section of the makeshift gag into Sander's mouth, who instinctively bit down and came close to retching when he found it was moist. 'You mages, you're all the same.' Malachy tied the ends tight at the back of his head. 'Think you know everything, but you've never actually lived, have you? Never had to worry about your next meal, or who's going to pay the taxes and tithes? You should've listened to me, mate. Kept your head down, done your job, and you'd've been all right.'

'Mahagy,' Sander said through the gag. 'Fees poifoning him. Owwen. Fee garnt be twufted. Wiffen to me.'

'I know what she's doing,' Malachy said as he took the rope binding Sander's hands and knotted them around a wooden post.

'Wha? Den why don you ftop her?'

'I have a sneaking suspicion,' Malachy said, baring his black and yellow teeth in what passed for a smile from the old crook, 'that she's on the winning side. You don't get as old as me in this game without knowing who to back in the long run.' He patted Sander's cheek. 'Now sit there and shut up and you might just get through this in one piece.'

Unlike last night, sleep came easily to Sander. Despite everything, it felt like a weight had been lifted. The failure of this mission would all be down to Gunnar. The king would have *him* executed instead. Though, now Sander thought about it, they'd probably *all* be executed. Another reason to leave this party at the first opportunity.

Then he remembered the gap-toothed smile of Princess Brianna when he told her his stories. Her voice when she called him silly and her sincere thanks when he bade her good night. If he ran, he was condemning her to die. But if Malachy was right, if Orren really was on the winning side, then the poor girl was dead already. Yorath had planned to sabotage this mission from the beginning and the king would have no choice but to go to war. A war that the Faith would blame on magic, a war that would drive mourning mothers into their churches and fill their coffers with coins soaked in blood and—

'Will you shut up?' Malachy barked from where he stood, leaning on the open door.

Thinking aloud again. Sander shivered and opened his eyes, exhaling loudly through the gag and surprised to see his breath form little clouds on the air. It was cold. Too cold for a spring night.

A tiny crackling noise made him glance down. The nettles pushing up through the cracks in the floor had tiny spikes of ice growing on them right before his eyes. A small puddle of water froze over, and there was a smell in the air that he thought he'd never experience again, a kind of metallic burning smell.

Magic! Someone nearby was using magic.

'Mahagy! Mahagy! Unfie me!' Sander called, but the old elf was sliding down the wall, his eyes shut as he fell into a cold slumber. 'Oh, ffit.'

Sander wriggled his wrists and hands to undo the rope, but the knots were tight and the wriggling only made them constrict even more. Eventually, the wooden post started to budge a little. Sander glanced up to see that frost was already forming where the post met the ceiling joist. That would make it weak. He shuffled around the post until he was facing one of the outhouse's walls, pressed his feet flat against the decaying wattle and daub and pushed.

There was a crack followed by a shower of dust and particles of ice as the post began to move. He pushed against the wall again, his legs trembling with the effort. The post gave way and he fell on his side, snapping his eyes shut as he was covered in the plaster dropping from the cracked ceiling.

He rolled onto his knees, then stood on shaking legs with his hands still bound around the remains of the post now balanced on his back. He was carrying it like a giant wooden caber and he had to be rid of it. He rested the bottom of the post on the floor then shimmied down, the wood scratching against his arms. When his bound wrists reached the bottom, he twisted them free and the post fell away. He got back on his feet and rushed to Malachy, slipping on an icy puddle, righting himself and kicking the soldier where he lay slouched against the door.

'Mahagy! Mahagy, wake up!'

Malachy jolted awake, instinctively gripping his halberd, then shuddering in the cold, rubbing his arms. 'What's going on?' He saw Sander, upright, free of the wooden post but still gagged and with his hands tied behind his back.

'Magic!' Sander managed through the gag. 'Unfie me!' He saw Malachy glance around at the creeping frost on the floor and the ground outside, most likely wondering which choice would keep him on the winning side. He pulled Sander's gag loose but left his hands bound.

'Someone's using magic.' Sander spat the taste of the gag away and waddled off like a duck with his hands tied behind his back. 'We have to wake the others.'

'Oi, get back here!' Malachy caught up with Sander easily, grabbing him in an armlock. 'Wait!'

'What are you doing? We have to—'

'Shh! Look.' Malachy nodded to the nearby stables. All the horses were flat on their sides. 'Someone's knocked 'em out.'

'Oh gods, this is happening, it's really happening.'

'And out there…' Malachy narrowed his eyes, looking into the darkness across the fields like a hunting dog. Sander looked, too, but had no idea what he was looking for.

'Where? What?'

'There!' Malachy said, pointing into the cornfield.

Sander saw it. Something cutting a path through the corn. It was joined by two others, three, four, more. 'What are they? Dogs? Foxes?'

'Foxes don't hunt in packs.'

'Wolves?'

'Wolves with swords.'

'Wolves with—?' Sander frowned, then he got it. 'You mean *men*? Why don't you just say so? We're about to be massacred, Malachy, we haven't got time for elaborate metaphor.'

Malachy readied his halberd.

'Untie me, Malachy, please, I won't stand a chance with my hands behind my—' It was Sander's turn to spot something. Beyond the edge of the field, among the trees, he could see a blue light glowing. A Lapis blue. The colour of magic. Malachy saw it, too, and knew that the already bad odds had now tipped overwhelmingly in the enemy's favour.

'Magic,' Malachy said, the word sending a tiny cloud of breath into the dark.

'A stone from the Lapis Moon,' Sander said, his voice a whisper. 'It has to be Rosheen. She's drawing from its power.'

'How much power?'

'Not as powerful as, y'know, before,' Sander said with a sigh, nodding up at the ribbon of stones in the night sky. 'But enough to make a mage dangerous.'

'Can you use it?' Malachy asked.

'Not from here. I'd have to be so close as to touch it.'

'Can you get your hands on one?'

'Oh, yeah, let me just pluck one out of my arse,' Sander snapped. *'Do you think if I could, I would be in this situation?'*

'Fair enough,' Malachy said, before running back around the building, into the field and out of sight.

'Malachy?' Sander's voice wavered. He was unable to believe that the decrepit old elf would abandon him. 'Malachy, you bloody coward!'

There was a rapid rustling in the field. Whoever it was, they were closing in fast. Sander's legs were telling him to run after Malachy. It made complete sense. Flee and live to flee another day. Keep running. Don't think of the consequences. Stay alive and figure out how to fix everything later. He thought of Norrey's terrible food, Rasmus's awful laugh and Gunnar's blind devotion to orders and he knew they wouldn't last long at the mercy of any wolves with swords. Sander dashed from one farm building to another, hissing his companions' names as loud as he dared, but clearly not loud enough for anyone to hear him.

He found them sleeping in a circle around the embers of a dying fire by the stables. Frost was already forming in clumps on their lips and hair. Despite his fear, he took some little pleasure in kicking Gunnar's backside.

'Captain! Wake up, we're under attack!' He moved to Rasmus, Norrey and Orren, kicking and nudging them in turn. One by one, they began to rise.

Rasmus was first, squinting at Sander through his piggy eyes. 'How did you get free?'

Sander's words came in a tumble. 'Someone's using magic – look at the frost, see how cold it is? That's magic. I don't know how, but there's a blue light in the woods. A Lapis stone or something, and no, before you ask, I can't use it myself. There are men coming, wolves with swords, not literally, that's just a figure of speech, and now Malachy's buggered off and the horses are all unconscious. Come on, we have to get up and run. Actually, first you need to untie me and then we can run. Up, up, now, c'mon!'

Rasmus frowned at Sander like he was mad, then his eyes flitted to something behind the mage and he got to his feet with such speed he almost pirouetted in the air. 'Captain! To arms!' he screeched at the top of his voice.

Sander spun to find three men moving towards them across the farmyard, their swords drawn. 'Rasmus, untie me now, untie me now!'

'Captain! Norrey! Awake and to arms!' Rasmus rummaged among his clothes, folded neatly by the fire. For a moment, Sander thought the second-in-command was also readying to flee, but then he found his sword in the pile, drew it from its sheath and ran towards the invaders in his long johns.

It was the clang of steel that finally woke the others. Orren was instantly alert, her head darting about like a bird's, sensing danger and scrabbling to her feet. 'Captain!'

Gunnar was bleary-eyed, snorting in a waking breath as he tried to make sense of what he was seeing: Rasmus taking on a trio of black-clad attackers in nothing but his night things.

Norrey was like a child waking from a nightmare. He kicked his legs and stumbled twice before getting to his feet. 'Where's my sword? Where is it?'

'Never mind your sword, Norrey, untie me!' Sander begged.

There was a strangled grunt as Rasmus sliced one of the attackers across the stomach. The man fell to his knees and Rasmus finished him with a decisive chop that sliced clean through his neck.

'Gods!' Sander jumped back as the head of the decapitated man rolled across the hay and dung in the farmyard and came to a rest near his feet.

Gunnar staggered into the fray now with the fearless confidence of the half-awake. He was followed by Norrey who had found his sword, though the frost had stuck it in its sheath. He tugged at it but it wouldn't move. One of the attackers saw this, kicked Gunnar away and rushed the cook.

'Norrey, watch out!' Sander yelled, but the lad looked at the former mage and not his attacker. Before he knew it, Norrey was sent falling to the ground by a slash across his back, followed by an ugly barrage of hacks that bit into the meat around his neck and shoulders.

THE END OF MAGIC

'Oh gods, oh gods, oh gods.' Sander's legs felt boneless. He looked for Orren.

She was rushing for the wood, holding a small leather-bound copy of the Word of the Goddess as her only shield as the chaos unfolded around her. 'I shall not fear blade or bow,' she chanted, 'for the Goddess will welcome me into her embrace and—'

'Orren, look out!' Sander called as one of the attackers ploughed into her, grabbed her by the neck and dragged her around the side of a barn.

Sander flushed cold. Gunnar and Rasmus were at least armed as they fought their pair of opponents. And their hands were free! How could Sander defend himself if someone grabbed him in the darkness? Gunnar and Rasmus were the only things between him and death at the end of a sword, and they were fully occupied.

Run, he had to run, even with his hands tied, he must run. His legs moved, trembling at first, but then he found some last reserve of strength and was pelting through the farm buildings, past the crushed farmhouse and the dead dragon and into the fields.

Where he found two more black-clad assailants rushing towards him.

Without a moment's hesitation, he turned tail and began running back the way he came. He arrived in time to see Gunnar finish off a second antagonist. Gunnar and Rasmus now flanked the lone remaining swordsman.

Sander whooshed by. 'Two more! That way! Run!'

But a captain of the King's Guard does not run, and nor does his second-in-command. They stood their ground as three men in black now circled them, swords raised.

With the first clang of steel, Sander dared to look back. He saw Gunnar moving like a whirlwind, spinning with his sword flashing in the moonlight. Made delirious by Orren's poisoning, he moved with a strange, unpredictable grace, sending the attackers skittering back, ducking his flashing blade.

Rasmus, though, was as orthodox as ever. Even Sander could see his learned-by-rote moves coming a mile off, and it wasn't long before one of the assailants stabbed him in the back. A move definitely not approved of in the King's Guards' training manual. Rasmus fell to his knees with a look of genuine disappointment in the unsporting manner of his death.

Something grabbed Sander's arm and he yelped like a dog. 'Malachy!' he said, baffled but overjoyed to see the old rogue. 'You came back for me.'

'Course I did, you loon,' Malachy said, trying to pull Sander away. 'I found a coupla wide-awake horses in the next field. Let's go, c'mon, shift.'

Sander knew he should be running but his legs had become jelly again. 'No, we can't. Look at him. Look at Gunnar – he's going to win.'

Gunnar was hemmed in against a barn wall, his sword zigzagging as it knocked back each attacking blow from the trio of men shuffling back and forth, taking turns to jab and slash. Outnumbered though he was, he was clearly the better swordsman, and despite all their differences, Sander desperately wanted Gunnar to win.

'He'll be dead in three moves,' Malachy said. 'You can waste time here and watch him die, or get a head start with me. Choice is yours. I was stupid to come back.'

'No, you're wrong, he'll—'

One of the attackers deliberately ran his belly into Gunnar's sword, as if he had some kind of insane death wish. Even in his heightened state, Gunnar hadn't expected that. The man gripped Gunnar's sword hand and now the captain's only weapon was stuck. Then the other two came at him and he didn't stand a chance.

Malachy had been wrong: the captain was doomed in only two moves.

Sander was already running after Malachy into the fields as Gunnar Jarl, captain of the King's Guard, screamed then began to choke on his own blood. At the sound of another strangled cry, Sander dared to glance back and saw Gunnar, in a final act of defiance, shaking his sword free and sticking it through one of his attackers. The second man died, but the sole survivor calmly despatched Gunnar with a blade through the throat.

Sander let out an involuntary noise, a rasping sob of fear. He found his breath again and kept running, hands still tied behind his back.

'Untie me, Malachy, untie me now, please!'

Malachy didn't answer, slipping between the rows of corn with all the guile of a rodent. Sander, by contrast, tripped and fell head over heels into the field. Pollen filled the air and got into his nose, and he fought the urge to sneeze. When Sander staggered upright again, Malachy was nowhere to be seen. The farm was behind him and there was a line of trees ahead of him. He saw the blue light again some way back in the wood and ducked out of sight. If that was Rosheen, why hadn't she joined the fray?

Sander moved in a running crouch, keeping his head down. There were shouts from the farm. He couldn't make out the words, but someone was taking charge and they knew they hadn't killed every-one. It wouldn't be long before they figured out where he'd run to. Gods, if that was Rosheen, then she could be tracking his heartbeat even now. Sander ran blindly.

He found Orren slumped against a tree in the woods. Lying next to Orren was her would-be kidnapper with a dagger buried in his crotch. He had made the mistake of underestimating Orren's resourcefulness in a crisis and, if the astonished looked on his dead face was anything to go by, it had come as something of a shock.

Orren had paid a heavy price. Her yellow robe was stained with blood across her left side. Her face was white in the moonlight but, even so, she was smiling.

'What are you so happy about?' Sander asked as he turned and hunched down to yank the dagger from the dead man's groin. The handle was slippy with blood, but Sander was able to start cutting through the ropes binding his wrists while doing his best to avoid slic-ing one or more of his fingers.

'The soil, the sun and the sea.' Orren's eyes were dull and her voice was a whisper, but she was full of that unwavering certainty. 'I kept my faith, Brother, and soon I will join the Goddess. She will welcome me with her loving embrace and together we shall spend eternity in everlasting love.'

The dagger finished cutting through the rope and Sander's hands were finally free. He crawled to Orren's side to check her wounds and found a cut on her back. It was a thin slash, but it had bitten deep into her flesh and thick blood oozed slowly from it with a horrible cease-lessness. Already there was a bad smell. She wasn't going to live and she knew it.

'The soil, the sun...' Her voice faltered.

'And the sea, yes,' Sander finished for her, sitting back and catching his breath. Even though every fibre of his being was telling him he should run, there was something he had to know. 'Why did you do it, Orren?' Orren's head dipped, but Sander gently took her face in his hands and looked into her eyes. 'What did Yorath promise you?'

'A place at his side.' She smiled. 'As magic falls and the Faith rises, he said I would be there with him. In the chaos of war, the people would need succour and the Faith would be ready. Together, the First Minister and I would build the church anew. It is the Goddess's bidding.'

'You'd let a little girl die?' Sander said. 'For a promotion?'

'She would be welcomed in the garden of eternity by the Goddess and live for ever in—'

'No, Orren, she won't. And neither will you.'

Sander heard shouts in the field beyond the trees. Rosheen and one of the attackers were exchanging notes and closing in. He'd know her voice anywhere. This was one time he hated to be proved right.

'You will pray, Brother,' Orren said, her voice little more than a gasp. 'Before the end comes, your fear will make you pious. It is only at the end that the truth is revealed.'

'The truth? You want the truth? You're cold, yes? Your sight's fad-ing.' Days of pent-up frustration with Orren's pious certainty was coming to a boil. 'Everything's losing its colour, it's becoming more difficult to hear? Am I right? I've sat with the dying before and it's not like stepping through a door, there is no warm embrace, no garden of eternity. There's only death, Orren.

'Not long from now, you will cease to exist, your mind will no longer function, your organs will fail and everything you've ever done, everything you've ever believed in, will have been a complete waste of time. A lie. Imagine all the good you could have done instead of spreading your poison, hmm? Why don't you think about that in your last few moments, eh?'

Then he saw it. A flicker of doubt as Orren's face fell. A brief flush of fear. He felt a pang of self-loathing at spitting his anger and frustration in the face of a dying woman. And, for a moment, he wished he had her simple confidence.

'The Word…' Her voice was little more than a cracked hiss as she reached for her leather-bound copy of the Word of the Goddess.

'Goodbye, Orren.' Sander snatched up the book, placed it in her bloody hand, then got to his feet.

Her fingers entwined with his, gently at first, then she closed her grip with every last ounce of her strength. '*He's here!*' she called out, her voice bellowing like a sergeant-at-arms on drill duty. '*I have him, he's here!*'

Sander shook her hand away and she began to cough and spit specks of blood onto her robe. She was utterly spent and, as he stood, she looked at him through heavy-lidded eyes. 'You will pray,' she said with a sneering grin. 'At the end, Brother, you will pray.' And with that, she breathed her last in a gurgling death rattle.

Sander ran. Ran as fast as he could. Ran to live.

The Hearts of Hunters and Prey

Bowden returned alone.

Rosheen's heart sank when she saw him. She had dared to hope that it might be over now. Bowden slumped towards the horses, head bowed, back bent. This was not the triumphant stride of a victorious man.

Still, she had to ask: 'Is it done? What happened?'

'Two got away.' Bowden's black hair was lank with sweat. He took the water gourd tied to his horse's saddle, drank deeply then poured more over his head. Whoever Bowden and his men had attacked hadn't been defenceless merpeople, or a frightened, powerless mage. Their prey had put up a fight. A good one. It was the first time Rosheen had seen Bowden look so dispirited, as if he was convinced that this mission might never end.

'Where are the rest of your men?'

'Dead,' Bowden said matter-of-factly as he began to untie the dead men's horses.

'Dear gods,' Rosheen said, glad that she hadn't been in the thick of it. Though a part of her wondered if she might have been able to stop it. She had argued strategy with Bowden beforehand. She told him that she could send a frost, causing the group to remain in a deep slumber, and they could simply kidnap Sander and end his mission without any further bloodshed.

Bowden had ordered her to stay back. It was a job for blades, he told her, and his orders said nothing about kidnapping. His loathing of magic and his stubborn insistence on brutality had already made this mission unnecessarily long and savage. So she sent the frost anyway, as a warning to Sander's group. She had naively hoped that he would see it as a sign, wake the others, flee and avoid a massacre. Her blood ran cold at the thought of how badly everything had gone wrong.

'What about the mage?'

'The mage wasn't among the dead.' The mercenary slapped the hindquarters of the dead men's horses, sending all but his mount galloping back down the path to Haldor.

'Where did he go?'

'If I knew that, would I be here?' Bowden muttered an insult under his breath, replaced his gourd and reached into his jerkin, producing a small silver flask that contained something far more potent than water. He tipped his head back as he took a swig. Calm returned to his eyes, colour to his cheeks. 'We should have brought dogs,' he said in a rare moment of regret.

'I can track him.' Even as the words came out, Rosheen began to doubt herself. *Can I, still?* She would not have hesitated in the past, but the Lapis stone on her staff was growing dim.

'With that thing…?' Bowden nodded at the blue stone and waggled his fingers like a street magician. 'Bollocks.'

'Give me a moment.' She ignored his mockery and closed her eyes.

Rosheen listened for Sander's heartbeat. It wouldn't be easy. Even at night, the forest would be teeming with tiny hearts. Some puffed like bellows in slumber, others rattled like peas in a jar. She could sense hunters and prey playing out their nightly game of life and death throughout the wood. The human heart had a particular kind of timbre, especially one in flight. It was fast and heavy, every beat like the flap of a bat's wings, and she found one pounding in terror a little over a mile off.

'That way.' She opened her eyes and turned her horse towards where the Connal River tumbled down through the woods on a bed of rocks and rapids. Bowden mounted his horse and took position beside her. 'Follow me,' she commanded.

Orren's words rang in Sander's ears. 'You will pray,' she had told him. 'Your fear will make you pious.' Well, she was wrong about that. Fear had given him what felt like unlimited reserves of energy. The terrifying image of Gunnar, Norrey and Rasmus being run through would haunt him for the rest of his days. It was one thing reading about battles and skirmishes in the Chronicles, but another thing altogether to see humans, people he had been bickering with only moments before, turned into nothing more than slabs of meat before his very eyes. The fine line between a happy and fulfilling life and becoming a feast for worms had never been thinner.

So, no, he wasn't praying. He was cursing. Cursing the day he ever agreed to become a mage, cursing the first time he walked through the gates of Taranis, and, most of all, he cursed Malachy's name again and again. The old bastard had come to his rescue, then disappeared at the first sign of trouble.

And Sander cursed himself for losing Malachy. He wasn't much of a rider, but any horse would have been better than his heavy feet slapping around in sandals that pinched at the skin between his toes and threatened to fly off with every step.

He had no idea where he was going. Only that he had to put as much distance between himself and Rosheen and those murderers as possible. Especially Rosheen. If she still had magic and was within close range, she would be able to track him – through his heartbeat, or the warmth of his body, or the racket he was making as he crashed through the thickening undergrowth of the wood.

So he kept moving, his bad ankle flashing with pain with each footfall, all the while trying to formulate a plan that would see him survive not just tomorrow, but for many years to come. He could fake his death somehow. Change his identity. Disappear.

The whinny of a horse bounced around the labyrinth of trees. He couldn't pinpoint where it was coming from, though it was close by. He dared to glance back and saw that blue glow again, bobbing and weaving through the trees, sending long shadows swirling around it.

It had to be a Lapis stone, a fragment from the shattered moon. Rosheen must have got her hands on one somehow. This wasn't unheard of. Throughout history, these stones had been dug up or found in river beds or on beaches, and some mages attached them to impressive-looking staffs carved from rare woods to make them look twice as pompous as they already were. These stones never had any effect on the strength of their power, but magic had been all around them back then. Now it only came in small, rock-sized doses.

He had to get one of those stones for himself. The world must be littered with them. Magic wasn't gone. Sander simply had to work harder to find it.

Of course, he had to get away from this lot in one piece first.

The long grass snagged at his feet and he lost both sandals. The brambles tugged at his robe, the nettles stung his hands and his progress was agonisingly slow, but Sander knew there was no way their horses could follow him through this mire. Even if Rosheen knew where he was, they wouldn't be able to run him down.

Sander didn't recognise the man she was with, the sole survivor of the farm massacre. He certainly couldn't be part of Torren's guard, not unless the old fool had gone completely mad, and what little Sander had heard of his voice suggested he was from the north. That meant she was working for the warlord Haldor. Why the blazes would she do that? He recalled her saying something about her brother, though at the time he was too busy trying not to be eaten by her griffin to take much notice.

She was doing what she needed to in order to survive. It's what Sander would do. Sly compromise was better than death any day of the week. And then he thought back to the frost that appeared right before the mercenaries did. Was it a warning? Her way of alerting Sander and giving them a fighting chance? Maybe she thought that if Haldor's men died in the attack, then she would be free, too?

All this speculation was enough to distract Sander from the pain of his aching bones and muscles, but it also meant that he was running blind and so he was completely unprepared when the undergrowth gave way and he found himself tumbling through the air and landing with a heavy splash in the rapids of the freezing cold Connal River.

'I've lost him,' Rosheen said.

Bowden pulled on his horse's reins and Rosheen caught a glimpse of his weary look of disdain. She reckoned he had probably killed people for less, but she put his hatred to one side and concentrated on the task at hand.

Sander had hurtled off like a frightened rabbit. Rosheen was astounded by the energy he was able to summon, but he soon slowed down as he became tangled in the wood's undergrowth. They couldn't get close to him, but they could ride parallel, and she knew that sooner or later he would come to the river.

She just didn't expect him to run headlong into it.

That was the only explanation. No one would willingly dive into the Connal River, even on a spring evening, *even* when pursued by deadly hunters. The water came from Connal Lake, which in turn came from the ice and snow of the Conloch Mountains. It was so cold it burned, and if Sander was in the water now, he had either drowned or was doing his best to get out as quickly as possible.

'He's in the river,' she told Bowden. 'We follow this path, there's a bridge ahead. We cross it, bear left, follow the bank and we'll pick him up somewhere downstream. Make sense?'

Bowden muttered some kind of begrudging acknowledgement, kicked the flanks of his horse and thundered ahead down the path.

Rosheen held back for a moment and dared to wonder what would happen if she just turned her horse around and went the other way.

Her brother would die, that's what.

She supposed there was something admirable in Bowden's dogged determination, even if the cause was so despicable. How do you fight that kind of will without becoming the very thing you despise? Rosheen thought to ask Anzu when they next…

Grief consumed her, taking her breath away like a punch to the belly.

How could she have forgotten that Anzu was dead? How was it possible to be such an empty vessel that she could forget the fate of her best friend? Rosheen's cheeks burned and her body rocked with sobs as tears came freely. She hated herself for crying, she hated herself for not thinking of Anzu until now, she hated working with this cold-blooded bastard, and she hated what she had become. Rosheen needed her friend's shrewdness and wisdom more than ever, but they had disappeared like a morning frost.

The wood fell quiet, the only noise the fading gallop of Bowden's horse.

I love you, Rosheen. Anzu's voice came to Rosheen. *Whatever happens, never forget that. Love, forgiveness, mercy… none of these need magic to feel real.*

She knew it was only a memory – some of Anzu's last words to her – and they should have given her comfort, but they only reminded Rosheen of how far she had fallen. Love, forgiveness and mercy were in short supply these days. Rosheen tried to conjure Anzu's voice again, but it wouldn't come. Rosheen puffed her cheeks, blinked the tears away, geed her own horse and set off after Bowden.

Having stumbled into the river rapids, Sander was swept away by the rushing water, banging his bare scalp on a series of boulders and sending lightning bolts of pain around his skull. He began gasping uncontrollably, his heart beat like a hummingbird's wings and he started to panic. This might have killed any other poor soul in the clutches of the icy river, but for Sander it was merely another panic attack, and he utilised all his usual breathing techniques to bring it under control. Much more worrying was that he had lost all feeling in his fingers and toes, and any attempt to clutch at a passing branch or stone to stop his inevitable doom was foiled by his useless hands. Soon all he could see was a flurry of foaming bubbles around him. The unforgiving river had Sander in its grip and wasn't inclined to let him go.

He went tumbling over a small weir and landed on a damp wooden ledge underneath it. Sheltered from the rushing water, Sander's heartbeat returned to something like his normal erratic anxiety. He got on all fours and coughed up what felt like half the river from his throat, the tumbling water brushing against his face.

A deep sleep felt like the best idea in the world right now. He knew he might never wake from it again, but even death's embrace would be warmer than this, surely? Shivering, his teeth chattering, Sander wondered if he was visible to Rosheen.

And then he felt it.

The power of the stone.

With it came the approaching clop of horses' hooves and voices muffled by the white noise of the falls, but there was no doubt that Rosheen was there and she carried the stone with her. He could feel its energy in the same way you might get a taste of coriander in a soup. It made his skin tingle, his muscles warmed a little, his hearing and sight improved, and he was more alert and aware of the space around him than he had been in days. Oh gods, this was almost more cruel than taking magic from him. This was a tease, the fates tormenting him before he died. Even with this tiny morsel of magic, he was no match for Rosheen. It was barely sufficient to keep him alive long enough for him to be found and slaughtered. He could wiggle his toes and move his fingers again. Maybe, in the moments before he died, he would be able to make a final, defiant, rude gesture with them?

Rosheen almost rode straight past Bowden, little more than a silhouette between willow trees by the riverbank.

'Found him?' she asked, bringing her horse alongside Bowden's.

'You tell me, witch,' Bowden said. 'Do your thing.'

'I can't sense him anywhere now,' she said. 'He's an old man. If he fell into the river, he's as good as dead.'

'Not good enough. Haldor will want his head.'

'So we're doomed to search every inch of a rushing river to find him? He could have gone over Muirne's Falls and broken his neck. Dead or alive, he's most likely halfway to the Sugar Sea by now.'

'Then we search the Sugar Sea,' he barked, then gestured at her stone. 'Unless the power in that thing is too weak? Have you spent your usefulness?'

'Would you like to find out how much power I have?' Rosheen raised her staff, the Lapis stone's blue glow illuminating the trees around them and sparkling on the rapids.

Bowden didn't move, and Rosheen felt her heart sink as she mourned the passing of possibly her last gesture of power. 'I'll find him,' she said, lowering the near-impotent stone. 'There are ways.'

There were indeed, but if her power was almost spent, she needed to use what remained sparingly. She could try without magic. She needed a clear mind to think. Rosheen closed her eyes and raised the staff. A little bit of show for Bowden while she thought.

If she were Sander, what would she do? What if she had no magic, but knew how magic worked? He would know that she'd be looking for a heartbeat, sensing his body heat. He would try to fade to nothing, throw his pursuers off the scent. And to do that, he would need to be cold.

She opened her eyes again. The river was shallow and offered few places to hide. He could be skulking behind one of the bigger boulders, or in the thick foliage on the far riverbank, but she would have sensed him immediately. She felt a trembling glimmer of a heartbeat.

Wherever it was, it began to crescendo. Like someone was about to attempt something monumentally stupid.

Her eyes were drawn to an old weir a little way upstream. A tiny waterfall and the perfect place to hide. She raised a finger to her lips, caught Bowden's eye and tilted her head towards the weir. He understood immediately, waded into the rushing water and drew his sword with a loud scraping noise that set Rosheen's teeth on edge and silenced every creature in the wood.

The foaming water was up to Bowden's knees, and as he levelled the sword at the weir, something burst from behind its shimmering veil.

Sander, fugitive and former mage, came flailing out of the water, clumsily knocking Bowden onto his back, and flopped with all the grace of a newborn foal into the rapids, which swept him away.

Sander knew he was a coward. He had been called that plenty of times before and did not take it as an insult. Instead, he embraced the concept like an old friend. He knew that cowardice would keep him alive. Skulking under the weir was the stupid option. Simply waiting for the mercenary to stick him with that sword, or hoping that he would somehow miss Sander and move on, was a fool's death. The brave would fight, or make some kind of defiant speech or gesture before meeting their end. Cowards fled to live another day. Cowards ran and learned to live with blazing self-loathing, which he knew he could douse with ale, wine and whisky.

Sander waited until the mercenary raised his sword, then sprang from behind the falls and made a run for it. Almost immediately, the churning water took his feet from under him and sent him precisely where he didn't want to be: straight into the mercenary's arms. Sander lashed out blindly and was astonished to see the man go tumbling back into the water. Sander had little time to enjoy his accidental victory, though, as the water grabbed his legs and yanked him away.

Once more, he found himself bouncing between stones that used his head for sport. As he spun, he saw the mercenary was back on his feet and making for the riverbank. Rosheen was already riding parallel to Sander, no doubt looking ahead for some bend in the river or a bridge where she might corner him, but the water cut a straight, fast and deadly path.

As the whole world whirled around him, he saw a row of boulders ahead where a grey mist rose in the moonlight and the river disappeared. With a sudden sinking sensation in the pit of his stomach, Sander realised that this was Muirne's Falls. A drop of over a hundred feet into deep water.

He was stuck between a maniac with a sword and a fall leading to almost certain death.

In the blink of an eye, he chose the fall.

This was it. This was his way out. In moments, he would either be free or dead. It was an exhilarating thought. Sander's arms began to flap in a feeble attempt at swimming in the falls' direction, but it didn't matter. The river was taking him there whatever happened. It was only yards away now. He took a deep breath, steeling himself for the drop, trying to remember if there were any big rocks below.

And then he stopped.

The water continued to rush around him, but he no longer moved. He tried flailing his limbs some more, but while his arms and legs rose and fell with the water, he remained defiantly in place.

His robes had snagged on something.

'There!' a voice called.

Sander turned to see Rosheen come galloping to a halt by the riverbank. The big bastard mercenary with the punished face was already off his horse, soaking wet, sword drawn and wading through the water to kill Sander.

Meanwhile, Sander was becoming increasingly entangled in his robes. His belt had caught on a broken tree branch. As he reached behind him to unravel the mess, the wet and heavy robes merely tightened around him like a Sachari finger puzzle.

The mercenary was almost upon him. He raised his sword for a killing blow. Sander was about to be slaughtered like a farm animal.

Sander twisted the other way and slipped out of his robes completely. Now naked save for his thin linen underpants, Sander flung himself back into the rapids and made a decision not to fight them. As he closed his eyes, relaxed his arms and legs and prepared for death, the icy-cold water took his breath away, cupped him in its hand and threw him over the edge of the falls like a child flinging a ball.

The moment Sander tipped over the edge and found himself tumbling through the misty air, he knew he had made another monumentally bad decision. He had merely switched one grisly death for another. If the fall didn't kill him, then the frothing water below would.

His stomach turned over and he felt an unreal tingling all over his body as every nerve prepared for the worst. The last thing he remembered was a strange thought. How the water that was about to kill him had no malice towards him. It didn't care if he lived or died. It simply continued, oblivious, on its way to the sea where it would return to the air, rain down again in the mountains and start its journey all over again. Sander wondered if he should have chosen to live that way. Let life carry him along in peace and not fight it at every turn. Would he have been happier? He longed to be happy again, to be content with his lot. And he wondered if that thought qualified as a kind of prayer. And if it did, then he was angrier than ever that Orren had been right, and he wanted to live more than anything just to prove her wrong...

He hit the water and it knocked everything out of him.

Killing Sander Bree

Rosheen looked on as Sander tumbled like a rag doll over the edge of the waterfall.

'This way!' She didn't wait for Bowden to clamber out of the river but used her magic to glide to the base of the falls. Landing gently, she ran to the riverbank and closed her eyes, listening for Sander's heartbeat, some sign that he was still alive.

'Well?' Bowden hollered from above. He was soaked from head to toe and surrounded by a ghostly halo of spray, his sword drawn as he jogged down the narrow path that zigzagged from the top of the falls.

'I think...' She opened her eyes. 'I think he's dead.'

'You *think?* Not good enough, witch. We search the river. All night if we have—'

'Good idea. You search this side. I'll do the other.'

Before Bowden could object, she leapt into the air with her staff in one hand, soaring high over the wide river and landing gracefully on the far bank. She glanced back to see Bowden spit into the water before beginning his own search.

She was glad to be away from the aura of hatred he carried with him. She puffed her cheeks and took a cleansing breath, and the tension began to ease. And the truth was, she *could* sense something out there, a glimmer of life. Not much, but it might be him. If Sander was alive, she wanted to be the one who found him.

Rosheen searched all night. Every sandy bank, every bend in the river, every burrow and dam and weir. Nothing. The glimmer she felt had been very faint, and now it was gone for good.

Every so often, Bowden would call from the other bank, 'Anything?'

'No!'

The first hint of daylight was glowing on the horizon and Rosheen wondered if her Lapis stone would see another dawn. And then would she even see the day after that? With nothing to use for self-defence and no dead mage to deliver to Haldor, she was as good as—

Oh.

Something out there kicked into life. Like someone waking from a bad dream, heart pounding, lungs gasping. Rosheen closed her eyes and it shone like a beacon.

The thing that Rosheen found crawling into the woods was barely alive. Its pale, bare scalp was dotted with nicks where it had been shaved with a blunt razor, blotchy skin hung off its emaciated ribs and it muttered nonsense to itself while its teeth chattered.

'Abbey, there's an abbey, Barrow Abbey, Faylen will be there, Faylen, she'll know, Barrow Abbey...'

To kill it would be a mercy, she told herself.

Love, forgiveness, mercy. Anzu's words came to Rosheen once more. 'Sander?' she whispered.

He jolted like he'd been bitten, brought his knees up to his chest and crossed his arms, 'Nopleaseohpleaseohpleasedontkillmepleaseoh-pleaseohplease,' he babbled. When no death blow came, he opened glassy eyes that had sunk into dark sockets. 'Rosh— Rosheen?' His eyes widened with a combination of shock and hope.

He could feel the magic coming from the stone.

He could feel it and he was going to use it.

Before Rosheen could back away, Sander flexed his hands and a small ball of white energy appeared and flamed in his palm. He scurried to his knees and raised his arm to hurl it at Rosheen, but then the flame died as quickly as it had appeared and he fell back to the ground.

'I can't...' he gasped, exhausted. 'I can't even... Too bloody weak, even for... Oh gods, look at me. Look at me, Rosh. I'm sorry. I'm so sorry.' He bared his teeth in a pitiful smile, laughing at his pathetic attempt to use the stone. The laughter turned to tears and his body shuddered with sobs. 'Oh, Rosheen. You don't have to do this. I know they have your brother, but do you know who you're dealing with? What kind of people they are? I've seen what they do – they butcher people like meat. Do you think for one moment that they'll keep their word? Warlords don't make deals or keep promises. They make war.

They *literally* lord it over war. That's how they get their name. That poor boy is as good as dead, if he's not dead already.'

'Shut up, shut up!' she hissed at him, but her stomach knotted at his words. She needed time to think, and if his little fireball hadn't drawn Bowden's attention, then his pleading soon would. It didn't matter how wide the river was, the bloodthirsty mercenary would make up her mind for her.

'You're not a killer,' Sander said, lowering his voice. 'I know you, Rosheen. You're a good person. Please. Let me go. My sister is nearby. Barrow Abbey. Downriver then follow the Andraste Road. You'll never see me again, I swear. I'll disappear. You can't do this. I know you can't.'

She could do it with a thought. Rosheen had the power. He wouldn't feel a thing. He'd be dead before his head hit the ground. The longer she drew this out, the worse it was for him.

Rosheen brought her staff around, the glowing stone aimed directly at Sander's head, giving him a ghostly glow. He scuttled away, cowering beneath his arms and now on his knees.

Love, forgiveness, mercy. None of these need magic…

'I'm sorry, I'm sorry. Make it quick,' he said. 'But know first that you're condemning that poor girl to death. I'm the only one who can help her, the only one, Rosheen, you know this. You're the truth-seer – look into my heart, tell me I'm lying, I won't resist, I'm an open door, do it, Rosheen, look into my mind, do it.'

So she did. Closing her eyes, she found the light of his mind easily. Images, memories, some vibrant, some faded, came rushing by in no order whatsoever. The assorted mess of Sander's thoughts. She found his knowledge of merclan medicine. Little shining bubbles of skill and expertise. They were swept aside by more visceral, visual memories. Sander's friend Ragnall hanging in a village square; a cave where a dog came pouncing onto Sander; Princess Brianna's smiling face bursting into giggles; the disapproving expression of the young Sister of the Faith who had accompanied Sander on his journey; the same Sister dying, slumped against a tree, followed by a flash of grisly vignettes showing each of Sander's companions cut down or run through.

Rosheen broke the connection, finding her breath with a shudder.

'You see who they are? What they do?' Sander's teeth were chattering again. 'Course you do. They've changed you, too, haven't they? Boring goody-two-shoes Rosheen wants to lash out and kill.'

Rosheen shuddered. As much as she had looked into him, he had seen her ugly side, too.

'Use that.' Sander nodded at her staff. 'I know you want to. Kill them now.'

'And my brother dies—'

'Send them to sleep, make them think they're chickens, do whatever needs to be done to buy us some time to think, just don't kill me. Please Rosheen, I'm begging you. If not for me, think of that girl.'

Rosheen lowered her staff.

'Anything?' Bowden's voice cut through the moment. 'Witch! Anything?'

'No!' she called back and took a step towards Sander. Okay. This was it. She was actually going to do this. There was a spot in the brain. Shutting it down brought a peaceful death. She had used it a couple of times when tending to elderly patients in pain. She just needed a moment. To be sure.

'Let me go,' Sander pleaded. 'This never happened. You never found me. Or tell them... tell them you saw me sink into the water!'

'They need a body. I'm sorry, Sander.' She raised the staff.

'Please, show a little love, forgiveness, mercy!' he pleaded.

'What did you say?' Rosheen said, quite breathless, and lowered the staff.

Sander's bony hand grabbed hers. 'A body? I can get you a body, I can get you a body!' he said. 'How much power is left in that thing?'

Sander watched from a hiding place in the reeds, exhausted, though his encounter with the stone had given him some little strength. Not enough for magic, but perhaps enough to get away from here. He had agreed with Rosheen that he would start running as soon as they parted ways, but he needed to be sure that she would keep her part of the deal. She had started behaving in a peculiar way. Looking off into the distance, as if hearing voices. As he watched, he had no doubt that she could sense his presence and would be furious that he was watching, but he didn't care. He had to see this.

Rosheen met the mercenary by a sandbank where she claimed to have pulled a body from the water. Apart from its undergarments, the body was naked, to match what they had seen tumble over Muirne's Falls.

Orren's body.

Even as Sander had suggested the idea, it made him feel nauseous, but he was desperate.

'Use a glamour,' he told Rosheen. 'Show them Orren's body but make them see me. The illusion won't last, but you only need to sustain it long enough to convince them, then leave the poor girl where she lies.'

Rosheen curled her lips in disgust as he outlined the plan, but this was the least appalling way out of their mess. Further draining the power of the Lapis stone, she sped back a mile or so through the woods to where he had told her she would find Orren, then carried the dead Sister over her shoulders and placed her on the sandbank.

She called for Bowden, and he arrived to inspect the body.

The trick to a glamour was to make the onlooker do all the hard work. Experience had taught Rosheen that if you pushed too hard on someone's mind, then they instinctively knew something was wrong, and Haldor said he had prepared his men for such tricks.

And Bowden's disposition was permanently set to one of suspicion. He was no fool.

'That's him,' Rosheen said, trying to keep the tremble from her voice as she gestured at the body lying face down in the sand. Her mind was queasy after the intense magic and she did her best to hide it. 'Drowned.'

Bowden ignored her, tilting his head and squinting at the body. Rosheen held her breath as he rolled it over.

He expected to see a dead mage and so that's what the glamour reflected back at him. Rosheen only saw Orren, slain Sister of the Faith.

'Good.' Bowden sniffed, drew his sword and in one swift movement sliced through Orren's neck. The Sister's head appeared to shake in disapproval as it rolled to one side. 'Bag it up. We're heading back.'

New Orders

Petra was crammed into a cage mounted on a long cart pulled by four dray horses as big as the ones Oskar used to watch ploughing the fields in the farms around Sabley. They exhaled great billows of steam as they trudged north along the King's Road from Port Byle.

The King's Road dated back to Ceezan times and was wide with smooth flagstones, perfect for their heavy load, and so they made good time. At every checkpoint, Bingham produced his bona fides with a flourish, a scroll with the king's seal declaring that he was on the king's business and should be given free passage. They were waved through each checkpoint without fuss by weary-looking soldiers who nevertheless stopped to stare at the caged wyvern as it passed.

'I could get used to this.' Bingham grinned as he flexed the reins and set the horses on their way once more.

Oskar said nothing, still trying to equate the perky Captain Bingham, the man who had generously given Oskar new boots, trousers, a shirt and a waistcoat, with the cold-blooded murderer that Gudrun had accused him of being. She'd clammed up immediately after telling him and wouldn't answer any of his questions, so Oskar chose to put her finger-pointing down to some kind of past resentment. Oskar had been on a ship full of killers and the captain wasn't anything like those men. This man couldn't be a murderer, surely?

They passed a dead unicorn. This was the most fascinating part of the journey for Oskar. He had only ever dreamed of seeing a unicorn, and now here was a real one, in the flesh, slumped by the side of the road, its eyes closed in eternal sleep. Oskar was struck by a sudden sadness that these beautiful creatures would now be a thing of the past.

'Bingham, can we stop and see the unicorn, please?'

'Sorry, lad, no time. Wars wait for no man, or unicorns, even. And besides, unexpected stops confuse and upset Gudrun, and we don't want her crying and wailing and banging her head, now, do we?'

Oh, for gods' sakes.

Gudrun's voice broke into Oskar's mind. She had been quietly

283

seething for the whole journey. Oskar knew how frustrating it was to keep up the stupid act, but she had been so unwelcoming to him that he had little sympathy for her.

They rode up front on the cart next to Bingham, sitting on a bench in a row, gently rocking with the rhythm of the road. He and Gudrun took turns to nod off, though Bingham was permanently perky and never needed to rest. Not when he was giving himself regular top-ups of snuff, anyway.

Gudrun was silent for the remainder of their journey. Oskar tried to see if he could somehow speak to her with his mind, but if he got through, she didn't reply.

They heard the king's army long before they could see it. A low rumble of marching boots, cartwheels turning, officers barking orders and the rhythmic scrape of blades being sharpened on whetstones. As they left the King's Road, Oskar glimpsed banners whipping in the wind further down the valley. Behind them in the haze were peaks of tents and yurts clustered together.

They found themselves at the end of a long queue of carts, many laden with post-magic contraptions, the essentials of war now that mages were no longer around to intervene in the fighting: siege towers teetering slowly along the road, battering rams squatting on giant wooden wheels, giant mobile cages for prisoners and horse-drawn ambulances for the wounded.

Oskar's mind tripped over the idea of a world without magic. If there *was* no magic, then what was happening to him? To Gudrun? Did these strange quirks count as magic? He wanted to talk with someone about it, with Gudrun, but she remained obstinately silent.

They eventually reached the head of the queue and were waved down at yet another checkpoint where a handful of King Bhaltair's men were gathered around a small shelter at a turn in the path. Petra hooted and shook her wings, prompting the soldiers to stand and draw their swords, spreading out as the cart rocked to a clumsy halt on the uneven path.

Bingham held his scroll aloft. 'Gentlemen, I am on the king's business.'

One of the soldiers, a man with large eyeglasses perched on his nose, sheathed his sword and took the scroll from Bingham to inspect it. 'Your orders are to report to the quartermaster at the camp where you will receive your ordnance. A detachment of infantry will accompany you to Canwick Tor, where you will launch your wyvern.' He glanced up from his notes to the great beast caged on the cart. 'Looks like a dragon to me.'

'It's a wyvern,' Bingham declared. 'Two legs and a forked tail. And what do you mean, ordnance? What ordnance?'

The soldier returned his attention to his notes. 'All it says here is "Where you will launch your wyvern and attack the targets given to you by the detachment's sergeant-at-arms". Is that clear?'

'Yes, uhm, no. I think there's been some kind of mistake.' Bingham's smile was still present, though somewhat diminished. 'General Kentigern requested that we perform missions of reconnaissance. There was nothing about ordnance – whatever *that* is – or targets, or any of that nonsense. Now, if you'll kindly point me in the direction of the general, I'm sure we can sort this all out to everyone's satisfaction.'

'That won't be possible.'

'Why not?'

'That's not for me to say, but I do have orders to commandeer your creature if you refuse to cooperate.'

'Oh, do you now? You and whose...? Actually, don't answer that. Why can't I see the general? I'll cooperate if I can see the general.'

The soldier's shoulders dropped, his head dipped, then he puffed his cheeks. 'Right, come on, then.' He beckoned for Bingham to follow him. 'I'll take you to the camp, and someone with more stripes on his arm can explain why you will obey these orders, and why, in future, if you disobey them, you can be killed on the spot.' He stalked off, muttering to himself, 'I don't know, bloody civilians, haven't got a bloody clue.'

Bingham hesitated and looked ahead to where the noise of warcraft came drifting down the valley, and Oskar could see that he was wondering if he might ever come back alive. 'Er... yes. Oskar, Gudrun, why don't you to stay here and look after Petra and the horses, hmm?'

'Yes, Captain.' Oskar took the reins and gave him a reassuring smile.

Bingham had to scurry to catch up with the soldier who was already some way down the path. The soldier's comrades-in-arms returned to the shelter where they played a game with dice, and Oskar and Gudrun were left together on the cart's bench.

'So...' Oskar started.

Shut up.

'How do you do that?' Oskar kept his voice down so as not to draw the attention of the remaining soldiers. 'And why bother now? He's not here, and I know you can speak so you can drop the pretence.'

Gudrun remained silent, her face turned away from him as she looked to the sky.

'I was a moon child, too,' Oskar said, not caring if she wasn't listening. It was a relief to unburden himself of all the changes he'd experienced over the last few days. 'I can do things now that I never imagined possible. Healing, strength. I can see like never before, I can hear the thistles on those rocks shaking in the breeze, and I have a voice. Even without the strange stuff, I'd be happy with a voice. I think I'd die if that was taken from me again. I think about the years wasted as a simple fool—'

'And you don't want to waste a minute longer,' Gudrun said, her own voice dry and rasping.

'Yes.'

'So you can see why I don't want to fritter away any more time speaking to you?'

'I understand what you're going through. We can learn from each other.'

'Water.'

'What?'

'Pass the water, I'm parched.'

Oskar unhooked a gourd from the side of the cart and handed it to her. Gudrun swigged some water, sloshed it around her cheeks then spat it out on the dirt below.

'You have no clue what I'm going through,' she said, her voice warmer now.

'Okay, no, but I can guess what your life was like before. Being patronised by everyone around you, even the ones who love you. Doing the jobs no one else would do, carrying buckets of shit and piss because you were the only one dumb enough to do so. Being beaten and abused and mocked in the streets—'

'I didn't carry shit,' Gudrun cut in, before taking another quick gulp of water. 'I shovelled it. Where they tied the horses around the back of a whorehouse in Port Byle. Bingham took pity on me. I owe him that much, I suppose. But I just ended up shovelling different shit from different horses.'

'At least he's family, of a sort.'

Gudrun laughed so hard that the soldiers looked up from their dice game. 'He's not family,' she said with a sniff. 'He was a regular at the knocking shop. No, my family gave me up. Runt of a big litter, and they didn't have the time, patience or coin to look after a moon child, gods forbid.'

'Then why does he say—?'

'Because he's the biggest liar you'll ever meet. Talk about horse shit – that man deposits more of it in one day than the entire King's Cavalry.'

'Why don't you tell him the truth? Tell him how you've changed. I'll back you up. The same thing happened to me and—'

'Are you out of your tiny mind?'

'I know it feels difficult, and he won't like it at first, but you can't live a lie for ever.'

'I won't be. Not for much longer, anyway.'

'What does that mean?'

'Nothing.'

'Gudrun, tell him.'

'I can't!'

'Why not?'

'He killed his brother!'

'I've met killers, Gudrun, and that man does not look like a murderer to me.'

'They come in all shapes and sizes. Trust me.'

'You saw him do it?'

287

'Yes.'

'So how—?'

'Did you ever wonder how he managed to bag a wyvern?'

Oskar glanced back at the forlorn creature in the cage behind them. It hardly looked fierce, but it had taken the three of them over an hour of cajoling and whipping to convince Petra to get into the cage on the back of the cart.

'Bingham and his brother Oddmun are – *were* – swindlers. Crooks from the coast who used to steal wyvern eggs and pass them off as Parthalan dragon eggs to gullible apothecaries who would pay big money—'

'What's the difference?'

'What?'

'Between a wyvern's egg and a Parthalan dragon's egg?'

'Do you want to hear this story or not? Then shut up and let me finish.' Gudrun took another gulp from the gourd. 'After the Lapis Moon was destroyed, we went egg hunting as usual. I was still trying to figure out what in the world was happening to me, without letting on that anything *had* actually happened to me, and I didn't notice that the wyverns were behaving differently. Bingham did, though. They were tired, sluggish. Weak. We'd already heard stories that mages and magical creatures were losing their powers, so Oddmun reckoned the moon was what gave the wyverns their strength and now it was gone. So Bingham had this brilliant idea: let's get ourselves a wyvern, flog it to the highest bidder. Oddmun's iffy, but Bingham talked him round, reminding him of a baby wyvern that was sold in Cerwidden last year for more than a thousand silver coins. So, they send me back to the cart to fetch some rope while they sneak into a cave where there's a nest but no mother about, and they set about stealing a baby.'

'Petra's a baby?' Oskar glanced again at their enormous caged passenger.

'Runt of the litter,' Gudrun said. 'She's grown a bit since then, mind. Anyways, before they can get her out, Mummy comes home with a mouthful of fish, only to find these two idiots trying to steal her baby. Now, wyverns ain't as fierce as dragons, but you've seen this one's teeth? Imagine being on the end of ones twice the size of Petra's.'

'Where were you?'

'Getting the rope. When I heard screams, I came running. Mother had them both cornered, and I got there in time to see Bingham shouting, *I'm sorry, I'm so sorry!* before shoving his screaming brother right into the jaws of Mummy Wyvern and running off with her bundle of joy.'

'Why would he do that?'

'A thousand silver coins. The patronage of a king. Bingham is such a sad bastard that the good word of a king is worth more to him than his own flesh and blood. They hated each other anyways, Bingham just needed the right opportunity.'

'How can you be sure? Maybe it was an accident?'

'You sound like Bingham. *Poor, dumb Gudrun saw Oddmun sacrificing himself to save his brother. May the gods bless Oddmun for his bravery and selflessness.* You know when you tell a lie so many times you start to think it's true? Bingham reckons poor, dumb Gudrun doesn't know what she saw, so he's not worried about poor, dumb Gudrun telling anyone. But if he figures out that I'm anything other than poor, dumb Gudrun... then he'll kill me, too.'

'You can't be sure – let me talk to him, I—'

Shut up. He's coming.

Gudrun's voice was in his head again. Oskar looked down the valley to see the unmistakable gangly frame of Bingham heading back towards them. He was gesticulating to the soldier and another man walking with them.

When Oskar looked back to Gudrun, she was staring into space with heavy eyelids, a slack jaw and a vacant expression. A moon child once more.

A Nun, a Mercenary and a General Meet in an Abbey and Gang Up on a Mage

Sander could sleep through the screams and unexpected wails of pain so long as they weren't his, but it was the smells that eventually woke him. He was trying to piece together his recent memories into some kind of order, but an unholy mix of pungent vomit, acrid piss and steaming shit kept clamouring for his attention and distracting him.

He tried to put them aside as flashes of his escape from Rosheen and the mercenary came to him: watching from the riverbank with bated breath as Rosheen showed the mercenary Orren's body; wincing as the man cut Orren's head off with all the bored efficiency of a village butcher; then his flight – scurrying into the woods, half-naked, barefoot, chattering to himself, nauseous with fear, cold, wet and convinced he would be dead before sunrise.

He found a lone horse silhouetted in a cloud of its own breath, idly chewing hay in a field with no owner in sight, and so he claimed it. Riding it unsaddled, he took the Andraste Road south towards Barrow Abbey. His sister's abbey.

And even though he had no recollection of the remainder of the journey, he knew that's where he must have arrived, for one other scent wove itself through all the others: the sharp sting of incense. An odour that triggered much older memories of visiting Faylen here when she was a noviciate, of the candlelight glistening on proud tears as they rolled down their father's cheeks, and of the downcast sadness of their mother, who always stood in Father's shadow.

There had been no screaming in the abbey then. No bodily fluids stinking the place up. Only a solemn quiet that had always bored Sander when he was a boy, though he rather fancied a healthy dose of tranquillity right now.

'Ah, you're awake at last,' said a familiar voice. 'Thank the gods, I couldn't bear another moment with only these poor wretched bastards for company.'

Sander hadn't realised he had opened his eyes. It was so dark in this corner of the abbey that his vision had taken a while to adjust, and he could now see a handful of green weeds and grey mushrooms huddled against the stone wall. He was on a wooden cot stuffed with straw that had long lost its spring, but it was warm and dry, sensations he'd thought he would never experience again after his recent adventures. He could feel the weight of round earthenware bed warmers wrapped in hessian sacks by his head, belly and feet. Cool to the touch now, but with a hint of warmth when he slipped his hand inside one of the sacks.

'Bree? Sander Bree? That *is* you, isn't it?' The insistent voice was clearly not used to being ignored.

With a series of involuntary groans, Sander propped himself up on one elbow to acknowledge the voice and survey his surroundings. He was in the abbey's great hall. Domed and circular, it was normally a place of worship with prayer mats arranged like rays of the sun around the central altar. The altar remained, but the mats were covered with bodies. Maybe a hundred combatants from both sides of the conflict were scattered in the dappled light of the tall stained-glass windows. Many were writhing in the eternal fidget of the injured, looking for that one position that might take the pain away, if only for a short while. They were tended to by Brothers and Sisters of the Faith in their yellow robes, all stained with blood.

A lucky few of the wounded were in beds pushed against the wall. Sander was in one, as was his pestering neighbour, whom he was surprised to find was none other than General Kentigern. For a man who was known for his ruddy complexion and kaleidoscopic nose, the general looked dangerously pale, his once-beady eyes now sunk into dark sockets, and his ample body slowly rose and fell under the sheets like bellows as he laboured to breathe.

'Been through the wars a bit, eh, Bree?' Kentigern chuckled a cough. 'I like what they did to your hair. A vast improvement.'

Sander instinctively ran his fingers over his scalp. No longer shiny bald, but now peppered with tufts and patches of tiny hairs. It gave him some small hope that he might get his full head of hair back one day.

'Well, fancy seeing you here,' Sander croaked with a dry mouth. 'How goes the war, General?'

'Very badly, if truth be told. The mercenary Frang has an endless supply of men. A rabble who know nothing of the rules of war.'

'The rules.' Sander shook his head in despair. 'You expect them all to line up and march slowly towards your blades like civilised soldiers, don't you? If the first of rule of war is "Know your enemy" then you lot are doomed, General.'

'I see your failure hasn't dimmed your flippancy.'

'*My* failure? If I had gone alone as I wanted to, I would be done by now. But no, you had to send me off with the golden boy of the King's Guard who barely knew one end of a sword from another until he ended up skewered on the pointy end of someone else's.'

'Gunnar is dead?'

'Yes, I'm sorry to say. He wasn't a bad soldier, just... naive.' Sander took a breath a let his anger dim. He didn't want to ask the next question for fear of bad news, but he had to know. 'How's... how's the princess? How's Brianna?'

'She's a fighter. Still alive and defying all pessimistic expectations.' The general's voice dropped to a sorrowful low. 'She's survived longer than anyone might have hoped, though last I heard, she was failing.'

A little fire kindled in Sander's belly. 'She's alive? Gods, how long have I been resting? I can still... I can...' Sander tried to heave himself out of the cot, but his head spun and he fell back, panting for breath. Kentigern's look of pity robbed him of any remaining energy.

'Truth be told, we had scant hope that your mission would succeed,' Kentigern said, 'but it was a hope all the same.'

'Oh, that's great,' Sander said, slowly getting his puff back. 'So, while I was wasting all my time and energy only to end up half-dead, not one of you ungrateful buggers thought I could do it anyway. Well, fuck you very much, General. Who died and made you morale officer?'

Somewhere, a man started to scream. It was a wordless, gargling noise, as if he were biting down on something, and it bounced off the dome and around the circular walls straight into everyone's ears as if he were in the next bed.

'An unfortunate by-product of Barrow Abbey's excellent acoustics,' Kentigern said, pulling back his sheet. Both his legs ended below his knees, wrapped in bloodstained bandages. 'They do the amputations in the Lady's Chapel. Out of sight, but there's no escaping the noise, I'm afraid.'

'Gods.' Sander drew a breath. 'I'm sorry.'

'I'll live, don't you worry. Not even your magic could have healed this.'

'Can they ease the pain, at least?'

'They try. They constantly tell me they're praying for me, which paradoxically creates only anxiety as I feel I'll be letting them down should I drop dead, but their hearts are in the right place.'

'Yorath sabotaged the mission, y'know?' Sander leaned forwards, beckoning the general closer. 'His little favourite, Orren, she poisoned Gunnar. You have to warn the king, send word and—'

'You're too late for that, Bree, far too late.' Kentigern made a wheezing rasp of disapproval that ended in a spittling cough. 'Yorath…' He glanced at the robed Faith around them and lowered his voice. 'Yorath already has his claws in the king. Bhaltair has taken a vow of the Faith. He claims the Goddess is on his side. He's having entire battalions baptised.'

'Doesn't sound like Bhaltair's style.'

'War does strange things to people. Most men will only march willingly to their deaths if they think they're going to a better place.'

The screaming stopped, but the silence was broken by a new voice. 'That might be how they practice the Faith in Taranis, General, but that's not the way of the Goddess we recognise here.'

Sander knew the voice like his own. He slumped back on his elbows to find his sister Faylen standing at the foot of his cot in her yellow robes of the Faith.

'Hello, Sander.' She smiled.

'Faylen.' He tightened his lips into a thin grimace. He'd always wondered how he would feel when he saw her again. Their last meeting, which he realised with a shudder was over ten years ago, had ended with accusations of betrayal, tears and declarations to never speak again. She was smiling, which boded well, and he couldn't deny he was happy to see her. Like all younger brothers, he was quick to notice that she had something he did not. 'Hey, you have hair. Why can't I have hair?'

She did indeed have shoulder-length chestnut hair, and Sander only now realised that all the brethren in the great hall had their own hair. Not a shaved head among them.

'Brother Yorath's interpretation of the Word differs from ours regarding certain tenets of the Faith. He prefers a more... severe demeanour for his siblings.'

'You mean he's an arrogant tosspot and a tyrant? No argument from me, sis. You're looking plump.'

'As charming and tactful as ever.' Faylen self-consciously tucked her hands into the pouch at the front of her robes. 'The food here is good, I must admit.'

'I'm sure Father only brought us here for the meals. Mum said that's what the brethren do best.'

'Food, yes, and picking up the pieces of other people's messes.' Faylen glanced around the hall. 'We've been rather busy these past few days.'

'Haven't we all.'

'Hmm, I heard about your little adventure,' she said, and Sander looked sidelong at the general who shrugged and shook his head, *I didn't tell her anything.*

Faylen sat by Sander. 'Right, let's see how you're doing.' She rested one palm on his forehead and another on his chest, then thrust her hands into his armpits.

Sander wriggled as it tickled. 'What're you doing? Stop!'

'You were blue when your friend brought you in and I could barely feel a heartbeat. Any longer out there half-naked and wet and you might have died, but you're warming up nicely. I'll get you some hot sugar water.'

'Lovely. Can't wait.' Sander grimaced at the thought of it. 'Hang on. *Friend?* What friend?'

'He's awake, then?' Malachy arrived behind Faylen. Hat firmly in place, he gave Sander a wink. 'By the gods, man, you look like death warmed up.'

'Malachy! You came back for me.'

'If you like. Truth is, I found you out like a light on the back of some mare in a field. I knew the abbey was nearby and reckoned they'd be more likely to let a soldier in if he had some poor wretch at death's door with him.'

'That's not true,' Faylen interjected. 'We welcome all in need.'

'I know that now, don't I?'

'That's almost noble of you, Malachy, thanks,' Sander said, rubbing the sleep from his eyes. 'How long have I been here?'

'Four hours and a bit,' Kentigern chipped in, nodding to the altar in the centre of the hall. 'Thing acts as a sundial, and there's blessed-else all to do here but mark the passing of time.'

Four hours. Sander's stomach turned. Fours hours of sleeping like the dead while the princess inched closer to her own real demise. Four hours of a warm, dry cot. The guilt gnawed at him, not least because he liked it here. He was safe, among what might be classed as friends or loved ones. He could stay here and never be troubled by the blade of an enemy ever again.

'And how are you today, Lasse?' Faylen asked.

'Very well, thank you, Sister.'

Lasse? Sander knew the general must have a first name, but he would never have guessed that one in a million years.

'That's good to hear.' Faylen smiled then nodded at Sander. 'This one been giving you any trouble?'

'All my life.'

'I know the feeling.'

'Hey.' Sander pouted. 'When you're quite finished slagging me off...'

'Aww, my poor little brother.' Faylen pinched his cheek. 'Right, you're fine. Out you hop.'

'*Now?* I'm wounded.'

'Cuts and bruises, nothing more. Come along, we need the bed.'

'I'm not going anywhere.'

'Oh yes you are, matey,' Malachy growled. 'We have a little girl to save.'

Sander frowned. 'Who are you and what have you done with Malachy Nye?'

'I'm a soldier. I follow orders, and my orders are to save that little lass. I go back to Taranis without a cure and the king'll have my balls in a vice, am I right, General?'

'Only if he's feeling generous,' Kentigern agreed.

'And by circumstance and attrition, I reckon I'm in charge,' Malachy said. 'So, unless you fancy a slow death from having a halberd shoved up your arse, you'll do as I say.'

Sander narrowed his eyes at the old soldier. 'Or maybe... maybe you think that by sticking with me you're on the winning side? Is that it, Malachy? Orren let you down on that front, didn't she?'

'Give an old soldier the latitude to change his mind.' Malachy bared his overlapping, tobacco-stained teeth in a crafty grin.

'If our former mage's night terrors are anything to go by,' Kentigern wheezed, 'he knows he has to save the girl.'

'What in all the realms are you babbling on about now, you old fool?' Sander sneered.

'All bloody morning, talking in your sleep!' Kentigern said. '*Have to save her, have to save her!* I wish you'd get off your arse and get on with it, if only to give me some decent kip.'

Sander looked from Malachy, to Faylen, to Lasse, and all of them were staring back at him with expectant eyes. Sander liked it here. Every part of him was telling him to lie back in the cot, huddle in the straw and never come out again.

'I don't suppose there's any chance of a hot bath before I go, is there?'

Faylen led Sander to the south transept, a quiet nook well away from the screams of surgery, where the air was thick with moisture and wisps of incense drifted in the dark. They found a large tin bath filled with pink water, a colouring that Sander hoped was from local Barrow bath salts and not the diluted blood of a previous occupant. It was warm, as promised. Malachy had insisted that he be quick, so Sander was in and out in short order, still sore and aching but feeling more alive than he had in days. Faylen brought him towels, boots and fresh yellow robes.

'Oh, please, not the standard-issue pants,' he said, taking the towel and wrapping it around himself as Faylen looked away. 'They ride right up my crack.'

'You took a vow of the Faith. That's a serious promise to the Goddess. You're one of us now, Brother.'

'Ah, here it comes.'

'Here what comes?'

'The lecture. From the first moment I decided to come here, I knew I'd get a lecture from you. Fair enough. Let me have the robes and you may begin.'

Faylen shrugged. 'If you want righteous indignation, try the zealots in the citadel. I'm here to patch up the wounded.' She handed him the folded robes. They were clean, stiff and still had that warm whiff of the laundry about them. 'You don't have to do this, you know,' she said. 'You can do good here. No more pain, no more fear, just peace and the love of your brethren and the Goddess.'

'A child will die if I don't—'

'Children are dying every day, Sander. She's one of many. It's a tragedy, but at least here you can help the living.'

'I made a promise and I intend to keep it... Oh, don't look at me like that.'

'You promised to visit, but never did. You promised you would send Mum and Dad money regularly, but frequently forgot. You didn't come to their funerals—'

'A lecture. You can't help yourself.' Sander turned his back on her to put on the robes.

'That's not a lecture, it's a series of facts.'

'I know who I am, Faylen. I was a terrible son and a terrible brother and a terrible mage. So, be angry with me. Hate me. I want the pious lecture, so give it to me.'

'The Word teaches forgiveness, Sander. We don't lecture, we heal. With time, you will learn to—'

'I killed a man.' Sander pulled the robe's belt tight, folded his arms

in a knot and sat on the edge of the bath, his eyes fixed on little bubbles popping in the water. 'Can you forgive that?'

More little bath bubbles winked out of existence during the silence
that followed.

'The Word says not to kill,' Faylen said finally. 'Several times. It
couldn't be clearer on the subject. But you're not beyond the Goddess's love or forgiveness, so yes. Yes, I *can* forgive that, but you have
to earn it.'

'I was going to leave Taranis, y'know? Travel, enjoy a bit of freedom, no worries, no cares, but I killed a man. Didn't mean to, but I
did. I try to forget, and sometimes it works, and sometimes the guilt
goes away, but when you're least expecting it, there's a little voice
– your own voice – that reminds you you're a liar and a killer, and
nothing I do will ever change that.' Sander had never said this out
loud before and he felt like he was in a confessional. He had never
understood why people did that, but now he could sense a little bit
of weight lifting. 'I catch myself babbling out loud – and I talk in my
sleep, apparently – and now a little girl is going to die because of me
and I'm not sure I can bear another burden like that, Faylen. I'm doing
this because I want to sleep at night.'

'You want to silence that voice? You can do that here, with solitude, prayer—'

'How? By bowing and scraping to your—'

'Oh, will you give it a rest?' Faylen snapped, her voice trembling.
'Do not confuse us, or me, with the cretins you know from the
citadel,' she said. 'My Goddess is one of love, and if you accept her
into your heart, you will find peace. It won't be easy, but I promise
you it will happen.'

'I think Malachy's halberd up the arse is more likely, to be honest.'

'Everything's a joke to you, isn't it?'

'One long, sick one.'

Faylen reached out to Sander, her fingers touching the hard, scaled
skin around his neck. 'Someone tried to hang you?'

'They were scared. There's a lot of it about.'

'Sander, you'll die if you leave here.' Faylen's voice softened and
she rubbed the tears from her cheeks. 'Your magic is gone and war is

blind. It neither knows nor cares if you're on a mission of murder or mercy, you'll be dead before you the reach the coast. You can claim sanctuary here. If you fear Malachy's halberd, I can send him away—'

'I fear not being able to look at my reflection in a mirror,' he said, taking a deep breath and inhaling a lungful of incense. He felt light-headed and relaxed. He *could* stay here. It didn't have to be for ever. He allowed himself to wallow in a momentary fantasy. Waking each morning in the peace of the abbey, three meals a day, a life of quiet contemplation, some light gardening and laundry and, once the war had washed over them like a storm, he could maybe seduce one of the less committed noviciates and get himself banished. He could pick up the pieces, rebuild his life and travel the world. It was, like all his plans, subject to the intrusions and flaws of others, but the thought of it was as warm and comforting as a hot bath.

Yet there was a voice in his head that wouldn't be silenced. Not by staying here.

'She's still alive, Faylen. They all thought she would be dead by now, and they all thought I was going to fail. Let me keep one promise, let me finish this, even if it kills me,' he said, wondering if it was possible to condemn oneself to death with a handful of words.

Faylen exhaled and all her fight went with it. As children they would argue non-stop for days about nonsense. The names of things, the meaning of stories, the words of songs, the rules of games. He teased and provoked, and she took the moral high ground with all the certainty of the devout. Now, when it came to a final life-and-death decision, it all ended with a sigh. She threw her arms around him.

'Will you look at that? My little brother has finally grown up.'

'And all it took was a relentless string of near-death experiences.'

'You have to come back. Promise?'

'I'll think about it.'

'That's progress, I suppose.'

'What do you mean?'

Faylen stepped back and smirked. 'A while ago, you would have promised to return and then broken that promise.'

'A while ago, I would never have come here in the first place.' He smirked back. 'It's good to see you, Faylen.'

'The soil, the sun and the sea, Brother.' She hugged him and pecked him on the cheek.

'Yes.' He smiled, finally appreciating the simplicity of that little homily. It really was all anyone should ever desire. 'The soil, the sun and the sea.'

'Now, what do you need?'

'Horses, water, a day's rations, a hat to keep my head warm in the cold evenings, a vial for the blood, one teaspoon of salt to preserve it and some proper clothes.'

'We can only spare robes.'

'In that case, I want the ones with a pouch,' Sander said, then snapped his fingers. 'And, most important of all, undergarments that won't chafe.'

How Do You Lie to a Truth-Seer?

Haldor's new camp was far from the model of efficiency that Rosheen remembered from a few days ago. Tents that had once been pitched with purpose were now arranged haphazardly, raised in a hurry, their guy ropes slack, their canvas sagging. The men who had time to laugh and jeer before were now sidestepping their wide-eyed comrades coming the other way as they hurried about on countless urgent errands. And as Bowden led her through the maze, Rosheen saw a familiar shape in a blacksmith's forge. Haldor's pride and joy, the great brass telescope, was being melted down. Rosheen wondered about the fate of the astronomer, if Haldor had double-crossed him, and if the man could have possibly foreseen the chaos that was unfolding now.

The camp was nestled in a field behind the protection of a ring of trees that would slow any potential attackers, but it didn't take a military genius to realise that it would also hamper an army's retreat. If anything were to go wrong, Haldor's men were stuck here.

The field beyond was empty, but she knew they were near the Alar River and a number of bridges that would be the focus of any army's attack. She was sure she could hear the distant clatter of arms drifting from the battlefield, but she didn't dare use any more of her Lapis stone's power to enhance her hearing to be sure. She wanted to save every drop left in it for what was coming next.

Rosheen knew Haldor would try to cheat her somehow, and she knew that whatever he tried to pull, and however she reacted to it, would determine whether she and Oskar lived or died. She didn't much care about herself; she had seen and done things these last few days that would haunt her for the rest of her life. But Oskar was innocent in every sense and she would not rest until he was safe and free.

Haldor's marquee was positioned at the point of the camp's arrowhead. Other warlords and generals might choose to surround and protect the headquarters of their army, but Haldor was no shrinking violet and his presence, front and centre, was a clear message to any of the enemy's spies: *I'm here, come and get me if you dare.*

His back was to Rosheen and Bowden as they approached. He was studying an enormous map spread across a long table, each corner held down by a stone, but every now and then, a breeze got under it, causing it to flap and threaten to fly away. He was flanked by a disparate array of fur-trimmed warlords, leather-clad mercenaries and Torren's defector generals in dull armour. One of them gestured towards Rosheen as she approached and Haldor spun like a top, his face lighting up as he saw them.

'Rosheen Katell, my witchy-warlock, I'm so happy to see you.' He rushed to her, embracing her and slapping her on the back. 'Bowden, my brother.' He held the mercenary at arm's length, then tapped one of the tattoo tears on his face with his index finger in some kind of secret gesture of brotherhood. 'I knew if anyone could do this for me, it would be you. Come, we have much to discuss,' he said, then turned to his strategists, waving at them dismissively. 'You bastards have till I get back to make up your minds before I make them up for you. Get to it.'

He steered Rosheen and Bowden away from the table, but she was able to get a good look at the map. It was from the Torren surveys of twenty years ago, compiled by the explorer Captain Kit Cox, whose life's work was to chart every nook and cranny of the Newlands. Considered quite mad by other explorers, he was last seen heading over the White Sea in a dirigible made from silk knickers donated by the women of Arranrod. Woefully out of date, the maps were most likely stolen from the old king's archives at Castle Agrona, but they still offered a fair representation of the surrounding landscape: fields broken up by woods, the Alar River and several hills. Haldor was using chess pieces on the map to represent the armies. His men were mostly clustered by the river, with Bhaltair's men opposite. There was a smaller cluster of both armies on a hill a few miles downriver. Before Rosheen could take in any more, Haldor gently clasped her arm and kept her moving. 'In a moment, Rosheen Katell, in a moment.'

She soon found herself with Haldor and Bowden around the back of the marquee by a glowing brazier. Haldor fell into a chair draped with bearskin. Rosheen and Bowden remained standing.

'I can't believe how pompous these bastards are.' Haldor shook his head and gestured somewhere into the distance where Bhaltair's army clashed with his own. 'Honestly, they're complete imbeciles. A man should know when he's beaten. Do you know, we've—'

'Where's my brother, Haldor?' Rosheen said. 'We did what you asked, and at great cost.'

For a moment, Haldor's face was frozen, unreadable. Then it burst into a smile.

'I wish I had a dozen like you, witchy-warlock,' he said with a chortle. 'You would make my life so much easier. May I...?' He nodded at the canvas bag slung over Bowden's back. The mercenary shrugged it off his shoulder and it fell to the ground. He untied its string and shook the bag. Orren's severed head came rolling across the patchy grass. Her skin was almost translucent now; the grim odour of rotting flesh made even Haldor recoil, and immediately flies began buzzing around it.

Rosheen held her breath, silently hoping that her glamour still worked, that they would see a likeness of Sander's head.

'That him?' Haldor asked Bowden.

'That's him,' Bowden nodded.

'Good.' Haldor clapped his hands twice and his guards appeared around them. He gestured at one of them. 'Spike it.' The guard obeyed, nudging the head back into the bag with the tip of his boot before drawing the string tight around the bag and dashing off with it. 'Put it in sight of Bhaltair's camp,' Haldor called after him. 'You never know, the arrogant ass might see it and kill himself in despair.'

Rosheen noted that the other guards remained, surrounding them in a circle. And they had their hands on the pommels of their swords.

For what it was worth, she raised her staff with the pale blue Lapis light. No one backed away this time.

'Haldor,' she said. 'My brother.'

'A moment.' Haldor stood, raised a finger at her, then turned to Bowden, gripping the man's arms. 'Bowden, my friend, you know I value your service to me, and I know we had an agreement regarding your family, but things have happened while you were away and I must hold them a while longer. Okay?'

Bowden gave a tiny nod, but his brow knotted in unspoken confusion.

'Before we go any further' – Haldor was talking to both Rosheen and Bowden now – 'I want to make one thing absolutely clear. If anything – *anything* – happens to me today, here, this moment, then Bowden's family will die.'

A numb feeling of cold dread started in the pit of Rosheen's stomach and began to eat her from the inside.

Haldor continued as if explaining the rules of a game. 'His children, Elena and Jakob, and his wife Audri – all beautiful, by the way, Bowden, you should be very proud – all of them will die. The children will watch their mother's throat cut, the younger brother will witness his sister stabbed through the heart, and as for the boy... I think they're going to take out his eyes then bleed him, I can't remember, it's been a long day. But they all die. Understood?'

Bowden nodded numbly.

Rosheen's body was trembling with the now-familiar rage and fear coursing through her. She felt light-headed, her heart pumped in her ears and the world around her felt unreal. She was a white-hot knife ready to lash out.

'My... my brother...'

'Your brother is dead,' Haldor said. 'Lost at sea.'

A handful of words, but they confused her beyond all reckoning. One in particular.

'Sea?'

'The Sugar Sea, they said. I can't begin to tell you how sorry I am, Rosheen. I had every intention of honouring our deal. Ask anyone here, I am a man of my word. I left the job in the hands of an old friend, Yanick Heck. Bowden, you know Yanick? A good man, trustworthy, wise, experienced.' Haldor's face dropped and he puffed his cheeks. 'The old fool thought the sea would be a safe place. He kept the boy on a ship, the ship sank. How? I don't know. The Ocean's Hand can be deadly.'

He approached Rosheen, one hand reaching out, then gently entwined her fingers with his and spoke softly, though his words came to her through a fog of her own bewilderment. 'I couldn't lie to you, Rosheen Katell, not to a truth-seer, and not to someone I know is no fool. I knew you would want to kill me as soon as you heard and I understand that feeling completely, but the rage and the sorrow will fade, I promise you. One day, the pain will pass and you will feel whole again.' He stood back, releasing her hand and resting his on Bowden's shoulder. 'I know you are a good person, Rosheen Katell, and will not allow this man's innocent family to die. Bowden, my brother, I am sorry. I would gladly offer you Yanick to skin alive, but I suspect he's at the bottom of the Sugar Sea, too.' Haldor then pressed his hands together as if in prayer and rested them against his lips, his eyes fixed on Rosheen. 'So… we have an understanding?'

Feeling came back to Rosheen, the ground slowed under her feet and she looked back at Haldor Frang.

'There is a simple solution to this,' she said, her voice barely a whisper.

Haldor cocked his head, ready to listen, or pounce. 'Which is…?'

'Kill Bowden,' she said. Out of the corner of her eye, she could see Bowden stepping away from her, his hand reaching for his sword. 'He dies and his hostage family has no value. The innocent live and two bad men die.'

Haldor threw his head back and laughed. 'Oh, you are wonderful, just wonderful. You have learned so much in this reprobate's company. You will go far, witchy girl, you will. But…' He grinned, wagging his finger. 'If you were serious, you would have done it by now and I don't think you—'

There was a noise and a movement on the edge of Rosheen's vision. The squeak of a leather jerkin twisting, the clatter of a blade, the heavy *flump* of something hitting the earth like a sack of potatoes.

Bowden fell face first to the ground.

Dead.

She had found that spot in his brain. The one that had brought peace to some of her elderly patients in the past. She wondered what, if anything, he would have felt. He was most likely dead before he even began tipping forward.

A few days ago, under the light of the Lapis Moon, Rosheen would not have even contemplated such a move, but now she calmly accepted what she was capable of and was ready to kill not only Bowden, but Haldor, the guards and everyone around her, everyone in the camp, everyone on that distant battlefield. Before she could even raise her staff, Haldor was on her. He crossed the small distance between them in a flash, knocking her onto the hard ground, emptying the air from her lungs. He had a knee pressed into her belly and a knife at her throat. The staff fell from her grip and one of his guards scurried over, snatched it up and backed away, the stone's power now out of her range.

'Please, Rosheen, please believe me, I did not want this to happen.' Haldor's face was so close to Rosheen's that his eyelashes fluttered against hers, and every word he spoke puffed breath onto her lips. 'Your brother was an innocent pawn, but if this war doesn't stop now then many more like him will die. Your magic will soon be gone for good. Look at it. Look.' He glanced to the guard holding her staff with the Lapis stone. 'So dim. A candle in the fog. I need your magic more than ever. Yes, you can use it to kill me, that is your right, but why not use it to end this conflict, hmm? Join me on the battlefield and bring King Bhaltair's army to heel. I will negotiate a peaceful ending. We will save lives.'

'And you will become king.'

Haldor's eyes flashed. 'I prefer emperor,' he said. '*Emperor* Frang. Has a nice ring to it, no?'

Shouts came from Haldor's marquee, overlapping voices, but one commander's yell broke through the jumble with a panicked cry of, 'They're attacking the bridge!'

Haldor never even flinched, his gaze fixed on Rosheen. 'I can see you hesitating,' he said. 'Considering every option, which includes killing me, and I know you could do it, stop my heart in the blink of an eye. But what would it mean? Don't think about it too long. You want to save lives. I know you do, you're not like me. Come on, Rosheen Katell. What will it be?'

King Bhaltair's Flying Corps Volunteers

After hearing Gudrun's story, Oskar couldn't bring himself to look Bingham in the eye.

Where Oskar had first seen charm and enthusiasm, he now detected an edgy nervousness, and what he thought was Bingham's exhaustion due to overwork now looked more like the hollow eyes and bowed head of a haunted man.

Bingham was a murderer.

Killer of his own brother, Oddmun.

That's if Gudrun was to be believed. Oskar glanced at her sitting next to him on the cart's bench, swaying with its movement over the uneven road, her green eyes staring into empty space. She had been silent since Bingham's return and was now back in the role of moon child.

They had set off without saying a word. Accompanied by a King's Guard and another officer of some rank Oskar didn't recognise, they turned the cart around and headed back the way they'd come, eventually taking a fork along the eastern road which became a steep and narrow zigzag with thick woodland on either side. Progress was slow as the long cart negotiated the tight bends. The guard and the officer hopped off the cart and walked ahead of them, hands on their swords, surveying the darkness between the trees, watching for an ambush.

Bingham had returned wearing a peaked cap with the king's sigil stitched into it. As he drove the cart, he rested a small crossbow on his knees, a quiver of bolts at his feet. Oskar knew that now might not be the best time, but he was bursting with questions.

'Where are we going, Bingham?' he asked.

'*Captain* Bingham. Can't say.' Bingham tipped the cap back on his head and reached into his coat pocket. 'We're in something called the Royal Flying Corps now, Oskar. They give me orders, which are secret. Until we get where we're going, I can't say any more. Understand?' He took a small box from his pocket, the same ivory-patterned one Gudrun was carrying when Oskar first met her, and flipped open the lid. There was a grey powder inside, with a tiny little spoon shoved into it. Bingham caught Oskar's inquisitive look.

'Poppy powder. You know poppy powder?' he said. Oskar did not know poppy powder, but he nodded as if he did all the same. 'Course you do. This stuff's from the Jooey Valleys in Eru. You're from Eru, aren't you?'

'My family are. Mylar. I've never been.'

'Ah, well, you should try some. It'll banish hunger and you'll feel like a new man. I can spare a little. Help yourself.'

Oskar looked from Bingham to the powder.

'It's perfectly safe. In very... small... doses.' Bingham extended his little finger into the powder. Oskar noticed that the nail on that finger was longer than the others, and Bingham used it to scoop up a tiny amount of the powder, then raised it to one nostril and sniffed loudly. His eyes widened and watered momentarily, but then his cheeks flushed red and he was back to normal. 'There. Nothing like a little pick-me-up.'

Bingham used the tiny silver spoon to dig up a portion for Oskar and held it under the boy's nose.

Oskar looked from the spoon to Bingham.

Bingham the murderer. The liar. 'No, thank you,' he said.

Bingham frowned. Oskar could see that he sensed that something had changed between them, though the flyer couldn't quite be sure what. 'Suit yourself,' Bingham said, snapping the lid of the box shut and slipping it back into his pocket. 'Let me know if you change your mind.'

Wise decision, said Gudrun's voice in Oskar's head. *Ask him why he has a crossbow.*

Ask him yourself, Oskar thought back, and he saw Gudrun's eyes flash to his. *You heard me! I can do this, too.*

Oh, great. Nice while it lasted, I suppose.

I have no idea how I'm doing this. How am I doing this?

Just ask him about the crossbow, will you?

Yes, yes, of course. Oskar turned on the bench to face the flyer. *Bingham, why do you have—?*

With your voice, not your mind, idiot!

It was too late. A connection had been made and Bingham was looking at Oskar with narrowed eyes.

'Anything wrong?' Oskar asked.

Blame it on the poppy powder, Gudrun's voice said in Oskar's head. *No, tell him he looks tired. He'll think he's hearing things.*

Oskar continued to play dumb, simply smiling as Bingham shook his head, pinching his nose. 'I could swear...' Bingham trailed off. 'Never mind.'

'What's with the crossbow, Captain Bingham?'

'It was given to me by the corporal.' He nodded ahead at the new officer.

Ask him why he needs it.

'Is it because you're a soldier now?' Oskar asked.

'No, I'm not a soldier. Definitely not a soldier – I made that clear to them several times over. I'm a civilian, a *deployed* civilian volunteer—'

'You volunteered?'

'Gods, will you give it a rest with the questions, Oskar?' Bingham huffed, and Oskar could see that his eyes were watering and bloodshot. An after-effect of the poppy powder. 'Yes, I volunteered... eventually. And, as such, I'm an officer in the Royal Flying Corps with temporary duty status for the next few days. Which means I am your commanding officer, which means that you do as I say without question. Understand?'

I know why he has it, came Gudrun's voice.

'Yes, Captain, I understand,' Oskar replied to the flyer.

We're going into battle, Gudrun continued. *And that's to defend himself when he tumbles out of the sky. Only a few bolts, though. He won't last long. His volunteering is going to get us killed.*

Oskar didn't reply and began to wonder if there was some way to block Gudrun's thoughts from his mind when the guard up ahead called for them to slow down. They had come to a checkpoint with more of the King's Guards. Papers were inspected and they were waved through. The woodland began to clear and they found themselves halfway up a grassy hillside, a prominent tor in the patchwork of farmland around them, and quite some distance from the fighting. Oskar could see several spirals of smoke rising from cookfires in an encampment about three miles away that looked like the one they had just left.

The horses whinnied as they struggled with the weight of Petra and her cage, and so Oskar and Gudrun hopped off to lighten the load and push from the rear.

They saw a dirigible first, a rope-bound patchwork of grey fabric with a basket hanging underneath for the flyers. It drifted aimlessly in the breeze and its ground crew pulled on the ropes and dug their heels in to stop from being whisked away. There was another behind it, a flaccid gasbag being inflated with hot air wafted in from a bonfire.

There were other caged creatures, too, a copper-coloured simurgh dog-bird, a lizard-like ropen, a winged white foal and a griffin. This last one excited Oskar as, for a moment, he thought it might be Anzu, but it was too small and its feathers and fur were too dark. They were all so beautiful and awe-inspiring to Oskar, but none was as big or as impressive as Petra the wyvern. Oskar caught Gudrun looking at the wyvern from under her fringe, her bright green eyes sharp and calculating.

You want to steal Petra, he thought.

Gudrun checked herself and dropped back into her moon child persona, head down as she pushed the cart. *How did you know?*

You told me yourself that you wanted to get out. I figured you were waiting for the right moment, and I think that moment is upon you. Us.

You're not coming with me. Gudrun glared at him.

Fine, I'll tell him what you're planning and—

Okay, okay, you can come… I'll need ballast.

So, how do we do it?

I have no idea, Gudrun replied. *I was planning to steal it when he was asleep.*

Looks like they want us to fly now.

I know, I know. Let me think. I need time.

'Halt!' the corporal commanded, and the cart came to a stop. As the horses panted to cool down, a group of the King's Engineering Corps came hurrying over and circled the cart and Petra. Oskar and Gudrun stood back, trying not to get in the way. 'You will release the beast,' the corporal added.

Bingham lured Petra out of her cage with a series of increasingly frustrated orders and whip-cracks.

She's not flying anywhere, Oskar told Gudrun. *Look at her, poor thing.*

Petra shuffled out, lethargic, her head and neck stooped as Bingham struggled to fit her with a bridle and reins. A pair of engineers strapped a three-seater saddle and harness on Petra's back.

She needs to rest, Gudrun thought. *We all do.*

The engineers unpacked small, black jars from a straw-lined crate and proceeded to hang them on hooks attached to Petra's saddle.

'Captain, what are those?' Oskar asked.

Bingham finished pulling Petra's bridle into place and looked around, befuddled, at the jars. His mouth started to form an answer for Oskar, but then he frowned and beckoned the corporal over. 'I say, Corporal, what are those?'

The corporal was conferring with two men sporting fur-lined coats and woollen hats. A little overdressed for a spring day, Oskar thought. The corporal either hadn't heard or was ignoring Bingham, so the flyer had to insert himself between them.

'Corporal, if you please, sir, what exactly are you attaching to my wyvern's saddle?'

'Ordnance,' the corporal said. 'A dozen bombs for your first run. Fly the beast to the targets on your map and my men will do the rest.'

'Your...?' Bingham's eyes darted to the men in the woollen hats and saw them for what they were. 'Your men? What about my crew?' Bingham jabbed a thumb back at Oskar and Gudrun.

'I thought I had made this clear.' The corporal spoke slowly, as if talking to an unruly toddler. 'Your crew are not military personnel and this test run will be essential experience for my men as they are to be the first flyers in the Royal Air Corps. If today is successful, then you will be taming many more of these creatures for His Majesty's Royal Air Corps.'

'I didn't agree to that.'

'You did when you signed the contract.'

'Well, I... I didn't see that clause. I would never have agreed to that. I take it back.'

'I would advise against that,' said the corporal.

'Oh, really, would you now? And why's that?'

'You would be disobeying a direct order, and that's punishable by death.'

Once again, Bingham found himself mouthing words but momentarily unable to speak. He turned his back on the corporal, reached into his pocket, pulled out the ivory-patterned box of poppy powder and took a sniff. Bingham turned back to the corporal, his eyes watering. 'Very well,' he said, with the gaunt and haunted look of a condemned man. 'Let's get this over with. You two' – he pointed at the corporal's men – 'get on board, I'll show you the ropes.'

'What do we do, Captain?' Oskar asked, and Bingham turned to look at him and Gudrun with a wince, as if he had only just remembered they were there.

'Oh gods…' Bingham puffed a breath and waved vaguely at the horses. 'Look after them, will you? Keep them fed and watered and—'

'We want to fly,' Oskar said. 'We're ready to fly. Gudrun can—'

'Oskar, not now, please. Let me—'

They were cut off by a noise from the bottom of the hill, overlapping battle cries mixed with the low rumble of heavy footfalls. Every head on the hilltop turned to see.

From the treeline below came rushing dozens of Haldor's mercenaries, spilling from the dark woodland like an infestation of ants. As Oskar joined the king's soldiers and engineers standing and watching in disbelief, he was astonished to find the mercenaries were already halfway up the hill and completely unchallenged.

There was a *whit-whit* noise like a shepherd whistling for a dog and Oskar glanced over to see the corporal's two flyers fall to the ground, arrows buried in their chests.

The corporal was the first to come to his senses.

'To arms!' he bellowed, then grabbed Bingham's elbow and spun him towards Petra. 'You, get that thing up in the air now, that's an order!'

'Yes, yes,' he muttered. 'Wait! My crossbow.' He ran to the cart, snatched up the crossbow and bolts and turned to find Oskar and Gudrun in his path.

'You can't leave us, Bingham,' Oskar said, his eyes darting from the captain to the hill below where the mercenaries were cutting a swathe through the first wave of the corporal's men. 'Please, they'll kill us.'

'No, of course, look... take this!' Bingham offered Oskar the crossbow, but the boy shook his head.

'No!'

'It's easy, watch.' Bingham pulled on the whipcord bowstring, his muscles straining with the effort, but eventually it locked into place. Hands shaking, he placed a bolt in the flight groove.

The corporal yelled at him. 'Bingham, get moving!'

'Please, Captain, don't leave us,' Oskar pleaded. 'We'll die.'

Bingham looked at Oskar with his watery eyes, then at the corporal, who had drawn his sword and was moving purposefully towards him.

'I'm sorry.' Bingham spluttered the same words he had uttered to his brother. 'I'm so sorry.' And with that, he shoved the boy to the ground and clambered onto Petra's saddle.

The mercenaries were already upon them, clashing with the king's soldiers, the clanging of their swords ringing in Oskar's ears.

One voice rose above the clamour of battle.

'Abel Bingham, you gutless bastard!'

It was Gudrun. She was standing atop the cart and pointing an accusing finger at Bingham. 'I know what you did to Oddmun, you son of a bitch. I know that you killed your own brother and now you're going to let us die to save your own neck.'

Bingham froze, utterly astonished, his eyes fixed on Gudrun. Then his face contorted in agony and he convulsed and spasmed.

Oskar couldn't be sure what caused Bingham's pain, but Gudrun's hand had become a fist and she was tightening her grip.

'Gudrun, what are you doing?' Oskar got to his feet, climbed up on the cart and grabbed her arm. As he did so, he saw the colour come back to Bingham's face.

Gudrun shoved Oskar off the cart and reached out again. Bingham's back arched, the tendons in his neck went taut, he screamed in agony and his own hands gripped tight.

Triggering the crossbow.

A bolt flew from the weapon and punched into Gudrun's chest,

315

sending her tumbling off the cart to land next to Oskar in a cloud of dust.

'No, gods, no!' he cried and scrabbled over to Gudrun. The bolt was lodged deep in her chest and blood was already oozing from the wound. 'Help, please, somebody help!' He looked around in desperation, but everyone was busy fighting. The corporal fell to his knees, an arrow in his eye.

The mercenaries were making short work of the remainder of the corporal's men and Oskar knew he had only moments left.

He looked to Petra, where Bingham was desperately cracking his whip at the young wyvern's neck, but she remained defiantly on the ground, hunched, head low as she hooted fearfully at the chaos around her.

Oskar slapped the hinds of the two carthorses crying, 'Ya! Ya!' and sent them careening towards the advancing mercenaries. This bought him a few moments as the animals punched a gap through Haldor's men.

Oskar gathered Gudrun up in his arms then ran for Petra, quietly praying that none of the arrows whizzing through the air would hit him. Gudrun was a dead weight, and he drew on all his strength to heave her up onto Petra's saddle. She slumped sideways, threatening to topple off.

Oskar clambered up onto the wyvern's back, lashing the long reins around Gudrun to keep her steady, ducking as an arrow whizzed by. He could see the mercenaries rushing towards them, some with their swords and axes held high, others firing more arrows.

'I'm sorry,' Bingham cried over his shoulder from the front saddle. 'You have to understand – I had no choice, I—'

'Get us in the air,' Oskar commanded.

'She's too scared,' Bingham yelped. 'Our test flights were in a nice, quiet field by the Andraste Cliffs. She's not used to all this noise.'

Something caught Oskar's eye and he reached out, closing his eyes.

The first wave of mercenaries were passing the other caged animals, and Oskar knew what he had to do.

Bingham watched amazed as the cages fell apart, unleashing the once-magical creatures on the advancing enemy in a wild frenzy of unfettered teeth, kicking hooves and savage claws.

'Oskar, was... was that you?'

As the mercenaries screamed, Oskar turned to face forwards and reached out to Petra. He found her mind, a dim light in the darkness, and offered her his strength.

Petra began to move. Slowly at first, lumbering across the tor, making the saddle creak and twist.

'What's...? What's happening?' Bingham cried. 'How are you doing that?'

The wyvern threw her wings open, pushed away from the earth and they were briefly airborne—

'Yes!' Bingham beamed. 'Go, Petra, go, fly, my beauty!'

—before hitting the ground running with a shudder that threatened to tip them all off. Oskar wrapped one arm around Gudrun's waist while holding the reins with his free hand.

Petra's mind was a confused mess and Oskar could feel the wyvern's fear, her overwhelming urge to hide away and curl into a ball until all the noise was gone, but he needed more than that from her if they were to survive.

'Petra, please, up!' Bingham screeched. 'Fly!'

As arrows whistled through the air around them, Oskar shut out Bingham's panicked wailing and the imminent danger and tried to find a corner of Petra's mind that wasn't in turmoil.

There.

The part of her that kept the wyvern breathing, the part of her that didn't need to think but was always working. He found that part of her which had known since she was a fledgling how to do one thing and one thing only.

Fly.

They lurched into the air at an incredible speed that took Oskar's breath away and made his stomach turn.

'Reins!' Bingham called over the buffeting wind.

'What?' Oskar opened his eyes. Looking back, he saw the tor fall away behind them, the battling soldiers and mercenaries now as small as a child's toys.

'Pull back on the reins!' Bingham hollered and Oskar did so, sending Petra ever higher, soaring into the clouds. Gudrun began to slip on the saddle. Oskar gripped her tighter and, as her head flopped back, he caught sight of her pale face, spotted with blood.

The Unusual Battle of the Alar River

If you were granted three wishes, what would you wish for?

It was a question Mother teased Rosheen and Oskar with when they were younger. Oskar could never answer, of course, so Mother would try to coax one from him by wishing that she could go back home to Eru. She always did so loudly, and within earshot of Father, who would get angry and tell her to stop filling the children's minds with nonsense, and the argument would escalate, often leaving Rosheen without having given her reply.

As a child, Rosheen knew the best and only answer was to wish for infinite wishes.

It was advice she kicked herself for not thinking of sooner as she watched the glow at the centre of her Lapis stone fading to nothing. She should have used this stone to find more stones, infinite magic, but she had been so intent on finding Haldor and saving her brother that the thought hadn't even occurred to her. As the sun passed behind the ring of Lapis stones overhead, she wondered if she ever had the power to draw them down and rain magic back upon the world, returning the balance it had once kept.

Another piece of advice, this time from her father, was not to cry over spilled milk. Something she knew all about after their exile from Eru. What's done is done and this was the world she lived in now. One where her power would soon be gone for ever. What could she possibly do with this last ounce of magical energy?

She could end a war.

Haldor hadn't given her much of a choice. Since agreeing at knife-point to help him, her hands had been bound behind her back and his guards kept their blades ready to strike if she tried to escape.

'And Bowden's family,' she said, 'they'll be unharmed?'

'Of course.' Haldor splayed his fingers across his chest, looking mortally offended at the very idea. 'What would be the point of hurting them now? I'm not a sadist, Rosheen.'

She wasn't exactly reassured by his lack of self-awareness, but

Rosheen was hardly in a position to insist. 'We'll do this my way,' she told him. 'No bloodshed.'

'Fine, fine, just get it done.'

Haldor and his guard escorted her through the trees to a rise with a better view of the battle. Unlike the skirmish at Canwick Tor, the combatants here were in far greater numbers and spread over a much larger area. There were men clustered on both sides of the Alar River by an old bridge. For the most part, the surrounding countryside was unspoiled, squares of farmland in contrasting shades of green and yellow divided by neat lines of ancient hedgerows, but around the bridge was a bruise of conflict. Grass turned to mud, fences and hedges were broken and trees felled as countless men surged back and forth in the tide of war.

'I should have taken the hill first,' Haldor told her. 'Look over there.' He pointed further upriver, where there was an encampment much like Haldor's. 'More of Bhaltair's men, possibly even the king himself, but this lot at the bridge were closer, and I thought if I moved quickly and decisively here, I could capture half his army then wipe him out on the hill.'

Echoes of screams drifted up from the bridge. Rosheen could see downriver that some of Haldor's men were trying to cross in boats, but they were being slaughtered by hidden archers.

'As you can see, it's been far from quick and decisive. And the small number I sent to the hill were forced back and they've asked for reinforcements, which I don't have as they're all rather busy at the bridge. I should have taken the hill with superior forces and *then* moved on the bridge.' Haldor sucked air through his teeth. 'Hindsight. It's a bugger.'

The sound of a sputtering horn came from the bridge and dozens of horses thundered over from the other side. Bhaltair's cavalry sliced through Haldor's mercenaries, scattering them into the fields on the other side of the bridge road. The cavalry then flanked them, hemming them in as they were cut to pieces.

One of Haldor's generals couldn't help himself. 'Sir, they're breaking through!'

'Yes, I have eyes. Thank you.' Haldor took Rosheen's elbow and whispered in her ear. 'I'm losing, Rosheen. You need to end this now.'

'I... I'm not sure I can.'

'Of course you can. Give them the fear, do to them what you did to my men.'

'That takes incredible power. More than I have in this stone.'

'Make them sleep, make them dance themselves to death, blind them, do something, or we'll all be dead before the sun sets.'

'You don't understand,' Rosheen said. 'To control so many minds takes too much power. I didn't know there would be so many.'

'What about one mind? You can control one mind?'

'Perhaps.'

'Then find Bhaltair. Kill him. Cut the head off the snake. Start there.' Haldor pointed at the encampment on the hill.

Rosheen turned away from the battle to the cluster of tents on the distant hill. It wouldn't be easy, but she was sure it was within her power. Nevertheless, she gave Haldor the nod. 'I'll put him to sleep,' she said. 'I won't kill him.'

'Fine. Leave that to me. Untie her,' Haldor commanded and two of his men rushed to comply. 'Give her the staff,' he told another, then drew his dagger and pressed the blade into her back, right below the ribs. 'A little insurance. I'm sure you understand.'

Rosheen closed her eyes and began searching for King Bhaltair.

'We're losing height. Drop the bombs, Oskar, drop them now!'

It had almost slipped Oskar's mind that they were flying into battle on the back of a wyvern. He had shifted Gudrun around so that she was upright, her back slumped against his chest.

'Oskar, drop the bombs!'

Oskar felt for the crossbow bolt buried in Gudrun's chest. He recalled watching the hunters when they brought dead deer to his father for skinning at the tannery, and the blood that seeped from the creatures when their arrows were removed. He needed a quiet place to concentrate if he was to remove it safely.

'Oskar, now!' Bingham screeched.

Gudrun spasmed, her bright green eyes blinked open and she began to foam at the mouth as she convulsed.

'Oh gods, Gudrun, I'm sorry, I'm sorry,' Oskar told her. 'I should never have doubted you, I should have helped you stop him.'

'Oskar, the bombs!'

'If I don't help Gudrun soon, she'll be dead.'

'We'll all be dead if we don't lose some weight,' Bingham shouted as they dropped sharply, making Oskar and Gudrun briefly weightless. By concentrating on Gudrun, Oskar had to leave Petra to fly with her own strength and now she was exhausted. 'We're too heavy for her, so drop some bloody bombs!'

Oskar placed his hand on Gudrun's head and whispered, 'Rest,' sending her into a deep, hopefully painless slumber.

He looked up and the horizon was missing. Petra was banking at a steep angle and he could only see clouds in the sky, then she lurched to one side and a battlefield swung into view, presenting Oskar with two swarming masses of men and horses mingled together on a field stained with splashes of blood like spilled wine on a rug.

It was almost too much to take in. The clang of swords and war cries were strangely distant and Oskar wondered if this was what it was like to be a god, looking down on the pointless scraps of humanity. Then – *thwip* – an arrow whizzed past his head and he didn't feel so omnipotent any more.

Rosheen drew on the Lapis stone's power as she searched for Bhaltair among the tiny pinpricks of light floating in the void, each one a living soul. Not only humans, but horses, dogs and, she was surprised to find, an underground warren full of terrified rabbits halfway down the hill. She focused on Bhaltair's encampment and found one light that remained still while all others moved around it like drones servicing a queen bee. It had to be Bhaltair. Aware that every moment was draining what little magic she had left, she tried to block out the other lights and voices. She couldn't hear his voice, or perhaps he wasn't speaking, but she knew it had to be him.

'I think I have him,' she told Haldor, keeping her eyes closed.

'You *think*? Can you be sure?'

'Give me a moment,' she said. 'I need to hear him speak.' And then he did. Only a few words, but uttered with such authority that he had to be the one in charge. And then another voice came, one that called him 'Majesty'. 'Yes. It's him.'

'Kill him,' Haldor growled in her ear. 'Do it now.'

'Sleep,' Rosheen said. 'I won't—'

'Kill him now, or I kill you.'

Rosheen felt Haldor press the blade against her back. It pierced her leather jerkin and pricked her skin. She nodded and reached out with her staff.

And then there came another light in the darkness. One brighter than all the others. As dazzling as the sun and moving across the sky, and Rosheen knew it could only be one person.

'Oskar, bombs! Now!'

Oskar reached for one of the black jars tied around the saddle, then stopped himself.

'Aren't we supposed to drop these on specific targets?' he yelled over the whipping wind.

'Oskar, if you think for one moment that I'm following orders, you're out of your bloody mind. We drop these, lose some weight, then we go.'

'Where?'

'Anywhere but here!'

'Then we help Gudrun?'

'Yes, yes! Do it now.'

Oskar pulled on the strings, releasing the bombs. He watched them tumble in silence, wondering what they would do.

What followed was devastating. Great flashes of orange and white burst among the combatants below, obliterating many and sending severed limbs spiralling through the air. Oskar felt numb, bile rising from his belly as he slapped a hand over his mouth to stop himself puking. All those deaths because of him. The shockwaves came less than a heartbeat later, flapping across Petra's wings, threatening to flip them over.

Oskar instinctively squeezed Gudrun's body. 'Sorry, sorry,' he told

THE END OF MAGIC

her, taking her hand. It was chilled. He closed his eyes, pressing his ear against her back, listening for her heartbeat, but he couldn't hear one, not above all the screaming from below.

'Bingham.' Oskar's voice broke as his chest began to shudder with grief. 'I think she's dead. What do we do, Bingham, what do we do?'

There was no time for Bingham to answer as a hail of arrows came battering Petra, stabbing into her thick hide. The wyvern was now a target for both armies.

Haldor's commanders had all instinctively stepped back when the bombs landed, though Haldor stood his ground and jabbed his blade into Rosheen's back. She heard him utter a northern curse. Not even he had foreseen this.

'Oskar!' Rosheen cried as the smoke cleared from the explosions and she found the wyvern spiralling above the battlefield.

'What?' Haldor said, pressing the blade harder, making her wince as it cut into her.

Somehow, Rosheen's brother was alive and flying a wyvern. She had no idea how this could be, but she couldn't stay here any longer. The creature was falling and Oskar with it.

'Witchy-warlock, what are you—?' Haldor began, but was knocked back by a wave of energy from the Lapis stone. It wasn't much, but enough to give Rosheen a head start as she ran from Haldor's encampment towards the thick of the battle, all the time calling to her brother.

'I've lost control,' Bingham yelped. 'We're going down, hold on!'

Petra was spent. The arrows in her side had weakened her and she was tumbling to the ground.

'Oddmun, I'm sorry, I'm so sorry!' Bingham babbled as they fell. 'Forgive me, brother!'

Oskar, is that you?

When the voice arrived in Oskar's head, at first he thought it was Gudrun, and it took him a moment to realise that it was a voice he had known all his life.

Rosheen?

324

The crowded battlefield rushed up to meet them and soldiers from both sides scattered to get out of the way. Then Petra stopped falling and Bingham screamed as he was thrown clear.

Rosheen was vaulting over the stone wall bordering the battlefield as the wyvern slowed its descent and came to a halt in the thick of the action, throwing one of its passengers from its back. It wasn't Oskar. The terrified wyvern was suspended in the air only a few inches from the ground, gently bobbing like a lure on the end of a fishing line, with two passengers still on its saddle.

The soldiers around it, enemies in war but united in their fear of magic, backed away, weapons ready. The creature gently settled on the ground and a young boy hopped from the saddle as if he was just popping out on an errand.

Rosheen's heart soared when she saw her little brother alive and well.

Then it sank as she saw the soldiers and mercenaries around him cry out and raise their swords to attack him. She swung her staff around, unsure what power she had left, sure she was ready to do anything to save him.

Oskar didn't know how he did it, he only knew that he could. Being moments away from smashing into the ground and certain death had released something in him. A change almost as grand as the one triggered by the destruction of the Lapis Moon. A confidence to do and try anything.

His sister Rosheen was out there somewhere. She had spoken to him and he had to find her, if only to learn what she was doing here. He closed his eyes again to locate her, but he was overwhelmed by the cacophony of the minds of the baffled and angry soldiers around him, the blazing lights of their souls in the void blinding him from seeing her. There was too much noise, too many competing thoughts. He needed clarity. And so he would silence them.

Rosheen had barely raised her staff when she saw Oskar sweep his hand in a circle.

And every soldier and mercenary on the battlefield clattered to the ground.

Asleep.

The tranquillity was sudden and eerie. The wind whistled around her and she could hear birdsong again. Somewhere in the sea of slumbering bodies, a soldier began to snore. Dozens of horses, now riderless, whinnied in confusion and many galloped away.

There she was. The only one left standing, protected by her magic.

Hello, Rosheen, he called to her with his mind.

'Oskar!' She called to him across the field, her voice distant and flat through the clearing smoke. Oskar wondered why she couldn't use her mind for communication, or if she chose not to. 'They told me you were dead! Where have you been? What's happened to you?'

I've changed.

'How?' she asked, thinking back to Anzu's mad idea that the boy might be a demigod of ancient myth. No, he wasn't a demigod, but he certainly wasn't the simple boy she had left behind, either. Rosheen started to weave her way through the tangled bodies on the field, using her staff to stop herself from falling more than once.

How long have you had a staff? Oskar asked her. *Is that a Lapis stone?*

'Oskar, please speak to me. I need to hear your voice.' There was a clearing in the bodies and she began to rush towards him.

And that's when he felt it. Like a cloud passing in front of the sun, the light in his mind began to dim. He staggered back, rushing away from her.

'Back, Rosheen, please stay back, don't come any closer!' Oskar raised his hand, waving her away.

Rosheen kept coming and he found himself struggling to create thoughts in his mind, to coordinate his limbs, to form words. He stumbled back and only slurred sounds would come from his mouth, until somehow he managed one word: 'Stop!'

The sheer panic in his voice made Rosheen halt in her tracks.

Oskar backed further away from her and his mind was clear once more. 'The Lapis stone,' he told her as he caught his breath. 'It clouds my mind, Rosheen. Please don't come any closer.'

Rosheen glanced at the weak blue light at the centre of her Lapis stone. 'The curse of the moon child,' she muttered to herself, then dropped the staff to the ground before stepping over rousing soldiers to be with her brother.

'No, please,' Oskar called to her. 'Stay there.'

She stopped and found herself slowly raising her hands as if she was approaching a wild animal. She didn't have anything to fear from her brother, did she?

'Come with me, Oskar,' she said. 'We have to leave. Now. We can go home.'

'Home?' He gave a sad smile and shook his head. 'They burned it to the ground, Rosheen. When they took me. Father's dead, but mother might still—'

'Mother's dead, too, Oskar.' Tears came freely as Rosheen spoke. 'I'm sorry.'

'How… how do you know?'

'I… I saw her,' Rosheen said, desperately hoping that he wouldn't ask for more details. 'She's gone, Oskar. I'm so sorry.'

Oskar felt his heart go cold. He had known, he supposed. He had fooled himself that more of Yanick's men might be holding his mother hostage, too, but the truth had always been there, and he had tried to put it away to confront at another time. Now it was here, and it nearly broke him. He felt his knees weaken and his eyes water.

'You left me behind, Rosheen,' Oskar said, his voice straining and rising in pitch. 'You left them to die. And now you want me to come with you? You snap your fingers and expect me to come running? No, Rosheen. I'm no longer a moon child. I've changed.'

'I see that, Oskar,' she said, wiping the damp from her cheeks. 'Your powers are unique.'

'Powers? I don't want them. What good are they? Gudrun is dead!'

I'm not dead, you idiot.

Gudrun's voice burst into Oskar's mind as clear as day, as if she were standing next to him.

You're alive? Gods, Gudrun, you're alive!

Only just. Take me to Tofa's Peak. It's the tallest mountain in Arranrod.

I can heal you here, Gudrun. Let me help you.

This is a battlefield, Oskar. It's tricky to heal people when everyone else wants to kill you. And I need time to heal properly. Please, take me to Tofa's Peak.

Rosheen's voice broke through. 'It's going to be difficult for you to understand what to do with them, Oskar. You're so young, so inexperienced—'

'Shut up!' Oskar waved her into silence as he tried to concentrate on Gudrun's voice.

Follow the King's Road till you meet the mountains and take me to the volcanic pools, Gudrun told him. *It's where my people come from.*

'Oskar, please listen,' Rosheen said. 'You don't have the training to cope with your powers. If you misuse them, it could lead to terrible consequences. Let me help you.'

Don't let me die here, Gudrun pleaded. *We have to go now, Oskar, this minute. I'm bleeding out, I can't hold on much longer.*

'I'm sorry about your friend, Oskar, but you can help me. A princess is dying. A little girl. You can help me right a wrong.'

Oskar ignored her and rushed to Petra and Gudrun.

'You have to understand, I did it for you,' Rosheen called to Oskar, but he wasn't listening. Instead, he clambered onto the back of the wyvern, where a young woman was slumped forward in a blood-stained saddle.

Around them, dazed soldiers were getting to their feet and the muffled cries of commanders barking orders echoed across the fields. Oskar's magic was wearing off. It wouldn't be long before this was a battlefield again.

'Haven't got time for this,' Rosheen muttered to herself and turned back for her staff. If he wouldn't listen then she would have subdue him. She could contain his power, get him away from here and then they could speak properly.

She snatched up the staff and began running towards her brother and the wyvern.

The clouds came again.

Oskar saw Rosheen sprinting towards him with the staff and its Lapis stone. What was she thinking? He had to stop her now.

The wave of energy that hit Rosheen was like being slapped in the face with a stone wall. She was knocked off her feet and the staff went flying. She shook her head clear and got herself upright, only to find Oskar reaching out to her. A moment later, he sent a bright ball of light surging towards her and she staggered back, but not fast enough to evade it and she was bowled over once more. She landed near her staff and snatched it up, and returned her own feeble ball of light to stun him, but he batted it away like a ball. Back and forth they sent bolts of energy. Oskar unleashed a terrible storm of magic lighting up the field, each blast more intense than the last, more power than Rosheen had ever encountered before. Rosheen could only summon weak crackles to defend herself. With a final zigzag bolt of lightning that cracked like a whip, Oskar sent his sister reeling, blown across the field like a leaf on a breeze.

Every part of Rosheen convulsed in agony. The ground tipped and rolled below her and any attempt to get upright simply saw her falling again. As she collapsed on her back, she watched the wyvern shake its head awake, flap its wings, then, despite the arrows in its side, rise effortlessly into the sky with her brother pulling on its reins. The two of them soared away in a graceful arc above the clouds and over the horizon.

Haldor hadn't slept like that since he was a child. Certainly not since before his family and entire village had been wiped out by Morven raiders all those years ago. He felt more refreshed than he had in years, his body was revived, his muscles buzzing with energy, though his mind was still somewhat muddled. He recalled explosions, a wyvern, Rosheen sending him and his men flying, then she ran towards the battlefield, and then what had happened?

He looked for her now.

There she was, in the middle of the battlefield, surrounded by the slumbering forms of every soldier in the field. Some, like him, were already awake, but drowsy. She had lied to him, the bitch. There was more power in that stone than she was letting on.

'My lord?' a confused voice called and Haldor turned to see a messenger dismounting a horse, frowning at the awakening warlords and commanders around him.

'What is it?' Haldor beckoned him closer.

'Urgent intelligence from your eyes on the roads south,' the messenger said. 'Bhaltair's mage is riding south to the merclan commune on the Andraste Coast.'

Now it was Haldor's turn to frown. 'That's not possible. He's dead. I have his head, I saw it with my own…' Haldor faltered. What had he seen? Rosheen had magic. She could have shown him anything. He grinned as he realised he had been duped by such an obvious trick. 'Oh, you are such a clever witchy-warlock, and I am such a fool. You!' Haldor snapped his fingers at the first of his guards to get to his feet. 'Bring me the head of the mage. The one on the spike. Now!'

The Lapis stone was dead. Its light was gone, and what little magic it had contained was now extinguished for good, drained by Rosheen's clash with Oskar.

Around Rosheen, soldiers were now awake, if drowsy. Her own mind reeled with mage's delirium. This was the worst case she'd ever had, her fingers trembling, her body aching all over as she craved the magic that had kept her going these past few days. She stumbled over to the man who had been thrown clear of the flying wyvern.

'You.' Her voice slurred as she pointed at him. 'Y'flew tha' wyvern for Bhaltair?'

'I am Captain Bingham of the—'

'Y'know Oskar?'

'Uh, Oskar? Yes. Where is he?'

'Good. I'msister annaneed your help.' Rosheen shook her head to clear it and tried to act sober, but her words kept tumbling into one another. 'I wanyou totake amessage to the king.'

Bingham winced as he checked for broken bones. He was too worried about himself to notice her odd behaviour. 'Not without my wyvern.'

'S'gone. He took it. Take a horse,' she said, waving vaguely to one nearby. 'Ride asfastas you can.'

'Are you all right?' Bingham was squinting at her. 'You're acting a little peculiar, if you don't mind me saying so?'

'Yes'm fine. Here's message...'

'You lied to me, you bitch!' Haldor Frang's voice carried across the battlefield and Rosheen turned to see him standing on the stone wall surrounding it, holding something aloft.

A decapitated head.

Orren's decapitated head.

'First, I'm going to peel the skin from every inch of your body, and then you're going to beg me to kill you,' Haldor called to Rosheen across the battlefield. 'Then the mage. I know where he's headed.'

He watched as she clambered up onto a horse and rode away, face down, clinging to its neck. The man next to her did the same, riding full pelt on another horse towards Bhaltair's encampment.

Haldor inspected the head in his hands. A young woman. No more than twenty years old, perhaps, with a shaved head. Probably the Sister of the Faith who had accompanied the mage on his mission. Haldor wondered how had he not seen that before?

'Magic,' he muttered to himself. 'Thank fuck that's a thing of the past.'

The sound of steel clashing drifted from the field. Some of the soldiers and mercenaries had already resumed the battle, engaging in clumsy, drowsy combat. Bhaltair's cavalry had the advantage again and were pushing forward.

'Sound the retreat,' Haldor told his commanders. 'We'll fall back. We've lost here, but we're not done yet.'

Smudging the Firmament

Sander and Malachy rode overnight, south from Barrow Abbey, as soon as their horses were ready. Rather than following the longer coast road, Sander insisted that they take a short cut through the marshes, much to Malachy's dismay.

'I've only just got meself dry,' the aged elf complained.

'It'll cut half a day off our journey,' Sander told him. 'Trust me, I grew up there, and we've pissed about enough as it is. We can't waste any more time.'

Around mid-morning, they came to a Kelish village. They left the horses by a freshwater pool with a bag of feed, and Sander quietly promised them that he would return before nightfall. He almost believed it himself. He and Malachy continued on foot, wading into ever deeper stagnant marsh water. The whiff of damp mud and rotten vegetation made Sander think of Ragnall's little hothouses where his tomatoes and squashes would ripen and sometimes die when he forgot to harvest them. Being here brought back memories of playing in the marshes as a child. The warnings from parents and elders not to stray too far or too deep.

The Kelish were renowned fisherfolk who lived in conical houses teetering on stilts all through the marshland, their entire lives ebbing and flowing, rising and falling with the tides and annual floods. The funnel-shaped bottoms of the houses also doubled as a hull, so if the floods were too severe, the Kelish families could simply float until the water subsided. They stayed close to the land and kept their distance from the merclans. They knew enough to give them a respectful amount of space.

The Kelish were friendly if cautious with outsiders, and Sander knew their customs well from his childhood. He had brought fresh bread, milk and tobacco from the abbey and was able to trade them for an old coracle that he and Malachy steered through gently swaying reeds eight feet high. Once they cleared the reeds, they were in open swamp with white lilies floating on the surface. Dragonflies darted around them, their iridescent wings catching the light of the sun, and the salty breeze of the nearby ocean mingled with the damp earthy scent of marsh water.

'This is where we need to be careful,' Sander told Malachy, who was using his halberd as a pole to nudge them ever forward. 'Merpeople often wait in the shallows here. Even when you only see one above the surface, there'll be two or three under the water.'

'Like that poor bugger?' Malachy nodded ahead where a cloud of flies were circling a body in the water.

'Keep your distance,' Sander said, slowing the coracle for a better look.

'Bait?'

'Could be. Look at the scales on its tail,' Sander said. 'All the colour's gone. Whoever they are, they're long dead. I think we're okay.'

'That's as may be, but you said yourself there could be more under the surface.'

As they drifted by, Sander gazed at the dead merman's wrinkled features, the saturated beard, his staring white eyes. The top half of the body was as bloodless and pale as unbaked pastry. A beetle with green and blue wings came crawling out of the merman's mouth, then buzzed away.

'One of the elders,' Sander said. 'Probably exiled himself to spare the others the burden of looking after him. They do that sometimes.'

'No wounds,' Malachy noted. 'He ain't been massacred like the other lot.'

'No, but without the magic of the Lapis Moon, they're dying, and we don't have much time.'

Considering it was the tallest mountain in Arranrod, Tofa's Peak was a bugger to find.

Gudrun had told Oskar to follow the King's Road, which, having been built by the ancient Ceezans, was straight as a die until it hit the mountains, where it began to twist and spiral around the various crests and valleys. He found it was almost impossible to tell one mountain from another when he was flying above them, especially at night, and Gudrun had long since fallen silent, so he couldn't ask her for directions.

Instead, he kept Petra below the clouds and, as the morning sun started to break through the canopy, they found themselves weaving between the jagged snow-capped mountains and dormant volcanoes. They passed over Gerdas monasteries, with their red and blue banners flapping in the wind. He thought about asking for directions at the hamlets huddled near the roads but decided to keep Petra going, not wanting to break his link with her, sure that it was only his energy keeping the wounded wyvern aloft. Confused mountain goats watched him glide silently overhead as they munched on the crabby weeds that grew on the steeper faces of the mountains.

Flying Petra felt effortless for Oskar. Once he was up, it was simply a matter of choosing not to go down again. He could stay here. Perhaps for ever. All his problems were down there, and up here he hadn't a care in the world.

Except for the small matter of the dying girl slumped in the saddle in front of him.

He was beginning to lose hope when he crested another peak to see threads of steam rising up from a cluster of craters. He passed over them to find dozens of small volcanic pools with cloudy blue water at the bottom that made him think of the tannery back in Sabley, giving him an unwelcome and unexpected pang of loss for his mother and father. Pushing the heartache away, he descended. The pools were bubbling like pots on a stove and he could feel the heat intensify as he came closer. By the time he landed, his shirt was drenched with the moisture in the air. Petra collapsed in a heap, utterly exhausted. He put a hand to the wyvern's head and sent her into a deep sleep. She had earned a long rest.

Oskar then carried Gudrun to one of the pools. He dipped his hand into water as hot as a freshly drawn bath. Without any further hesitation, he gently lowered Gudrun's cold body into the water, which hissed and foamed around her.

Gudrun remained silent and still. Oskar wriggled out of his waistcoat, rolled it up, placed it on a rock at the edge of the pool and rested her head on it. He wondered if these pools had any kind of healing properties. Could they have some kind of magic?

Magic. If magic was gone, then what explained his abilities? His sister's power came from the Lapis stone on her staff, and that was exhausted now. He could sense no other mage or moon child in all the Newlands, so were he and Gudrun the last ones with any kind of power left?

And what power. Healing, strength, speaking with his mind, flying a wyvern. Thinking about how far he had come in the last few days left his mind spinning. What else could he do with it?

Rosheen had warned him about the consequences of his power, and of course he knew that she was right. He was no fool. He had been treated like an idiot his whole life, and that would stop now. He knew what he was doing. If only he had an inkling of what he was capable of even this morning, then Gudrun might not be injured. They could have left Bingham and that pointless war behind and started their lives anew.

He could have found Rosheen and met her on his own terms, instead of enduring her patronising advice. He was no longer her baby brother, no longer a prisoner, a slave. He was Oskar Katell and he would show her what a moon child could do.

He felt a chill and was astonished to find that he had risen high above the healing pool craters.

He was flying. He was bloody flying!

No wyvern, no wings, only him, rising higher and higher.

Despite his sadness for Gudrun, he found himself laughing at his newfound skill. He could float like a feather on a breeze, or soar like an eagle.

He wondered how high and fast he could fly, then decided to wait until Gudrun was well again. They would take to the air together. Explore the world.

He closed his eyes and reached out, slowly rotating in the air.

Rocks, boulders and pebbles rose from the ground, spiralling up to join him, then they began to spin around Oskar like the Greystone Moon orbiting the world. The clouds above began to gather and blacken the sky, rumbling and cracking as they came together. From deep within their darkness came silent flashes that left bright impressions on his eyes.

Oskar released the rocks whirling around him and they hurtled through the air with a whoosh, then careened into the sides of mountains all along the Arranrod Range, triggering avalanches and rockfalls followed by a booming noise that sounded as if the world itself had cracked open.

As the noise died away, all the colour drained from the world, and Oskar looked up to see the sun passing behind the ring of Lapis stones orbiting high above.

Rosheen had been riding south all night and all morning as fast as she could on the King's Road when her horse whinnied, reared up and came to a stuttering halt. The grass on the road around them became bleached as the sun passed behind the ring of Lapis stones again. Rosheen had grown accustomed to the daily event even if her horse had not.

She was surprised to see the colour return as quickly as it had gone. She glanced up into the sky, shielding her eyes from the glare with her hand, and what she saw made her blood run cold.

The Lapis stones were no longer in a tight band. They were smeared across the sky, blown and scattered like dandelion seeds.

Sander and Malachy looked up, drifting in their coracle in the marsh water. Sander could see that gravity was already drawing some of the stones back into the main band, slowly turning them over as it did so, but he couldn't for the life of him figure out what had happened. Another rock smashing through them, perhaps? It didn't matter. It was a worry for tomorrow and he dug his paddle in the water and kept moving.

Haldor happened to be looking skywards at the time and had seen the stones move with his own eyes. It was an unnatural sight, sudden, as if a child had lashed out at toys during a tantrum. One moment they were in place, the next they were sprinkled across the bright blue sky. His men around him, supposedly ruthless mercenaries, were already babbling about signs and portents, and Haldor regretted killing the astronomer, missing the old drunk's grounded perspective.

Haldor wondered what kind of power it took to dash them across the sky. Whatever it was, he wanted it. But first, he had unfinished business.

'Snap out of it, you pathetic bastards. We have a pair of mages to kill!' He waved his men forward. Two dozen of them on horseback, trailing Rosheen as she headed south.

Oskar's power invigorated him. He thought he would be tired after such excesses, but he felt stronger than ever.

He came to rest by Gudrun in her pool. She remained motionless, silent, but some colour was returning to her skin.

While he was in the air, he could sense his sister moving south. And she was pursued by men on horseback. The same men who had been fighting in that battle. Her power was gone completely, and yet she still rode into danger. Something to do with righting a wrong.

Oskar couldn't worry about that now. He joined Gudrun in the warm pool and took hold of the bolt in her chest. He could sense where it was lodged in her ribs, the inflammation around it causing her so much pain. It had to come out. She would bleed more, but he would heal her, he could do this. Slowly, firmly, he pulled on the bolt. Blood seeped from the wound as the shaft slid out. He felt the arrowhead scrape against bone and stopped, not wanting it to come loose from the bolt. Closing his eyes, he could see where it had caught against her rib. He carefully angled it around and allowed himself a moment of joy when it slid free from the wound. Then the blood came, thick, dark and warm. Oskar pressed his hands against her skin, the blood oozing between his fingers. He desperately wanted to rest, but he summoned every last ounce of energy, cradling her in his arms as he muttered, 'Heal, heal, heal.'

Effie of the Jeltse Merclan

Sander and Malachy passed more bloated corpses in the water. Carrion birds pecked at the bodies' soft flesh, witnessed by long-legged, dispassionate red-crowned cranes wading nearby, but the former mage and elf didn't stop to inspect them. They came to a sandbank rising up out of the water, a thin, golden island stretching east down the coast to where it would eventually grow to meet the Andraste Cliffs. Here it was only yards wide, flanked by the green murk of the marsh on one side and the crystal blue of the Sugar Sea on the other.

'This it? Where are they?' Malachy asked, hoisting the coracle on his back.

Sander found himself smiling. 'You look like a turtle.'

'Yeah? Well, your head looks like a badly shaved bollock, so we're even.'

'Charming. This way.' Sander led him further down the sandbank to where a coral reef rose from the water, curving around like a sickle blade. As they climbed the coral, they could see merfolk nests lining the huge underwater sinkhole within, a black void in the water, an abyss without an end.

'Down there,' Sander said. 'They nest here but live in caves out of sight from the surface. They only come up to feed. Or when summoned.' Sander made his way down the remains of some well-worn steps to an old brass horn chained to a rock.

'What the bloody hell is that?' Malachy said.

'The door knocker.' Sander lifted the horn, wiped the mouthpiece clean with his shirt, dipped the horn into the water and blew. The water bubbled and a sound like whale song reverberated through the depths.

Sander and Malachy peered into the darkness of the sinkhole.

Nothing. No movement.

'Nobody home,' Malachy said.

'There must be.' Sander blew again. No response.

And again. And again. The noise he made went from a vigorous trumpeting to a desperate, croaky rasping.

Sander began to feel faint. He released his grip on the horn, dropped to his knees and buried his head in his hands. 'They're dead,' he said, his voice barely audible over the wash of the waves around them. 'We're too late, Malachy. I'm sorry. We came all this way for nothing. I'm clearly going mad.'

'Nah, if anything, I reckon you's getting better.'

'How's that?'

'You ain't been talking to yourself since you left the abbey, for a start.' Malachy dipped his halberd into the water. 'How did you know this lot so well, anyway?'

'One of them tried to kill me and my father when I was a boy,' Sander said, then he caught Malachy's worried expression. 'Oh no, she's mellowed a lot since then, we're fine now. I think.'

'You *think*? When did you last see her?'

Sander closed one eye as he tried to recall. 'Fifteen... no, twenty-something years ago?'

'You haven't seen her for over twenty years?' Malachy said. 'It's lucky this ain't a life-or-death situation, mate, otherwise I'd be worried.'

'No, seriously, it'll be great. She always liked me.'

'Make it personal,' Malachy said. 'Call for her by name.'

'You can't, there's a protocol to this. You use the horn and they—'

'Protocol be bollocksed, we ain't got time for that,' Malachy said, and he started slapping his halberd on the surface of the water. 'Hey, fishy, fishy!'

'Stop! Gods alive, you're an insensitive sod sometimes, Malachy.'

'Not much call for sensitivity in the army.'

'So I've noticed.' Sander got to his feet and cupped his hands around his mouth, shouting down at the water. 'Helfina Glenna Grizel of the Jeltse Merclan,' he called.

'That's a mouthful,' Malachy said.

'Effie, are you there?'

'Who?'

'It's what I called her as a boy.' Sander cupped his hands again, 'Effie, can you hear me?'

'Yeah, I can hear you,' came a serrated voice from behind them.

Sander and Malachy spun to find Effie resting on the coral. She must have swum around them from the ocean side. 'Been here for some time.'

'Why didn't you answer?'

'I ain't at your beck and call, wizard.'

'Effie, we need your help—'

'I know why you're here,' she said. 'And I ain't bleeding for some royal bitch.'

If Effie had been old and haggard when Sander was a boy, she looked like one of the undead of ancient myth and legend now. A few wisps of white hair were all that remained of her once-golden locks, her skin was so pale as to be translucent, her ribs and gills shuddered with the simple effort of breathing, and her once iridescent tail was pale and dull. Sander was heartened to see that she still had a wicked glint in her eye and her colourful way with words.

'I thought we were friends, Effie.'

'And I thought you was a mage.' She curled a lip. 'Guess them days is over.'

'I guess they are.'

Malachy leaned close to Sander. 'The sinkhole, son,' he muttered. 'Take a look.' Sander glanced over to see the ghostly forms of mer-people, at least twenty, rising from the deep. 'This might get ugly, mate,' Malachy said. 'Make it quick, eh?'

'Oh, it'll be quick, soldier boy,' Effie said. 'The answer's no. Now fuck off.'

'I don't need much, Effie,' Sander told her. 'A few drops. You'll be saving a little girl's life.'

'That'll be the princess?' Effie asked, already knowing the answer. 'That poor girl. Terrible thing to happen. What a tragedy.'

'Then you'll do it?'

'No.'

'Come on, Effie. Where's your humanity?'

'I ain't human!' Effie snapped. 'All my life, humans have told me where to live, where I can fish, how to behave, and when we said no they sent mages to do their dirty work. They killed us, caged us, dried us out, watched us as we died.'

'That wasn't me, Effie.'

'Would you have been any different? My little girl breathed her last in a travelling circus in the Arranrod Mountains. Didn't know that, did you? They stole her from me for some freak show. Scared and all alone she was when she died. When they brought her back to me...' Effie faltered, her voice trembling at the memory. 'The things they did to her. Where was your humanity then, Sander Bree? Humans.' She spat on the sand. 'They've done nothing but bring misery, and now at the end they send a human for my blood. The answer's no. Now fuck off.'

Water lapped gently on the coral and Sander glanced down to see merfolk circling under the surface, their large, black eyes fixed on the confrontation above.

'Effie.' Sander stepped forwards, prompting a flurry of splashes in the water behind him as her fellow merfolk broke the surface and swam closer to the coral, baring their teeth and ready to pounce if he tried anything. 'If you give me this blood, I'll offer you something in return.'

'I can't think of a single thing you have that I might want,' she sneered.

Sander took a breath. He had been contemplating this since he woke in the abbey, since he left Taranis, if truth be told. There was only one thing he could offer. One thing he could be positive that he knew she wanted.

'I'll give you me,' Sander said, not quite sure if he said it out loud. And, if he had, he wondered if it was too late to take it back.

Malachy swung his halberd from the water to Effie and back again, unsure where this was going. 'What are you doing, Sander?'

Sander gestured for Malachy to be quiet and kept his eyes locked on Effie's. She hadn't immediately insulted him, so he knew he had her interest now. 'Ever since that day on the beach,' Sander continued, 'I know you've felt humiliated. Outwitted by a boy, for gods' sakes. You lost your standing in the clan. You never recovered, did you, Effie?'

'I've done all right for meself.' She raised her chin, summoning every ounce of pride she had. Around her, the merpeople began to climb onto the coral with slow, deliberate movements, hunters stalking prey.

'You should have been matriarch, but it never happened.' Sander chose his words carefully. He couldn't afford to crow. 'Take me, Effie. Get your revenge on the arrogant little prick who made you look a fool. Once we have your blood, I will come willingly, I promise.'

'I could kill you now and be done with it,' she said.

'Oh no you won't.' Malachy levelled his halberd at her as the merpeople began to hiss in unison, closing in on Sander and Malachy, ready to launch themselves at the interlopers.

Sander held out his hand to her. 'Give me your blood, do some good, save a life, stop a war. How many people get a second chance like that, Effie? What do you say?'

Effie's stern face began to fall and her eyes flickered from Sander to the merpeople. She waved a hand and silenced their hissing.

'I understand if you want to consult the clan,' Sander said, and gestured at the sinkhole with an open hand. Effie nodded, took her cue, flexed her tail and dived into the water. The other merpeople followed her into the depths.

'You know what they do to people, don't you, mate?' Malachy said.

'Trying not to think about it,' Sander said, keeping his eyes on Effie.

'First they drown yer,' Malachy continued. 'Then they feast on yer flesh, starting with the neck or the belly.'

'Yeah, I did say I was trying *not* to think about it, but thanks all the same. Anyway, I read somewhere that drowning is a peaceful way to go. Virtually painless, it said.'

'And what am I supposed to do when you're dead?' Malachy asked.

'Prepare the blood.'

'I don't do magic.'

'Add this.' Sander handed him a small paper packet folded like an envelope.

'Wassat?'

'A teaspoon of salt, pop it in straight away, give it a quick shake. Keep it at room temperature, try not to spill any, and when you serve it to the princess, simply dilute in water.'

Malachy frowned. 'Is that it? I thought there'd be thunder and lightning or something.'

'It's not magic, Malachy, it's a remedy.'

'So all that bollocks about you being the only one who knew how to cure her—'

'It's not bollocks. Just easy when you know how.'

'Now I know why you kept it to yerself for so long.'

'Take the blood back to Taranis, Malachy. That's an order,' Sander said. 'Tell them whatever tales of sword and sorcery you want. Return as the sole hero of the expedition, save the princess's life and redeem the name of elves everywhere. And if that bastard Bhaltair doesn't give you at least a dukedom for that, then he deserves to fail.'

'Well, son.' Malachy sniffed and leaned on his halberd. 'I've got to admire your—'

Sander instinctively turned to the splash as soon as he heard it, but Effie was too fast for him, even at her advanced years. She came hurtling from the water, through the air, slamming him onto his back.

She pinned him down with arms that were more sinew than muscle, and before he could get his breath back to ask her what she was doing, she leaned forward and whispered into his ear, 'I'm putting on a show for the others,' she said.

'A what?'

'I can't just give you my blood. It's forbidden. We fight, you cut me, honour is satisfied, so be quick about it.'

Malachy came running with his halberd, but Sander waved him back with one hand while fumbling in his robes' front pouch for his knife and vial with the other. The elf kept coming and Effie whacked him with her tail, sending him tumbling onto his backside on the coral.

Sander glanced at the water. The other merpeople had returned, watching from under the surface as they circled.

Sander and Effie struggled as he unfolded his fishing knife.

'Where do you want it?' he asked her.

She grabbed his wrist and stabbed the blade into her own forearm with an anguished cry. The blood, a dark claret, came slowly, thick as treacle. Sander had to squeeze her arm to tease more of it out. He held the lip of the vial to her wound and soon had all the blood he needed.

He twisted its cork back in the top and looked for Malachy, who by now had twigged this was all a ruse. 'Malachy! The blood, take the blood, save yourself!' Sander tossed him the vial.

Malachy snatched it from the air, untwisted the cork and tipped the salt from the paper packet into the vial. He replaced the cork and shook the vial as he gave Sander a nod.

'Ready to die?' Effie clasped her bony hands around Sander's neck.

'No,' he said with all honesty.

'You were such a handsome boy,' she said, tightening her grip. Her fingers were soft and clammy, yet peppered with grit and sand. 'I've been looking forward to this for—'

A horn sounded. At first, Sander wondered if it was coming from a ship at sea, but it was soon followed by the rhythm of galloping hooves. Sander, Effie and Malachy craned their necks around to see who was joining them.

'Maybe twenty of 'em.' Malachy shielded his eyes and looked further down the beach where they could see men on horseback thundering towards them, kicking up plumes of sand and hollering war cries as they came. 'No banners, and a bugger's muddle of arms and armour.'

One rode ahead of the others. He didn't have the usual trappings of a warlord – no furs or gold – but as he waved his men forward to the coral, Sander had no doubt that this man was in charge.

'I reckon that's Haldor Frang,' Malachy said, tucking the vial of merblood safely inside his jerkin.

'Oh no, not yet, not now,' Sander muttered, his heart racing. This was not part of his plan. 'Malachy, run!' he cried, but the old soldier stood his ground and raised his halberd. 'Effie, please,' Sander begged. 'They'll kill Malachy and this will have been for—'

'Sorry, boy, a deal's a deal,' she said, before grabbing his arm, flexing her tail and yanking him away from the coral. He tried to take a deep breath before he hit the water, but the impact knocked all the air out of him, and before he knew it, she was dragging him down.

Fuck You, Haldor Frang

Haldor's men had caught up with Rosheen on the southern road. Her horse's legs buckled with exhaustion, sending her tumbling into the dust on the side of the highway. As she gave the poor beast the last of her water, Haldor's riders surrounded her, stirring up clouds of dust as they circled, drawing their swords and uttering curses and promises of grisly mutilation. Rosheen's head was pounding and sparkles of light danced in her vision, but her body had at least stopped shaking. Her mind was less foggy now, and she could appreciate the terrible irony that just as she was recovering from her worst case of mage's delirium ever, death was only moments away.

Haldor joined Rosheen in the centre of the squall, looking down at her from his saddle with his usual grin. She expected some quip about her cunning and how much he admired her, but he simply raised his boot and kicked her in the face. Before she could get to her feet again, she was bundled into a sack and tied over the back of his stallion.

All she could do was hope that she didn't come flying off and crack her head open on one of the many rocks on the road. Thankfully, it wasn't long before the uneven surface became something smoother. The sound of crashing waves and the smell of brine told her that they were galloping along the beach. Rosheen reached for the neck of the sack, hoping to loosen it and pull herself free.

'There!' Haldor's voice bellowed and the horses accelerated to a sprint. 'Sound the horn. Let the bastards know we're coming. Put the fear of the gods into them.' Haldor gave the first war-cry and his men joined in, creating a wordless, tuneless howl.

Rosheen thanked the gods that the chase was brief, though Haldor's horse reared up as it came to a stop, tipping her off its back and onto the sand. She barely had time to get her breath back as she was pulled from the sack by her hair. The sunlight pressed on Rosheen's eyes like thumbs.

'Is that him?' Haldor said.

Rosheen tried to open her eyes, but the brightness burned intensely and she shut them again. Streaks of green and purple danced across the inside of her eyelids and she was convinced that her skull was going to crack open.

'Witchy-warlock, is that the mage?' Haldor asked impatiently.

'Give me a moment, I can't see,' she said.

'I ain't no mage,' said a grizzled, no-nonsense voice that she didn't know.

'That's not Sander Bree,' she told Haldor.

'Then who is it?'

'I'm Sergeant Malachy Nye of the Wayland King's Guard,' said the voice.

'Hey, I know you.' The menace in Haldor's voice was gone and replaced with boyish admiration. 'You survived the Siege of Fourfoot, yes? And you led the charge at Ragomar?'

'I did.'

'My father was at Ragomar!'

'Oh, yeah?' Sergeant Malachy Nye replied cautiously. 'On whose side?'

'I forget. Probably not yours, I suspect.'

'It was a bit of a mess.'

'That's the understatement of the century. Hey, look at his ears,' Haldor said, sounding genuinely surprised. A first for him. 'You're an elf!'

'That I am,' Malachy replied.

Rosheen could squint her eyes open now, and she got to her feet to find the silhouette of a stick insect of a man – or an elf – standing on top of a coral reef, wielding a halberd. She was sure she recognised him as part of Sander's group. There was no sign of Sander.

'Well, shit my bed.' Haldor threw his arms wide. 'I thought you were all dead?'

'Not yet, I ain't.'

'It's a pleasure to finally meet one in the flesh, my lord.'

'Ain't no lord. Just a soldier.'

'So modest.' Haldor smiled, then his voice became all business once again. 'Where's the mage, Malachy Nye?'

'Snuffed it,' Malachy said a little too quickly. 'Died at Barrow Abbey. Came crawling in, cold as a witch's tit and almost as blue. His dying wish, he asked me to come to this place and get the blood, but I pitched up here and found the merfolk all dead, too.'

'You're lying, Malachy Nye,' Haldor said.

'Not my job to lie,' Malachy said. 'I'm a soldier, son. Have been for more years than I care to remember. I've fought for elves, for magic, for men, for love and for kings. In all that time, I've learned two important rules: follow orders and watch your back. That's how I've managed to—'

Something whistled through the air past Rosheen's ear and cut Malachy off. He stared down in puzzlement at a knife buried deep in his chest. Rosheen hadn't even seen Haldor throw it.

'Honestly, these people… They must think I'm a fucking idiot.' Haldor sounded even more exasperated than when Rosheen met him on the battlefield. 'I haven't got time for lies and riddles and bullshit, I really don't.'

Malachy looked up at Haldor with a glare of disapproval, like the warlord had broken some unwritten rule of warfare. Malachy dropped his halberd and tumbled off the coral, falling face first onto the sand.

'Last of the elves,' Haldor puffed. 'No wonder they all died out, yap-yap-yap… *You!*' A boot in Rosheen's back confirmed that Haldor was talking to her. 'Go and check.'

Squinting, head thumping and body aching, Rosheen clambered up the coral. She had never been here before, but the sinkhole of the Jeltse Merclan was a famous sight, visited only by the more daring tourists, and tales of its beauty and depth were told in taverns across the Newlands. Rosheen found its swirling deep blues hypnotic and wondered how many travellers had met their end looking wide-eyed into its abyss.

Sander was nowhere to be seen, but there were strong ripples on the surface and she was sure there was something moving down below. These merpeople were alive.

'Well?' Haldor called.

'My eyes are still adjusting to the light,' she called back. 'There's definitely something down there. I need to get a better look.'

'No tricks, witchy-warlock,' Haldor told her.

Rosheen clambered down the coral to where the summoning horn was chained to the rocks. She had one chance to end this. She ran to the horn, grabbed it in both hands, dipped it in the water and blew as hard as she could.

'Hey!'

Rosheen glanced up to see two of Haldor's men rushing towards her, their swords drawn.

'People of the Jeltse Merclan,' she called to the still water. 'These are the ones who killed your brethren at Connal Lake. Avenge your brothers and sisters now!'

Sander was drowning. He knew. He recalled fishing trips with his father when he was a child. How they landed the fish on the deck of the boat, and Sander watched, indifferent, as they writhed about, gasping in the open air. Now the tables had turned, as the merpeople looked down on him like he was the landed fish.

Effie had dragged him into to a cave in the pool wall to drown. She pinned him in place with her stringy yet incredibly strong arms as the rest of the clan gathered above her in silent approval. The boy who had humiliated her, and the clan, so many years ago was now paying for his impertinence.

Sander's lungs were burning, his ears ached with the sudden pressure and the salt stung his eyes. He was fighting every instinct he had to open his mouth and gulp for air, knowing that once he did, it was all over. He had hoped that he would face his death with a heroic, calm acceptance, but Haldor's arrival created only panic and Sander's sacrificial gesture now felt foolish.

Someone sounded the summoning horn and it reverberated around the coral. The merclan looked up as one, and Sander heard someone calling to them from the surface. His ears couldn't make out what they were saying, but whatever it was, it caused every member of the clan to bolt for the surface.

All but Effie. Though even she was distracted, momentarily loosening her grip on his throat. He batted her hands away and reached for his knife.

Rosheen's cry to the merpeople bought her only a couple of heartbeats as the approaching mercenaries hesitated, wondering who she was calling to. Their confusion was soon dismissed as unimportant to the task at hand and they raised their swords again.

The air filled with the bodies of merpeople bursting out of the sinkhole. Some careened over the coral to the sandbank. Two came flying straight at Rosheen's attackers, who were the first to die. A pair of merwomen bit down on their necks, sending arterial blood spraying through the air. Then, as quickly as they came, they flipped back into the water, swam down into the dark, then came rushing up again, flying even higher through the air.

Rosheen snatched up a sword from one of the dead mercenaries and rushed to the top of the coral, where she could see the fight below. It was suicide mission for the unarmed merclan. They knew their time was short, but they would not go quietly, and she shared their determination if not their desperate savagery. They moved with astonishing speed, flexing their tails to move across the sand and pitch themselves at the mercenaries. Some fell under the soldiers' blades; others ripped throats open with their multiple rows of razor-sharp teeth and gouged eyes out with their long, sharp nails. Her own blood began to rush at the sight of the massacre, but this time she would not fight the bloodlust. With aching arms, Rosheen raised her sword and ran into the fray screaming.

There were clouds of blood around Effie's arms where Sander had stabbed her repeatedly, but she refused to let go of him. With a wince, he went for her eye with the blade, plunging it in, feeling the eyeball pop as the point cut into it, meeting little resistance except where it scraped against the bone of her eye socket. She moaned in agony and released her grip on him.

Sander kicked for the surface, but he was so weak that he could do little more than flounder. He felt a lightning bolt of agony as Effie's bony hands tugged on his bad ankle. She wasn't letting him go anywhere.

There was a darkness at the edge of Sander's vision, his head was pounding, his lungs screaming for oxygen. He couldn't fight it any longer. With an odd feeling of incredulity that this was really happening, he quietly acknowledged to himself that he had to open his mouth. And so he did, and water flooded in.

Rosheen swung her sword into the mercenaries' bodies without hesitation. Banishing fear and replacing it with a cold certainty that if she didn't do this to them, then they would do it to her. She had learned that much during her time with Bowden. Be swift and merciless. Rosheen had only ever received the most basic swordcraft training and had forgotten almost as much as she'd learned, but in the midst of this chaos, she doubted any of it would have helped anyway. All around her were blades swinging at empty air as the merpeople revealed themselves to be ferocious, merciless fighters, tearing into the soft flesh of the mercenaries' necks and faces.

Rosheen found Haldor fending off two merpeople. One merwoman was despatched swiftly with a strike that sent her head spiralling away. Her brother merman dug his claws into Haldor's skull, but Haldor stuck him in the gut with a dagger drawn from a sheath strapped to his leg. As his attackers' bodies fell away, blood streamed from the head wound down Haldor's face, and he gave Rosheen a manic grin.

'Isn't this fun?' he said, running towards her with his sword at the ready.

A kind of calm inevitability washed over Rosheen. She knew there was no way she could survive this encounter, but she wasn't going to run and she wasn't going to beg. She tried to remember her basic sword training and took a defensive position.

Her sword's blade made contact with his and a jolt of pain shot from her elbow and up her arm. It was like hitting a wall. He followed through, cutting into her jerkin and left biceps.

It was only a minor wound, yet the sudden, stinging pain sent a shock of pure agony through Rosheen, brief but more intense than anything she had ever known, and she involuntarily dropped her sword. Haldor backhanded her across the face, and the blinding crack she felt told Rosheen her nose was broken. A boot pounded into her belly and she fell breathless to the sand.

'Well, witchy-warlock, it's been a joy getting to know you,' he said, looming over her, the sun creating a halo directly behind his head. 'Don't take this personally.'

'Fuck you, Haldor Frang,' she spat. 'I hope you burn in hell.' Not particularly clever words, but they were, if nothing else, from the heart.

He raised his sword for the kill.

Rosheen kept her eyes open. She wouldn't give Haldor the pleasure of cowering, so she was astonished to see him convulse. He dropped his sword and grabbed at his stomach. When he looked at his hands, they were covered in blood. A wound had appeared across his midriff and blood was already soaking through his tunic.

For one baffling moment, Rosheen wondered how she was doing this.

She heard a voice in her head. *That is for Father,* the voice said.

Oskar's voice.

Haldor fell to knees, arms splayed out before him, as more blood seeped through the back of his shirt in criss-crosses. Like welts from a whipping.

That is from me.

Then came loud crunches as bones were fractured and Haldor howled in pain, his body contorting as his arms and legs were broken by an unseen hand. The fighting around them had stopped now. Those of his men who hadn't fled already were watching in horror. The merpeople reared up on their tails and held back. They knew powerful magic when they saw it.

And this is for Mother.

Rosheen was briefly blinded by a sudden bright light. She felt heat bloom across her face and turned away. When she looked back, Haldor was completely aflame, a hunched silhouette, crouched in a mockery of prayer.

A shadow flickered above and, wincing into the sun, Rosheen could make out something descending from the sky. She wondered if it was a bird, or Oskar's wyvern, but then she saw her brother Oskar himself descending to the ground like a new god.

What remained of Haldor's men fled back down the beach.

The merpeople stayed, unsure if they should flee or fight.

Oskar had been unable to rest.

Since he sensed his sister heading south, the shining yellow light of her being refused to move from his mind. It pulsed with pain and fear. Whatever gripe he had with her, he couldn't bear to see her suffer.

Nor did he want to leave Gudrun alone. He had watched her all morning, shivering, turning pale, twitching in her slumber, muttering and thrashing at unseen demons. If she woke and he wasn't there, she would be afraid and he wouldn't be able to forgive himself.

In his mind's eye, he saw his sister surrounded, trapped in a sack like an animal.

He told himself he would be quick. He would go, he would help, he would return within the hour.

He left Gudrun snuggled in the curled embrace of Petra's tail with a promise to return as soon as he could and sent himself flying over the clouds, heading south. As he descended to the sandbank by the coral reef and saw his sister kicked to the ground by a man armed with a sword, he was thankful to whatever gods were listening that he hadn't waited a moment longer.

Fuck you, Haldor Frang.

Rosheen's words struck Oskar like a slap.

This man was Haldor Frang? The initiator of all Oskar's pain. He had known without hesitation what had to be done, and it had all come so easily. Oskar, who only a week ago would not have harmed a fly, had just systematically broken a man's body, lacerated him, then burned him alive.

Oskar knew he should be feeling some kind of anguish, but instead he was filled with a deep sense of satisfaction. A happiness that this man was dead. Another problem solved.

'Oskar, please listen!'

He snapped out of his stupor. Rosheen was waving at him.

'Oskar.' Rosheen pointed to the coral. 'Sander, can you help him? He's—'

'I have him,' Oskar said, raising a hand.

Sander had never died before, so he didn't know how to do it properly. There was water in his nose, his throat, his lungs. His larynx spasmed violently, then there was a horrible burning sensation in his chest.

Yet, at the same time, he felt a curious bliss.

Sander was dead now. He was pretty sure of it. Though a tiny part of his brain reminded him that if he was thinking this then he couldn't be dead yet. Which meant that this was going to be more painful and drawn out than he had hoped.

A rising sensation turned his stomach.

Ah, here we go. So there is an afterlife, Sander surmised as he rose to what he thought was the hereafter. *That's nice. I was never much of a believer. Well, none at all if truth be told, but I'm certain I can straighten this all out with whoever's manning the gates of paradise. I'm sure they're reasonable people.*

He burst out of the water, tumbled head over heels and found himself coughing up the water from his lungs on the sandbank.

Not so dead after all.

There was a long moment of fear and confusion during which his lungs refused to work and he thought he was going to die all over again, but then they began pumping oxygen through his body once more.

And that's when he saw someone floating in the air before him. For one confused moment, he thought that his old mentor Ragnall had returned from the dead and was up to his old party trick, but on closer inspection, it turned out to be a young man.

Rosheen helped Sander as he coughed up the last of the water in his lungs. His voice, when it came, was hoarse and faint.

'Effie.' His arms flailed at the gathered merpeople. 'She needs help.'

There were only four of the merfolk left. Three women and a man.

Around them lay the bodies of their clan and the men who had tried to kill them. Rosheen might otherwise have feared for her life, but they had all seen what Oskar did to Haldor and the fight had left them. One of the women extended a hand. The man took it. They all held hands and the woman led them back to the coral reef, where they leapt into the sinkhole and vanished.

Leaving only Rosheen, Oskar and Sander.

Oskar was still hovering inches above the ground. The effort would have exhausted Rosheen at the peak of her powers, and she wondered how her brother managed it now. She wanted to embrace him, but the simple, huggable Oskar she had grown up with was gone. In his place was something that frightened her.

'Thank you,' she said to him.

'Why did you come here?' Oskar asked her. 'Why would you put yourself in danger like this? You don't have magic any more. Don't expect me to do this again.' Far from being a god, Oskar was starting to sound like their mother.

'I told you, Oskar – a girl's life is at stake because of something I did,' Rosheen said. 'I have to put things right.'

'The blood.' Sander's voice was barely a whisper. He staggered on legs of jelly over to Malachy's body, his soaked boots kicking through the dried merblood on the sand, all of it useless to him now. Only the blood in the vial mattered. Sander fell to his knees by Malachy and began rummaging through the old elf's clothes. He found the blood-filled vial, showed it to Rosheen with a smile, then turned back to the old soldier, his friend, and tears came quickly.

Sander wiped the wetness from his face and was surprised to find himself laughing. The final expression on his friend Malachy's face made him look little more than mildly annoyed that he was dead, as if it were only one more impediment to doing his job properly.

'Fare thee well, Malachy Nye.' Sander closed the elf's eyes. 'I'll make sure you're mentioned in despatches.'

'I'm not dead yet, you big tart,' said a voice as faint as a nib scratching on parchment. 'There's magic close by and I'm healing, or I'm trying to, so do me a favour and piss off and leave me be.'

Sander's face broke into a beaming smile and he squeezed Malachy in an embrace.

'Ow, for fuck's sake. What did I just say?' Malachy groaned.

'Sorry, sorry.' Sander gently lowered the elf to the sand.

'I'll be a while, so go and help your friend,' Malachy told him.

'Yes, yes.' Sander nodded and got to his feet, every muscle in his body burning in complaint as he did so. He found Rosheen with the boy who was floating a few inches above the sand.

Show-off, Sander thought.

'You going to introduce me?' Sander said, disappointed that the cocksure voice in his head didn't match the rasping noise that came from his mouth.

'This is my brother, Oskar,' Rosheen said.

'The moon child?' Sander extended a hand. 'Pleased to meet you. I'm—'

'I know who you are, Sander Bree,' Oskar said, remaining airborne and folding his arms.

'Okay...' Sander stopped in his tracks as pieces of a puzzle fell in to place. 'You have magic? You can fly?'

'I am only beginning to understand what I can do.' Oskar rose higher as he spoke. 'I believe these powers to be greater than the magic that you and my sister once—'

'Yeah, yeah, great. I don't care. If you can fly, you can get this to Taranis before sunset.' Sander offered Oskar the vial, but the boy backed away from it.

'Don't drag me into your politics, Sander Bree. I—'

'There's a child's life at stake,' Rosheen chided him. 'Worry about politics later.'

'Yeah, don't be a dick, son,' Sander agreed. 'You've got years to perfect that. Take this to the king. Just add water to drink.'

Oskar remained unmoved.

'Show the people you can do some good, Oskar,' Sander said. 'It's better to be loved than feared. Trust me, I know.'

'The man who flew with you on the wyvern—' Rosheen began.

'Bingham?' Oskar cut in, his eyes narrowing. 'He lives?'

'Yes – at least, I hope so,' Rosheen said. 'I told him to get word to the king that I was going for the blood. They're all waiting, Oskar. It would take us days to get back, but you could save a life before the sun goes down.'

Oskar's eyes fell on the vial.

Without a word, he took it from Sander's palm and rose silently into the bright blue sky. Up and up and up he went, and Sander and Rosheen watched him as he became nothing more than a dot.

'No one person should have that much power, Rosheen,' Sander said eventually. 'Especially if the uppity bugger doesn't even offer us a lift home.'

A Week Is a Long Time in Politics

'Why in the name of the gods would you come back here?' Rosheen greeted a hooded Sander as they met at the crossroads on the outskirts of Lugham Village. 'Didn't these people try to hang you?'

'On this very spot,' Sander said, patting the trunk of the silver oak. The tree was dying. Silver oaks had magic properties once, but this one's bark was weak and faded. A brittle piece came off in Sander's hand and he tossed it into the bluebells. 'I passed through the village on the way here,' he said, his voice still hoarse from his near-drowning.

'Are you mad?'

'Hood up, head down. I'm not an idiot.'

'Hmm.'

'I was oh-so-tempted to pop into the Jolly Cooper for a pint of Night Mary, but I managed to resist. It's so strange down there.'

'It's the same everywhere,' Rosheen said. 'Business as usual. Like none of this happened.'

'Yeah, like they all had this collective madness and then agreed to forget about it. Though I saw the old mages' temple has burned down. They've left it to rot. It's all black, hollow and crumbling.'

'I know how it feels.' Rosheen brushed her hand against the hanging tree's trunk. 'You're not worried someone might spot you, string you up and finish the job?'

'Yes. Very,' Sander said. 'But someone had to come back for Ragnall's notebooks and, more importantly, I left this behind at Springtide,' he said, producing a bar of soap from his knapsack.

'Jasmine soap? You risked life and limb for jasmine soap?'

'This stuff is expensive.'

'Gods, you're such a narcissist.'

'Grooming is important, more so now I'm self-employed. Anyway, that's not why I asked you to meet me... I need to show you something.' He pulled back the hood of his blue cloak. He was going for intriguing and mysterious, but Rosheen couldn't help her giggling when he revealed his shiny bald head and wisps of white hair on his chin.

'Oh, are you trying to grow a beard?' she said, brushing at the hairs. 'That's adorable. Or is it that the hair on your head refuses to grow back and you're compensating for it with this delightful shrubbery?'

'I prefer to be smooth on top, and the beard is a disguise,' he said huffily, batting her fingers away.

'Yes, of course, excellent disguise. No mage ever wore a beard and a big, dark hooded cloak, did they? You'll blend in perfectly.'

'Oh, shut up and follow me.'

'Dear gods, is that an earring?'

'It's an ancient Andraste design. I'm honouring my elders.'

'Y'know, if you're worried about your virility, I recommend some ginseng.'

'Shut up.'

'It's quite common in men your age and nothing to be ashamed of.'

'You're still not shutting up. Come on.'

Sander took Rosheen away from the crossroads, over the covered bridge where he and Ragnall had teased poor Cleff the troll and through the wood. Spring was in full blossom and warming up for summer. He sneezed profusely as they made their way through the pollen-filled air.

'Where are we going, Sander? I like to know where strange, bearded men in cloaks are leading me.'

'Ragnall has – *had* – a cave in the wood.'

'Oh yes, your little mushroom retreat. Where you two would hide away searching for mystic revelations.'

'You can mock, but I had some pretty insightful moments in that cave.'

'I bet you did,' Rosheen said as she followed him up a steep mossy incline. 'Look, if you're thinking of starting that again, then count me out. Bhaltair hates former mages enough as it is without us getting intoxicated and scaring the villagers.'

'No, nothing like that.'

'Did you speak to him yet?'

'The king?' Sander shook his head. 'I got two scrolls from him. An official pardon, followed by a warning to keep away. I'm barred from Taranis for life.'

'But the princess is okay, yes?'

'Oskar did us proud, I hear. There's talk of betrothal already, poor girl. Wayland and Parthalan will be united, so hopefully their combined strength will be enough to ward off any future Haldor Frangs.'

'You know it won't.'

'Of course it won't.' Sander shrugged. 'Just means the next war will be bigger.'

'Can't wait.'

They passed the boulder that blocked the main entrance to Ragnall's cave without a word and kept going until they found a sinkhole. 'Here we are,' Sander announced as he rummaged in the ferns, eventually producing a long coil of thick rope with one end wrapped tightly around an oak tree. He tossed the rest of the rope down into the black of the sinkhole. 'Down we go.' He grinned, carefully lowering himself into the cave.

A single beam of sunlight came through the sinkhole in the cave ceiling revealing a milky pool below. Rosheen clambered down the rope to find Sander waiting for her on the shore by a few old pots and pans on a scorched, ad hoc fireplace. 'That's it, steady now, the water's not that deep.' Sander's voice echoed off the walls. This space was much bigger than Rosheen would have imagined from the outside.

Rosheen jumped the last foot or so into the water, which only came up to her knees. 'Right, I'm now wet and cold, Sander, so this had better be worth it.'

'Oh, it is,' Sander said in an excited whisper. 'Can you feel it yet?'

'Stop pissing about, Sander, just show me.'

'Follow me.' He smiled. 'You need to see this for yourself.' He took off his cloak and waded into the water. 'It's a bit nippy, but it's worth it,' he promised.

Rosheen reluctantly followed him across the pool to a dark shore, where he pointed towards a narrow crawl space between the rocks. 'Through there,' he said.

Daylight leaked in from an underwater tunnel. No, not daylight,

Rosheen realised – it was something else. Something familiar. And from Sander's wicked grin, she knew what it was. The only thing it could be.

She could feel it before she saw anything. As she and Sander wriggled through the crawl space, a familiar and welcome sensation of serenity returned to her, making her skin tingle.

Magic.

Real magic. She felt stronger, more relaxed, more agile. Oh gods, she hadn't realised how much she missed this feeling. It stirred something inside her, a well of power and invincibility, and she felt as if she could raise the roof of the cave and hurl it at the Greystone Moon.

The feeling grew stronger as they left the crawl space and found themselves in a smaller chamber flooded knee-deep like the one they'd just left. One that glowed a bright blue with the light of countless Lapis stones piled up against the cave wall.

'By the gods,' Rosheen whispered. 'How?'

'Listen.' Sander raised a finger to his lips. In the distance, they could hear something moving through water. 'Yes… yes, I think we're in luck. He's back from another trip.'

There was a hole in the cave wall, with a cloudy green subterranean river beyond. Sander poked his head through the hole, calling, 'Gorm! That you, old friend? We have a visitor. Don't be shy.'

A hulking shadow emerged from the gloom, moving towards them between the amber stalactites. It was a troll, and he was cradling half a dozen glowing Lapis stones in his arms. Beckoned by Sander, he came to the hole in the wall but did not step through. Instead, he added these new Lapis stones to the pile, gave Rosheen a suspicious glance and headed back into the murk.

'Can't stop for a chat, then?' Sander called after him. 'Fair enough. A troll's work is never done, eh?'

'The White Sea,' Rosheen said, figuring it out. 'Anzu and me, we watched fragments from the moon, millions of them, fall into the White Sea. We thought they were lost.'

'There's an underground river that runs between here and the White Sea.' Sander bit his bottom lip, barely containing his excitement. 'While we've been out there putting our lives on the line, Gorm has been quietly collecting these rocks and stockpiling them here, the only place he knows is safe. A lifetime's supply and it's ours to share.'

The possibilities of what to do with this news whirled around in Rosheen's head. 'Have you told anyone but me?' she asked him.

'You, me and Malachy.'

'Malachy?'

'He's working for me now. Looking after the horses in town.' Sander grinned. 'After his near-death experience, Bhaltair pensioned him off. Can you believe that? He's older than most mountain ranges and he got early retirement.'

'But no one else knows?'

'I'm not an idiot, Rosheen. Of course not. Things are only going to become more dangerous for mages and we need all the help we can get. I propose that we travel the land and spread word among former mages about this place. Maybe one day we can restore a bit of order?'

'Order?' Rosheen quietly repeated to herself.

'I'm not saying we hire town criers to sing it from the rooftops,' Sander said. 'We'll be selective, of course. People we trust.'

'When did you ever fully trust a mage, Sander?' Rosheen asked. He didn't answer. 'Let's… let's think this over before we get too excited. Maybe save this for when the time is right. When there's some kind of imminent danger.'

'Or we could *prevent* imminent danger. I could take this to the king and—'

'Sander, those days are gone.' Rosheen tried not to snap, but an idea that had been vying for her attention since she last saw Oskar finally took shape. 'Y'know what, Sander? This might sound insane, but after all that's happened, I have to admit I'm *glad* that magic has gone. It… it feels like a weight has been lifted.'

'You're not flaking on me, are you, Rosh?' Sander said. 'We can't let these people tear each other apart. We have a responsibility to—'

'To what? Yeah, the world will go mad for a while, but some kind of balance will return eventually, and then there will be peace again. And you never know, these idiots might actually grow up and evolve in ways that don't rely on magic curing their dose of the pox, or mages turning the tide of battles. Kings might actually think twice before sending their citizens to kill one another, knowing that the fight will be infinitely longer and bloodier without magic.'

'Do you have any idea how naive that sounds?'

'I have to hope that the end of magic might actually change this world for the better.'

'It might. But not if one person, one *boy*, holds all the power,' Sander said knowingly, trying to hold her gaze, but Rosheen found herself being evasive. 'Not only would our kings and warlords fall back into their old ways, but the balance of magical power would be so one-sided as to spell complete disaster.'

'I've been thinking about that,' Rosheen said. 'This place has to remain a secret, Sander. No one can know except you, me, Malachy and your troll friend. Let's take what we need and block up the sink-hole. Then you can go off travelling, and I can go home.'

'Fine, we've got the rest of our lives to argue about this, but there's one thing we need to take care of first.'

The God of the Mountain

When Oskar returned to Tofa's Peak, he found Petra awake, standing over Gudrun like a guard dog. He embraced the wyvern, happy to see her alert and energised again, then he turned his attention to the young woman curled up on the ground.

Gudrun's chest wound was fully healed, but Oskar was sure that her blood was somehow infected. Perhaps some poison on the tip of the crossbow bolt? He couldn't be sure. Her body was shutting down and there was nothing he could do to stop her decline.

He wrapped her in a woollen blanket and lay next to her to keep her warm, giving her his healing energy for as long as he could before passing out in exhaustion.

After two days, there were some signs of improvement.

Don't leave me.

Her eyes opened briefly as her voice came to him.

'I won't.' He gently squeezed her hand. 'I promise. Except... I must fetch food and water sometimes.'

Of course you can get food and water, you fool.

The corners of her lips twitched in a smile. The green in her eyes twinkled. A glimmer of the real Gudrun.

I meant don't ever leave me. For good.

'I swear it.'

Oskar was heartened that she was getting better, but soon after, she closed her eyes again and said nothing for the rest of the day. He began to worry.

The mention of food had triggered a gnawing in his stomach that he tried to ignore, and he endured a night of hunger before accepting that even a moon child needs to eat.

The villagers had seen him flying back and forth and began leaving him food and gifts at an altar at the foot of the mountain. He was wary about accepting them at first, but the woollen blanket they gave him probably saved Gudrun's life and the food was heavenly.

They were Salm People. A peaceful faith, sharing much in common with worshippers of the Goddess though less zealous, theirs was a much older religion that had endured the Ceezan occupation, the Mage Wars and now the destruction of the Lapis Moon. Oskar envied their quiet stoicism. He tried speaking to some of them, to tell them not to be afraid of him, but with every word he spoke, he could see them becoming more agitated. They preferred to relate to their gods at one remove.

Food. He needed food now.

He checked on Gudrun. Still and silent, but breathing. He kissed her forehead. He felt uncomfortable doing so, sure that if she were awake, she would probably thump him, but it made him feel better about leaving her.

He began to walk down the mountain path. He wanted to moderate using his magic. Flying was almost too easy, and it simply reinforced the unease the Salm villagers clearly felt towards him.

After an hour, he came to a tight bend and found his way blocked by a rockfall. He could have removed the rocks with a thought, but it occurred to him that they ensured his and Gudrun's privacy, and so he flew the rest of the way down to the altar.

As he did so, he thought back to his encounter with the king in Taranis.

Oskar had soared over the citadel walls only to be greeted with a hail of arrows, which he deflected with a wave of his hand. Oskar soon found the princess's chambers and gave the vial to the child's nanny, who listened carefully to his instructions before rushing off to dispense the cure.

The king was away at the battleground. His courtiers and advisers apologised for the hostile welcome and were grateful enough, but Oskar had seen the fear in their eyes, and he knew that their agitation would inevitably boil into conflict. They insisted that he stay the night as their honoured guest, but he felt their eyes watching him, studying him for weaknesses. The man in the yellow robes, the leader of the Faith, was the most frightened, glaring at him from under hooded eyelids like a snake waiting to strike.

No one mentioned Oskar's flying. His powers. Not one word.

The king returned the next morning with his entourage, which now included the ever-ambitious Bingham. The captain of the Flying Corps had been given a room in a high tower that once belonged to the king's mage. When they met, Bingham boasted to Oskar about the view from the balcony. Oskar learned that the flyer was off in the morning to hunt for more wyverns to tame for the king. He had been appointed Keeper of the King's Wyverns.

'Congratulations,' Oskar said. 'And it only cost your integrity and your brother's life.'

'W-what?'

'You haven't asked about Gudrun yet.'

'Oh... gods, yes. How is she, poor thing?'

'I think she's dying.'

'That's... horrible.' Bingham backed away to the far edge of the balcony as Oskar slowly advanced on him. 'Bring her here! They have physicians who can cure almost anything. Now the mages have gone, these people have come into their own, you won't believe—'

'Are you really so unrepentant? You murdered your brother, left us to die, ignored Gudrun as the blood spilled from her body, and now you've promised to kidnap innocent creatures from their mothers and force them to rain fire from the sky,' Oskar said. 'I can't allow that to happen.'

'Now look, you don't know me or my brother or what happened between us,' Bingham snapped. 'I took you in, you ungrateful little urchin, and this is how you repay me? I don't care how sick she is, you two were up to something. How long had she been able to speak, eh? And you, how long have been able to do all this... stuff?'

'Not long.' Oskar glanced down.

Bingham did the same.

And realised that they had somehow drifted away from the balcony. They were floating, suspended in the air. Oskar could make out smoke from chimneys, pinpricks of orange light from the houses at the lowest levels of the citadel far, far below.

Bingham tried to speak, but he had lost his breath.

'I'm still getting used to these powers,' Oskar said. 'Learning what I can and cannot do. How much I can carry through the air, for example.'

'No,' Bingham begged, his voice a hoarse whisper. 'Please.'

'Happy landings, Bingham.' Oskar released his hold on Bingham and he dropped like a stone. He fell surprisingly fast, turning over like a circus performer. And he was silent. Oskar had expected him to scream but was glad that he didn't. Oskar didn't see where he landed but heard the impact clearly. Flat and heavy.

Word came that the princess was awake. Bright-eyed as if refreshed from a good nap. She was hungry and asking where Sander the mage was. She wanted to hear one of his silly stories.

Oskar's task here was done, and he left without saying goodbye. He knew they would find Bingham's body soon, so Oskar had decided to avoid what would doubtless be an ugly confrontation and returned to tend to Gudrun.

Oskar arrived at the altar at the foot of the mountain to find an offering of freshly baked bread, some hard pears and a gourd of red wine. He'd never tasted wine before, but recalled his mother and father treating themselves to Eruish wine on special occasions. He popped the cork and sniffed it. A fruity aroma.

He heard the dull *clonk* of a copper bell and turned to find a young goat herder and a dozen or so goats staring at him in frozen terror. The boy had the same striking combination of brown skin and green eyes as Gudrun.

Oskar smiled and raised the gourd. 'Thank you,' he said.

The boy ran and the goats followed him, their bells clanging as they went.

Oskar, can you hear me?

Oskar nearly dropped the gourd. *Gudrun?* he replied, but no, that wasn't her voice.

Oskar, it's Rosheen. We need to talk.

At first, Oskar was irritated. He was too busy looking after Gudrun to be bothered with his sister's trivial life, but then it hit him. How was she doing this? Did she have magic again?

Oskar, I don't know if you can hear me. Please reply. I'm with Sander Bree.

The pull of his curiosity was too much, and he used his mind to speak to Gudrun. *I won't be long,* he told her, unsure if she could even hear him. *I promise, I will return soon.*

Oskar found them in a remote, bluebell-filled glade in the hills near Lugham Village. They stood in its centre, craning their necks back to watch him descend.

He chose not to land, preferring to remain above the treeline.

'Where have you been?' Rosheen asked.

'What do you want?' Oskar ignored the question. The less they knew, the better. 'And how did you call to me? I didn't think mages could sense moon children.'

'You're not a moon child any more, Oskar,' Rosheen said. 'You've changed and we need to talk about what's happened. Your powers. You're unique and people are going to try and harm you.'

'Or exploit you,' Sander chipped in.

'I'm not a fool,' Oskar said.

'No, but you are inexperienced,' Rosheen said.

'Let us help you.'

'I don't need your help,' Oskar said, the thoughts that had troubled him for the last few days beginning to come together. 'I can do almost anything. I moved the stones in the sky, did you see?'

Rosheen didn't reply but shared a look with Sander Bree, and Oskar saw the same fear in their eyes that he had seen in the king's courtiers.

And Rosheen saw the same dead look on Oskar's face that she had seen on Bowden's men. A cold, nihilistic lack of warmth and it troubled her. She had never believed the stories of the moon children and how they had laid waste to the world before the rise of mages, but she was sure she was looking at one now and it gave her chills.

'I know people are frightened of me. Kings, soldiers, former mages,' Oskar continued. 'They shouldn't be. I'm going to make things right. Where there is war, I will bring peace.'

'Oh really?' Sander asked. 'How?'

'I shall smash their war machines, destroy their castle walls. If they make war, then I will stop it.'

Sander made an *I told you so* noise to Rosheen who raised her hands to her brother. 'Oskar, think about the consequences. Magic kept the peace, yes, but mostly through the threat of what it *might* do. It was only ever used as a last resort. Please don't do this.'

'I've seen their fear, Rosheen, and yours. This is the only way. I will succeed where you have failed, I—'

Oskar felt weak all of a sudden. Dizzy. Why did he feel so tired?

He was slowly falling. He couldn't rise.

He saw something around his sister's neck. A silver necklace with a pendant. There was a blue stone in the pendant and it glowed like the Lapis Moon.

'Where...' Oskar's head was light, and he tried to shake some life back into it. 'Where did you get that?'

'I'm doing it now,' Sander muttered to Rosheen, thinking he couldn't be heard.

'Give me more time,' Rosheen pleaded, 'let me convince him.'

Sander caught Oskar's eye. 'He knows. I'm doing it right now!'

The older mage raised his arms and shadows began to shift in the trees surrounding the glade. Countless Lapis stones flew in from the forest, gliding between the trees, guided by Sander's hand, swarming around Oskar. They were Sander's Mage's Moons in miniature, trapping the boy and draining him of his power.

Oskar tumbled to the ground, the Lapis stones hovering above him. He landed hard on his back, banging his head and unsure which way was up or down.

Gudrun, help me, please! He desperately called to her, but had no idea if she could hear him. *Gudrun, please!* There was no reply. *I'm sorry, I shouldn't have left you, please forgive me, Gudrun, I love you.*

'She'll die without me!' was what Oskar meant to say out loud to his sister and Sander, but all that came from his mouth was a slurred moan. 'Please, I beg you, let me go back to her, please, she'll die, she needs me, she's dying, oh gods, please.' He kept trying, but his mouth couldn't make the words.

His vision was blurred, his hearing dulled and his mind began to break apart like dandelion seeds in a breeze. Soon, all that remained was the dumb moon child he thought he had left behind. He made more noises like the moaning of an animal in distress. He found himself curled into a ball, saliva dribbling from his mouth, as his sister stood over him with tears in her eyes. For a moment, he thought he could hear her voice in his mind, the words *love, forgiveness, mercy,* then darkness.

Epilogue: Passage to Eru

A woman and a young man cross the Sugar Sea on a merchant ship to Eru. They pay good coin for passage and even more for privacy. The porter thinks she looks a little too young to be his mother. Perhaps they are brother and sister? Or something sinister? More money quenches his curiosity. They carry a heavy trunk with them everywhere they go. Six locks keep it secure. The cabin boy says a blue light glows from within like the old Lapis Moon.

The young man doesn't speak. The woman rarely says anything at all. The first officer says the woman wears a pendant around her neck with a Lapis stone and he thinks she used to be a mage.

Every night, when the sun sets and the moon rises, the woman and the young man make their way to the ship's bow to watch the new colours in the sky. And they huddle together, hand in hand. Homeward bound.

Acknowledgements

Big love and thanks to...

Claire, Emily and George for understanding that when my door was closed, or when the headphones were on, I was in another world and probably best left alone. I love you so much.

To Ed Wilson for declaring that this is 'the real deal!' and finding the perfect home for it at Unbound.

To Edit Mage Simon Spanton for weaving his powerful magic.

To Lisa Rogers for her impeccable copy-edit work. She never ceases to amaze me, and she always prevents me from looking like a complete numpty on the page.

To Xander, Andrew, Kwaku, Georgia and Sara at Unbound for their patience and skill.

To Graeme Williams and Kit Cox for early reading and feedback.

To Dominic Currie for the theme tune.

To Tim Jessey for generosity above and beyond.

To Jeremy Mason, Jon Wright, Steve Mayhew, Andy Bowden, Phill Bingham, Julie Wassmer, Mark Desvaux and my friends and colleagues at Orion for being cheerleaders throughout.

To Rich Boarmen the Steam Wizard for his magical staff (that's not a euphemism).

To John Fox-Smythe for the flying advice, which I never really used in the end (a glider became a wyvern in later drafts, but thank you anyway!).

And to everyone who pledged: you are amazing. This book simply would not exist without you.

Acknowledgements

My love and thanks to...

Patrons

Eric Ahnell
Emad Akhtar
Giles Alderson
Kimi Armstrong Stein
Bilbo Baggins
Jason Ballinger
RJ Barker
David Barnett
Julian Barr
Victoria Barsham
Gavin Bell
Alex Bell
Neil Beynon
Nirpal Bhogal
Louise Bishop
Jeffrey Blomquist
Michael Bowden
Joe Brothers
Matt Brown
Brian Bruinewoud
Chris Burgess
Thom Burgess
Jason Burwood
Jeanette Cake
Amber Caraveo Oliver
Yvonne Carder
Viki Cheung
Daniel Churchill
Jasmine Churchill
Gail Cleaver
David Clipston
Edward Cox

Kit Cox
Noel T Cumberland
Miles Cumpstey
Dominic Currie
Marion Dante
Lilian Darvell
Anna Dawson
Morgan Delaney
Mark Desvaux
Laurence Doherty
Linda Doughty
Nina Douglas
Shaun Dovaston
Samm Downing
Frances Doyle
Jack Dudman
Paddy Eason
Michael Ebison
Brioney Euden
Edie Evans
Juliet Ewers
Natalie Field
Russell Finch
James Fisher
Jo Furlong
Joshua Gardiner
Craig Garner
Linda Gawley
Laura Gerrard
Kirsty Gonzalez
Jenny Gordon
Steve Gowland
Mark Grant
Ben Green
Caroline Green
Jess Gulliver

Ben Gutcher
Gretel Hallett
Andrew Hally
Kate Hames
Petrina Hartland
Tim Harwood
Kevin Hawkins
Deborah Haywood
Mark Hodgson
Rob Hopkins
Jon Howard
Robert Hudson
Rachael Hum
Ella Hunt
Marissa Hussey
Stephanie Indykiewicz
Victoria Innell
Richie Janukowicz
JCMcDowell JCMcDowell
Brenda Jessey
Darryl Johnston
Judy King
Tina Kinsella
Jackie Kirkham
Fiona Klomp
David Knill
Jo Krnic
Stefanie Lamprinidi
Duncan Larter
Simone Lazarus
Kevin Lehane
Dean Lines
Daniel Lloyd-Squires
Scott Lynch
Maggy
Ria Mancey

Jeremy Mason
Katherine May
Steve Mayhew
Sam McCarthy
Tony Mcgrath
Mel Melcer
Hannah Methuen
Michael Miller
Alastair Monk
Glen Moy
Lauren Mulville
Genevieve Narey
Larissa Nash
Carlo Navato
Nick, Olivia, Lelia & India x
Carmel O'Donnell
Steve O'Gorman
Jason Obee
Gareth Owen
Ruhee Padhiar
Sophie Painter
Charlie Panayiotou
George Parkes
Isobel Pearson
Hetty Perkins
Thomas Phillips
Laura & Miles Poynton
Henry Rawlinson
Rebekah Reade
Keegan Reynolds
Andrew Riddell
Phil Saunders
Jenny Schwarz
Kevin Selfe
Dan Sellars
Laurence Shapiro

Avril Silk
Jon Small
Gavin Smith
Danny Stack
Paul Stark
Chris Stay
Helen Stickland
Annie Stone
Genn Stone
Susan Strachan
Raakhee Stratton
Michael Stuart
Kristian Sullivan
Arzu Tahsin
Ceri Teasdale
Jillian Tees
Piers Tempest
Tom Toner
Lucy Tucker
Chelle Vess
Lucy Vine
Philip Walberg
Jon Wallace
Carole-Ann Warburton
Ellie Warmington
Grace Warmington
Sneha Wharton
Vicki Whatson
Billy White
Pandora White
G.M. White
David Whitecross
Lucy Wilkins
Sharon Willis
Andy Willmott
Ina Winteridge

Jon Wood
Jon Woolcott
Jon Wright